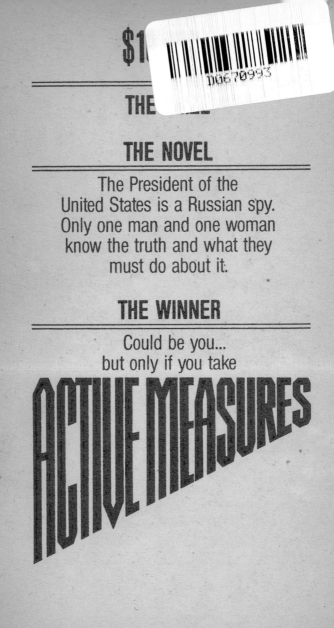

$1...

THE ...

THE NOVEL

The President of the
United States is a Russian spy.
Only one man and one woman
know the truth and what they
must do about it.

THE WINNER

Could be you...
but only if you take

ACTIVE MEASURES

THE CIA IS PLANNING TO ASSASSINATE THE PRESIDENT OF THE UNITED STATES

. . . but you won't know how, or why, until you read *Active Measures*. Along the way you'll discover why, in 1999, American families are eating krill and soy protein while vast harvests of U.S. grain are sold to the Soviet Union at bargain prices . . . why radical blacks are demanding outright ownership of six southern states . . . and why only one man and one woman can stop the U.S. from sliding into ruin.

You'll also be well on your way to solving seven key questions—and winning $10,000! See details, page vii.

ACTIVE MEASURES

JANET MORRIS & DAVID DRAKE

BAEN science fiction BOOKS

ACTIVE MEASURES

Copyright © 1985 by Janet Morris and David Drake

A Baen Book

Baen Enterprises
8-10 W. 36th Street
New York, N.Y. 10018

First printing, April 1985

ISBN: 0-671-55945-1

Cover art by Vincent Di Fate

Printed in the United States of America

Distributed by
SIMON & SCHUSTER
MASS MERCHANDISE SALES COMPANY
1230 Avenue of the Americas
New York, N.Y. 10020

OFFICIAL CONTEST RULES

A. **Entries.** Complete the Official Entry Form on following page and attach it to any 8½″ × 11″ paper(s) on which you have *printed* or *typed* your answers to the following seven questions:

(1) What was the probable city of manufacture of the Czech motorcycle Fox drove in Istanbul?

(2) Which police or security force had ultimate responsibility for investigating Albert Stevenson's murder?

(3) Who killed Genya Posner?

(4) What was the nature and purpose of KAFIR?

(5) Who was GLAVA?

(6) Was Luftsen's death suicide or murder?

(7) What did Gallen hear on tape which caused her to take the action she did regarding Sonny Quaid? WORD YOUR ANSWER AS CLOSELY AS POSSIBLE TO THE FORM THAT SHAI GALLEN WOULD HAVE USED IN AN AFTER-ACTION REPORT *IF* SHE HAD ALL THE RELEVANT DATA.

Print or type your name, address and telephone number in the upper right corner of each sheet. Answer all seven questions completely and mail entry to: ACTIVE MEASURES, P.O. Box 1391 Ridgely, MD 21683.

You may enter more than once, but each entry must be accompanied by an Official Entry Form plus a 50¢ processing fee* (cash, check or money order payable to Active Measures). Official Entry Forms may not be copied or mechanically reproduced. Entries must be in English, legibly *printed or typed only* and must be received by September 30, 1985.

B. **Judging.** Contest answers in the authors' own words are sealed in a bank vault. All entries will be reviewed under the supervision of Beaumont-Bennett, Inc., an independent judging organization, whose decisions will be final. If more than one entry, or no

---

*Processing fee not required for Canadian residents only.

entry, has the correct answers to all questions, contest winner will be the entrant who, in the opinion of the authors, has best expressed the correct answer to question 7, using the fewest words. The best answer to question 7 will be the one that is closest in meaning, logic and style of expression to the actual words the authors have used, which will be found in the bank vault. The authors' decisions will be final.

C. **Prize Winner.** Contest winner will be notified by mail on or before November 30, 1985 and, upon verification, will be awarded $10,000. Winner, and parent or legal guardian if a minor, will be required to sign and return an Affidavit of Eligibility and Release within 14 days of receipt, or prize may be awarded to another contestant. Taxes on prizes are winner's responsibility. For name of winner, send a stamped, self-addressed envelope to: ACTIVE WINNER, P.O. Box 667-P, Ridgely, MD 21660. Requests received after December 31, 1985 will not be fulfilled.

D. **Authors' Answers.** For a copy of the authors' contest answers, check appropriate box on Entry Form and send 50¢ for postage and handling to: ACTIVE MEASURES, P.O. Box 1391, Ridgely, MD 21683. Requests for this answer insert, which can become a permanent part of your book for future reference, will be fulfilled after October 15, 1985 but not later than December 31, 1985.

E. **Eligibility.** Contest open only to residents of the U.S. and Canada (excluding residents of Quebec Province), except the authors and authors' families, judges and employees and their immediate families of Simon & Schuster, its subsidiaries, advertising agencies and Beaumont-Bennett, Inc. *Contest is void in Florida and Vermont* and wherever prohibited or restricted by law. Subject to all federal, state and local regulations. Awards will be made to parent or legal guardian of a winning minor.

Official Entry Form

Mail To: ACTIVE MEASURES CONTEST
          P.O. Box 1391
          Ridgely, MD 21683

Use this form to enter contest and/or request authors' solution. Check appropriate box(es) below and *print or type all information requested.*

☐   *Please enter me in the contest.* I am enclosing the following:
     a) My answers to the 7 questions (see back of this form) on one or more 8½″ × 11″ sheets; plus . . .
     b) 50¢ processing fee.*

☐   *Please send me the authors' answer insert* (available after October 15, 1985). I am enclosing 50¢ for postage and handling.

Note: To enter contest *and* obtain authors' solution insert, enclose $1.00 cash, check or money order payable to "ACTIVE MEASURES."

Name of Entrant _____
Address _____
City_____ State _____ Zip _____
Telephone (   ) _____

To Be eligible For $10,000 Contest Prize . . .
clearly *print or type* your answers to the following 7 questions on one or more 8½″ × 11″ sheets. Be sure your name, address and phone number are on the upper right corner of each sheet.

Question 1:   What was the probable city of manufacture of the Czech motorcycle Fox drove in Istanbul?

Question 2:   Which police or security force had ulti-

---

*Processing fee not required for Canadian residents only.

mate responsibility for investigating Albert Stevenson's murder?

Question 3:   Who killed Genya Posner?

Question 4:   What was the nature and purpose of KAFIR?

Question 5:   Who was GLAVA?

Question 6:   Was Luftsen's death suicide or murder?

Question 7:   What did Gallen hear on tape which caused her to take the action that she did in regard to Quaid? WORD YOUR ANSWER AS CLOSELY AS POSSIBLE TO THE FORM THAT SHAI GALLEN WOULD HAVE USED IN AN AFTER-ACTION REPORT *IF* SHE HAD ALL THE RELEVANT DATA.

Important: If more than one entry, or no entry, has the correct answers to all seven questions, contest winner will be the entrant who, in the opinion of the authors has best expressed the correct answer *to answer* 7 using the fewest words. The best answer to question 7 will be the one that is closest in meaning, logic and style of expression to the actual words the authors have used, which will be found in the bank vault. The authors decisions will be final.

NOTE: This Official Entry Form may not be copied or mechanically reproduced and must accompany all entries and requests. Be sure to enclose appropriate fee. Residents of Florida, Vermont and the province of Quebec, Canada, are not eligible. See Official Contest Rules for complete details. *This entry must be received by September 30, 1985.*

PROLOGUE: 1975

One week after James Crossfield had been elected senator, the man who would become his KGB case officer made his way to the Crossfield home through a premature Midwestern snowstorm.

When the doorbell rang, Crossfield paused with his glass raised but the toast unspoken. His eyes glanced across his wife and their guests—though Marie and Owen Neely were more family than guests, which is why they were present this first night in almost a year that the new senator had to relax.

"Oh, God," said Crossfield's wife, closing her eyes as she patted her blond hair with her free hand. "Not *more* reporters. . . ." Professionally cool again, she rose from her chair and said brightly, "Well, I'll see who it is, and I suppose I should bring them. . . ?"

"I think," James Crossfield said as he strolled toward the door himself, "that I've fawned to the

1

press for long enough to be forgiven for telling one of them what I think of their constant intrusions. After all—" and the smile he threw over his shoulder was a chill one "—senators only have to run every sixth year."

Crossfield was tall and aristocratically thin, his temples touched with gray hair which was natural— but was also too useful for Crossfield not to have aided Nature had she been less obliging. The Constitution might permit a thirty-year-old to be elected to the Senate, but the conservatism of voters in Crossfield's state made even his actual age of thirty-five something of a drawback.

The porch light had been left off deliberately to make the house uninviting. Crossfield turned it on now, though condensate on the triple windows of the main panel and frost across the storm door left his visitor no more than he was already in imagination: a dark bulk on the open porch. Crossfield swung open the inner door and called, "Yes?" to the figure across the remaining barrier of glass, aluminum, and cold.

"Dear, dear, my boy, I could have hoped for a warmer greeting than that," responded the figure, a heavy-set man with a tweed overcoat, waxed moustache and a very recognizable voice.

"Well good *god*!" blurted the senator-elect, so startled that he made three increasingly-violent attempts to open the storm door before he remembered that he had thrown the little pin lock after he let in the Neelys. "God *damn* it, Janelle!" Crossfield shouted back into the livingroom. "You locked the *door*."

He pushed it open at last; the man on the porch entered with a smile and a nod—and without touching the storm door himself, though his gray suede gloves already showed the dark blotches of snowflakes they had met between the rental car parked on the street and the Crossfields' porch.

The trio in the livingroom had advanced to the edge of the tiled entrance hall when they realized that Crossfield was not going to turn away the source of the interruption. They waited now, Marie Neely still holding her wineglass and a look of vague recognition on the face of Crossfield's wife.

"Janelle, of course you remember Doctor Blaustein," Crossfield said, smiling but with an edge in his voice at the fact that she had obviously fuzzy recollection of the man on whom all of Crossfield's undergraduate memories were centered. "Doctor Blaustein, this is Owen Neely and his wife Marie. Owen was my campaign manager and the main reason that I'm Senator Crossfield now and not Crossfield, the guy who used to be Representative from the Second District."

"Kurt, please, Jimmie," said Blaustein, stepping aside so that Crossfield could close the front door. "I'm always Kurt to my special students—once they graduate. And Jimmie here," he added with a nod toward Neely, "was very special, a man certain to go far."

"Well, glad to meet you, Kurt," said Owen Neely, extending his right hand without notable enthusiasm.

The two men were much of a size, but there the similarities ended. Neely was an athlete gone fat in his early thirties, his belly a noticeable protuberance above the trousers of his doubleknit leisure suit. This late in the evening, Neely's solid jaw was shadowed by whiskers as black as the hair of his head—though that was receding in sharp warning of baldness. He might have been a car salesman or the owner of a hardware store; in fact, Neely had trebled the size of the family paving business in the eight years during which he had been actively involved with it.

Kurt Blaustein was older by a decade than Neely, but the gap between the men was wider than that, than the Trinity College tie Blaustein wore, or even the professor's overall appearance of puppy-ish softness. Blaustein removed his right glove with care before he took Neely's hand—the delay too natural to be an overt insult, any more than was the hint of a smile when Blaustein's eyes flicked across the American flag pin in the younger man's lapel. "Charmed to meet you too, Mr. Neely," the professor said. "Any friend of Jimmie's must have hidden talents."

Even as he shook the contractor's hand, Blaustein turned to James Crossfield and said, "Jimmie, I'm *terribly* sorry to interrupt your evening, of course, but I really must have a few moments of your time." He looked around again, adding to Neely and the women, "Alone, I'm afraid."

"My study's at the end of the hall, ah, Kurt," said Crossfield whose palms were suddenly sweaty through fifteen years of acquired poise. "Owen, I depend on you to deputize for me with the ladies— we'll rejoin you as soon as we can."

"You know," said Neely as he and the women turned away from the entrance hall and the foot-steps rapping toward the study in the other direc-tion, "I never yet met a man with a waxed mous-tache who was worth a shit."

Blaustein paused and, before stepping from the hallway into Crossfield's paneled study, examined the door. It was satisfactory, a solid oak panel rather than an ordinary hollow-core unit. The lower edge fit snugly against the threshold and the inner face was felted besides for soundproofing.

"I work odd hours," Crossfield explained, "and the bedrooms are just across the hall."

Blaustein latched the door and smiled, stroking his moustache, but did not speak.

"It's been a long. . . ," began the senator-elect, driven by unease into the gap which was really the other man's to fill. A better point of entry struck him and he said, "But here, Kurt, let me take your coat."

He stepped toward Blaustein, and the professor froze him in his tracks with, "It's bad news, in a way, that brings me here, Jimmie. But it's good for you, you'll see, that it's me here. Instead of someone from the FBI; very nasty people, they are. Or even from State itself."

"Has this," Crossfield said, articulating very carefully while he settled his weight back onto his heels, "anything to do with my campaign records?" All the blood had drained from the layers close to his skin. "Because if it does, the man to ask is right out there in my livingroom."

The older man deliberately shrugged out of his overcoat unaided and draped it over the leather back of an armchair. His suit was pale gray with a stripe of maroon too thin to be recognized as a separate color at any distance; it gave him the smooth, quiet elegance of a caterpillar stuffed with mulberry leaves. "Obtuse, are we, Jimmie?" he said as he laid down the overcoat.

When he looked back at Crossfield, his pale eyes had in them the hard, cruel glitter that the younger man remembered from classroom dissections—but always somebody else, never Jimmie Crossfield the cringing target. . . . "I hope that's not the case, Jimmie, because if we've become *obtuse* there isn't any need for me to have made this trip. You represent a *stinking* part of the country, you know . . .

except for my faith in you, I would just have let my associates give the proper authorities all the information on Julio Ortiz."

"What?" said Crossfield, genuinely confused by the name.

Blaustein made an angry motion with his hands, a petulant child scrubbing the wrong answer from an invisible chalk board. His tension was well concealed, but it was not less real for that. Kurt Blaustein knew far better how important this conversation was than did the man he was addressing. "Luisa Guzman, then," he snapped, "Ortiz's sister— your mistress when you were vice-consul in Manila ten years ago. And Ortiz is the man whose visa you approved even though you knew he was wanted by the Philippine authorities."

"Good God," said the senator-elect. He pulled out the swivel chair at the rolltop desk—phone and power connections had been built into what was otherwise a careful reproduction of a 19th century original—and sat down heavily. "Good God," he repeated.

"You see," the professor went on, the fingers of his left hand touching the door jamb too lightly for support but perhaps in affirmation of physical reality, "Ortiz didn't only have political problems as the woman told you; though I don't know how cretins like your campaign manager out there will react—but I should say, *would* react, Jimmie—to the news that you knowingly slipped a member of the Philippine Communist Party into this country for a bit of pussy . . . *wog* pussy."

Crossfield looked up and his slim fingers tapped a quick demand for notice on the arm of his chair. "Doctor Blaustein," he said crisply, "I haven't the faintest notion of what you're talking about, and like a gentleman I'm simply going to ignore what can only be a symptom of overwork on a fine mind. Now, I suggest we join the others for a drink before you go on about your—" He broke off because Blaustein smiled, and the younger man knew very well that there was no bluff in that ferret-cruel smile.

In the silence, the professor said, "Ortiz had assassinated a village policeman, you see, shot him down from behind and shot his wife for good measure. And, of *course*, I wouldn't be here if there weren't proof, Jimmie. Brother and sister are both here in this country, quite safe and perfectly willing to testify to any court or investigating body if they're told to. They know very well what would happen if they refused to obey my associates." His voice was smooth and mellow, but the claws behind it were ready to tear at the least further hint of resistance. Crossfield could behave, or—

The younger man chuckled with every appearance of friendly amusement. "Kurt, have a chair and let's discuss this like two adults, shall we?" His hand opened in a gesture that took in a pair of armchairs, including the one Blaustein had used for a coatrack.

Crossfield had not said, "You can't prove it," words which would have provided that very proof in the likely eventuality that his visitor was taping the conversation. Just as he had not blurted an admission earlier, he did not lose control of his tongue now as he continued easily—but Blaustein remained standing—"Your associates, you say. Well, certainly not Justice, and I presume not State?" He raised an eyebrow for the question, relaxing himself into a negligent sprawl which tilted the back of his chair.

Blaustein said nothing, but his right index finger beckoned—"Proceed," a familiar gesture from Crossfield's past.

Obedient now as then, the senator-elect went on, "Yes, a little hardball for State, I thought, too." His eyes narrowed. "There's Defense, I suppose. Certainly enough people in the Pentagon who'd like the, shall we say, ear of an up and coming young senator ... But you know, Kurt, I can't picture a man with your mind working for Defense, even as a—" he grinned, briefly, falsely; as false as his appearance of leisure "—civilian recruiter. Brass on the cap, concrete between the ears; that's been my experience, and neither of us would care to work for people we couldn't respect."

"You realize, Jimmie," said his visitor somewhat unexpectedly, "that this can mean a great deal *for* your career. Money, of course. But there are forms of influence which money quite literally can't buy, and planning focused on making *you* successful, not on advancing the aims of an entrenched bureaucracy. It's important to all of us that you rise as high as possible, Jimmie ... and we think that anything is possible."

Blaustein paused, and his smile broadened into what Neely, had he seen it, would have called a shit-eating grin. "With our help, Jimmie," the professor went on, "anything at all is possible. Your little peccadillo in Manila may turn out to be just the most fortunate action an ambitious politician could have taken. So long as you remember who your friends are."

"You're CIA, aren't you, Kurt?" said Crossfield who smiled in the first sign of true relaxation he had displayed since he watched his visitor check the soundproofing of the door. "Well, if you play ball with me, I'll guarantee that you have no cause to regret it."

He leaned forward, raising an index finger to point toward his former teacher, and said, "But I want *you* to realize something too, Kurt: with you or without you, I *am* going places. This country needs me, because it needs a leader. That's where all the talk of principles and policies breaks down—on the man. And I'm the man America needs."

Blaustein looked at the man seated across from him, and for a moment the prepared words caught in the practiced, professorial throat. But then he stroked his moustache, swallowed, and said, taking a slip of paper from a breast pocket, "We'll be in touch with you, of course, and we might have some suggestions for staff appointments—people we can *both* trust implicitly, you'll understand."

He handed the slip of paper to Crossfield who took it impassively, the momentary fire gone from his eyes and leaving behind only the coals of watchfulness. The number written on the paper was not in Blaustein's own handwriting, though his former student neither cared for nor realized that fact.

"But any time you feel you need to get in touch with me, Jimmie," continued the KGB agent, "you can through this number. Any time, day or night."

He smiled again. "We're going to accomplish great things, my boy," Blaustein concluded. "Greater things than the world has ever known before."

OUTSIDE

If Larry Fox had known the defector was dying of emphysema, the initial meet would not have been set for the top of the Galata Tower.

If anyone had realized the defector was Abdulhamid Kunayev, the meet would have been run out of Ankara if not Langley. Larry Fox, "Vice-Consul" in Istanbul and a CIA officer with only six years service, would have had no involvement beyond chauffering the heavy hitters who were not familiar with Istanbul.

But since intelligence collection in an imperfect world is often equally imperfect, it was Fox who lounged against the tower's railing, trying to look like a tourist while his hands sweated on the rusty iron. He had gone as far as checking the schedule to make sure no Soviet reconnaissance satellite would be overhead, but he had no real hopes for the meeting. His Turkish agent, Mehmet Sabanci, had said he knew a Soviet who wanted to talk to

the Canadians but not at their consulate. It was
too much to hope that the Russian walk-in would
be a diplomat at the Soviet Istanbul mission. There
was a fair chance that he would be from the Aeroflot
offices, though, somebody with knowledge that
might be of use ... perhaps enough of a coup to
get Fox and his wife back stateside, out of this city
she had come to hate.

Though in all truth, Kathie would probably hate
McLean too ... and the walk-in was most likely a
truck driver and a Bulgarian besides. If that turned
out to be the case, the initial meeting would be the
last Fox saw of him. The fellow would never need
to know that Fox was Canadian only by virtue of a
year's study at Calgary—and that tradecraft demanded that Fox keep as much distance as possible between himself and crazies like Sabanci.

Mehmet Sabanci was high up in the local coun-
cils of the Gray Wolves, the best-funded of the
terrorist organizations whose murders and bomb-
ings had brought Turkish democracy to its second
collapse in fifteen years. The fact that the Gray
Wolves were nominally rightwing—as their victims were nominally leftwing—did not keep them
from funding their operations with Soviet money.
And the fact that Sabanci now considered Larry
Fox a close friend—dear God!—did not keep Fox
from wanting the Turk to look for him someplace
other than the American Consulate General if anything should go wrong between them.

Sabanci came through the door to the circumfer-
ential viewing platform first. The elevator ended
at the night club one floor down. The Soviet's
wheezing breaths preceded him, audible despite
the breeze and the sound of traffic echoing from
the two nearby bridges over the Golden Horn.

Sabanci smiled beneath his bushy, down-turned

moustache, but that did not make him look any less bloodthirsty, and the sight of him gave Fox the usual twinge of fear. He knew the Turk's right hand under his coat was on the grip of a Browning Hi-Power, and that there was a smaller pistol in the purse in his left hand as well as a US Marine combat knife with a seven-inch blade sheathed inside the waistband at the base of the Turk's spine. Sabanci had displayed them all over a bottle of raki one night. Fox was perfectly willing to credit the man's stories about how and how often he had used the weapons in the past.

The Russian behind Sabanci made Fox's skin draw up as if he had just been dropped into cold water. The American had been keeping his face blank in order to buttress a claim of innocence if a squad of security police muscled onto the platform after Sabanci—always a possibility, and the more so now since the declaration of martial law. That preparation served Fox well now, because it kept his face from blurting the fact that he recognized the Soviet.

It *had* to be Kunayev. The round flat face and bow legs were similar enough to those of a million other Tadzhikis and Azerbaizhanis, Soviet descendants of the Golden Horde. The missing right earlobe, though. . . . if not unique, then surely, when added to the other features, it made alternatives hugely improbable.

Almost as improbable as the chance that Larry Fox was meeting a member of the Politburo who wanted to defect.

"This is Selim," said Mehmet Sabanci in Turkish. The grin as he waved—with his left hand—would have suited a pasha demonstrating a pyramid of skulls to his sultan. He winked. "We have friends in common. He wanted to talk to somebody British, but I said why not Canadian? The Canadians are trusty people. Because you're my friend I do this for you, eh, Alvin?"

There was no real Alvin Stevenson in the Canadian mission in Turkey. Fox had sometimes wondered whether he would warn an unfortunate of that name if one were transferred here.

The immediate problems were much more serious. "Good afternoon, Selim," Fox said. "We're looking forward to an opportunity to help you." He extended his hand.

The Soviet, who wanted to be known as Selim, ignored the offered courtesy. His face was scrunched in a mixture of anger and pain. If he was really Kunayev, he looked a decade older than the 55 or so he should have been. The lung condition could explain that, just as allergy medications could have caused the puffiness in his face. He stepped to the railing and looked down at the red tile and dingy concrete of the surrounding buildings. The quarter had been old when the tower was built, whether that was by the Genoese in the 13th Century or by the Byzantines in the 6th. Some of the streets had been broadened into boulevards, but a warren of more than a dozen separate ways still knotted close to the base of the tower.

Selim turned grimly. "Are we alone?" he asked Sabanci in Turkish of a dialect unfamiliar to Fox. The paymasters of the Gray Wolves were Turkomans born in the USSR. It was easy enough to guess who Sabanci's "friends in common" were.

"I checked to see there's no one else on the deck with us," said Fox. The lead-sheathed conical roof of the tower hid antipodal portions of the walkway. "And there's only the one door, so we can't be surprised. If you'd like to go—"

The Soviet flicked a hand and grimaced at Fox

to silence him. Sabanci drew the heavy Browning—
it was cocked—and stamped around the walkway
with an enthusiasm that demanded something to
kill. Selim, staring after the departing Turk, looked
nonplussed. The men who give certain orders do
not always understand the sort of men who carry
them out.

"No one," said the Turk as he returned in obvious disappointment. He slipped the weapon into a
crossdraw holster and stood with his back to the
door. "You treat Selim well, Alvin," he warned.
"His friends are very good to me."

Larry Fox watched the scene from the distance
of his mind. Instead of taking charge, the CIA officer was being threatened by his agent and ignored
by the Soviet walk-in who could be the biggest
coup in intelligence history—if handled correctly.
Fox could imagine his superiors' lips curl at his
performance—everyone from Ed Platt, his Chief of
Station, to the Deputy Director for Operations about
whom he tried not to think. Somebody as inexperi-
enced as Larry Fox shouldn't be here!

Aloud, and with the coolness made easy by his
present sense of dissociation, Fox said, "How can
my country help you, Selim?"

The Soviet pointed a puffy finger and scowled,
but the threatening posture collapsed in another
paroxysmal coughing attack. Fox had seen dying
men before. The future was as clear in Selim's
eyes as it had been in those of the Lebanese child
with no hands and whose lungs were riddled with
steel wire from the bomblet she had picked up. . . .
Fox stepped toward the man and his own past
with his arms out in support.

"No," Selim whispered. He waved the handkerchief, but the word was not really directed at Fox.
"No." The Soviet straightened by an effort of will.

In a voice stripped of arrogance, he said, "The Americans must not learn of this, do you understand? You have normal channels. They must not be used. I will die if the Americans learn, *any* American. And you will die as well."

Mehmet Sabanci was beaming from his post at the doorway. The Turk might have been able to hear the defector's warning, but there was no sign that he cared. Again Selim shuffled to the rail and peered over morosely. The observation platform gave an excellent view of a quarter without particular interest. The Golden Horn itself was almost curtained by the height of the buildings which fringed it.

At least the Soviet seemed to be able to understand Fox's Turkish. The young CIA field collector would cheerfully have promised the defector anything—a Politburo member!—but that would have been inconsistent with his cover identity: a Canadian intelligence officer who had just met a claimed defector calling himself Selim. The last thing Fox wanted was to frighten Kunayev by acquiescing too quickly. The muscles on the left side of Fox's ribs tightened as a sniper rose in old memories.

"That can be arranged if it is necessary," he said to the Soviet's gloomy profile. "Relations between my government and our—neighbors to the south—won't be jeopardized without a reason, however. And I think you'll agree that the reason would have to be a very good one, eh?"

The whole statement was a delaying action while Fox's mind raced, planning the next stage. He'd set the follow-up meeting for 1800 hours. With luck, there could be a C-130 airborne from Incirlik within minutes of the time Fox got back to a secure phone. He and his station chief, Ed Platt, wouldn't be manpower enough to immobilize

Kunayev when the Soviet realized he'd turned himself over to the US after all. Daniels, the third member of the Istanbul station, was on leave ... but they could co-opt the six Consulate Marines for something this hot. Once they had Kunayev wheels-up from Istanbul, the real problems were over, but it might be good to suggest that something faster than a turbo-prop C-130 be standing by in Rome to—

"You want to know the reason?" said the Soviet's harsh voice through the shimmering of Fox's imagination. He moved closer to the American.

Fox was thin but a head taller than the defector. Nonetheless, the Soviet's stark personality drove before him like a sledge. His breath was sour and medicinal. "You want to know. The President of the United States is one of ours. Yes. Ours." The flat Tartar face beamed with pride which momentarily overcame his awareness of death. "James Crossfield—" the accent would have made the name unrecognizable had Fox not known it so well "—is a Soviet agent. And KAFIR. . . . Anyway, you see why I don't want to go to the Americans, yes?"

"I don't—" said Larry Fox's mouth with almost no prompting from his intellect. He swallowed.

The Soviet began to laugh. His arms spread on the railing to brace the stocky body. The laughter turned to spasms of coughing that pounded the man against the iron.

"I don't blame you for that," Fox said. It was all play-acting. None of this was real. The Red Queen would appear at any moment, or perhaps Ed Platt would slap him on the back and tell Fox how badly he'd just failed the test. "We'll need some evidence, of course," said the mouth that pretended it was part of a CIA officer handling a routine contact.

The Soviet lifted himself from the railing. If he had heard Fox, he gave no sign of it. His eyes were focused on something below.

"That is," said Fox, "we—"

The babble of Turkish which the Soviet suddenly threw at Mehmet Sabanci was too rapid and too harshly accented for the American to catch the words. Fox's mind, wrestling with the implications of the Soviet's statement, had no capacity to deal with unexpected occurrences of another sort.

Sabanci snatched open the door to the stairs. The Soviet bolted through it.

"Wait!" Fox cried. He jumped forward. Sabanci slammed the door and met the American's chest with his shoulder.

"Mehmet, for God's sake don't let him go!" Fox said. He touched the Turk's arms in an effort to guide Sabanci out of his way.

The Browning punched Fox beneath the ribs like a blunt steel finger. He gasped, not at the blow but at its implication. There were ways to disarm a gunman in situations like these, but Fox had never been very good at them. One slip and Mehmet Sabanci would put fourteen rounds through the man who had been his friend thirty seconds before.

Fox backed away with his palms spread toward the gun muzzle. "Mehmet, I want to help him," the American officer said, his voice falling into the cadences with which he would have tried to calm a screaming child. There was only one elevator in the tower. The stairs had been blocked for office space years ago in spite of whatever fire laws the city might have. If Kunayev—if Selim—reached the ground, then he was gone. It was that simple. "If he's in danger, you mustn't let him go alone." Fox was sure he heard the elevator, though intellectually he realized that the thick walls and breeze made that impossible.

Sabanci waved his pistol playfully. Nothing could give a Hi-Power a hair trigger—the magazine face itself is a bearing surface—but the motion still made Fox's face slacken.

"I told you, Alvin," Sabanci said, "his friends are very important to me. I don't want to hurt you, eh? But if Selim wants to leave, you don't get in his way. I think we just stay here half an hour or so." The gun waggled in the motion of a finger chucking Fox under the chin. "They've arrested Gulnus, had you heard?"

"Fuck Gulnus!" the American snapped, turning his back on the gun to leaning as far over the railing as he could. The tower's corbelling obscured the sidewalk directly surrounding its base. Fox began to sidle around the circumference of the observation walk, praying for a glimpse of Selim so that at least he would have a direction for later inquiries. He saw nothing in the least unusual except a Skoda taxi, one of a number of Czech motor vehicles built in Istanbul under license, with its hood up and apparently abandoned.

"Now Alvin," Sabanci said, "he'll be back in touch, I'm sure. We mustn't crowd him. He's an important man, I think."

"That's what I'm afraid of," Larry Fox said grimly. "That's exactly what I'm afraid of."

Fox had cheerfully walked the half mile from the Consulate General to the Galata Tower. He rarely rode his motorcycle to initial meetings with agents, and today Kathie had the car. Besides, neither driving nor parking was a pleasure in the old city.

Walking back with failure for a companion was

no pleasure either. The dingy, six- to eight-story row-houses built along Mesturiyet Street did nothing to lift Fox's mood. He wasn't sure what he *could* have done to save the situation. Mehmet wasn't bluffing. Maybe Kunayev really would get in touch with them again. Maybe Selim would turn out to be somebody minor after all, merely a truck driver with a missing earlobe and a crazy story to get asylum. Crazy.

The bastard looked just like pictures of Kunayev, only older.

"Good afternoon," said the Turkish gatekeeper. Larry Fox blinked back into the present.

The Consulate General had been built as a *palazzo* in the 1860s by an Italian merchant. A ten-foot fence of iron palings separated the paved forecourt from the street. The court, which continued around the right side of the building, now provided parking for the vehicles of the staff. Separate vehicular and pedestrian gates were controlled by the local guard who had just startled Fox enough to keep him from walking past his destination.

"Right, hi, Suleyman," the CIA officer said as he wondered what the hell he was going to put in his report. The gate squealed back. Within the courtyard were four soldiers in fatigues and a national policeman whose garb would have passed at a distance for a Wehrmacht dress uniform of 1940. The policeman carried a submachine gun, and the soldiers were armed with automatic rifles—SAR-80s bought from Chartered Industries of Singapore when Turkey converted to 5.56 mm. There had been no serious anti-American incidents in the months since the declaration of martial law, but the army wasn't taking chances. The troops stared at Fox, but they said nothing since the gatekeeper had recognized him.

Fox wasn't going to mention Kunayev or the statement Selim had made. He'd only report that a Turkish agent had put him in contact with a disaffected Soviet, and that, though the initial meeting had been unproductive, there was a possibility of further contact initially through the Turkish go-between. That wouldn't make Fox look like a blundering, gullible fool; and such a report was more likely to be correct than the wild-ass nonsense that had filled Fox's mind on top of the Galata Tower.

The male Turkish receptionist inside the front door could only nod as he talked on the phone, but the Marine guard called a cheery greeting as Fox started up the sweeping staircase to his office on the second floor. The ground floor was given over to consular business. If Fox had really been a vice-consul, his office would not have been upstairs; but anyone who had made that connection already had more than a suspicion about who the CIA personnel were.

Half the volume of the second floor was taken up by the Grand Ballroom at its center, whose rococo ornamentation had been recently restored. Though it might not have been the most practical use of the space, Fox liked to stand in the ballroom on rainy days and look up at the painted ceiling high above.

The Communications and Records vault was at a corner, beside the office Fox shared with Joe Daniels. On the other side of the vault was the dusty staircase which gave access to the roof where the communications antennas were. So were the burn barrels for disposing of classified papers if an emergency blew up too fast for the shredder in the vault to handle the load. In the closet beneath the stairs was a case of thermite grenades to incinerate with enthusiasm and certainty the barrels full of documents.

The vault door was open and, though the air conditioner in the bricked-up window alcove was on, the room was still unpleasantly warm with waste heat from the equipment operating within. "Hello, Mitch," Fox called to the Communicator relaxing for a moment in his swivel chair.

"Hey, the Mad Bomber," said Mitch Dolby as he swung upright and alert. "How'd your meet go, Larry?"

"Jesus, don't call me that, Mitch," the officer said. "Right now I think I met a truck driver, but my agent swears the fellow'd be worth talking to again."

Fox and Mitch Dolby had trained together at Camp Peary. There was nothing unusual about a collection trainee like Larry Fox talking his way into a course in booby-traps and explosives—it was a macho thing to do and therefore normal for many who joined CIA. It was, however, very unusual for anyone to know his way around blasting caps and det cord as well as Fox had when the course began. That skill had caused enough comment to be embarrassing even at the time. Dolby had just been transferred to Istanbul from Mexico City, bringing with him a near-certain revival of rumors Fox had hoped were buried years before.

The stories about Fox and explosives weren't the ones which particularly concerned him now.

"Thought I'd keep current on the Politburo," Fox said casually. "Do we have the bios in hard copy or will you have to print it out for me?"

"The Prime Target we've got in hard copy," Dolby said as he rose and headed for one of the fireproof, padlocked file cabinets. "Anybody in particular, or you going to work your way through from Aardvark?"

"How about Kunayev?" Fox said as the Communicator began working the combination of the Sergeant and Greenleaf padlock. "He's Turkish by nationality, isn't he? Tadzhik?"

"How the hell would I know?" Dolby replied.

The Communications Vault was, among other things, the bolt hole for the staff of the consulate should a fire or riot trap them within the building. The room was of decent size, but Fox still found it hard to imagine twenty-odd Americans and God knew how many of the local staff all perched inside on the dozen filing cabinets and such of the carpeted floor as the cabinets and other equipment did not cover. The vault did, however, have the basic requirements: electricity, the radio, the shredder, the classified documents, and a door that could not be forced in less than two hours by any technique which did not reduce the whole building to a smoking crater.

The vault did not have water; its ventilation was only marginally adequate for the two hour period; and there was no way out except through the main door. In twenty years of Requests for Proposals and testing, the State Department had still not found an escape-hatch design it would approve. Diplomatic personnel—and personnel operating under diplomatic cover—had to be able to trust their host country for protection beyond a certain minimum. Fox was not alone in thinking that a few other options might have been useful in Tehran and elsewhere.

"Here we go," said Dolby as he withdrew a file folder with a red-bordered cover sheet. He locked the cabinet before he carried the folder over to the desk to log it out. "Hey, Larry," he said as he entered the number and description of the folder in the log, "just between us, you know, men. Is it true you knew our Deputy Director of Operations when you were in Israel? Before either of you joined the Company, so to speak?"

Fox's hand twiddled with the pen he had taken out to sign the log. Dolby was not meeting his eyes. "They tell you that at the Farm?" Fox said instead of answering.

"No, well," the Communicator said. He finally looked up, "You know, you hear things around."

Around *here*, Fox realized. Jesus. "Look," he said aloud, "when I was nineteen I thought Israel was the last best hope of freedom. Only people in the world who really knew how to deal with terrorists. When Sharon went into Lebanon, I paid my own way over. I had two years of ROTC, and they needed warm meat too bad to worry long before they found me some khakis and a Galil to carry."

"Pretty rough over there, I guess?" Dolby volunteered to keep up his end of the conversation. He had been Air Force before he joined the Agency. The closest he would have been to war was ninety rounds of qualification firing on the rifle range.

"Rough was learning we were shooting firecracker rounds into civilian areas," Fox said. He stared at the Communicator. Dolby blinked, waiting for an explanation he could understand. Fox sighed and wrote his name. Toward the paper he said, "Artillery shells with eighty-eight separate bomblets in each one. There's always a few that don't detonate."

He straightened. Fox was an inch or so short of six feet. At a hundred and forty pounds, his joints and cheekbones stood out sharply. "The kids dug up shrapnel to sell for souvenirs," he went on. "It was the only goddamn thing there was to sell for food, that or themselves. When they found a piece of a firecracker round, nine times out of ten it went off in their hands. I volunteered for ordnance disposal when I saw the first little girl whose luck had run out that way. It made me feel better about what *I* was doing, at any rate."

Gathering up the folder on Kunayev, Fox started to walk back to his office. Behind him, Dolby said, "So you didn't know her after all—the DDO? Shai Gallen?"

The collection officer turned. The left side of his chest ached as if the cracked ribs had not healed thirteen years before. "I'm a peon, Mitch. Would I be here if I knew somebody that high up? Not that she'd let it matter anyway."

Dolby did not call again for an answer. Perhaps the Communicator realized that he'd been given one already.

When Fox set his elbows on his own desk, he cradled his face in his hands for a moment. The room smelled of stale cigarettes; Daniels was a smoker. There didn't seem to be any way to air the room out, even in the other man's absence. Today, the harsh odor was just one more damned thing. It was a wonder that Mehmet hadn't shot him.

The file told him that Abdulhamid Kunayev had been having the worst kind of luck recently also. He had risen fast as a member of Romanov's New Dedication team in 1987. His daughter's husband became Minister of Defense in maneuvering that was as much to Kunayev's benefit as a result of it. His status as a Politburo alternate, then a full member replacing his own cousin, was impressive enough. In fact Kunayev was actually one of the Party Secretary's half-dozen closest confidants. The file photo of Kunayev showed him standing di-

primary links to the Washington area—though in theory the chain of command passed through Ankara in both cases.

Fox tapped on his superior's closed door, then walked into the outer office. There should have been a U.S. national, a secretary. Deirdre had left abruptly three weeks before for personal reasons she hadn't confided to Fox. It wasn't that easy to replace staff with the required Top Secret clearance, so the three officers were doing their own typing until further notice. "Ed?" Fox called. "You were looking for a file?"

Instead of speaking, the station chief—about a decade older than his thirty-two year old subordinate—motioned Fox into the inner office. Fox had never been sure whether his distrust of the man stemmed from any better reason than Platt's curly, palpably false, hair. Apparently even that judgment was faulty: from the way Platt's forehead had risen over the past three years, his hair, at least, was real.

"Mitch said you were looking for the Kunayev file," Fox explained after he closed the door behind him. "I just returned it."

"Marvelous what a grade-school education can make of the simplest question, isn't it?" the station chief sneered. "I asked him what *you* were working on. Why on earth *were* you wasting your time in the dead files? I thought you had an agent contact this afternoon?"

Fox sucked his lips in. He kept his eyes unblinking and seemingly candid. "Right, I met. Nothing much to write up, but something may come of it in a week or two." He cleared his throat. Platt had not gestured him to a seat, and Fox wanted to cut the discussion short anyway. "The file, well . . . the damnedest thing. Just a few blocks from here,

I ran into a guy who could've been the spittin' image of Abdulhamid Kunayev. Well, not too surprising—he's a Turk, more or less, and we're in Turkey, the features aren't that rare. But I thought I'd check the file photo while the face was fresh in my memory."

Platt tapped an index finger on the polished teak surface of his desk. "Well?" he said.

On the wall behind the station chief was a framed group portrait from the Consulate-General archives. The photograph was of the staff of what had been the U.S. Embassy Istanbul in 1920 or so. Allen Dulles, the man who had made the CIA into an instrument of presidential policy, was one of the beaming figures. Fox recalled Dulles' autobiographical anecdote—told after he had risen too high to be harmed by it—about how he'd turned down a chance to meet with Lenin on the eve of the October Revolution. "Oh, the guy did look like Kunayev," Fox said, "but he was way too old. Need anything from me? Otherwise I'm going to knock off and go home—we're having the Barkers in for dinner tonight."

Platt gave him a look as flat as a petroglyph and rose from behind his desk. "Sure, Larry," he said accommodatingly, "you want to knock off, that's fine. I'll even give you a ride back to the apartment."

The Chief of Station kept up a running, catty patter as they walked down to his car. Fox noticed that while they were in the building, his superior's targets were Turks or personnel in Ankara. As soon as they reached the courtyard, however, Platt began to pick at Sam Barker, the new Deputy Principal Officer. Platt's take-off of Barker trying to greet the receptionist in Turkish was accurate enough, but Barker had been shipped to Istanbul with only six weeks of language training. At least the fellow was making an effort.

The ride back to the apartment block was as uncomfortable for Fox as the three-block distance made it unnecessary. Ed Platt drove the station's bulletproofed car everywhere—for safety reasons, he said. That meant the vehicle was unavailable for any real Agency business, which pissed off Daniels no end but was fine with Larry Fox. The vehicle was a black Chevy four by four. The sheets of Lexan would probably stop pistol bullets fired into the windows, but they also made them impossible to clean. Urban fumes grayed both inner surfaces even when no one forgot and lit a cigarette inside.

The plates of T-6061 aluminum in the body panels would have impressed Fox more if he hadn't seen what real projectiles did to the same material in Lebanon. Whatever the test range results might have been, at least part of a burst of jacketed nine-millimeters—like those from Sabanci's Browning—was going to come through tumbling.

Ed Platt was housed in the same apartment block as the Foxes, the Barkers, and several other Consulate-General families. The owners, a family of Turkish industrialists, had kept the top floor for themselves. Platt had insisted on a space in the enclosed garage under the apartment building rather than in the fenced courtyard behind it. That way he could enter and leave his armored vehicle without exposing himself to terrorists.

It also kept him from getting wet when it rained, of course. The rain was a far more common problem.

The driveway into the building was not chained, but there was a mixed handful of troops and police on duty as there were at the Consulate General itself. Fox cringed as his superior bounced over the curb-cut and brushed past the soldier who had bent over to check their identities. "Wogs will be wogs," Platt muttered. "You'd think they'd have learned by now not to interfere with me."

"Thanks for the lift, Ed," Fox said as he got out of the car. He half-expected the Turkish soldier to follow them, shouting, into the garage. Silly games with cars were bad enough at any time. When the victim of your joke was an 18–year–old kid with a Thompson submachinegun, your rank and diplomatic passport were a good deal less than adequate protection. Fox opened the stairwell door.

"Ta, lad," the station chief called as he pushed the elevator call button. His apartment was on the second floor, just beneath the Foxes'.

The door that closed behind Larry Fox made him feel more relaxed than he had been all day. Then he began to climb the stairs. With the welcome exercise came the memory of the Galata Tower: "The President of the United States is one of ours. . . ." Selim was crazy or a liar, whatever else he might be.

He wished that the Soviet hadn't run off that way. He wished that the Soviet had provided some concrete evidence as to who he was instead of being so damned coy. And most of all, he wished that Larry Fox had stayed in his office all this afternoon and didn't know a damned thing about whatever was going on.

"That was a delicious lamb roast, Kathie," said Sam Barker as he slid his chair back from the dinner table. He patted his stomach, already ample. "Delicious."

"Anybody for another drink before the evening's entertainment?" Larry Fox asked. He was already strolling to the sideboard that served as a liquor cabinet. "More Irish, Sam? And Susan?"

"I hope you're not just saying that about the lamb—for your own sake," Kathie said, leaning nearer to the deputy principal officer. "It's the *only* decent meat you can find in this miserable country."

"There isn't the French influence we're used to from Tunis," Susan Barker said in what Fox found an entrancing British accent, "so I presume there aren't the specialty horse butchers here."

Kathie looked at the other woman and blinked, then blinked again.

Only a ghost of a smile showed that Mrs. Barker was aware of the rise she had gotten. "Yes, Larry, another gin and tonic," she said.

"And sure, another hit for me too," her husband agreed. He got up when Larry did, but he walked to the television set instead of the sideboard. "I didn't think American TVs would work here," Barker said. "Or does, ah, your agency leave you in one country long enough that you just go ahead and buy one for while you're here?"

"God, it does seem like forever," Kathie said as she began clearing dishes. "And Larry says it's going to be another year and a half."

Fox formed his mouth into a smile. He ignored his wife and sidestepped the foreign service officer's question on CIA policy. "This is actually a mission TV, not ours," he said as he handed the Barkers their drinks. "We pass it and the VCR around on a schedule. Turkish TV isn't much, and what you might pick up from Greece and Eastern Europe here isn't a great deal better. In the southeast, some people have sets to watch Syrian broadcasts. Sesame Street dubbed in Arabic, for instance."

Susan Barker laughed unaffectedly. Sam knelt to browse through the box of video cassettes beneath the TV stand. "These look like private tapes. Doesn't the mission provide them, too?"

"The mission!" Kathie hooted angrily from the kitchen—but she *was* clearing the table. Kathie had been less prickly the past couple weeks than, hell, ever before in their marriage.

The light built into Fox's desk in the livingroom was on the fritz, and the glare of the overhead fixture on the TV screen was irritating. Fox walked quickly into the bedroom for the lamp on the nightstand. "There isn't a whole lot in the official library, no," he said as he returned. "We borrow tapes sometimes from residents with recorders of their own. The past year Glenn Alden, a lawyer friend of mine in the States, has been taping off the air. For the whole mission, really. He sent the Superbowl and a couple tapes of Saturday morning cartoons." He smiled. "Ads and all. It gives you a feeling for what foreign service means to families when you see Daniels's eight–year–old girl hug her daddy because the TV has a McDonald's ad on it."

Three years in Istanbul married to Kathie gave Fox a viewpoint on the family question, too, but fluent Turkish speakers were too rare to waste. Unlike Arabic, say, or Spanish, the slots in which they could be utilized were limited to Turkey itself and a few positions in the Agency's central bureaucracy. For a variety of reasons, Fox preferred Istanbul to Langley. He had never openly admitted that to his wife, however.

"What I thought we'd do tonight," Fox continued, "was to check something that came in the last batch. Glenn says it's a *Panorama* program on current controversies that caused quite a stir. He thought it—" Kathie came back into the living-dining room—"Glenn thought it was important for people who'd been out of the country for the past few years especially."

"Larry, you've got to remember not everybody's been stationed forever in West Bumfuck," Kathie said in the hard tones which she had managed to suppress so well for most of the evening. "The Barkers have probably seen it already."

"No, really, I missed it," Sam Barker said with an easy diplomacy which overlooked everything but the surface content of Kathie's outburst. "I did hear about it, though. Quite a *cause célèbre* back home. If we hadn't been running about getting things shipped to Istanbul, I would have looked up a copy of it myself. We'd like very much to see it."

"But I'll beg you for mercy on the Superbowl," Susan said, "even though we were in Tunis when that played, thank God."

"*Panorama* it is," Fox said without looking at his wife. He clicked the tape into the recorder.

"I don't care what they say about the United States," Kathie muttered as she poured her own Scotch. "They don't know how good it is till they've been stuck in a place like this."

The tape hissed in the recorder; then the screen bloomed into a 900-line, U.S. standard picture which always seemed to Fox, after weeks of Turkish television, to be amazingly bright and sharp. The logo of *NPT Panorama* faded to a liquid blue which at once coalesced into two faces on a blue background.

"Welcome to *Panorama*," said the male face. "I'm Don Welles—"

"—and I'm Rachel Joplin," continued the female, a shaven-skulled Black. "Tonight, we have something different for you."

The blue screen dissolved and the camera dollied back sharply, to show four people seated at a very ordinary broadcast desk, Welles and Joplin in the center and a pair of older white males flanking them.

"Ugh, that Welles makes my skin crawl," said Kathie as she stared at the TV.

"Rather reminds me of Ed Platt," Sam Barker commented, giving his attention to his drink for the next moment.

"We at *Panorama* have picked what we consider to be the major *continuing* stories of the past year," Welles was saying.

Kathie shot a hard glance at Sam Barker, but the foreign service officer preserved at least the appearance of innocent unawareness. Aloud, the blond woman said, "Well, I liked MacNeil and Lehrer."

"Goodness, they've been—" began Susan Barker with a giggle. She broke into a fit of diplomatic coughing as she realized that her intended remark, 'retired for years,' was absolutely the worst thing to say to a woman who was already complaining about how long she'd been away from the United States.

"—Owen Neely, President Crossfield's National Security Adviser and long-term political ally," Welles was concluding with a gesture and professional smile to the heavy, perspiring man beside him.

"While across the table," picked up Joplin with a gesture of her own, "is Professor Kurt Blaustein—"

"Jesus!" whispered Fox, startled to get his first look at the Deputy Director of Central Intelligence— in Fox's chain of command the way the Army Chief of Staff is in a sergeant's chain of command—in this fashion.

"—currently on leave from the Political Science Faculty of Harvard University where he some years ago taught a brilliant young undergraduate named James Crossfield," the anchor woman continued.

"Far too many years ago, I'm afraid, Rachel," Blaustein interjected with an engaging chuckle. His face sobered and he stroked one tip of his moustache. "I think I should add, though," he went on, and the director switched to a close-up of Blaustein's smooth face and seraphic white hair, "that both Mr. Neely and I are here representing ourselves, not Jim Crossfield and not the U.S. Government—in any of its branches or, ah, agencies."

The professor chuckled and looked away from the live camera to the two studio anchors. "Do we have to be quite that circumspect, I wonder, Don? Rachel?"

Welles joined in with a laugh of his own and said, "I guess that's really up to you, Kurt—" the camera drew back so Blaustein and the two anchors were in the shot; Welles looked toward the lens and said, "Professor Kurt Blaustein, ladies and gentlemen: private citizen and, during office hours, Deputy Director of Central Intelligence; here with us in the studio tonight to comment on the major continuing stories of 1995."

"What's a university professor doing in a job like that?" asked Susan Barker idly as she fingered one-handed through her purse for her cigarettes.

"He's not being asked to penetrate the Kremlin, is he?" said Larry Fox more sharply than he had intended.

"What's a paving contractor doing as National Security Advisor?" Sam Barker said, reaching for his wife's hand without looking at her directly; he patted the cigarettes back into her purse. "The President has known them for thirty years or more; they have his confidence; and for that matter, anything I've heard about Blaustein indicates that he has a very incisive, non-doctrinaire intelligence."

"—the extraordinary growth of the Friends of Survival," Rachel Joplin was saying and, in time with her words, the wall behind the participants flared with "FRIENDS OF SURVIVAL" in expanding white letters. The people at the broadcast desk did not disappear, but they were shrunken to a minuscule lower border of the screen which now showed a sea of pedestrians sweeping up the curving drive to the Pentagon. Blue and white Capitol Police helicopters dipped low enough over the line of march to appear in the shot, fluttering banners and sending straw hats sailing like leaves in October.

"July Fourth," said Don Welles, "and a march estimated by the police at two hundred thousand—"

"—and by the organizers themselves at a full half million," added Joplin on cue.

The camera angle shifted to a closeup of a middle-aged man wearing a plain T-shirt, old-fashioned, heavy-rimmed glasses, and a sun disk of metalized mylar held three inches above his head by a balance of static charges. "There are five hundred thousand of us here today," the man was saying as his fellows streamed past behind him, "but we are only a tiny fraction of those in this country and across the would who want to say this to the U.S. military: you will not dig our graves!"

Barely audible beneath the words of the Chairperson, as the caption described him, Owen Neely's voice rasped, "The two hundred thou was right. Hell, generous."

Sam Barker sniffed. "My God," he said.

"Yeah," said Fox in what was not quite agreement, "I'd give long odds the police figures were correct, but he doesn't seem to have any sense of when to speak and when to keep his mouth shut."

The television screen split into three sections behind the tiny figures at the broadcast desk. The aerial shot in the upper left showed the brightly clothed marchers as a snake miles long which seemed to reach all the way back to the Arlington Memorial Bridge. The picture in the upper right focused on the rank of soldiers wearing camouflage fatigues and incongruous blue riot helmets as they stood in front of one of the Pentagon entrances. The rifles which the troops carried ported across their chests had no magazines inserted, and plastic sheaths covered the fixed bayonets. All the soldiers appeared to be black, though the reflection from lowered face shields made it difficult to be sure.

The bottom half of the screen was filled with the front ranks of the Friends of Survival stripping off their light clothing and beginning to anoint themselves and one another with bottles of cooking oil. The participants were a total melange in age and sex—one young woman slung an infant on her back, the straps of the carrier crossing between breasts pendulous with milk—but Fox did notice that the vast majority of the naked bodies were Caucasian. The half picture expanded to full screen as the demonstrators flooded across an empty parking lot chanting what focused microphones picked up both as, "We will not let you dig our graves!" and "We will not dig *your* graves!"

The troops braced to stop the crowd, a task for . which they had as little chance of success as the ramparts of a sand castle do of holding back the sea. Men in uniform hindered by their rifles tried to grasp oiled bodies one-handedly as demonstrators squirmed past and under and even between the legs of the soldiers. Even then there might not have been significant damage to the building had not the double doors been swung open from the inside in an attempt to reinforce the cordon of troops when it was already too late to do so. The demonstrators roared, and the whole huge column ran to follow its naked leaders like a Viking wedge exploiting the breach torn by its front rank of berserkers.

The screen fragmented again as it displayed separate views of office windows being smashed out from the inside and a confetti of paper and electronic components showering down from them. Against that background, fading slowly to blue, the broadcast desk swelled again to normal size.

"To begin with, Mr. Neely," said the anchorwoman as a fresh scene began to form on the background, "how would you respond to critics who say that the government's response to peace protesters has often been extremely heavy-handed—that it was during the Fourth of July march we just watched, for example?"

Neely hunched forward and turned his head for a better view of his questioner instead of keeping one eye on a studio monitor. The close shot brought out the grim set of his jaw and the sweat glistening on his bald scalp. "Well, what *I'd* respond, honey," Neely said against a slow-motion background of an infuriated soldier clubbing a naked woman so fiercely that the light butt of his M16 broke away and pinwheeled over the crowd of demonstrators, "is that the security forces used quite *remarkable* restraint, too *much* restraint for some people to like it, if you ask me. Why, do you realize that it cost over a million dollars to clear up the mess those jackasses made? Out of pocket, I mean—not even thinking what the disruption and the *preparations* cost the taxpayers."

It was probably the audible gasp of incredulity from the studio crew which caused the presidential advisor to glance up at a monitor. He blinked and said, "By the way, there weren't but two hundred thou on that march, whatever they say."

"Well, Professor Blaustein," said Don Welles with a smile and a shake of his head, "do you agree with your colleague?"

"On the question of whether this particular march was five times as large as the town in which Owen grew up," said the white-haired professor, "or just twice as large, the way he insists, I really have no opinion."

Blaustein's smile faded as quickly as it had appeared, quenching Welles' ripple of laughter. "I think," he went on soberly, "that we can all agree with the organizer, that however many individuals may have been in Washington that weekend, they were only a hint of the numbers worldwide who sincerely long for peace.

"But—" and Blaustein's index finger extended at a 45° angle, above Welles rather than threateningly at him "—I also think, Don, that it's important to note that the Friends of Survival recognize their quarrel is with the military establishment rather than with the present administration. And I'm afraid that the same factor explains—though of course it cannot excuse—violence of the sort your cameras caught. There are men and women in the military who feel threatened by talk of peace and by our growing rapprochement with the Soviet Union ... and not all the, the *victims* of this fear, I must call them, are mere private soldiers like that one."

The professor looked straight into the live camera which locked his righteously-determined face in a close-up—and cued a quick-cut to a wide-angle panorama of the broadcast desk with a summoning motion of his raised index finger.

"Wait a minute," Susan Barker said. "Run that back. The last—the movement he made."

Larry Fox fumbled for the VCR controller, backed the tape too far, and then advanced it jerkily to the point Blaustein faced the camera.

"*There*," Susan said. "He's acting as director of the show, isn't he? Isn't that what it looks like?"

"Wonder if Neely knew that?" Larry Fox commented, disquieted.

As the tape continued to roll, the background seethed green and, as Owen Neely said, "Blaustein, Miss Joplin, I think you've got to recall that governments have the right to self-defense too...," the green formed itself into the verdant letters FARM POLICY.

"The next of our continuing controversies is the Farm Adjusted Parity Program," said the anchorwoman, with a bright smile for the camera and no sign at all that she had heard the National Security Advisor. "March 10, 1993—the Food Producers Union marches on the Mall where one hundred thousand members of civil rights and poverty groups are already gathered to protest food prices."

The background which swelled to fill the television picture was momentarily an impressionistic garden scene, great blurs of pastel color—until they congealed into a column of giant farm machinery, tractors and combines with enclosed cabs, rolling up 14th Street four abreast. The police cars leading the march with headlights and barlights flashing were dwarfed by the vehicles which followed, gay in coats of orange, yellow, chartreuse, true green, and a handful of other vivid colors.

The sirens and the blat of diesel engines powering the procession drove a wedge through all human sound, but there were too many throats on the Mall for their thunderous chant, "Bread and *Free*dom! Bread and *Free*dom!" to be silenced by mere machinery. The protesters were bundled against the cold; as they shouted, mist from their breath drifted across the sea of their black faces.

"Scarcely a triumph of planning," said Susan Barker, snapping the taut concentration of the others in the Istanbul apartment on the scene from their own past and country. Susan noticed the blinking confusion of her host and explained, "Well, it's no secret that neither group could have gathered in such numbers if the government hadn't helped transport them. And to have both arrive simultaneously, well—the right hand not knowing what the left was doing, I suppose."

On the screen, a double line of policemen on foot linked arms to hold back the crowd, but from just behind the front ranks on both sides of the street objects began to fly at the vehicles: eggs, tomatoes, balls of slush and mud trampled from the grass of the Mall. The organized chanting fragmented into something bestial and no less loud.

The shots, which everyone watching the videotape knew were coming, were only a dim popping. The screen filled with a blow-up, fuzzy despite computer enhancement, of glass in the cab of an Allis-Chalmers combine starring in splashes of blood red that complemented the orange enamel.

The framing of the television picture was backed to show the vehicle lurching to the right, through the line of unsuspecting policemen. Either by chance or the dying will of the driver, the twelve-foot reel of cutting blades began to rotate as the combine made its bloody way into the midst of the packed demonstrators.

The camera held on the scarlet waste of body parts in a zoom shot which finally became so close that it was a blur—which switched to green and was again the neutral background of the desk and the four studio participants.

"Professor Blaustein," said the anchorman in the funereal hush, "that tragedy was the real beginning of the program which some critics would say is overt Fascism: a direct copy of the Corporate State of Mussolini's Italy. How would you answer such criticisms?"

"I think, Don," Blaustein said, patting rather than stroking his moustache with one hand, "it might be more accurate to say that the necessary decision to governmentally develop red-meat alternatives—krill, soya, and—" he paused and flashed a smile, but did not attempt a euphemism "—squid fisheries for protein was the real genesis of the Farm Adjusted Parity Program. What that terrible, saddening event did—" Blaustein gestured to the background, and for a moment the innocuous letters were replaced by the carnage displayed earlier "—was to force the Legislative Branch to realize that things could not be permitted to muddle on the way they had been."

For an instant, Owen Neely appeared to be trying to speak at the other end of the desk, but the sound was not picked up. The director switched to a close shot of Blaustein as the professor enumerated his points, raising the fingers of his left hand, "By the common marketing provisions of FAPP, producers are guaranteed a wage commensurate with the back-breaking labor which farming entails—something the so-called free market never did. Consumers are guaranteed cereals, protein, and garden truck at prices well below those they would have had to pay in the days before the government rationalized marketing—and in the days when protein meant steers which required ten pounds of high-grade feed to provide one pound of beef. Finally, the United States now dominates world grain markets to a greater extent than OPEC ever dominated oil—with all the attendant benefits to American foreign policy."

He smiled again and folded his three fingers loosely against his palm. "There are critics of FAPP to be sure, but not among producers, consumers, or those who wish to have the rest of the world looking toward our country for reasons other than our life-threatening military might. They are critics of the cost—" Blaustein gestured to the screen, and the bloody background reappeared "—though what the cost in lives of the alternative would have been is clear to anyone."

"Well, I certainly find that persuasive," said Rachel Joplin as the camera dollied back to include her in the shot. "Does it persuade *you*, Mr. Neely, since you're rumored to be one of the strongest opponents within this administration of adjusted parity?"

"Rumored, hell," muttered Neely to his hands locked in front of him, "but I couldn't stop that either, could I?"

The heavyset man glared into the live camera, and for just a moment the picture was that of a man who had fought his way early to business success, then turned the same power and talent to political fund-raising and an organization which always had the right people ready to meet Candidate Crossfield, and which saw to it that the candidate had been fully briefed before each meeting.

Then the director cut away to a shot over Neely's shoulder toward Welles's manicured smile, as the National Security Advisor continued, "What I think about FAPP is that the *average* price of an acre of Iowa farmland sold last year was thirty-eight hundred dollars. Figure that against a two-hundred acre farm and you'll see what a crash there's going to be when we roll back FAPP because *everybody* sees the country can't support it."

The background was sharpening into the scene of the riot again but Neely, fully aware this time, waved at it brusquely and snapped, "I'm not against social programs or farmers, and god *knows* I'm not in favor of riots. But the country can't *afford* FAPP."

"Well, Mr. Neely, there you differ with our elected representatives," said Joplin, "who just passed President Crossfield's request for expanded funding for farm parity."

"I'll tell you something else we can't afford," Neely said so forcefully that habit drew the camera to him in a close shot. The fringe of remaining hair from his temples around the back of his head was fiercely black, a minor vanity since he had never been comfortable in a wig. "You talk about beef, but grain sold for *any* animal feed's at the full new price—that's chickens that could otherwise compete pretty damn well with your processed sea-uglies."

Neely pointed at Joplin with his palm down and index finger extended. "You try and buy a real steak now because you can afford it and you're lucky if people only spit at you. It's like parking your Mercedes in the ghetto. People who used to eat hamburger and chicken, *poor* people I'm talking about, they get patties that smell like the freezer went out two days before. And you know what the *real* joke is, honey? The real joke?"

The big man's stabbing finger was causing Joplin to flinch away with a fixed smile. The male anchor, seated between them was blinking in surprise.

"We're selling grain to the Soviets, thanks to FAPP," Neely continued, "*giving* it to them at a third the price the U.S. government pays for it. And they're using it to build up their meat and dairy herds!"

The cutting motion Kurt Blaustein made at the edge of the present frame was unmistakable and obeyed with alacrity. "I think we can agree," the professor said as a camera focused on his smoothly comfortable body, "that the Soviet Union *has* become increasingly dependent on the United States for its food supplies. What I'm frankly puzzled by is the fact that Owen objects to the way we have pushed our superpower rivals out on a limb which is ours to saw off upon any failure of the detente process."

"Sam," said Larry Fox to the foreign service officer beside him, "maybe it's just because it's not my field that I don't recall anything, but just what *have* we gotten from the Soviets in exchange for our grain shipments the past three years?"

"—a new militance of the women's movement," Welles was saying from the television, echoing the blazing red letters of WOMEN forming on the background.

"Well, they deigned to sign SALT IV," said Barker with more bitterness than the CIA man had expected, "but—since in the course of the negotiations we conceded every point they made an issue of—I suppose the real marvel is that *we* signed. Other than that. . . ."

On quadrants of the screen, women battled police against four separate urban backgrounds which Fox could not identify.

"Other than that," Barker concluded thoughtfully, "I suppose you could talk of a general easing of tensions. But nothing concrete, no."

"How do *I* feel about it?" demanded the black-haired woman whose head and shoulders now filled the expanded background scene and the picture on Fox's set. "I feel that there're twenty thousand more chances of life and happiness than there were a few minutes ago."

The camera dollied back to show the huge vat of an arc furnace over which dangled a crane-slung electromagnet. The magnet jounced again and a few more tiny objects, clinging by residual effect, fell away into the furnace before the crane operator swung away for another load from the first of a line of dump trucks.

"Every one of those had a life in it," the woman said in a voice-over as the camera zoomed to a close shot of the magnet as it was energized and the whole truck body leaped up against the springs as the crane lifted away. "One life or a hundred lives," continued the woman, while the magnet rose followed by tangles and festoons of handguns—barrels nickeled and stainless and blued, grips of wood, plastic, ivory, and a score of more exotic materials—which swung with it over to the arc furnace and then fell away. A uniformed supervisor on the truck bed waved and the vehicle moved so that the next load could advance into position.

The picture shifted to another camera and a flat angle on a long rank of placard-bearing women; the closest and only legible sign read "End Male Violence—Before It Ends YOU!" The group was mixed in age, though younger faces predominated; and it was noticeable that, though the members had dressed for the media event in their best, that "best" cut a wide range of social classes.

The dark-haired woman, captioned as National Chairperson of The 52% as the shot closed on her again, said, "The handgun ban wouldn't save a single life if it were up to male-dominated police authorities to enforce it. It's up to those of us who are overwhelmingly the victims of macho violence to first *inform* the authorities of where illegal weapons are being held and then to stand behind, pushing, until somebody takes proper action on that information. Voluntary compliance with gun laws would be a *joke*, a brutal joke, if it weren't that thousands of gun-owning swine have already learned that any house with a woman or a child in it is a house that the police may search for guns at any moment."

The camera returned to the magnetic grab as it rotated again toward the arc furnace with what was conservatively a quarter million dollars worth of handguns dangling beneath it. Then the scene folded back into itself and reemerged as the fiery letters WOMEN behind the broadcast desk.

"Professor Blaustein," said Joplin, "how do *you* regard this new female militancy?"

"I'm glad you chose to focus on The 52%, Rachel," said Blaustein with an approving nod, "rather than on the street violence which has been the most visible aspect of some of the other "New-women's" organizations. I think that violence is a natural result of dedicated people frustrated at trying to correct thousands of years of injustice instantly— but what The 52% and similar groups have done is to throw their weight behind an identifiable and critical facet of this administration's domestic policy. Their reward has been stunning success in place of frustration—and a safer nation for all of us to live in."

"Mr. Neely," asked Don Welles with his swarmy grin, "would you care to comment on news reports that you had a brush with federal investigators over handguns you retained illegally after the amnesty period?"

"What the *hell* is this?" bellowed Owen Neely, his head coming erect from the glowering slump into which he had let himself slip. His right hand clenched, though it did not quite rise in an open threat. He caught himself and spread his fist in what was an obvious effort of will rather than relaxation. "No," Neely said in a voice like rocks grating, "I don't want to talk about my personal life, buddy—and if you want to learn how a camera tastes, you just push that crap once more."

Welles blinked again. "Ah," he said, "then on to a less personal topic—"

"No, wait a minute!" the National Security Advisor demanded loudly, drawing the camera back onto him. "Doesn't anybody care about what this really means? I mean, okay, pistols have been outlawed, that's the law and I'm not going to argue about it here. But we've got some tight—some—some woman bragging that she's training every wife and kid in the country to be a *fink*, and we're supposed to cheer? You talk about families nowadays when kids are taught in school to turn in the old man for a three-year fall if he happens to take the Second Amendment seriously?"

"Not the Second Amendment on which the *United States* Supreme Court has ruled, I'm afraid, Mr. Neely," Welles closed. "But now, from domestic violence on Earth to the peaceful development of outer space."

POWERSAT surged onto the screen in letters of

electric blue before it split into halves, the left side of the split so sharply delineated that Larry Fox was sure for an instant that it was an artist's rendering. It was too huge to be real—but the take-off seared space shuttle that sailed close by the camera's viewpoint was real, and it shrank down to bullet size as it neared the miles of gallium arsenide solar cells in corrugated ranks. Though he had probably heard the dimensions of the field of solar collectors—three miles by six— the CIA officer had not grasped the significance of that size in human terms. It was like looking across one of the vast valleys of northern Mesopotamia and realizing that you saw no men not because the land was barren but rather because men were too small to be seen against the scale of distance.

The other side of the split screen was more immediately recognizable; for, though the Kalahari Reception Antenna was huge in its own right— larger, actually, than the collector field above it in geosynchronous orbit—the foreground of the shot was a patrol of U.S. soldiers in desert-pattern fatigues.

"Rockwell Number One power-generating satellite," said Rachel Joplin.

"And the Kalahari Rectenna, which will provide southern Africa with five gigawatts of electrical power," continued Don Welles, "outside the control of the racist government of the Union of South Africa. Because of alleged threats by the white minority of South Africa, construction crews under the general oversight of the Texas-based firm PA&E are being guarded by troops of the United States Fourth and Twenty-third Infantry Divisions."

"Mr. Neely," said the anchorwoman, "do you think it's desirable to undertake an aid program which must be defended by American soldiers from third-party attacks?"

"Jes—" blurted the heavy man. "I mean, good God, *that's* not the problem—I'd be a whole lot happier if we still had our troops in South Korea. It's the whole *idea* that's crazy, spending this absolutely incredible amount of money on an idea that won't work and if it did work would destabilize the situation in southern Africa—which right now is beneficial to U.S. interests!"

"I don't know that support of racism has ever been in the American interest, Owen," Kurt Blaustein interjected in measured, reasonable tones which could be understood clearly because Neely's sound link had been switched off when the director cut away from him. "As for the workability of the scheme, the best scientific minds in this country are sure it *will* work, and the siting of the reception antenna in an unpopulated area is certain protection against the claimed fears of side-effects that some critics have raised."

"Yes, but what about the cost that so concerns Mr. Neely?" asked Don Welles with a friendly wave of his hand toward Blaustein, rhetorical support rather than an interruption.

"I'm glad you asked that, Don," said the professor with an approving nod. "Because the cost of this and similar programs already in the planning stages—gifts of energy, the most valuable aid our nation can give a Third World trying to industrialize in the face of shortages and uncertainty in the flow of oil—the cost of these programs is almost exactly what would have been wasted on the Stealth bomber system of which Owen was so open an advocate."

He aimed his index finger at Neely on the other end of the desk. "The only *desirable* function which

Stealth would have accomplished would have been to maintain the American aerospace industry and to mollify, to be frank, that important political lobby. The powersat program maintains our valuable pool of trained personnel, and it does so by bringing hope of a brighter future instead of threatening doom to the whole world."

"All right, you want to talk about doom?" rasped Owen Neely's voice from out of the frame. Those watching Kurt Blaustein, shocked for the first time out of his air of good-humored repose, assumed the director had turned the other participant's sound back on. In fact, when the camera was switched to a view of the entire broadcast desk, Neely was leaning angrily toward Don Welles from whose lapel he had snatched the button microphone into which he was snarling, "Let's talk about what these black Confrontation States—that's their own name for themselves—are really going to do with this so-called power satellite when they get their hands on it."

"As you know," said Blaustein, but not loudly enough because he was unused to having to speak over an angry opponent, "the satellite will remain under—"

"Wake up and read the *newspapers*, buddy!" snapped Owen Neely, whose voice faded and thundered as he gestured toward the professor with the hand which held the miniature microphone. "Namibia, Zambia, Mozambique—the whole Marxist lot of 'em, and if you don't believe *that*, you can't read either, the whole lot are already agitating for "national control of national necessities." If you think we're going to hang onto that pile of aluminum sheeting in an orbit that doesn't do *us* any good in the face of that brotherhood of man crap, you're even dumber than I've always thought you were."

Neely paused for breath. Blaustein opened his mouth again to speak, just as Don Welles attempted to grab his microphone back.

"Touch me again, sonny, and you won't know what hit you," the heavy National Security Advisor said. His voice was unexpectedly soft but just as threatening as the fist which he balled around the little mike. Welles jumped back as if he had been punched already, and Kurt Blaustein twisted speechlessly between thumb and forefinger the tip of one moustache. Rachel Joplin whispered something in the ear of her male counterpart.

"Right," said Neely with the measured calm of a tiger on its kill, "and so we hand the powersat over to the Angolans and company, and they tilt the sending antenna a degree or two—and that five gigawatts of microwaves cook Jo'burg to a turn, don't they? And Capetown, *and* Pretoria—and don't tell me they wouldn't fry their own black brothers, buddy, because I *saw* the footage from Bulaweyo last year when the Fifth Brigade decided to solve the Ndebele problem their own way."

Rachel Joplin winced and touched her own precisely-shaven scalp; she, too, remembered the bonfires and the black hands slinging screaming black bodies onto them.

Welles leaned closer to the National Security Advisor, keeping his fingers pointedly laced to avoid the suggestion that he was going to make another attempt on the microphone. He said, audibly though in an attenuated voice, "Ah, Mr. Neely, I think the fault in your own microphone has been repaired, so if you could return . . . ?"

Neely looked at the glossy, younger man scornfully. Instead of turning over the mike he held, he unclipped the unit from his own lapel and skidded it to Welles across the broadcast desk.

The anchorman fumbled twice before he managed to pick up the button-sized microphone; but as soon as it was attached, Welles was transformed again into a smirking plastic extrusion of a man. "Well, Rachel," he said, "our viewers tonight are certainly getting the diversity of viewpoints they expect from National Public Television." He coughed. "And now it's time for our final segment of the evening—the frightening increase in racial extremism."

The background screen again split as the desk shrank before it, but for a moment only the right half had sound. Blacks, both males and females though the sexes were in alternating ranks, leaped through what seemed a combination of calisthenics and rifle drill, though the "weapons" were wooden cut-outs. There were at least five hundred people visible through the camera's eye, pulsing in unison and chanting in a language Larry Fox could not even identify.

Then the sound came up for the left-hand picture, replacing the throbbing chant with clear voices that made Fox shiver for no reason he could have explained. A chorus of boys in short khaki uniforms on a stage beneath a tent or canvas marquee sang, "Die strasse frei den braunen bataillonen! Die strasse frei dem Sturmabteilungsmann...." as both sides of the screen began to reform. The CIA officer had barely enough German to catch the words, but nothing in his background fitted him to recognize the lilting song as the one Hans Heinz Ewers had ghostwritten for a dead man—Horst Wessel.

There was a bloody joy to the rhythms from both sides of the screen which were more disturb-

ing at an elemental level than the open slaughter
the tape had recorded earlier. The picture now
was of the steps of the Lincoln Memorial and the
torchlit figure of a giant black man thundering
through a sophisticated—and scarcely visible—
sound system. "But what do Onyx Justice say?
Onyx Justice say *no* white man frees a black man!
Onyx Justice say the black man frees himself!"

The roar of the crowd was so loud and all-
pervading that it appeared at first to be a fault in
the tape. A quick cutaway to an overhead shot
showed a sea of waving torches filling square blocks
between Constitution and Independence Avenues.

" 'How do I help my black brother?' the white
man say," continued the speaker. "Onyx Justice
tells him, 'We don't want your Detroit and Cleve-
land, white boy. We don't want your southside
Chicago, we don't even want your Little Havana.

" 'Give us Georgia, white man. Give us Louisi-
ana and Mississippi and Alabama, give us the
Carolinas. Then you'll be shut of us. But better
give them to us quick, my man—or you won't like
it when we come take them!' "

And the crowd roared like a dragon as the scene
blurred and shifted to different torches and a
similarly-excellent sound system booming from a
temporary stage on the Ellipse, "We ain't here to
protest Jim Crossfield, who's a real American just
like ourselves."

The lighted façade of the White House was out
of focus in the distance. The man at the center
front of the stage wore a business suit, but many
of those seated behind him on folding chairs were
in brown uniforms, as was the squad before the
stage holding standards and ceremonial rifles with
chromed metalwork. Overhead hung a banner of

luminescent cloth reading NATIONAL AMERICAN BUND.

"We're here," continued the speaker, a thin, intense man whose age was indeterminate in the torchlight, "because Washington, D.C. has got too many kikes and niggers in it trying to box real Americans in!"

The response of the crowd was savage, though distinctly higher-pitched than that of the gathering shown at the Lincoln Memorial moments before. The contrast was that of a cougar's shriek against a lion's.

"I can't *believe*," murmured Susan Barker, "that groups like these get government support."

"Well, it's probably easier to keep an eye on an umbrella grouping than it is on perhaps hundreds of little splinters going their own ways," her husband suggested, but Barker himself was frowning.

"But support?" Susan repeated. "*These*?"

"Jim Crossfield," shouted the television, "has to know that the real Americans *do* support him and that we won't let those others box him in. All over the country, in the towns and in the cities, there's men and women and true-blooded children ready to stand up for freedom on the Day! And if anybody says, 'Well, sure, but what about the Army?'—I say to them, go to a Ready Reserve drill, my friend, and recall that any one of the white men in the Reserve is worth ten niggers in a so-called active unit!"

And even as the screen began to dissolve to the black letters of RACISM, the camera pulled a closeup of the men seated behind the speaker. Most of them wore brown, but at least three of the stern-faced figures were in the green of U.S. Army Class A uniforms.

"Professor Blaustein," said Rachel Joplin, with

an arch smile, "don't you find this extremism to be frightening?"

"America was settled by extremists, my dear," said Blaustein in an avuncular voice, "and while I find some of the current manifestations sad—no, I can't say that they frighten me."

The professor paused and stroked his moustache with an index finger which he then raised as he added, "I don't mean to imply that I don't believe vigilance is in order. I was personally very greatly reassured when the last Congress gave the FBI national felony jurisdiction. Without a national, centralized control over the potential for crime and violence—yes, there would be reason for fear. But while the historical imperatives of our culture seem to be changing from the blandness of the melting pot to the vibrant individuality of distinct races, so long as the government is strong enough to lead and protect those separate facets of the new America, we will all gain by the changes."

"Mr. Neely, then," said Don Welles with the wary expression of a man feeding the dog which already bit him once, "do you have any thoughts on racism for the closing moments of our broadcast?"

Throughout most of the program, Owen Neely had lowered in his corner like a bull being goaded by picadors. Now for the first time the big man looked as though he were battered to the edge of submission—but by events rather than the trio with whom he shared the camera.

He lifted his head and said directly to the live camera, "Doesn't it bother anybody that there used to be a country called America that was proud of itself . . . and what we've got now is, hell, it's not the fifty states, it's more like there's a thousand different directions that everybody's going off in, f-screw the rest, I'm gonna get mine. . . ?

"Black, white, I wouldn't care about that if it was all, but *hell*," Neely wiped his brow with his left hand and said, looking down at the desktop, "I just pray it's not really like Humpty Dumpty. I just pray there's some way we *can* get back together again."

"And for those of us together at *NPT Panorama*," said Don Welles briskly through his slick smile, "thank you for joining us and our guests—Professor Kurt Blaustein of Harvard—"

"And Mr. Owen Neely," continued Rachel Joplin, "ex-campaign manager for President James Crossfield."

A burst of visual static closed that segment of the tape. The screen cleared into the title sequence of one of the network sit-coms Glenn taped for them. Istanbul *was* a long way away from what Americans had been raised to think of as civilization. Fox shut off the recorder.

"I'll tell you the truth," said Sam Barker from beneath a frown, "we were only back for sixty days this time. But from what we saw then, and what our girls tell me—they're in school in Philadelphia—I can't argue with what Neely says."

"I sometimes wonder," said Susan Barker, "just what the Russians could do differently if *they* were in control of the United States and wanted to take away all our freedoms." She laughed. "Of course," she added, "my dear father used to wonder the same thing about Clement Atlee."

Larry Fox did not laugh. His hands began to tremble so badly that he had to pause before pouring another round of drinks.

And he needed a drink very badly.

*　　*　　*

"Entrez," called Ed Platt from the inner office the next morning. When Fox did enter, his superior's bland expression became a smirk. "So the party boy returns to us."

"It was dinner with another consulate family, Ed," Fox said uncomfortably. "It wasn't some kind of drunken orgy."

"Whatever you say, boy, whatever you say," the Chief of Station commented. He waited with an expression at once inquiring and supercilious. Despite that, an unusual level of nervousness animated Platt's features. Fox knew Platt was ambitious and wondered if the senior man had heard rumors from the board meeting on his pending promotion.

"Look Ed," said Fox, "one of my agents has been making noises that he could deliver a high-level defector." He lowered his eyes from Platt's face so that he did not have to guess as to what was going on behind the smirk. "It's probably a crock, but . . . I wonder just how high I'm authorized to go if things were on the level. Nothing without hard evidence of intelligence value, of course." He looked up.

Platt was holding himself as stiff in his chair as if there were a broomstick up his ass, his lips pursed. "Well, Larry," he said carefully, "that would have to depend on just what you meant by high level, wouldn't it? A colonel might be one thing. The—" Platt's eyes held Fox as if the Chief of Station were using his gaze to troll for the truth in the other man's brain "—Commander of the Ural Military District, for instance, would be something else again. And there are some potential defectors for whom virtually no payment would be unreasonable."

He cleared his throat. Fox nodded in tight-lipped

agreement, though his question had not been answered.

"Does Sabanci say just how exalted this personage is?" Platt continued. "Frankly, I'd be cautious about what that man told me about yesterday's weather. I've met him, you know."

The Chief of Station had filled in at a scheduled meet with Sabanci when Fox was on leave. The Turk had thought Platt was a homosexual and berated Fox at the next meeting about his "friend." "I know what you mean about TICRAM," Fox said now, using Sabanci's cryptonym, "but he's really pretty accurate. The craziness gets in the way of believing him, sure." He took a deep breath. "He hasn't really said. Probably nothing to any of this."

"Or he's a phony, this defector," Platt said, pointing with both index fingers like a twin gun turret.

"I keep remembering," Fox said slowly, "that Colonel Penkovsky offered himself to CIA right here in Istanbul. And the folks here then turned him down because they figured any walk-in that high up in military intelligence had to be a Soviet plant. So a couple years later he went to MI-6. The Brits, thank god, showed a little better judgment."

The Chief of Station's paired fingers withdrew until they were part of a noncommittal steeple. His eyes were as flat and gray as boulders in an ice sheet. "Well, you'd better go for it if you're that sure, hadn't you, Larry-boy?" Platt said in a voice whose lilt belied his expression. "I want full reports of your progress, but we won't put anything in writing just yet. That might be a little embarrassing later, don't you think? But you *will* keep me informed."

"Ed, I'm not claiming we've got another Penkovsky," Fox said. "But I know my source, and I think it's something I ought to pursue."

He could see his superior getting ready to hang him out to dry. It made him mad rather than frightened as it would have done a day earlier. Larry Fox had been medevacked from Lebanon when a bullet struck the revolver in his shirt pocket and cracked four ribs. Sabanci's finger whitening on the trigger of his Browning had shunted the young line officer back to days in which "cut-throat" and "hard-ball" had nothing to do with office politics. The sneers of a little turd like Platt were not going to keep Fox from doing his job as ably as he could.

"Look," Fox added, "I've got people from Second Section coming in this afternoon. But I'm going to go see TICRAM tonight. I've got time to pick up the bike and some less obtrusive clothes from home right now." It struck him that the station chief had referred to the agent by his real name, Sabanci. The slip was odd, without being particularly important in context. "We'll know more after I've had a chance to thrash things out with him."

Platt nodded curtly. "I want you to report to me directly when you've seen TICRAM," the station chief said. "I don't want you to stop for dinner, I don't want you to change clothes again. Do you understand?"

"Clear as crystal, Ed," Fox said as he reached for the doorknob.

"Close the outer one and leave this open," Platt said. "And don't talk to anybody or do anything after the meet until you've reported to me. Do you understand?"

Fox suppressed his scowl, but he said, "Yo, baas," as he walked out of his superior's office. He had enough composure not to bang the heavy door.

Platt waited the better part of a minute without moving. Then he picked up the phone and keyed a number from memory. The connection was quick, surprisingly quick for a phone system which suffered, like all of Turkey, from a lack of foreign exchange to upgrade its plant. The fifth ring was cut off in the middle by a breathless, "Hello?"

"Kathie?" the Chief of Station said. "Look, baby, Larry's going to be home in a few minutes but he'll be going out again. Give me a call when he leaves, all right?"

He listened to her answer. "Yes, of course!" he snapped. "Here at the office." He slammed the phone down. Except for his petulant grimace at the last, his face had not changed since before Fox had left the room.

Platt gathered a fresh pack of cigarettes from the lower drawer of his desk. He had another call to make, but that one would not go through the Consulate-General switchboard. He had in his apartment a scrambler which did not come from Agency stores.

He was already rehearsing the way he would handle Kathie. Figuratively and literally.

It was a pleasure to crumple the ruffled flounces of the dress instead of letting her take it off first. The silly bitch had taken the time to change into it, blue and new and pretty, instead of coming downstairs immediately when he told her to. She could not know how tight his schedule was, but she didn't have to think, a task for which she was monumentally unsuited. All she had to do was obey him. He used gathered fistfuls of the fabric as handles to thrust himself deeper again.

The bed shifted, thumping the wall. Kathie moaned. She had braced her hands against the footboard. Her own feet were firmly on the floor with her legs splayed so that Platt could stand between them to enter her. Her face was turned sideways, eyes and mouth both slackly open.

Kathie's pleasure was a requirement of the operation. The necessity irritated him—she was *so* stupid—but Platt let go of the dress with his right hand. He reached around her pelvis with his freed hand and began to finger her clitoris as he thrust against her buttocks. She gasped, again, a third time—and let out the gathered breaths in a great wordless cry.

Platt smiled like a watersnake with a mouthful of frog. The expression would not have conduced toward the image Platt was aiming for at the moment, but Kathie was beyond consciousness of externals. He continued to pump. Her arms began to buckle. Platt shifted both hands to the knobs of her hipbones and lowered her directly against the bedboard without missing a beat.

Kathie was mumbling, "Oh God," over and over. Platt was as far from climax or interest in his own climax as he had been when he opened the door to her. She had at most been a diversion, and this today was not even that—just business. There were other ways to have accomplished the task set for him this afternoon . . . but circumstances simply made screwing her the easiest technique, irritating or not.

Enough. Platt withdrew and stood upright. No need to change the sheets, thank goodness for small blessings. Kathie knelt at the foot of the bed, supporting her arms and head on the upper rail. She drew in a deep breath and turned, opening her eyes for the first time in minutes. "Oh, God, Ed," she whispered. She reached for his penis, her mouth already opening to engulf its tip.

Platt twisted away, "Now, now, too much of a

good thing," he said. "You're far too much woman for me, darling."

"Oh, Ed," the woman repeated. She managed to stand up after the second attempt. "I want to spend some real time with you so bad. At least a night."

"Well, we have to be sensible, don't we?" the station chief said. Conditioned reflex kept the lilt in his voice ... though there *would* be some satisfaction in introducing this moron to the leather and chrome-plated steel in his locked suitcase. Platt ordinarily reserved that paraphernalia for paid partners, who could be silenced afterwards by a bonus—or a bonus to their pimps. Kathie's clinginess was beginning to grate very badly.

Aloud, Platt continued, "You have your car keys?"

"Yes, but I thought you wanted to borrow... ?" Kathie said. She caught the towel Platt threw her when he was finished with it. The blond woman looked fragile and awkward as she tried to keep her dress and slip away from her thighs until she had dried them.

"I *do* want to borrow the apartment," the station chief said. He opened the woman's purse and rummaged through it for her key ring without bothering to put his trousers on first. "What I want *you* to do, my dear, is to go straight downstairs and drive away. Don't stop at your room, and don't come back for two hours." The keys to the three door locks were easy to identify because they were similar to Platt's own. He removed them from the ring and handed the purse to its owner. "Remember," he lied, "this is a *very* important meeting or I'd be able to use an ordinary safe house. If Larry gets even a whisper that it's been held in his apartment, well ... you can't imagine how bad it will be."

Kathie held the purse in one hand and the panties which she had not had time to put on in the other, her face a complex of emotions which were less clear to her than to Platt—who had seen such faces many times before.

The woman blinked and stuffed the lacy blackness into the purse. "I'll show you you can trust me, Ed," she said as she stepped to him for the obligatory kiss.

Platt responded with practical enthusiasm. No point in ruining a successful performance by muffing the final scene, after all. "Now you scoot off and let me play the games Uncle needs me for," he said as he disengaged. He patted her rump. The dress had not wrinkled badly after all. "Remember, at least two hours." He guided her out the door without the pause that she would have tried to fill with another embrace.

Platt walked to the window overlooking the street. He set the copy of Spengler on the sill as agreed, then stepped back fingering the keys he had taken from Kathie. The people who wanted to check the Foxes' apartment did not need the keys to gain entry, but they did need some time to themselves. Kathie would not interrupt them if she could not open her own front door.

Ed Platt preferred that nothing go wrong. Sometimes the people hired to do legwork overreacted when things went awry. Kathie deserved anything her stupidity got her into, of course . . . but Platt got a little squeamish at some things.

Larry Fox was a head taller than most Turks. Certainly he was too tall for a Turk who weighed only Fox's 140 pounds stripped. On the credit side, his hair was black and his skin tanned to a swarthiness unremarkable among the locals. In any case, Fox was not trying to pass under close scrutiny as a Turk. He simply liked to keep a low profile on those occasions when he had to deal with his Turkish agents on their own ground.

For that purpose, Fox was dressed this evening in garments of local cut and manufacture. There was nothing about the clothing that would have set him strikingly apart anywhere in the United States. The cotton slacks were on the full side, similar to carpenters' jeans but without the extra pockets and loops. His rubber and canvas shoes were not Nikes, but they were styled in deliberate imitation. His shirt was white and long-sleeved. He wore a dark sweater and a wool blazer as well. The combination was ordinary enough—without a tie—and it added bulk to Fox's slim frame.

So dressed, and given his fluency in Turkish, he could poke around in Sabanci's hardware store until circumstances made it possible for them to talk. It wasn't ideal, but neither was the situation. What they might—*might*—be sitting on was hot. It was too hot to wait to be developed in the course of planned meetings or whenever Sabanci and his principal decided to resume contact themselves.

Fox's Jawa motorcycle stalled as he concentrated on backing it between the bumpers of a pair of parked Fords. The bike had the usual two-stroke problem of loading its plugs when it wasn't kept on the buzz. Istanbul's streets and traffic did not encourage spirited riding . . . but hell, they couldn't afford a second car, and Fox couldn't walk everywhere. Kathie didn't like to be left without transportation; and anyhow, she needed to do the shopping.

The American cursed the bike in Turkish—the men who built you do not resemble their fathers—and muscled it as a dead weight up the street's camber. He let the Jawa roll back to the curb just out of contact with the two cars. God knew how the cars could move with the bike between them. They probably had been parked too close to be maneuvered out even before the Jawa was inserted, though—room to park in the Pera district was always at a premium.

As Fox crossed the narrow street, he wondered what would happen if he walked in on Sabanci and "Selim" right now. His palms became clammy. He couldn't transport the defector on the little bike—certainly not if he expected to take the man against his will to the American consulate. Fox was generally a little afraid before meetings with Mehmet Sabanci. The better he got to know the Turk, the more difficult it was to relax around him. This business with Kunayev had just given Fox something new to worry about besides being split open by a seven-inch knife.

The shop was three steps down from street level. Repavings in the centuries since the building's foundations had been laid down had gradually raised the street. It was the modern equivalent of the process which had turned Troy into a mount, a tell, on the plain of the Scamander.

Lighting inside was from a single incandescent fixture and what sunlight filtered through the grimy windows. Tools and baskets of twine hung from the joists and cluttered the shelves. There were several men within the shop already, eliminating Fox's hope of an immediate chance to talk with his agent. Instead of a counter, the shop had a desk in one corner with an old cash register on it.

The heavy-set man at the desk was not Mehmet Sabanci.

"Excuse me," the CIA officer muttered as he turned and found it was already too late to get out of the shop. Two men stood between him and the door. They were short but broad enough that either could have filled the doorway. "I need fifty meters of electrical wire—" Fox said to the pair. Handsaws hung within reach, but nothing else with potential as a weapon "—for rewiring an apartment, you know, I am trying to save—"

The man who had been at the desk grabbed him from behind, and a fourth man caught Fox's right elbow when he jabbed backward with it. The Turk bent his right arm as if to use it for a hook by which to hang the American. His partner kept his grip on Fox's left arm with one hand and tugged upward on a fistful of hair with the other.

The men between Fox and the door stepped forward deliberately. One of them stubbed a cigarette out on his own left palm. There was a fifth figure in the shop, an elderly man who locked the front door and drew the blinds over the windows. Fox's eyes were wide open in an attempt to lessen the terrible tension against his scalp. He could not see clearly even so. His eyes had not adapted to the dim light and his brain was overloaded with adrenalin which he could neither fight nor run to burn away.

The fifth man had pale, non-Turkish features. His three-piece suit was Western and of very high quality. The four thugs who surrounded Fox like the jig of a drop forge were local in dress and appearance.

"Once," said the fifth man in accented Turkish. Each of the pair in front of Fox punched the American in the abdomen.

He had felt a blow like theirs once before, when a bullet from an assault rifle had struck the revolver he carried in his breast pocket. That round had torn the cylinder from the alloy frame and had made a good start at propelling the whole mass of steel and aluminum through Fox's rib cage. The two Turks got the same effect with muscle and bone.

Fox's legs buckled. He was no longer conscious of the pain of his scalp and the twisted arm which supported his weight. Even the gag reflex failed him, because his spasming diaphragm could not manage to drive the contents of his stomach up his throat. One of the men behind Fox chuckled.

"Who did you meet yesterday?" the fifth man asked in English too flat to be that of a native speaker.

Fox's belly muscles would not permit him to get his legs under him properly. The men holding the American permitted him to kneel, but their grips by no means loosened. The fifth man bent slightly to meet Fox's eyes. The man's face was narrow but unremarkable.

"What are you doing?" the CIA officer managed to gasp in Turkish. His lower abdomen was a pit of flame. "Where is Mehmet?"

The fifth man straightened regretfully. He crooked a finger. Hands jerked Fox upright by hair and twisted tendons as before. "Ali," the fifth man said.

One of the thugs slapped Fox with his open hand.

Fox had thought the Turk was showing bravado and contempt for pain when he ground a cigarette into his palm. In fact, the man probably had not felt the warmth. His calluses were so thick and harsh that they tore Fox's cheek like a handful of ground glass. The American's skull flexed. His vision blurred and he thought that he could feel his left eye bobbing wetly against his cheek. His mind disassociated itself from what was happening. He viewed the action from a point somewhere in the air of the shop. He even managed to feel a mild contempt for the victim who was being worked over beneath him.

The fifth man continued to ask his mild questions. Fox's body smiled slackly. He was not unconscious, though it seemed likely enough that he had a concussion. Hands like trip hammers, Ali had. Fox could see himself very clearly as his brain deduced his condition from the body's signals and fed them back to him in the form of false visualizations. His eyes were both in their sockets, but his cheek was slick with blood. The point of one canine had been driven through the lip so that he was beginning to drool blood.

Fox's training applauded the care with which his questioner was trying to avoid killing his subject. A corpse can't answer questions, nor can someone who has been battered unconscious. The questioner was keeping very tight control of the Turks who were his tools. It was not his fault that Ali was unthinkably strong, and that the previous situation already had Fox's mind flirting with the edges of reality.

"Why you wanna hurt nice Canadian boy?" Fox mumbled through a loose grin.

The questioner himself snarled a curse in Russian and slapped Fox. Blood and spittle sprayed. The questioner snatched a handkerchief out of his breast pocket and began angrily wiping his hand with it. "What did Kunayev tell you?" he shouted. "What did he say to you on the tower yesterday?"

Fox tried to smile to show that he felt sorry for his questioner. The American's jaw muscles were numb on the left side, so the smile twisted instead into a knowing smirk.

The questioner cursed again in fury and disbelief. He took a pistol from the side pocket of his suit coat and thrust it so close to Fox's face that his eyes could not focus on it. "Shall I?" the man snapped in English. "Do you doubt that I will, Lawrence Oliver Fox?"

The pistol was a gray blur with a fuzzy hole in the center of it. The glimpse that Fox had gotten as it came out of his questioner's pocket suggested it was the weapon Mehmet Sabanci kept in his purse. That possibility fit in well with the rest of what was going on. The pistol was a datum, not a threat. It could not threaten Larry Fox who watched it thrust in the face of an unfamiliar beating victim. The face dribbled blood and tried to smile.

Ali stepped forward, cocking his fist. The muscle-men were well trained but, as with the questioner who controlled them, their frustration level was building.

"No!" the questioner snarled in Turkish. He waved the pistol, a gesture that carried its muzzle across two of his own men. Either he was unused to handling guns himself—probable enough—or he was even closer to the edge of control than the cool analysis of Fox's mind had concluded. "Show him the Turk. If that doesn't do it, we'll have him up there himself."

The Turks holding Fox pivoted him with a deliberate brutality. It was as vain as the more formalized attempts to soften him up. The fifth man prodded the American spitefully in the ribs with the pistol as his minions dragged the victim toward the back of the shop. Fox tried to make his body walk, but his motor control did not appear to be up to the task.

The hardware store's toilet was of a type standard throughout the Moslem world. The floor of the closet-sized room was of cracked plaster. It sloped to an open drain near the back wall. There was a water tap on the left-hand wall, six inches above floor level. Near it sat a cup of enamelled steel. There was neither need nor provision for toilet paper.

The questioner and his gang had turned the room into an abattoir. The toilet was lighted by a grime-frosted window high in the back wall. It was protected on the outside by a grate, barely visible as a web of shadows, and on the inside by three vertical bars. Mehmet Sabanci's wrists were fastened to a bar with baling wire. His shoes and socks had been removed. His bare toes dangled just above the floor. Sabanci was otherwise fully dressed, but the waist-band holster on his left side was empty. Presumably one of the thugs had appropriated the Hi-Power as their leader had done with the pistol from Sabanci's purse.

"Do you want your complexion improved the same way, Lawrence Fox?" the questioner demanded. He was making an effort to regain his composure. "Come now, you are an intelligent man. I could not bear to have such a terrible thing happen to you as well."

Sabanci had been beaten. Even his solid body could be literally crushed by a man like Ali punching it back against a stone wall. The flattened nose and pressure cuts wherever bone lay close to the surface proved there had been blows to his head as well. Sabanci's lolling head bore only one visible bruise, a purple swelling from his left temple to brow ridge. The stunning blow that caused the injury would have been well within the capacity of Ali's bare hands. The arsenal Mehmet carried would have been useless to him if he were struck down as he approached a burly, unfamiliar customer.

Other bruises were only shadows of what they should have been. The blood that should have leaked through burst capillaries had instead been drained from the victim's ankle. Somebody with a sharp blade—Mehmet's own combat knife?—had cut a three-inch slit between Sabanci's left Achilles tendon and ankle bones. The cut had been deep enough to sever the arteries feeding the left foot. The victim's heart must have spent many minutes pumping itself dry in a stream of crimson that splashed and dribbled, thickening as it ran down the floor drain. Nobody had bothered to rinse off the plaster. Mehmet's stubble of whiskers stood out like flecks of ink on the sallow parchment of his chin.

The sight shocked Larry Fox once more into a unity of body and mind. Most of the former felt as if a disk sander were spinning across its nerves. His mind, on the other hand, slipped into the mode of icy calm in which he had functioned when he disarmed bombs.

There was a muttered order in Turkish. One thug let go of Fox's right arm so that his partner could step through the narrow doorway. Still holding Fox by the hair and left wrist, he forced the American's face against Mehmet's. The drained corpse swayed by its wrists like the clapper of a bell. Sabanci's open mouth stank of its last meal.

"Come now, you and I are reasonable men," said the old man without an accent. Fox tried to push himself back, but the thug holding him thrust him forward so that he had to grip the corpse to save his balance. "For your own sake, tell us everything you heard from the traitor Kunayev."

They hadn't used Mehmet's own knife to bleed him out, because that seven-inch Ka-Bar was still sheathed at the base of the dead man's spine.

There was no snap or other detent to hold the weapon in its sheath. Fox's hand closed on the leather hilt it had brushed when he flailed to escape the cooling corpse. Instead of trying to push himself away again, he rotated toward the man who held him.

The Turk began to smile when he realized his captive was struggling for the first time since Ali slapped him. Fox thus far has been a punching bag rather than a victim who made one's efforts worth-while with his screams and whimpering.

Fox stabbed up through throat, palate, and the base of the Turk's brain. The man's limbs spasmed like those of a pithed frog. Fox jerked the knife down, aided by the convulsion that lifted his victim's chin and arched his back.

Most of the blade's gray phosphate coating had been polished off in a half century of use and rubbing against its sheath. Now the steel shone liquidly in the muted light. No spout of arterial blood followed the withdrawn knife as Fox had expected. Muscles clamped off the neatly-severed blood vessels. Without the damage to his nervous system, the thug might have been as long about the business of dying as Sabanci himself had been.

The questioner had no idea that there was trouble, even when his subordinate arched back-wards in the doorway in a tetanic convulsion. "What are you—?" he began in Turkish. Then the heavy corpse flopped past him.

Fox struck for the extended right wrist, the gun wrist, using the heavy knife as a cleaver. The sharp edge carried the full depth of the steel into cartilage and brittle bones. It made a sound like a clean axe stroke.

The pistol dropped because the tendons causing fingers to grip it had been severed. The questioner screamed from shock, not the pain that was yet to arrive, and lurched away from the knife.

Two of the thugs—Ali still had not realized something was amiss—collided in the doorway with one another and their master. The older, slightly built questioner rebounded. He took Fox's artless knife-thrust in the small of the back.

Fox slipped and fell on the blood-slimed floor with the questioner shuddering against him like a gaffed fish. The American's free hand snatched at the pistol. One of the Turks in the doorway bent toward him, while the other stepped back to open a gravity knife of his own with the snick of a trap springing. Fox opened fire left handed.

The pistol was a Turkish copy of the Walther PP. Mehmet, since it could not reasonably have been the questioner's weapon before that afternoon, had carried it with the hammer down, safety off, and a round in the chamber—normal practice for a double-action pistol. Any other technique would have cost Fox the life which fate seemed determined to hand back to him.

The flash and muzzle blast of the .32 were stunning in the confusion. That and not the three bullets fired point-blank into his chest were what caused the nearest Turk to hurl himself away from Fox.

The man with the flick knife cocked his arm to throw. The short, upright blade of his weapon glinted like a shark's tooth. Fox swung toward him. The American was not left handed, but the pistol's curved backstrap shaped itself to him so that the barrel pointed like a steel index finger. Even so, it was luck rather than marksmanship that centered the second of the pair of little bullets on the bridge of the target's nose. The thug toppled onto his face, still clutching the knife.

Fox twisted to his knees. He switched the pistol to the right hand which he had cleared from the tangle of knife hilt and the questioner's corpse.

Three bodies were sprawled at the doorway. Another Turk lay in an aisle with only his boots visible from where Fox knelt.

Ali wore a grimace of horror as he wrestled with the right sidepocket of his coat. His big hands gripped Mehmet's Browning Hi-Power, caught in the lining of the pocket. The Turk was not a gunman, but the pistol's availability led him to snatch at it instead of running while the chance was offered.

Fox fired twice into the center of Ali's broad chest. The red muzzle flashes winked from the Turk's staring eyes. He turned and ran for the front door of the shop, brushing a display rack which teetered and cascaded hardware into the aisle opposite.

The American rose to his feet and for the first time became consciously aware of the punishment that his body had taken. Pain radiated from a dozen centers among his chest and stomach muscles. The arm that had been extending the pistol drew back reflexively as if to keep his ribs from bursting out in shards.

Ali stumbled on the bottom step and crashed against the outside door. The lock rattled as the Turk fumbled with it.

Fox leaned back against the bathroom partition to steady himself. He lifted the Walther copy in a two-hand grip. Even hunching over, the pain of extending the weapon to the full length of his arms was more than he could bear. The pistol cracked.

Ali lunged forward. The locks and the grate-protected door both held, but the old wood of the jamb on both hinge side and lock side tore out under the Turk's impact. The Turk blundered out into the street like Sampson carrying the gates of

Gath. It was dark outside. The splinters raggedly framing the opening reflected the interior light.

The police and army could appear at any moment, and Fox did not dare to be found with no identification in the midst of five bodies. He dropped the pistol into his coat pocket and began to stumble through the shop. The littered corpses were obstacles because of the pain that shot through his abdomen when he lifted his feet to step over them. By the time he reached the entrance steps, the throbbing muscles had relaxed enough to permit him to get out of the shop without having to crawl. It was a close thing, however.

The street was quiet. Chances were that the commotion had been interpreted as a police raid, an excellent reason to wait fearfully behind shuttered windows and pray that boots would not approach one's own apartment.

The door lay just beyond the shattered jamb. There was no sign of Ali. Fox's struggle to get up the steps had been so great that he had forgotten the Turk might be waiting outside in ambush. At this point, Fox hurt too much to really care. If two, maybe three bullets through heart and lungs were not enough to put Ali down for good, then there wasn't enough left in the pistol's magazine to change the situation.

The Jawa sat across the street where Fox had parked it. One of the Fords had driven off and been replaced—somehow—by a Skoda pickup, but the bike was uninjured. That put its evening a long way up on that of its owner.

Fox lifted his leg to swing it over the saddle. The pain, a purple environment for his thoughts, now became a pattern of blinding sheets that throbbed with his pulse. Fox lay for a moment with his chest on the bike's gas tank and his right leg supported at full length by the seat. Finally he could open his eyes again and lower his foot so that he straddled the bike.

The doorless shop was a lighted accusation. The American's luck was not going to keep police patrols off this street forever. The Jawa did not have an electric starter, and Fox could no more have kick-started the bike in his present condition than he could have flown under his own power. He stuck the key into its place in the sideplate and thought for a moment, supporting his head on his right biceps. Then he switched on the gas and power. The street sloped to the left, in the direction ultimately of the Golden Horn. He straddle-walked the motorcycle in neutral until it pointed down-slope. Then he shifted into second but held the clutch disengaged. The effort of keeping the clutch lever depressed was dizzying.

A car turned into the upper end of the street. Now or never. Fox stumbled ahead, letting gravity get a grip on the bike. Then he jumped forward, coming down on the seat instead of on the ground. Simultaneously, he let out the clutch so that the bike's forward momentum was transformed into a rotation of the crankshaft. The Jawa coughed itself forward. Fox declutched again and revved the throttle to bring the two-stroke to full, flaring life before he feathered the clutch in with as much delicacy as he could manage.

He was in one piece, more or less, and he was on his way home. That was almost perfect.

The qualifier was necessary because now he had to think about Abdulhamid Kunayev again—and other things.

His apartment was dark. Fox paused, supporting himself against the front door for a moment while his muscles trembled and his mind shivered in and out of alertness. At last he walked to the bedroom. Kathie was asleep across most of the mattress surface, her hair radiant in the moonlight. Fox shut the door carefully so that he would not disturb her. It was after 1 AM by the bedside clock.

Fox was actually feeling better for the motorcycle ride. The familiar physical activity used most of the body's muscles without over-stressing any of them. The beating had not broken any bones, not even ribs; the questioner had not wanted his subject to drown in blood filling a punctured lung. The bike's vibration had loosened cramps and started his swollen bruises on the road to reabsorption.

Fox's bloody cheek might have been a problem if the sleepy soldiers on guard had been interested in checking the motorcycle they'd seen leaving at the beginning of their watch. Apart from that, the CIA officer looked normal enough. He felt a great deal better than he had any right to; well enough that he could imagine being fully recovered in six months or so.

The desk light did not work—of course. If he turned on the overhead or got the reading light out of the bedroom, he would waken Kathie. He did not want to explain the situation to her. He was not certain that he *could* explain it. Instead, he turned on the kitchen fixtures which spilled enough light into the livingroom for him to work at the desk.

A pair of video cassettes were set out in an envelope already stamped and addressed to Glenn Alden. Fox had been waiting for a moment to write a note of appreciation to enclose with the tapes he was

returning. This was the time for a note to Glenn—
and to one other person.

Dear Owen Neely,

*I am an American Foreign Service officer stationed
in Istanbul. The person who forwards this letter to
you may be able to provide details which convince
you of my good faith. I cannot expect you to believe
me. I ask only that you read this and consider it with
other data on the subject. I suppose you're familiar
with the formal ranking of hearsay evidence. From
your standpoint, this will have to be an F-5—reliability
of source cannot be judged; information appears
improbable. But somebody in a position like yours
has to know, just in case the information is true.*

*In the course of my duties here, I met a would-be
defector with the appearance and ethnic background
of former Politburo member Abdulhamid Kunayev. I
don't have much time, so I won't tell you things
you've already got in your files. The defector did not
identify himself as Kunayev. He fled before we had
exchanged more than a few words. I have no way to
resume contact with the man and suspect, in any
case, that he has by now been returned to the Soviet
Union or killed. But before he left me, he said that
President Crossfield is a Soviet penetration.*

*I cannot believe that myself. Since I was told
that, however, the contact who brought the defector has been murdered. I was forcibly questioned
about my interview by a group of men led by someone whom I believe to be a Central European. They
knew too much about me, Mr. Neely, more than
my contact knew, more than anybody outside of
my own organization knew. They used the name
Kunayev. I am Kunayev. I am quite sure that I
was not expected to be able to tell anyone about
my questioning.*

I do not vouch for the truth of anything I have been told. But something is going on, and I'm not sure that I'm going to have another chance to pass the word along.

> *Yours truly,*
> *Lawrence Fox*
> *Vice Consul*

Fox folded the letter and sealed it in an envelope. He wrote Neely's name on the face of the envelope but did not attempt to address it himself. Instead he took out another sheet of paper and wrote:

Dear Glenn,
I need a big favor. Address and mail the envelope I'm sending along with this. Man, I don't know what's going on. I think you'd be better off not opening it first, no shit. If you just remail it, you'll be out and that's fine, no problem. If you tell the guy who you are and answer any questions he has about me, he'd probably like that. But that could get you pretty deep in this and that could be pretty bad.
Glenn, there's some stuff going on like I didn't see in the Lebanon. Some of it's real close to home. I guess they pay me for that, but they don't pay you. I just don't have anybody else to turn to.
Glenn, if I seem to be acting weird for a while, tell Neely that. If maybe I'm nuts, that's okay. I'd maybe rather deal with that than what I think I have.
Man, no shit. Keep your head down.

> *Larry*

The sweat on Fox's face was making his torn cheek sting. He folded the note to Alden around the sealed envelope and slid both between the pair of videotapes. He stapled the mailing envelope shut, feeling utterly washed out. There was still the official contact report to write, before his mind convinced itself that reality had not occurred. The previous hours had proved the degree of authority that his mind could exercise when it did not care for the objective reality of his perceptions.

The bedroom door opened, framing Kathie against the light of the bedside lamp. The thump of the stapler, sealing the heavy mailing envelope, must have awakened her. "Larry, where in *God's* name have you been?" she demanded in a mixture of relief and anger.

At least he'd be able to take a shower without worrying about waking her up. First the report, though. "Kathie, I can't talk about this right now," Fox said as he got up from the desk. "Maybe in a bit. I need to write things down while they're still. . . ."

The petite blonde flipped on the overhead, blasting from Fox's retinas the visual purple which had permitted him to work in the dim light reflected from the kitchen alcove. "Jesus, Larry! What *happened* to you? Look, Ed said for you to call him whenever you got back. You've really done it this time, haven't you?"

"You just might be right," Fox muttered, as much to himself as to his wife. He walked toward the bedroom to get the lamp. Kathie cringed against the doorjamb at his approach. "Look, honey," he added in a weary, reasonable tone, "I'll get back with Ed in the morning." Later morning. "Right now, I just need some time to get my head straight and, and all, okay? Go back to sleep, I won't make any racket."

He could feel his wife's eyes on his back as he

knelt to unplug the lamp. "Larry," she said in a cold voice, "you've done something really bad. Isn't that right? I could tell by the way Ed sounded. You've got us *all* in trouble!"

Fox turned in the doorway to stare at his wife. She flinched again, this time from his expression rather than because of the scabs and bruises pounded into the fabric of his face. "When did Platt call, Kathie?" Fox asked in a voice as mild as the snick of a sear releasing. "Was it maybe half an hour ago? Was that when?"

"No, it was just after you left," Kathie said, backing away from her husband. Her voice grew stronger with remembered anger. "You wouldn't tell me where you were going so I couldn't help. Do you know what goddam time it is now, Larry Fox?"

"I'm not keeping you up," he said in dismissal. He knelt by the desk to find the receptacle in the floor tile. There was a moment of vertigo as he lowered his head. With the dizziness came memory and a rush of the fear he had been unable to feel while his body was being beaten.

"Larry, goddammit," Kathie shrilled, "if you're not going to call Ed, I am. You need help." She picked up the receiver of the desk phone.

The CIA officer stood up more abruptly than he would have believed possible if he had paused to think about it. He had killed four men, probably five, within the hour, but the killings had been too surreal to burn away the frustrated horror of his earlier beating. He took the phone from Kathie, who backed away so suddenly that her heel caught on nothing at all. She hit the floor with a thud, still staring at her husband.

The telephone was Turkish, solid and old-fashioned. Fox slammed the receiver against the desktop. Bakelite cracked. The bell jangled as the base unit jounced. Fox pounded the instrument down three more times, until the mouthpiece was in shards and the desk was black with powdered graphite from the microphone. Fox blinked and tossed the receiver aside. "Go back to bed," he said very distinctly to his wife.

Kathie nodded, swallowing back more than the saliva that had been accumulating in her mouth. She crawled a few paces on all fours like a frightened dog before getting properly to her feet to obey. She did not speak.

Fox heard the bedroom door slam as he bent again to plug in the lamp. His head hurt in reaction to what he had just *felt*, rather than to the punishment he had received not long before.

"Honey?" he called. "Look, I'm sorry, I'm not in very good—"

The bomb in the bedroom closet blew out every door and window in the apartment. The interior walls of the building were more solid than anyone would have guessed—they held.

The world blotted itself red with the rush of blood to Fox's eyes. The heavy desk protected him from the shock waves caroming within the enclosing walls, but the desk itself shifted and pummeled Fox's aching torso. The kitchen and livingroom fixtures disintegrated in showers of glass. The light in the hallway shone into the apartment over the wreckage of the front door.

Fox gripped the desk to drag himself upright. The envelope with the tapes lay near the front door, at the end of a trail of rubbish which had lain on the desktop moments before. The lamp was gutted. Fox's convulsive grip on the cord had tethered the lamp firmly enough for the blast to flatten the thin brass instead of simply hurling it across the room. Something very similar would have happened to Fox himself if he had been standing in the direct path of the shock waves.

Jesus. *Kathie*.

There was no fire, but the bedroom doorway seethed with residues as black and lethal as the explosion which had spawned them. They welcomed Fox with beckoning tentacles as he staggered into the bedroom. He was barely alert enough to try to hold his breath.

The large bedroom window afforded some illumination now that the shutters were a cloud of splinters settling in the parking lot below. The bomb had not been built as a fragmentation weapon, but the closet door had been a thousand daggers of teak when it struck Kathie. There was almost as much of the petite woman splashed on walls and ceiling as remained to the ragged corpse.

His eyes saw Kathie and his mind blended the corpse with those of shell-maimed victims he'd seen in Beirut. The intervening thirteen years were sucked down in a vortex of blood and fire. Fox turned and strode away from the present carnage. His steps were firm because he no longer felt the punishment his body had taken.

Sam Barker burst out of the stairwell and skidded to a halt on the ruin of the Foxes' front door. "Larry!" he called. "Kathie!" When he saw Fox walking out of the bedroom, he darted to meet the CIA officer. "Thank God you're all right, Larry, but what on earth happened? Was it gas?"

Two soldiers holding Tommy guns followed a National Policeman with a gasoline lantern into the apartment. The white glare of the lantern's glowing mantle threw shadows sharp as knife cuts. Turkey was too poor a country for a security detachment like this to have a walkie-talkie, but there was probably somebody calling in an alarm from the nearest phone. None of the young security men in Fox's apartment spoke English, and Fox had no mind to attempt to explain the situation to them in their own language.

"They killed Kathie, Sam," he said to Barker. The poisonous combustion products of the explosion brought tears to Fox's eyes and made his voice catch, though he tried to speak normally.

"But—" Barker said.

A soldier thrust his gun in Fox's face and shouted for him to put his hands up. Sam Barker did not understand the words of the command, but the gesture was eloquent enough that his own hands rose reflexively.

Fox leveled his left index finger. "You!" he said in Turkish. "Are you trying to finish what the terrorists started? Is that why you were put on guard here?"

The Turk's jaw dropped and he lowered his Thompson. Even as Fox turned contemptuously, the other soldier was running toward the bedroom, calling for the policeman to come with the lantern.

Fox bent and pocketed an object gleaming among the remains of the lamp he had taken from the bedroom. It was an ordinary piece of intelligence paraphernalia, CIA standard and as likely as not from the stores of the Istanbul station: a line-transmitting audio bug. Because such units operated on wall current, they could be much smaller than bugs which required battery power. This one, scarcely pea-sized, had been nestled between one of the hot leads of the European-style 220-volt connection and the metal case of the lamp to which the bug was grounded.

There were disadvantages to a line-current installation. This one, for instance, would work if the lamp were not switched on, but it would have stopped broadcasting when the lamp was unplugged and being carried between rooms. A bug this tiny was probably not sensitive enough to pick up voices outside the room in which it was located, either. That drawback became an advantage only if you wished to be sure someone was in a certain room when you took some other action.

An action like setting off a command-detonated bomb, for instance, Larry Fox realized; and, as questions became answers in his mind, blood rushed to the surface of his skin. He felt hot all over, but he was no more angry than a bullet as it leaves the muzzle. He had a target now.

Sam Barker had followed the lantern into the bedroom. Now he stumbled back from what he had seen there, crying, "Merciful God, Larry! We've got to call Ankara on this! Merciful *God*!" He was distraught and half-blinded by the stinging smoke; otherwise he would never have tried to shove his way through the section of Jandarmas just deploying from the stairwell.

The paramilitary Jandarmas, wearing blue berets and leaf-pattern fatigues, were every bit as tough as the shock troops who had plunged through the breeched walls of Constantinople in 1453. One of them slammed Barker against the wall in a hammerlock. Another turned out the American's pockets, expertly if without result: Barker had apparently emptied them before going to bed.

The Jandarmas left their folding-stock rifles slung. Unlike the earlier trio of security men, the Blue Berets did not need their weapons as talismans in a tense situation.

"Sir, praise Allah you've come so quickly," the lantern-waving policeman said in rapid-fire Turkish to the Jandarma lieutenant. "Terrorists have killed a woman there in the bedroom. There're American diplomats here on all the floors but the top."

"We're here to arrest one," the lieutenant said with a nod. "Fox, he's supposed to be here in apartment three."

Fox stepped forward, his voice cool, his Turkish fluid . . . his mind molten: "Your men there—" he waved toward Barker who was now squawking in English, "—are holding an American citizen with diplomatic immunity, sir. He's Lawrence Fox, a vice consul here in Istanbul. There seems to have been an explosion here in his apartment, but I can't imagine Larry had anything to do with that. It must have been a gas leak."

"Hold that one!" the Turkish officer snapped to the pair who were about to release Barker. "And who are you?" the Blue Beret asked Fox in the tone of a man used to being obeyed.

"I'm at the Consulate General, also," the CIA officer said. "I'm the, ah, second in command there, Sam Barker. But what are you doing with Larry? You must realize that you can't arrest a foreign diplomat."

"I can carry out my orders, Mr. Barker," said the Turk coldly.

"Larry, for heaven's sake, get them away from me!" called the Deputy Principal Officer on a rising note.

The paramilitary police were not, apparently, issued ordinary handcuffs. One of the men holding Barker was tethering the American's wrists behind his back with a polyethylene pull strip that worked on the same principle as the ones that held electronics cords bunched for carrying. This one was larger, fiber-reinforced; it deformed when it was pulled tight so that the loop had to be cut to be removed. Until then, the ten-inch pigtail dangling from it made a useful come-along. The diplomat's struggles had absolutely no effect on what the soldiers were doing with him.

"My orders come directly from the Martial Law Command in Ankara," the Turkish lieutenant continued. He glanced toward Barker only long enough to make sure that his men were doing as they had been told. "We are to hold Mr. Fox under close restraint until he can be turned over to a team that is being sent for him."

Ordinary emergency equipment—an ambulance and a number of fire and police vehicles—was clanging to a halt in the street below. The lieutenant raised his voice to be heard over the racket. "You may protest through the Ministry of Foreign Affairs if you like, but I think you'll want to check very carefully before you do so. The men who are going to collect Lawrence Fox are being sent from Washington, you see."

Firemen, squat as trolls in their yellow bunker gear, pounded into the apartment ahead of a pair of ambulance attendants marked by the green crescents on their uniforms. One of the soldiers began directing the newcomers to the bedroom with thrusts of his Tommy gun.

"Section!" the lieutenant ordered.

"Section!" echoed one of the Blue Berets who had trussed Barker. That Turk had sergeant's pips on his collar, now that Fox had a chance to notice. The men of the section, including those who had stationed themselves in the kitchen and bedroom, came to attention.

With only their officer's nod as a further direction, the Jandarmas swept out of the bombed apartment, two of them holding Sam Barker by the elbows, and down the stairs. The emergency personnel trying to go the other direction cleared a path without objection when they saw the berets.

Larry Fox followed the Jandarmas out into the street.

The section had arrived in a closed van and a six-wheeled Bedford truck, both painted to match the leaf-pattern fatigues. As Turks hustled Barker into the van, Fox called in English, "Don't worry, I'm going to the Con-Gen and we'll have this cleared up in no time."

And then he repeated the sentence in Turkish, not for Barker, but for the security forces all around him.

Fox strode off toward Taksim Square. Behind him, the van and truck made U-turns with their sirens hooting on their way back to barracks with their captive. No one tried to stop the CIA man as he walked away from the scene of his wife's murder.

The listening device in his pocket was as dead as Kathie, but he felt it burning in his pocket.

The night gateman at the Consulate General knew Larry Fox about as well as his daytime counterpart did. As he locked the gate, he cooed in concern at the CIA man's appearance.

Fox had almost forgotten his injuries. He was running on adrenalin. The pain was a background to existence—too constant to be remarkable. "Ought to be more careful, shouldn't I, Murad?" he said to the guard.

The armored station vehicle was parked in its usual place, just visible around the corner of the building. Fox nodded toward it. "Mr. Platt been here long?" he asked.

"A few minutes only," Murad said. He shrugged and added, "Perhaps a little longer, but not long."

"See you soon, I hope," Fox called over his shoulder as he sauntered toward the main building.

The first thing Fox did after the Marine guard let him into the Consulate General proper was to wash himself from the waist up with cold water and soap in the ground floor restroom. He might not be able to afford the time washing cost him now, but there would likely be no time at all after his discussion with Platt, and he could not walk around in daylight in his present condition.

The water made Fox's muscles shudder and contract, but it did nothing to quench the fire in his mind or the image of what he had not seen: Kathie tumbling and disintegrating in slow motion as the shock wave lifted her.

The Marine was still waiting in the lobby. "Anything I can do for you, sir?" he queried hopefully. During the midwatch, there was usually nothing to answer him but the grumbling of the building itself.

"Teach me not to trip on stairs, maybe," the CIA officer said. "Thanks, but duty calls."

He was afraid that the watchstander might accompany him upstairs. The guard could go anywhere in the building since his duty included checking for security violations such as classified documents left out or safes unlocked during the absence of the responsible parties. Fox's combination of hurried friendliness and duty was enough to buy the privacy he needed, however. The Marine nodded in acceptance, then walked back to his kiosk in the center of the lobby—leaving Fox to mount the stairs alone.

Ed Platt's office was empty and dark. Fox eased the door closed again once he'd checked and, while still standing in the hallway outside, examined the pistol he had dropped into his pocket as he left Sabanci's shop.

Jesus, the hammer was back. He had been walking around with a gun as likely as not to go off if dropped—or if banged against a lavatory. That lapse from training and common sense frightened Fox in a way that the pain which ruled his body did not. The body wasn't *him*. . . .

Fox lowered the hammer by engaging the Walther-style safety. He did not trust his thumb to ease the hammer down while he was in his present debilitated state. As soon as the double-action pistol was uncocked, however, he took it off safe so that it would fire with a long, firm pull of the trigger.

The magazine was empty. Fox grimaced as he dropped it into his left coat pocket while returning the pistol itself to his right. There was still a round in the chamber, but additional support was called for. He should have checked sooner.

The trouble was that Fox had returned to a war-zone mentality for the first time since he left the Lebanon on a stretcher. When you become fully aware that there are people out there trying to kill you, you can react either by falling into abject terror—which is sane—or with a fatalistic acceptance which is not sane but which permits you to function. The process of realizing the situation takes time, but it was time Larry Fox had spent defusing live ordnance. It was no surprise that he had reverted to that mindset after his normal world had dissolved in death and flame.

But the same recklessness which permits you to do a job that has killed three men in your ordnance disposal section also makes detailed planning impossible. A mind already primed for a dangerous task cannot plot the details of that task without freezing into inertia. Fox had not had time to plan his actions before he became a tool of them. Now he was focusing down a tunnel, reacting to events with the precision of a gunlock—and with almost as little forethought.

There was a closet beneath the stairs which led to the roof and the burn barrels. The closet door was never locked: when classified documents had to be destroyed in an emergency, there would be no time to fumble with keys. Fox opened the closet and took from it two of the heavy, cylindrical thermite grenades in cases there. He dangled their safety rings from his left little finger as he stepped back to the communications vault. There was a smile of sorts on his face.

The vault door was closed, but the locking handle was in its open position, indicating that the bolts had not been thrown. Fox drew his pistol again, gripping it between thumb and index finger, then curled the other three fingers around the locking handle and swung the massive door open.

The suction drew a gasp of warm air and the attention of Ed Platt, hunched over the communications console at the far end. The Chief of Station turned with a look of fury. Then his gaze flicked from Fox to the gun; and back to the face of Larry Fox.

Platt had been speaking into an instrument the size of a small attache case, plugged into the consulate's ordinary equipment. Platt's unit was anything but ordinary if it was what Fox thought it was: the V/SIC/ MOSFET transformed an ordinary medium-wave transceiver into a burst-capable internally-encrypted microwave satellite communications unit. It was intended for use when neither security nor results could be compromised. Launching a nuclear strike was one such use. Obviously, Ed Platt's duties were another.

But while the V/SIC was not Station equipment, it *was* US forces only. Platt was not using it to communicate with the Russians. Not directly, at least.

Fox put the last bullet from his .32 through the set. The radio popped and sizzled nervously, but the internal amperages of the solid-state unit were too low to cause really spectacular death throes. The thought of what the V/SIC had cost gave Fox a grim satisfaction, though it had probably been bought with his tax money.

"La...," said Ed Platt. His smile was bright and ordinary, but his throat muscles were not working properly. "Larry."

Fox set the pair of thermite grenades on top of the filing cabinet nearest the door. He began to work the combination with his left hand. Because Fox had removed the magazine from his pistol, the slide had not locked back when the last round was fired. So far as Platt could tell, the pistol was fully loaded.

The communications unit hissed.

"You know, Ed," Fox said, "I thought when I came here that I wanted to talk to you. But I don't."

"Look, Larry," the station chief said. He started to rise from his chair. A bob of the pistol's muzzle sat him back down, but he never lost his engaging smile. "I don't believe the story about you fooling around with explosives in your apartment. I think something's very damned wrong, and that's what I was—ah—checking on." He gestured apologetically to the V/SIC. A wisp of smoke was trailing from the bullet hole in the center of the unit.

"That was the story, was it?" the younger man said. He had the drawer open now. Three of the files contained extra passports, made out with false names and Turkish entry stamps but with real photographs of the station personnel. "The Mad Bomber fucks up and blows himself to kingdom come. And his wife." He pulled out Platt's file.

"They told me they wanted *access* to your apartment, Larry," Platt said. Sweat was dripping from his curls and beading elsewhere on his face. His smile was becoming a rictus. The vault did seem very warm. "They needed to monitor you, they said; there were doubts about, well, your loyalty. But access only, a listening device. I—thank God you're all right."

"Kathie's not," Fox said as he thumbed open one of his superior's false passports. The facial features of the two CIA officers were not especially similar, but neither were there any differences too remarkable to be artifacts of passport photography. "Don't guess I really wanted to know how you got "access" without her telling me. Doesn't matter now." He slipped the passports into the breast pocket of his coat.

In the same drawer were packets of green dollars—US currency, twenties and hundreds. The money was untraceable except through the CIA's own records. It was intended for agent payments and did not, at the Istanbul station, aggregate more than $3000 at any normal time. Fox swept it all into his pocket, ignoring the disbursement folder with its signatures and counter signatures. He felt rather as if he had just broken the windows out of a church.

Platt tried again to stand up. Fox, a dozen feet away, smiled at him. The station chief subsided with a little moan. "Larry, look, we've got to work together on this. Somebody's *way* out of line, there'll be an investigation."

Fox was gently shaking his head. The gun muzzle did not move.

Driven by terror to the truth, Platt cried, "Shit, Larry, *shit*, I didn't know they were going to do *that*. It's Blaustein himself who must have ordered it, not me, shit, you can't—" He paused because the sob choked him. "Larry, baby, you won't shoot me?" he begged to his clenched hands.

"I won't shoot you, Ed," Fox said. He pulled the pin on one of the thermite grenades and dropped it into the file drawer. The grenade spoon flew up with a puff of smoke as the two-second fuze ignited. Fox slid the drawer shut and stepped back onto the vault threshold.

The thermite reaction is a simple one. When a mixture of powdered aluminum and iron oxide—rust—is ignited, it converts itself to aluminum oxide and molten iron with an incredible outpouring of energy. The reaction does not require external oxygen. It works perfectly well under water, within the closed tube of a cannon which must be welded into unserviceability—or in a barrel of classified documents.

Though the thermite grenades were intended for demolition, not combat, the one in the file drawer performed with spectacular enthusiasm. Heated air drove the heavy drawer open again in a roaring gush of white sparks, blazing iron spewed out by the force of its creation. White-hot gobbets sprayed the ceiling, the far wall, and the filing cabinets across from it. Fragments of folders and the documents within them were expelled, burning with more color but less intensity than the metals that devoured them.

Neither man was in the direct path of the curtain of fire, but it faded them to shadows in one another's eyes. Platt lunged backward onto the radio console, though the sparks were not falling dangerously close to his chair. His mouth was open to scream, but either panic gagged him or bellowing fire smothered all human noise.

The spectacle died away in a sequence of angry sputters. A white glare quivered within the vault. The normal overhead lighting was crespucular to eyes dazzled by the thermite. Patches of carpet and paint smoldered. The room had been warm. Now it was an oven, reeking with the smoke of plastics and other half-burned materials.

Fox coughed. "Going to be pretty hard for them to figure out which passports I took, isn't it, Ed?" he said, wheezing to avoid another series of coughs. The air conditioner was doing little more than stirring the competing banners of smoke into a uniform haze.

Fox pulled away the access plate covering the vault door's inner handle. A simple turn on the handle would slide open the bolts, bypassing the combination dial on the outside of the door. Fox set the remaining grenade into the handle niche.

"Wait!" Platt cried.

"Goodby, Ed," said Fox as he pulled the pin on the grenade.

He stepped out of the vault and set his weight against the door. Because the door itself was so massive, it had not quite slammed to when the thermite ignited. Through this fingers as he closed the lock mechanism, Fox could feel the blaze building to its lengthy crescendo. No sound was audible outside the vault, however. Certainly not the screams of the dying Chief of Station.

Fox dropped his empty pistol and its magazine into the base of one of the free-standing ash trays in the hallway. It would be found in a day or two, but that did not matter. At the moment, the weapon was excess baggage which would cause problems at airports.

As the CIA officer walked back down the stairs, he met the Marine guard coming up. "Guess I'm off for the night," Fox said with a nod. "I'll bet poor Ed doesn't get any sleep tonight, though."

"Man, I feel for him," the Marine agreed. His face twisted into a frown as he added, "Say, sir— did you hear some kinda noise a little bit ago? Water running maybe?"

"Maybe a jet overhead," Fox said without looking back. The guard scrambled after him to lock the front door.

Ed Platt would not burn to death. He could shelter behind the filing cabinets and stay safe from all but random sparks bounding and scintillating down the length of the vault. The fires which the thermite would set in the carpet and other combustibles would be low and nasty, barely self-sustaining. Their orange tongues and veils of smoke would suck all the oxygen out of the vault and replace it with a mixture of gases as lethal as cyanide and far slower in effect.

"Good night, Mr. Fox," said the Marine.

"Good night, soldier," the CIA man said as he stepped back out into the night.

The afterimage of thermite burning still threw purple blotches across Fox's vision. In his mind, the white gushing began to wash away the earlier memory of Kathie's ragged corpse.

The Istanbul-Frankfurt El Al flight was, as usual, almost empty. The exchange of flights between the national airlines of Turkey and Israel was still the only such direct connection Israel had anywhere in the Moslem world. At that, the aircraft which Turk Hava Yollari flew into Jerusalem twice weekly carried only international markings—and no sign at all that they were Turkish.

The political purposes of the State of Israel were now of more use to Larry Fox than had ever before been the case. He wanted desperately to doze on the flight—a real possibility, since he was alone on his trio of seats. There was one further arrangement to be made, though. Otherwise he could step out of the aircraft at 35,000 feet and not bounce any higher than he would if he returned to the States without preparation.

It was easy enough to spot the guards, one each at the front and rear of the passenger compartment. The older and presumably senior guard was in a seat just behind the cockpit from which he had watched the passengers file past to reach their places. He was a big man in a three-piece suit whose jacket was cut full to conceal the shoulder holster beneath it. His hair was gray with a white streak snaking from his temple to a tab of scar tissue just below his present hair line. His hands looked as if they could bend horseshoes but would rather break necks.

The Israelis—and the Turks, for that matter—had no intention of letting one of these flights be hijacked.

Fox waited until the aircraft had reached cruising altitude before he got up. He walked like an old man, and he felt like grim death. The adrenalin had worn off, and there was nothing left but pain.

The attendant in the forward cabin looked at him sharply. "I think I see a friend," Fox said with a smile. He gestured forward. The stitch in his side from the motion pulled a flash of agony across his face.

The guard was already crosswise on his seat,

watching Fox as he approached. "Excuse me, my friend," the CIA officer said, "but I noticed as we came in that you had the *Jerusalem Post*. I wonder if I might borrow it when you're through. My business doesn't take me through Israel very much any more, but I like to keep in touch."

The Israeli kept his face blank. He had not risen to meet Fox, but his right hand—concealed between the seat back and his torso—was in his coat pocket. "Take it, surely," he said, handing the paper over with his left hand. "You travel by El Al often, then?"

"Occasionally," Fox lied. Except in rare circumstances, American personnel were restricted to US flag carriers if they expected the government to pick up the tab. When exceptions arose, El Al with its bitter labor disputes was well down on Fox's list of personal favorites. "Here, let me give you my card."

The card he had prepared was in the breast pocket of his coat. It was one of his ordinary business cards. The side he held up to the Israeli security man was not the glazed front announcing that Lawrence Oliver Fox was a Vice Consul at the Consulate-General Istanbul. On the back Fox had written:

for Shai Gallen

> *Captain—I want to trade a spent AK round for an hour of talk. Best Western in Arlington, off Glebe Road. I didn't want ever to do this.*

The Israeli took the card and slipped it into his own pocket without a flicker of expression. Only Gallen's name would have meant anything to him, and perhaps not even that. "Happy journey," he said to Fox in dismissal. The American was blocking his view of the other passengers. The card had nothing to do with his immediate job.

But that didn't mean the message would not be delivered. Fox held the newspaper in both hands as he hunched his way back to his seat.

The note would reach Gallen, CIA's Deputy Director for Operations, through channels to which no one in CIA had access . . . except Shai Gallen herself. What happened then depended solely on what she decided.

If she made that decision as DDO, there would be a team waiting for Larry Fox as soon as he stepped onto US soil. He had made no arrangements as yet for the remaining leg of his journey home—he would do that in Frankfurt. That would not prevent them from taking him at whichever terminal, whatever port of entry, he chose. They had the resources, just as they had the resources to boil him down afterward until nothing remained but his bones and the information they had distilled out of him in the process.

So be it. There was nothing Fox could do now to change that future.

But it was just possible that the decision would be made somewhere else. Thirteen years before, Ariel Sharon's female aide had ridden back to Tel Aviv in the medevac bird beside a kid with cracked ribs and a collapsed lung. He had stepped between her and a sniper, the sort of stupid thing a kid would do. She was a short woman, the aide. The round that had smashed on a revolver in the kid's breast pocket would have taken her through the throat.

They had not spoken in the helicopter—said nothing that Larry Fox could remember, at least, through the morphine and the pinch of the oxygen mask. But she was waiting when he was released from the hospital two weeks later. He had gone to her apartment instead of to the airport as he'd intended.

He hadn't let it mean anything then. He especially had not let it matter when he heard the name Shai Gallen after he joined CIA and realized she herself had joined years before him—and far above entry level.

And it might not matter now, it shouldn't ... but just possibly, Shai Gallen and not Deputy Director for Operations Gallen would respond to Fox's message. That was the only hope in the world for Larry Fox; and it just might be the only hope for the United States as well.

His connections to DC gave Fox a three-hour stopover in the huge Frankfurt air terminal. That was long enough to buy clothes and a suitcase, but he didn't dare look for a hotel room—even to shower. He wasn't functioning well enough. If he fucked up—if he so much as lay down on a bed with his eyes open—he was going to lose it. He had to get back to the States before that happened.

He had to get to Shai Gallen.

The gray plastic seats in the boarding lounge were uncomfortable enough to keep Fox awake, though only just. Someone had left an *International Herald Tribune* on the seat beside him. The Pakistani who wanted to borrow it asked three times before the CIA officer understood the question clearly enough to wave the paper away with an attempt at a smile. He should have been composing an after-action report, but the words wobbled through his head like keyholing bullets, like splinters of the closet door tumbling through Kathie. . . .

The flight from Frankfurt to Kennedy was a long,

waking nightmare. Waking, because the aircraft was full and Fox was seated in the midst of a tour group of senior citizens. The husband in the aisle seat and wife by the window kept up a running conversation with one another and with their friends as much as three rows distant.

Perhaps it was just as well. It kept Fox from thinking about what was waiting for him when he touched US soil—and the possibility that the plane just might disintegrate over the middle of the Atlantic. They were playing for keeps. *Somebody* was playing for keeps.

Fox had thought that he would never again do anything as difficult as jump-starting his bike in front of Sabanci's shop. Picking up his luggage and walking it through US Customs was worse. They knew by now that he was coming in. *Shai* knew he was coming. This was the time for him to be politely shunted aside by men wearing the uniforms of Customs inspectors: young men, very hard, and at least six of them in plain view.

But nothing happened. Not then, not minutes later when Fox waited for the bus to his connecting flight among a crowd of civilians relieved to be on solid ground. They were totally unaware that in their midst was Larry Fox, multiple murderer, bomber of the US Consulate General Istanbul, target of at least one of the world's major intelligence services. At *least* one. . . .

The closer he came to what he had set before himself as success, the greater his fear became. The hop from Kennedy to National was lost in a haze of anticipation of the last stage—the point at which Fox would be truly alone. He was gritting his teeth so hard by the time he rented a car at National that the rental agent, a gum-chewing girl with bleached hair had to keep asking him to "Say that again, Mister Fox?"

For the rental slip, he used his own Oregon driver's license, mercifully still valid. That was hanging a target on his back—if they needed a target—but he didn't care about that now. He was not going to get in a taxi. He would not put himself in the hands of another driver without even the specious protection of a crowd around him.

He trembled as he walked through the rent-a-car parking lot looking for his car, out in the open twilight, waiting for the other shoe to drop in the form of a hand on his shoulder, a chrome bumper behind the knees . . . a bullet through his brain. He forced himself to stow his luggage before he slid behind the wheel.

Then he lost it for a moment and sat slumped, his forehead on the plastic steering wheel, fighting nausea and trying to catch his breath. *No scratch team, no babysitters, okay; maybe she's going to give me a chance.* He keyed the ignition and headed the stripped Dodge for Glebe Road.

It was pitch dark and cold as a nun's tit by the time Fox dropped his suitcase on one of the Arlington Best Western's twin beds, turned the room's heater on full-blast to chase the March chill, and walked to the offset bathroom. He flipped lights on as he went. The window curtains were rubber-backed. Nobody was going to be listening to conversations in the room by measuring vibrations on the glass with microwaves—not that Fox had ever heard of such gear working in the field anyway.

He'd registered in his own name—there wasn't any use in finessing it with a false passport when his name was on the car-rental slip. He hadn't had time to plan this, dear God . . . and Gallen's heavy-hitters could run him down no matter what. . . .

There was no team hidden in the bathroom. Fox stood in the lavatory alcove and tossed first his sport coat, then his tie, then shirt, out onto the carpeted floor. He was trembling with reaction. The whole business—lack of business—was surreal. He was being ignored as thoroughly as if he were one of the hundreds of Foreign Service types home on leave at any one time.

Like hell. He'd set the hook himself when he sent that message to Shai Gallen; the only thing now in doubt was the length of the line on which they played him.

When Fox lifted his right foot to take off his shoe, pain turned the room into a dazzling kaleidoscope. Its intensity surprised him: he could walk almost normally by now, but lifting that foot above knee-level put the wrong stresses somewhere. Gasping for a moment, eyes closed, he concentrated on the coolness of the wall and washstand against which he braced himself. Then, carefully, he bent from the waist to strip off his shoes and socks and used the black marbleized washstand to lever himself upright again. He let his trousers fall.

It is a cliché of interrogation that a subject becomes more vulnerable when his clothing is removed. Fox momentarily envisioned himself donning a suit of 15th Century plate-armor to prepare for what was to come. Then the spray of hot water from the showerhead struck him like a benediction, washing away his fatigue and what felt like several layers of fur covering his body. He'd never have believed that something so simple could feel so good.

After a time—his sense of duration was gone; it was probably between three minutes and ten—he shut off the water and stepped out of the shower. Even in the steamy bathroom, he could see the rainbow of bruises and abrasions on his body to remind him that everything he remembered was all too real, not the imaginings of a crazy. The hot water had brought out fiery blotches even on patches of skin which had seemed unmarked; and as bad as it looked, it was probably just a foretaste of what was to come when the home team got hold of him.

He didn't want to think about it; he didn't want to look at himself; he grabbed a towel and walked out into the lavatory alcove.

Shai Gallen, wearing gray slacks and jacket, her blond hair caught up beneath a beret, sat cross-legged in the chair by the front door. He remembered that her muscular legs had always embarrassed her, though they—the legacy of an aunt determined to raise a dancer if it killed them both—were spring-supple as well as strong. As a nineteen-year-old boy, Larry Fox had whimpered with delight while those toes stroked the back of his neck; he'd told her that she was a fool to hide limbs so beautiful, so liquid in the way they melded grace and power. . . .

Fox snapped back to alertness and found himself embarrassed by more than simply his nakedness and his memories. "Damn," he muttered, draping the towel around him. He felt even more of a fool when he had to flutter the towel loose again so as not to emphasize what it had been his intention to hide. Then a rush of anger at himself solved the problem.

The woman raised her eyes slowly from his groin and smiled like a wicked child. "So it *is* you—the Mad Bomber. Even for you, Fox, this must be some kind of record—five social indig kills . . . maybe six . . . your COS, blowing our Istanbul consulate's safe room *and* your wife." She shook her head slowly, her brow faintly furrowed with lateral lines that hadn't been there thirteen years before. "Would you like to tell me how you think I can help you—beyond the obvious, of course?" Her gaze flicked back to his crotch.

"I—" he said. He spread his hands helplessly, began again: "I wanted to tell somebody I could trust. You need to hear. Somebody needs to hear."

"What I heard," her voice was very low, "was from Mossad. Larry, what were you thinking of, involving the Israelis in this and me with them by implication? Now *my* ass is on the line. But never mind. We'll talk, okay? You will give me the *razvedka* now."

"The *what?*" Fox asked. Her eyes, behind clear glasses, fascinated him; it was as if he were staring down the throats of a pair of pistols; he couldn't look away. But he didn't know the word she'd used; it took him a moment to realize that it was Russian, with the implication that he was a Soviet agent—that he'd turned and been sent here to discredit her in some kind of complex double game. He'd forgotten how convoluted Langley logic could be. He said clearly, "I don't know Russian, Shai. I don't know what you mean."

"The word means 'true intelligence.' If you don't know it, then how can we discuss *seriozniye dela?*"

"I told you, my Russian's nonexistent. I'm a Turkish specialist, remember? You've got my file." He was beginning to weave on his feet; despite the heater warming the room, his skin was covered with goose-bumps.

"*Seriozniye dela,*" she repeated as if indulging him, then translated: " 'Things that matter.' What matters to you now, Larry Fox? When a man runs in the wrong direction, people wonder why. When the timing is so inopportune, and very busy people are pulled from sensitive analyses to deal with him, there is a tendency to suspect the worst—that you're either very smart, or very stupid. Which is it?''

Pushed to his mental wall, he blurted, ''I thought maybe saving your life was worth something—that you might acknowledge a personal debt of ... honor, I guess. By listening to me. That's all I want, somebody who knows me to listen. You don't have to pretend I'm a Soviet agent to get yourself off the hook—there *is* no hook. You're the only shot I've got. But doesn't it mean *something* positive to you that I came home after ... what happened—that's your thing, isn't it: positive intelligence—that I didn't run to Singapore or the Hindu Kush? ...''

Surprisingly, she nodded: ''Something, yes. But not what you think, perhaps.'' Her voice was throaty and penetrating, harsher than Fox remembered it. ''I've already gotten one Night Action cable from Ankara about you.'' She smiled, without humor this time. ''You're lucky it was garbled. Maybe it was garbage. You tell me.''

''Do—ah—you want me to get dressed?'' Fox said weakly. He'd been in bad physical shape when he got here; now he was feeling very naive and foolish as well. He made a tiny gesture toward the clothing strewn at the foot of the nearer bed.

''You wanted an hour,'' Gallen reminded him. ''You've got fifty-three minutes left.'' She reached up and fitted the tab of the door's chain bolt into its slot. The snick of metal on metal was no harder than her blue eyes.

''Check. I interviewed a Soviet defector who appeared to be ... *could be*—'' Fox said bluntly as he eased to the foot of the bed and sat facing the side wall rather than the woman by the door ''—Abdulhamid Kunayev." The bolt above her head wouldn't hold against a solid kick: it provided a symbol of the bargain Gallen had accepted; lighting a long fuze would have done the same. "In the course of the interview, the defector stated that President Crossfield is a Soviet penetration." Listening to his words, Fox realized how crazy he sounded and began quickly to explain: "He—"

She cut him off: "What evidence did this ... defector ... cite to support those statements?" Her voice was emotionless but it seemed to have risen an octave.

"Captain, I didn't *believe* them," Fox said despairingly in a low voice that trembled. There was a mirror over the long desk built into the wall opposite the bed; he closed his eyes rather than stare at his own face, battered by weakness and failure. The implications of the Kunayev contact were too important for validation to depend solely on him; but nobody was going to make decisions based on the information he'd collected until and unless he could convince Shai Gallen that there was some decision to make concerning Larry Fox, GS-11, field collector of moderate experience, beyond how deep under Langley to bury him.

He didn't know how in hell to begin doing that, but he realized as he monitored his thoughts that at least he was worried about it—human again, with human feelings, not just a computing gunsight, though somewhere in him that gunsight was locked onto his memories like a targeting array, waiting for someone to squeeze the red switch.

"Sir," Fox said a little too loudly as he attempted to override the quaver in his voice, "the defector broke contact almost at once." Gallen wasn't a girl he'd known in the Lebanon; she was his DDO—operations director for CIA: he *had* to handle this like the professional he ought to be. "He said he was afraid of the US because the President was a mole, then he took off as if he saw something in the street below. I was prevented from following him by my Turkish contact. So I didn't see what happened—I lost contact with the defector."

Gallen got up from the armchair with a look of cold fury on her face. Her glasses didn't distort the glaring eyes behind them: the lenses were clear, an excuse for the heavy frames. Fox was willing to bet that the attaché case beside the DDO held at least a recorder and a voice-stress analyzer. Gallen's glasses would house either an actual intercom connecting her to a crew outside the room, or an audio monitor giving her a readout from the stress analyzer. The tone in Gallen's ear would change as the level of stress in Fox's voice went up and down. There were more reasons for stress than the subject choosing to lie, however; he hoped she'd remember that.

Abruptly Gallen slammed the wall behind her with the the side of her fist: "Give me some *reason* that a man of Kunayev's resources would pick a low-level line operative to tell his story to ... some reason not to think you're feeding me crap which, based on the increased message traffic and troop movements on the Sino-Soviet and NATO borders, the Soviets know damn well that Blaustein's Assessment boys would love to believe. Come *on*, Larry—*find* something. Even you've got to realize that you're dead in the water if I can't help you and that I *won't* help you if it puts my credibility, and therefore hundreds of my field operators, in jeopardy. If anybody's going to get fucked here tonight, it's you, not me. We're not talking about flow-charts now, we're talking about extended chemical debriefing." Her fist uncurled and her hand cut a tight, angry circle in the air.

Fox looked at her and took a deep breath. The calm he'd experienced in Sabanci's shop was back with the memories of the beating he'd taken there. It was as if he were standing beside his tortured body in Istanbul and at the same time listening to his mouth make its report as logically as it could to Gallen in a cheap Arlington motel: "The contact agent—my agent—is . . . *was* unsophisticated. He believes—believed—my cover identity as a Canadian operative. The defector had no reason in our brief interview to doubt that cover either."

The operations director seated herself on the edge of the motel desk as smoothly as if she'd gotten up with that purpose in mind. "When was your next contact with the defector?" she asked mildly.

Her tone shook the younger officer out of the detached state into which her anger had propelled him. Flashback memories of Ali's fists faded. Fox answered: "No further contact."

Gallen shifted as if to make certain her body wasn't screening the microphones aimed at him from within the attaché case.

"I attempted to reach my contact agent, TIC-RAM," Fox continued, hoping it didn't sound like he was making excuses. "There was a wrecking crew waiting for me—for me specifically: they knew my name. TICRAM didn't know my real name; these guys did. Four Turks for muscle and a foreign national."

"What nationality?"

"Not American." Fox closed his eyes for information retrieval rather than self-defense. "He didn't have an accent in English or Turkish, but he wasn't a native speaker of either one."

"Best guess?"

"I thought he was Russian," the line officer admitted with a sigh. "He called the defector Kunayev. The defector was calling himself Selim, not Kunayev, and he had an accent in Turkish. This guy sounded like he came straight out of the US & Canada Institute or a Soviet broadcasting school."

Gallen shifted so that the heel of her right shoe hooked the desktop, leaned her temple against the raised knee, then propped the glasses up on her forehead so that the earpiece was not in her way. "What sort of accent did the defector have?"

"Eastern," Fox shrugged. "Maybe Uighur, maybe . . . I don't know . . . Tadzhik. I don't claim that. But they used his name—Kunayev—when they started to lose it with me."

"What did you tell them then?" Gallen asked. There was a whisper of reserve in her voice but no anger.

"They wanted to know about the meet, what the defector told me. They knocked me silly right away. Damnedest thing," Fox mused, "not out cold, but not all there, either. I didn't tell them anything, I think . . . I guess I can't really be sure." He looked at Shai Gallen, *at* her as a person, for the first time since he'd walked out of the shower. "You did the same thing to me a minute ago—made me a puppet, like. Only you didn't have to give me a tune-up; they did. Christ, Shai, what difference does it make what I said to them, if I can't make *you* believe me when I'm trying? I didn't *have* much of anything to tell them: Ku—the defector ran away too soon."

Gallen stroked the earpiece of her glasses with her right forefinger. "You look like you were trying out for tackling dummy, Larry," she said with a nod. It was only the second overt mention she'd made of the subject's body; his inference was that she was treating his physical condition as a piece of corroborative evidence in his favor. "You look like you're lucky you got out of there alive."

"You should see the other guys," whispered Larry Fox. The reaction Gallen had played for was raw in his voice with no need of the stress analyzer to evaluate it.

He stood up and took a step toward the bathroom, then stopped: "Shai, let's don't talk about that, okay?" His hands were wringing the ends of the towel at his waist. "I'll talk about Kathie or Ed, but not that, okay? I got away, I—they didn't carry any information back."

"What did they say about Kunayev?" Gallen asked in a neutral tone.

When Fox turned toward her again, breathing deeply, she was folding the glasses into a case she then pocketed.

"They asked me, 'What did Kunayev tell you when you met him?' " he replied, trying to quote a line distanced more by pain and shock than time. "That might be just the idea, not the words." His smile was wan. "I'm not sure whether he asked me in English or Turkish. Must have been English. But it wasn't any more than that—just a line, maybe a couple times in different ways." He stopped with a shake of his head.

"More," she urged.

Fox sat on the bed with a thoughtful frown: "They'd killed my contact agent, TICRAM, by then. But I don't think TICRAM knew the defector personally, just met him as a referral, probably through the Gray Wolves' Soviet contacts."

"Were any Turkish nationals involved in your escape from custody?" Gallen asked, inexorably bringing him back to the subject he'd begged her to let him avoid. That lapse of half-an-hour's worth of data might be critical if damage limitation were necessary.

"None," said Fox with a fierce shake of his head. "Nobody."

"Who *did* you report to after you made your escape?"

"Nobody. I went back to my apartment—I still had one then. There was—" Fox tried leaning his elbows on his knees, winced, then straightened and demanded almost urgently, "Did you know Ed Platt, Shai? My Chief of Station?"

"He was in my division four years ago," the woman said with a deliberate coolness. "What happened when you went back to your apartment?"

"I'd made one report to Ed before I went out that night," Fox told her, then looked at his hands. Her question had been a prod to return him to the subject. What he was about to say wasn't unresponsive to her intent: "It was a purposely sketchy report but Platt knew I was talking about TICRAM before I told him so. And nobody but Platt knew where I was going. TICRAM himself didn't know."

"That's why you killed Platt, then?" The wicked-child smile was back now and it was almost approving.

"No," said Fox. He knew he was answering the question she'd begged, but it didn't matter. He had surrendered all hope of keeping secrets when he decided not to try to run. "That didn't have much to do with it—I mean, what happened to me didn't."

"What *were* your intentions when you returned to your apartment, Larry?" Her eyes looked softer than they had with the clear lenses before them, but from his angle Fox could see the hammer of a cocked pistol in an upside-down shoulder holster beneath her jacket. Thirteen years ago, they'd been arguing about the propriety of shelling civilians when a sniper lifted over the top of the wall . . . .

"I was going to write my after-action report." Fox scowled as he tried to recall clearly a time for which he had very little serial memory because of what had followed: intentions, actions, and fears were scrambled. Even the reality of what had occurred had very little real-world referrent. "Dunno who I was going to turn it in to. Ed, I guess. Maybe. . . ." Eyes hooded in concentration, he trailed off.

"Go on," she ordered implacably.

He blinked and said, "There's a fellow I told." Christ, there *was* something he had to hide, someone left to protect—Glenn! "Owen Neely, Crossfield's National Security Advisor. Mailed a letter to him from the Con-Gen. I'd written it before the shit hit the—"

"What did you tell Neely?" Gallen asked. Nothing identifiable had changed in her face or voice, but the invisible curtain that had been between them at the beginning of the debrief was back again.

"What I told you just now," Fox answered. They were going to have a field day when they ran that tape through a stress analyzer at headquarters. The drugs would come once they had, but there was still a chance he could keep Glenn out of it: interrogation drugs disconnected the human discretionary override system but they also screwed up the brain's sorting mechanism. They were going to get Glenn's name for sure, but mixed in with a lot of garbage. Data collection is almost never as much of a problem as is analysis of the collected data. "That was all I knew when I wrote it. It was before Kathie—" His mouth clamped shut of its own accord.

"I need to know what happened next, Larry."

Fox realized he'd closed his eyes, opened them. Without looking away from Gallen he said, "I took a lamp from the bedroom when my wife woke up. This was in it." He knelt by his trousers; the movement jabbed him, muscles protesting unexpectedly.

He gasped and took the weight on his forearms. After a moment, his abdomen relaxed. He took the audio bug from his pants pocket, where he'd secreted it when he left his apartment, and handed it to Gallen.

She extended her left hand, not her gun hand, to accept it—habit, surely, for she *had* to know Larry Fox wasn't that kind of threat.

"I found it after the blast," he explained as he sat down again.

Gallen rolled the bug slowly between her thumb and forefinger but her eyes were on Fox, her face still as water in a pond.

He didn't notice; he was flashing back to his Istanbul apartment: "I said ... I *spoke*. That's what fucking killed her. I told Kathie to go to sleep and the bedroom blew up. That was the go signal: hearing my voice close by the bug meant that I was in the bedroom. Only I wasn't; I had the lamp in the living room. But they didn't know that."

"You know a lot about explosives, Larry," she cajoled. "What would you say they used on this one?"

"Christ, I don't know," Fox muttered. "Enclosed ... I don't know. Like blowing a one-oh-five in place but no fragmentation, just the door itself. . . ." Then his brain correlated the question with its context and realized why it had been asked. "Christ," he repeated very softly. Then: "I didn't kill my wife, Captain Gallen. I didn't grease her deliberately and I didn't fuck up fooling with blocks of tetryl, or whatever the hell it was. Somebody planted a command-detonated bomb in my bedroom closet, and if that's not what Tech Services tells you when they're done, then you'd better check out whoever did the on-site analysis and everybody between them and you."

"Don't worry, Fox, I will."

There was something new in her face and it frightened him; he was already experiencing respondent-syndrome: he wanted desperately to make her believe him or at least to know she was on his side. He stood up, moving with the effort and control of a bear on a chain: "Kathie's dead because somebody fucked up, lady, and it wasn't me. Ed Platt didn't have the balls to initiate a scratch order. He was reporting to somebody, and if it wasn't in-house then it was a parallel channel. For all I know, maybe it was you."

"Now that's the Larry Fox I remember," she grinned.

Fox's face lost its anger. "I hadn't any business killing Platt," he confessed, turning away from Gallen and the present. "The others, sure, but . . . hell, he knew things, Shai. He said the scratch order came from Blaustein and I didn't listen—I just blew the bastard away. I wanted him dead so bad—" He about-faced.

Gallen was standing a half-step away from him. She didn't back away; her lips moved with great care before she spoke, as though she were rehearsing her words. "Could you have misheard some other name?" she said at last.

"Than what?" said Fox, puzzled because the focus of his attention had been elsewhere. "Oh, than Blaustein. No, that was what. . . ." He paused, trying to retrieve the information to answer her next question before she asked it: "As best I can remember, Platt said, 'I didn't know what they were going to do, it must have been Blaustein who ordered it.' And he knew I was going to kill him when he said it, so I don't think he was lying. But you think he meant the Deputy Director of Central Intelligence, don't you? *That* Blaustein?"

"I think," said Gallen as she turned and walked back to the chair and her attaché case, "that it's just as well I'm debriefing you myself." It was the first time since Fox stepped out of the bathroom that she'd turned her back on him.

She sat down and set the attaché case on her knees to open it.

Fox stayed where he was.

"This is crazy, you know?" she said, her voice remote, her eyes assessing him over the top edge of the case's lid. Then: "Would you recognize the defector you spoke to if you saw him again?"

"Yeah," the standing officer said with a nod, answering both questions. He was beginning to drift again.

Gallen held up an $8 \times 10''$ glossy. Lighting was by strobe and straight on. The nose and forehead in the photo were faded by the glare and the eyes had a wild glint that could have been a result of the harsh lighting. But the face, even eight feet distant—

"That's him," Fox said, nodding again, giving her the positive ID she wanted. "He ... doesn't look as much like Kunayev as the file photo made me think."

"You mean, he doesn't look as much like the file photograph of Kunayev as you thought," the woman said. "One of the Communicators remembered that you and Platt both pulled Kunayev's file. That gave us a handle." Her blue eyes flared: "You didn't give us very many fucking handles, Larry."

Fox swallowed with difficulty. "Where'd you find him?" he asked. He could barely hear his own voice through the hot prickling waves which raced across his skin with every heartbeat. "The look-alike, I mean." His body stepped forward without conscious volition when Gallen held out the photo.

"He isn't a look-alike—or wasn't," Gallen said in a perfectly dry voice. "That's Abdulhamid Kunayev, six years after we got the last file photo." She paused as Fox took the 8 × 10.

He began to scowl as his eyes focused on the background detail in the picture.

"The Turkish police took it two nights ago on Taksim Square," Gallen told him. She reached back behind the top of her case. "They took this one—" she brought out a second glossy "—about thirty feet away."

The decapitated torso had been photographed from farther back. One arm was still attached. A huddle of cloth almost out of the flashlit area could have been Kunayev's legs. Dour, uniformed men were staring at the scene, their shoes gleaming in the photographer's light.

"And this," Gallen said, handing him a third photo, "we took ourselves last night at 12th and E, about four blocks from the White House."

The subject of the third photograph was a young man as dead as Abdulhamid Kunayev. One bullet of three to the head had punched through both cheeks, distorting his expression. Fox rubbed his eyes and said with utter certainty: "I've never seen him before in my life."

"What name did you use with your contact agent, this TICRAM?" Gallen asked as if she already knew the answer.

"Alvin Stevenson," Fox replied, wondering why the DDO was changing the subject.

"That," Gallen said with a dismissive gesture aimed at the third photo, "was a commercial attaché with the Canadian mission here named Albert Stevenson. Somebody was too nervous to miss a bet, however unlikely. It may turn out that they think they got you—my *reshet's* already at work on it. And you, my friend, are officially dead until I say otherwise."

Fox handed the photographs back. His face showed no emotion. He knew the meaning of the Israeli term *reshet*—network. If Langley wanted to stash him somewhere and kill him quietly later, Stevenson provided a corpse they could point to as the murderer of TICRAM, four Turkish nationals, and one unidentified foreigner. Larry Fox, whose wife was dead, would be logged out as being on special assignment. CIA personnel dropped out of sight regularly for as long as eighteen months at a stretch, no questions asked. The few friends he had in Turkey would forget about him—except maybe for Barker, who had reason to remember.

"Christ, Shai, what about Sam Barker? If you know all this, you know—"

"That's not the sort of question you should be asking, Larry. But Barker's safe and sound, back doing his job." Her expression, both arms folded on the attaché case's open lid, was oddly pensive.

"Okay, good for Barker," he said uncomfortably. "Now what?"

The woman unfolded her arms and closed the attaché case; its locks clacked simultaneously. "Now," she said, "we get you somewhere else."

She stood abruptly, again almost in contact with Fox.

His weight shifted, but at the last moment he decided not to back away. He wanted to ask her, point-blank, what was going to happen to him. He couldn't. He just watched the flutter of her nostrils as she gazed at him appraisingly.

"You aren't done with this, Fox—you haven't even started." She shook her head and her beret fell off; ignoring the beret, she reached up, unfastened a clip, and let her hair fall to her shoulders, saying ruefully: "Shit, Larry—Blaustein. Well, he may have saved your ass for the moment—I can't risk letting anyone outside my reshet near you until we've cleared this up. Right now—"

For the first time, he interrupted her: "I didn't *ask* to be done with it." His voice was very quiet; he'd already accepted her inference that there was no team in a panel truck somewhere hanging on his every word as they crouched over their monitoring equipment. But now he had to make it clear where he stood: "I'll tell you whatever I can. Hypnosis'll help." Fox swallowed hard. Best to offer freely what they'll take anyway if they want it. "You'd know better than me what drugs would—wouldn't distort. . . ."

"Ha. There are none, unless you don't mind the occasional tumor ten years later. But we'll use what circumstances require," Gallen added noncommittally. This close, she had to tilt up her face to meet his eyes.

"Shai, you're going to need more than just what I can tell you," Fox's voice was thick, so low it was almost a whisper, "if this is what it seems to be— what the defector said it was. If it's not the damnedest disinformation scheme ever. . . ."

"If you're not a dangle, you mean? Or a provocation. Maybe an unknowing one? That's my problem—figuring it out. I don't like you volunteering for chemical debrief. If you've got a death-wish, Larry, just hold the thought. We'll find a better way to spend you."

"You aren't really going to put in a report, are you? Eyes Only for the President?"

Her eyes were gun-blue and glinting dangerously again. "Somebody who thinks tradecraft is buttoning-down a matter of national security with Owen Neely ought not to question a superior officer about how that officer intends to do her job." Gallen's face managed the least increment of a smile to take the sting out of her rebuke. "When this over, you can pick your venue—I'll take you out of the Fig Leaf Brigade, send you to the Farm for retraining so that they can put enough weight on you to make you fit for a serious Operations assignment, and we'll use you like you ought to be used. You're wasted in Collection, Larry. You mentioned the Kush awhile back. We could use a good EO man to train the Afghan rebels; or maybe you'd prefer the Middle East? . . ."

"That's *not* what I want, Shai. What I'm trying to say is . . . count me in," Fox said in the same soft voice. "I'm owed it. If any of this is true, I'm owed it."

"Owed it? You want a shot at this? Think you can handle a serious debriefing—now—to my reshet? I'll help you, steer the questions away from Blaustein. Do it, and you're in the picture on Operation Lemon Pledge. Fuck up, and you're my house pet until we can figure out a safer place for you."

"Now?" Dear God, he wasn't in any shape to field questions. "Fuck yeah, lady. Lead me to 'em." He wondered who would be involved, and who besides Gallen *they* would be reporting to.

"You'd better get your clothes on first," she said and gestured toward his strewn garments impatiently.

"Okay," Fox said without inflection, trying not to think about what was going to happen: whoever

Gallen trusted enough to call her "reshet" weren't going to be flyweights. He turned.

Gallen's small hands on his shoulders stopped him. "Hey, cowboy?" she whispered.

Her breathy words tickled his spine.

Then her fingers tensed and in a slightly thicker voice she said, "Fox, do you always have to look like a truck just hit you when we . . . when we aren't arguing?"

Fox turned to face her. He was suddenly sure that no one would *ever* hear the tape now spooling its way through Gallen's recorder. His hands slid beneath her jacket and the cocked hammer of the pistol he'd forgotten about gouged at his right forearm. "We've got an insufficient sample," he said as he bent to kiss her.

RESHET

"Alden's name has come up way too many times for it to be innocent drug flotation," said Harrison Quaid, Deputy Chief of Operations/Counterintelligence Staff, to Gallen as she stared through one-way glass at what remained of Larry Fox.

It had been only three days since Gallen turned the young field collector over to her reshet for debriefing in the safe house; Fox looked as if he'd spent a month in Siberia. His normally thin frame was emaciated and even though he was sitting before a roaring fire in the cabin's fieldstone fireplace, he was shivering. He'd been on an enforced fast throughout the interrogation—food and truth drugs were a deadly combination. His lips were blue, his eyes sunken and roving beneath puffy lids, his cheeks hollow.

The pair of interrogators working at the moment included a woman whom Fox, in his drugged and debilitated state, obviously thought was Gallen:

he was weeping slightly, though he probably didn't know it, as he begged her in a hoarse, childlike voice to "make it stop, Shai, please. Okay? So sleepy . . ."

Gallen slapped off the intercom and turned her back on the interrogation in progress. "You're sure, Quaid? You're being pretty rough on him."

"That's not rough—that's the slow, easy way. And damn it, would I say something like that if I wasn't sure? Either he's a fag and this Alden's his lover, or the kid's got more balls than a bull elephant and he's trying to keep Alden's name out of this so hard it comes up every time he isn't looking. Shaitan," the deputy said softly, coming up behind her and putting his big hands on her shoulders— hands which, like the voice of the barrel-chested six-footer who outweighed her two-to-one, were capable of incongruous gentleness, "you don't owe this guy anything more. Beirut was a long time ago."

She turned in Quaid's grasp: "Are you sure, Sonny?"

Quaid took his hands away. He called her "Shaitan" because it meant, in Arabic, an evil spirit or fiend and because Quaid, as well as being an Arab specialist and counterterrorist, was Gallen's lover. He was her lover because Shai Gallen had long ago seen past the rough-hewn frame of the red-headed ex-paratrooper, under the jutting forehead of his craggy Jumpmaster's face, and into the unexpected intelligence behind Quaid's narrow eyes— and not because, as the gossip-mongers assumed, Quaid was a sterling example of what had come to be known as "Shai's type": Anglo-Saxon studs over two hundred pounds with bullish stamina, powerful positions, and passions to match her own. In fact, it was Sonny Quaid's quick wit and operational pragmatism which had ensured their continuing relationship. What Shai Gallen had needed was a lover who never mentioned the word "love," who could slip out of her bed and home to his wife and never think twice about it, who understood that Gallen's love was reserved for her work, for an abstract called democracy and for her line units and agents in the field.

If Sonny Quaid wasn't really such a man, he was doing a damn fine job pretending, and the passion they shared on joint ventures had naturally spilled over into midnight trysts that began and ended with analyses and estimates of Sensitive Intelligence operations to which both were privy—and which neither could discuss in intimate detail with anyone else.

Now Quaid stared at her pensively, eyes almost colorless in a weathered face that might have fought Caesar for Gaul and as relentless: *Come on, Shaitan,* the stare demanded, *don't shit the shitter. We know each other too well for this crap . . . or do I have to lay you flat to find out what's on your mind?*

Gallen let Sonny Quaid's interrogative gaze rest in hers until it locked up and Quaid looked away. She couldn't trust anyone right now, and she had to trust someone; since that someone was Sonny, her lack of response spoke volumes.

His broad forehead furrowed and his thin lips quirked before he said, "I deserve better than a non sequitur, Shai. I've been up for seventy-two hours straight, between this and my day-job at Langley. You want to fuck this kid, that's one thing: we'll wipe his ass and send him over to your place in working order. But that's not what you said you wanted—there's no "nice" way to sweat somebody, let alone squeeze out what they don't know they know. Now, which is it?"

"He's pretty well fucked already, Sonny, from what I can see." She sighed and let down her hair, then ran her fingers through it. "Everybody's tired. I've spent the last three days wrangling with the Capitol police, a Special Agent I know, and half of Justice, trying to get jurisdiction over the investigation of that Canadian hit at 12th and E. Nobody seems to be willing to admit that it's a Soviet Directorate V scratch-pattern, and that we're best qualified. I'm going to ask Noah Neely to intervene—they won't say "no" to a request from the President's own Intelligence Advisory Board."

"Or let it go," Sonny Quaid advised, sinking into a feather-stuffed black kid sofa and pouring coffee from a service on the table with hands trembling from fatigue. "You don't want to drag out your big guns until LEMON PLEDGE gets off the ground. And you wouldn't need to, but for Foxy-loxy there: the only value to us in handling the Stevenson case is to muddy the waters enough that we can claim Stevenson and Fox were one and the same."

"Maybe not." She'd told Quaid's CI people that was what she wanted, but she knew the legend wouldn't hold—Stevenson had family, Fox had family. It didn't have to hold, not forever, only until the effort to cover Fox's tracks had done its work. She was mildly surprised that Sonny hadn't sussed out where she was taking this—but then, maybe he had. Maybe he was indicating his willingness to catch the ball she'd thrown him ... here, in a safe house on nobody's budget that belonged to the LEMON PLEDGE interdepartmental task force alone. Thus she continued very carefully, "The scratch-artists that waxed Stevenson might lead us to the Oval Office. I hate like hell to go on line with LEMON PLEDGE without a shred of substantive evidence—especially being half-Jewish with ties to Shin Bet and Mossad." She bared her own teeth and took the coffee cup Quaid proffered. "I can see the headlines now: 'Israeli Double Agent Assassinates US President.' They'd probably reinstitute the death penalty just for little ol' me."

"That's not going to happen—we've had this discussion before." Quaid's brains might have landed him behind a supergrade's desk but his body would never forget the field: though he tended to restless moods when things were quiet, he was dead calm and cheerful whenever lives were on the line. "You're the youngest DDO we've ever had, Shaitan—*and* a woman. Nobody worries about your Israeli provenance but you. You're only half Jew; try to be only half paranoid. If there'd been any doubts about you renouncing your Israeli loyalties when you came over to us, you'd never have become DDO, let alone have the Israeli desk. Let me worry about the politics of protecting you, all right? You just run LEMON PLEDGE."

"And Larry Fox? Can you clear him high enough and quick enough for me to run him, too? Or is it a sacrifice we're looking at here?"

"He won't handle well, Shai. He's the wrong psychological type. A guy like that, all you can do is cock him and point him at the target...." Quaid stopped in mid-sentence, coffee cup to his lips. His narrow eyes widened slightly and he put the cup down as if it were filled with nitro. "Holy Mother of God! That's it, isn't it? That's what you're going to do—sic that walking grenade in there on Crossfield?"

"You bet, cowboy," Gallen tried to make her grin insouciant. "*After* I put him out there where Blaustein's—and/or Directorate V's—boys are sure to find him. We've got to take some risks if we want them to make some mistakes. That's why I don't care if it leaks that we've got Fox. I want Blaustein to really worry." If truth be known, she *wanted* it to leak. Gallen's distaste for her immediate superior, the Deputy Director of Central Intelligence, was unhidden in her voice.

"I still think," Quaid said in his flat, professional tone, "that it's as likely that KGB's orchestrated this whole thing to tie us up in knots as it is that this kid's information is A-1. It's a classic: disinformation of this nature could have the Agency biting its own tail for the next two or three *years*; with everybody worried that everybody else was a KGB double, communications and therefore operations would grind to a halt—we'd be all but neutralized."

"That's the trouble with you CI guys—*deformation professionelle*: years of double-think renders you too skeptical to perform your function. If you don't believe Fox, Sonny, then believe me: this is real. No one like Fox would be recruited by KGB as an agent—not as a provocation, or an induced double, or even as the contact for a dangle of the kind you think Kunayev was. Fox just isn't fucking credible enough."

"I've got to agree with that," her counterintelligence chief said with a chuckle. "But Shaitan, I don't like the sound of this. . . . What do you mean by 'out there'? You're not going to be anywhere near Fox while he's playing prime target, are you?"

"You mean you can't protect me? Come on, Quaid, this is nearly insulting. Talk about classic scenarios . . . given that we accept the premise that Crossfield's a penetration, then the only way for KGB to run Crossfield is through a handler or case officer close by—on-site would be best. And that handler or case officer would have to be a double, induced or not—somebody that Crossfield could hire as an apparent underling as he moved up. How long have Blaustein and Crossfield known each other? Twenty-five, thirty years? Blaustein was Crossfield's polysci professor at Harvard, for God's sake."

"You could be wrong. The Soviet handler you're postulating could as easily be Blaustein's boss—assuming it's anyone. Luftsen, as director of the Agency, has equal access."

"But not equal smarts. Maybe it's both of them—handler and case officer; maybe you're right and it's neither. In which case I'm grooming myself and everybody else involved in LEMON PLEDGE for Leavenworth. So if you want out, Quaid. . . ." As Gallen put down her cup, she caught sight of Fox through the one-way glass and felt as if she'd been rabbit-punched. For the first time, she sat down on the couch opposite Quaid.

Quaid was saying: "—stand by and let you run this yourself, you're deluded. You need me. I know that's hard for you to comprehend, Shaitan, but you can't float this Fox legend without plenty of support, and there's not another section with the security or technical expertise we've got."

"That's right, I forgot—counterintelligence: you weirdos down the hall with the locked doors and the nervous trigger-fingers."

"Be glad we've got 'em. Now, you want to lay it out for me?"

"Fox, at my place, with straddling babysitters and a backstopped legend of your choice, within forty-eight hours."

"Balls. You *are* going to run him."

"That's right, and you're going to help me. I want him blanketed like a rich man's son in a nursery. He likes bikes. Get him something hot that'll handle—" she paused for a moment to think

"—he used to talk about Suzukis; an ID down to pocket litter, and enough bugs that if he farts we'll hear it."

"It's hard to cover a guy on a bike unless you've got other guys on bikes.... How about I give you a maid and a houseboy?"

"Give me a Japanese gardener, for all I care." She stood up. "Forty-eight hours." She turned to leave, then turned back: "Oh, and Sonny: this guy Alden—Fox's lawyer or boyfriend or whatever. Bring him in. I want him and that damned letter. I don't care what you tell him—national security's at stake, whatever."

Quaid snorted softly and sat back, hands laced behind his head. "And then?"

"And then we've nailed down one loose end. Owen Neely's another, I'm afraid. Damn Fox for a GS-11 who really wanted out the hard way. Neely's got to be muzzled...."

"The National Security Advisor?" Quaid's tone dripped sarcasm. "Sure thing, Shai. You want me to have him captured by 'terrorists' or what?"

"I want you to go see *Noah* Neely—explain to him that his brother Owen's in receipt of information that an ex-hot-mix king just isn't suited to handle. Noah'll take it from there. He's not on Crossfield's Intelligence Advisory Board for nothing...."

"Noah Neely's *your* sugar daddy, not mine, Shai." Quaid's voice dropped an octave so that it was almost a growl. "But I guess I just volunteered. Want to tell me why you can't handle Noah yourself? He'll do anything for you, so I've heard."

Gallen didn't bother defending against the accusation. Her relationship to Noah Neely was privileged and Quaid didn't need to know more; Sonny, she thought, was more protective than jealous—it was part of his nature and part of his job, as well as a welcome sign of humanity she'd never criticize. Instead, she stood and picked up her purse, preparing to leave as she said, "Too busy, cowboy. This has got to be done fast. And clean. What with Fox's status being—"

"You want to clarify Fox's 'status,' while we're on the subject?"

Gallen was already headed for the door when Quaid's words snapped out, rapid-fire. She stopped and said very slowly, very clearly, "We're going to make it look as if we're doing our damndest to cover the fact that Fox is alive and ours for debriefing." Then she turned again to leave.

But Quaid's admiring voice stopped her: "Want to give me a strategy lesson tonight, Shaitan? About eight-thirty, dinner and whatever?"

She had her fingers on the doorknob. Because this was a dangerous moment— dangerous for everybody since Larry Fox had come in and phased them into operational mode too soon; dangerous because she couldn't fully trust even Harrison Quaid, the guy she was fucking, and yet the operation couldn't be run by a singleton and she *had* to trust somebody . . . trust Quaid, who held her security in his big hands—she was acutely aware of the coolness of the brass knob and the slowness with which everything around her was proceeding. Even her breathing seemed to be in slow-motion. And that was Shai Gallen's edge: in a crisis, her mind seemed to go double-speed; she had ages to consider a response to a question or an act of violence in a real-time situation measured by ticks of a clock's second hand.

"Let me get back to you on that, Sonny? I know you hate to play second fiddle, but since it's

Blaustein who might beat your time, I'm sure you can handle it."

Then, before Quaid could stop her, she slipped through the door and closed it on his objections, calling back, "A girl's got to do what a girl's got to do."

Watching the door close behind Shai Gallen's muscular ass, Sonny Quaid socked back his cooling coffee and shook his head admiringly at the woman who had just left. Yet the smile on his face wasn't fond. His square teeth gleamed through tight-drawn lips and his eyes were mere slits as he said silently to himself, "Right, baby, you do that. And I'll do what *I've* got to do."

Shai Gallen visited Langley as infrequently as possible. She'd made it a condition of her employment that the clandestine services no longer be run out of the multi-story office building whose employees could be identified by as simple a procedure as getting the license numbers of cars routinely taking the exit marked "CIA."

There was an executive garage underneath, however, and that was where Gallen parked one of her directorate's sterile operations cars, rather than in the outdoor lot.

In the elevator to Blaustein's office on the fifth floor, she clipped her clearance badge to her shapeless down jacket and took off her double-gradient Ray-Bans. The jacket was too warm and the sunglasses weren't much of a shield from prying eyes, but she wasn't really worried about who saw her come and go these days at Langley: the increased ComBloc message traffic, coupled with unusual Soviet troop redeployments along their borders, had bumped the Defensive Condition alert-status up a grade. Sensitive Activities reports were being given verbally until futher notice, so people from clandestine services like Gallen were bouncing in and out of Langley like pinballs.

If Blaustein, or his immediate superior, Luftsen, or both, *weren't* grouse, they might as well have been: a half-dozen KGB cars and commo vans were parked along the route to CIA headquarters, some feigning mechanical breakdowns or flat tires, some haughtily obvious; she'd even seen a car with six trunk-mounted antennae and a van with an exterior microwave dish. In a free society, there wasn't much that could be done about it.

But the freedoms of that society were being eroded daily, and Gallen, who'd been born in Israel of a sabra mother and American Diplomatic Corps father, knew better than most native Americans how precious those freedoms were and how very much was at stake. It had occurred to her more than once that she *wanted* to believe that Crossfield was a Soviet agent—that she'd believe anything that allowed even a flicker of hope that the man could be stopped before he dismantled not only the American space presence, but the entire Constitution.

And yet, in the elevator, it was Larry Fox and not President Crossfield or even Blaustein who haunted her thoughts.

When Shai Gallen had met Lawrence Fox thirteen years ago, she'd been about to marry an American, CIA's liaison to Shin Bet, Israeli Military Intelligence. Even then, she'd loved Larry Fox's voice. She'd found herself arguing with him about anything just to listen to it, that week she was down on the Green Line in Beirut taking the Israeli army's temperature for Sharon.

In Beirut, she'd been taking too many chances

for Sharon, just the way she was taking too many chances for her own sake now. She'd married her American fiancé, soon after Fox was released from the hospital and Sharon was removed as Minister of Defense. She'd married because Sharon, whom she loved platonically but passionately, had been hurt and that had hurt her; in her mind all Israel had been hurt.

She'd withdrawn, using her Israeli rank and American citizenship to hurt back—she'd entered CIA laterally, not exactly a traitor to Israel but one who said by actions what had to be said: Israel must be strong to survive; if weak, her strongest would leave her. As an intelligence professional, Shai Gallen could have gone anywhere; as a secular Israeli, only America was an acceptable choice.

But there had been Fox, thirteen years ago during the last great crisis in her life, as today there was Fox. He wasn't her type, even then—he was too young, too thin, too powerless. It had been part of her defection of the heart that had led her to wait for Fox on the day he was discharged from the hospital. She hadn't thought about him since, not even after her husband was killed on a field trip when the US Embassy in Kuwait was bombed.

Yet old instincts were deep in her: she wanted to save Fox as if by doing so she could save her countries—Israel, where she'd been born; America, where she'd chosen to live and work. She *wanted* Fox to be right, be vindicated, be the key to the puzzle that was Crossfield.

She wanted it enough to stick her head in Blaustein's mouth. Everyone in her reshet was risking life and career but her—Quaid had managed to keep her distanced from implication by his labyrinthine methods. So far, only her counterintelligence officers had taken actions which could be construed to be against the national interest, and those actions had been suggested, not simply authorized, by a tasking officer who was part of Gallen's reshet because he owed Quaid whatever Quaid chose to ask. Until recently, she'd let those loyal to her protect her, telling herself it was for the good of relations between the US and the State of Israel, because if Crossfield had to die it must not be a Jew who ordered it, not with the polarization between Jews and other minorities which was one of the effects of Crossfield's Equal Americans programs. Not with the NeoNazi "Bund" screaming for an end to American Zionism and Palestinian genocide. Not with so many Jews in the defense community who could be indicted out of hand as warmongers by the pacifist Friends of Survival, as elitist architects of doomsday weapons by the violently anti-gun female lobby called "The 52%," and as fascist purveyors of econometrics by those who supported the Farm Adjusted Party Program, who'd rather sell their grain to ComBloc and eat soy protein themselves than cut production. . . . And because, like all intelligence professionals, paranoia was her most intimate companion.

But then came Larry Fox, who'd blithely handed a business card with her name on its back to an Israeli sky marshal, and who flatly accused the President and his DDCI of being Soviet agents.

Fox had changed everything. It remained only to find out how much.

If Blaustein already had learned that Fox had gotten to Gallen through a subterranean Israeli connection, Blaustein might be baited into revealing what he knew. If so, she'd have proof positive.

And that was what she needed: positive intelligence. Her sort of intelligence, not Quaid's Machiavellian counterlogic.

Blaustein's office had a cork-papered anteroom housing a bank of phones, computers and expensive resin furniture. A pink-cheeked, androgynous-looking male secretary presided over everything like a Gulf State Emir.

"Yesss?" he said archly when she walked in: this high in Langley, during the day, the computer locks with their card slots weren't operational. All the supergrades had creatures like this immaculate weight-lifter with the cover-girl face to protect them from unwanted visitors.

"CAMEL from CS, to see the DDCI," she said levelly.

The pretty face frowned at her as if she were trying to check into the Madison without a reservation. "You don't have an appointment, Ms. CAMEL."

"Just tell him what I told you, and I will have." The sharpness in her tone wasn't intentional, but it brought out into the open her innate hostility toward male women.

"We'll see about *that*," Blaustein's familiar huffed. He stabbed an intercom button on his desk as if it were Gallen's eye.

"Sir," the secretary purred, "there's a person here to see you who isn't on your schedule who claims to be CAMEL from CS. I've already said that you were too—"

"*Who?*" came a tenor voice from the intercom.

The secretary began to repeat the message, but Blaustein's voice interrupted: "Send her in and hold everything else until I tell you otherwise."

The secretary's face wriggled, then settled into a mask of neutral courtesy. "Right through that door, CAMEL . . . ." he said, reaching under his desk to press a button which magnetically released the lock on the door behind and to his right.

When Gallen pushed past the door, Blaustein was already on his feet and coming to meet her.

He wore a chalk-striped blue suit and a Harvard tie, both of which enhanced his professorial air, as did his immaculate waxed moustaches, his short thin hair and his roly-poly girth.

He extended one plump, pink hand. "This is a surprise, Shai. Don't tell me CI's paranoia has infected Ops so badly that you were afraid even to let me know you'd be stopping by?"

The comment was merely intended to show that Blaustein was on top of things in the Agency which was virtually his to command—since Luftsen, his putative superior, was a political appointee who knew no more about running a shop like Langley than Gallen did about French cooking.

She returned Blaustein's strong grip with her own and let the warm palm fall. "I was in the neighborhood, that's all, Kurt. Though I must admit I'd like to bounce this hostile-threat analysis of recent ComBloc activity around with you before the Security Council meeting. What your Assessment boys are saying and what Counterintelligence is saying seem to be in direct contradiction. That's never good when the President is sitting in . . . makes us look like the right hand doesn't know what the left one's doing."

As if leading her into his parlor, Blaustein turned his chalk-striped back to her and gestured her to the seat before his desk.

Making his way back to his desk chair, he said, while she couldn't see his face: "That's what the 'National Security Council/Special Coordinating Committee/Working Intelligence Group' is for, Shai. By the time Jim Crossfield stops all visible and apparent progress in that meeting with a stream of idealistically laudable but realistically unreachable goals in the guise of Presidential Directives to 'reunify our Nation' and, Mother of God, Executive Orders further limiting the intelligence community's ability to do so much as requisition Kleenex here and abroad, we'll have come up with a united presentation that I can give in less than ten minutes—hopefully five—of the actual state of affairs and quick fixes for whatever is fixable—if anything is—with one eye on what's left of the Constitution and the other on our own behinds."

Facing her, Blaustein sank into his chair with an unctuous smile he usually reserved for members of the Senate Intelligence Oversight Committee.

"*Actual* state of affairs, Kurt?" Gallen said icily. "Do you have a crystal ball we lowly deputies aren't privy to?" Blaustein always treated her like an overachieving female graduate student. She half expected him to lean forward, lace his fingers, tap them against his beardless chin and tell her that she really ought to get married and start raising a family.

Instead, Blaustein only continued to smile as he said, "*Actual*, Shai, my dear, in that we'll naturally halve the overblown nature of your directorate's hostile-threat indices. President Crossfield wants his Summit meeting. He wants to be reassured that his administration's going down in history as the one that put the U.S. on a firm footing of 'friendly relations' with our ComBloc neighbors. And that's *all* he wants to hear. So that's what we're going to tell him. I've got several analysts who will point out that these new Soviet troop movements—and the message traffic increase—are just periodic. They indicate an updating of weaponry systems and exercises designed to accustom the Soviet army to related changes in Control, Communications, and—"

Blaustein wasn't going to be baited into revealing what he knew, that was obvious—*if* he knew anything about Fox and how he'd gotten to her. At least, not here, where the DDCI was in complete control. "Kurt," Gallen shook her head, "I've got substantive evidence supporting our CI analysis . . . not only on the numbers, but on *why* the Supreme Soviet is getting so damned ballsy." She looked at her watch. "Have you plans for dinner?"

"That sensitive, eh?" Blaustein's cherubic smile was vaguely out of sync with his words. "All right, Shai, if you think it's worth all this, I'll be glad to listen, one-on-one. La Maison suit you?"

She shrugged again; she wasn't going to have much of an appetite, but she'd worn a dress and suede boots in expectation that Blaustein wouldn't want to talk security matters at the nearest McDonald's. He did like his perks.

While Blaustein told his secretary to make a reservation for two in an hour and a half at the Washington restaurant and call his car, Shai gazed around the deputy director's office for something that seemed out of place. There was nothing. The walls were covered with memorabilia—photos of Colby and Bobby Inman, the space shuttle, a KH-15 surveillance satellite rendered by an artist, and a prototype of the developmental transatmospheric spyplane, nicknamed "Peregrine," that the Skunk Works had been building for the Agency. Crossfield had let Congress kill the spyplane three weeks ago.

Finished with his secretary, Blaustein followed her gaze: "Pity, isn't it? Such a beautiful aircraft . . . Mach 42, high-resolution surveillance pictures of the Politburo paring their bunions as they sun themselves on the Black Sea—all gone in the scribble of a signature." He sighed with heartfelt angst. "Ours is not to make policy, my dear, but to carry

it out. You ought to remember that. Your directorate isn't known for tweaking its reports hard enough
to please certain of our very particular customers."

Here we go, Gallen thought with satisfaction, *a
little hardball.* Blaustein was warning her to come
into line and "yessir" whatever his conclusions on
the threat and vulnerability estimate were to be.
She said: "We're doing our best, sir. Data, unfor-
tunately, doesn't always support the conclusions
some policymakers would like to be able to reach."

"Particularly in the matter of this apparent Soviet escalation, you mean. My National Intelligence
Officer for the Soviet Union vehemently disagrees
with your shop there, Shai." He levered his bulk
out of the chair and crossed to his coat closet in
the peculiar, rolling gait of a short man with pre-
tensions of stature. Out of the closet came his
trenchcoat and with it over his arm he turned and
caught her off guard: "Do you want to tell me
what kind of 'substantive evidence,' I believe you
said, you've got, Shai? Or is it something that
makes you think my office isn't secure? I hate
surprises when I'm eating, and if it's serious, we
can start talking about it on the way."

Gallen stood up: "HUMINT, Kurt, is all I'm willing to tell you now—it's Human Intelligence. We
brought in a field collector who, before he died,
reported a contact with a high-level Soviet—also
dead now—claiming to confirm every one of our
counterintelligence boys' worst nightmares."

"Such as?" Blaustein snapped in peerless interrogator's style.

"Later," Gallen promised casually. "I think better anywhere but Langley. And I don't know about
you, but I hate sitting in traffic. If we leave now,
we might just beat the Beltway rush."

"Whatever you say, my dear girl," Blaustein

agreed pleasantly and came around to open the door for her.

He wasn't sweating, yet, but his movements weren't quite as fluid as they'd been when she came in. She wanted Blaustein hurting by the time this evening was over. If Blaustein *was* a Soviet penetration, he would either have to play an overt card against Fox, or her, or both . . . or he would have to muzzle his Assessment boys at the meeting. Without the Pollyannas from Assessment, President Crossfield would have to dismiss the counterintelligence component's concerns personally—or allow countermoves to begin that no Soviet agent could sanction.

There was feed, and there was feed, in a double game. If President Crossfield was what Gallen thought he was, what Quaid suspected he was, and what Kunayev had told Fox he was, he couldn't possibly accede to her imminent request at the upcoming NSC meeting for clearance to begin flushing grouse in the White House.

Not if Crossfield was the grouse in question.

Kurt Blaustein couldn't believe the balls of that Jew-bitch Gallen. To sit right across from him at his table in La Maison, leaning over her tournedos and paté—which *he* was paying for—and tell him, "that the Soviets have somebody inside our politico-military establishment—somebody high enough that the Soviets *know* we can't or won't do anything now that they've doubled their troop strength in the last eighteen months on both their NATO and Asian borders—that if they move in any direction, whether to neutralize the "Chinese threat," stop the "civil war" in Pakistan or help "reunify the Germanies," we have neither the military strength nor the national will to stop them."

Then she'd sat back, sipping her Montrachet, and waited for him to respond, those un-Jewish sapphire eyes as steady on him as a laser-guidance system locked on target. When he didn't, she'd said in a voice like sandpaper on silk, "Kurt, this collector—Fox, Stevenson, whatever you want to call him—buttoned this down outside normal channels . . . he sent out at least one duplicate report before he died. We can't bury this. We've got to source it and disprove it or it'll do us as much harm, in-house, as if it was God's own truth."

Then he'd had to respond: "The ravings of a psycho? First you tell me this . . . line officer, if that's what you want to call a GS-11 gopher . . . of yours killed half a dozen people, his wife included. Then you tell me he's credible. I—"

"Kurt," she'd interrupted with an almost sensual pout, "I didn't tell you how many people that collector killed before he died. And I didn't mention grade level."

Blaustein recovered neatly: "Stevenson/Fox isn't exactly a low-signature fuck-up, Shai. The damage report's on my desk right now. Sonny Quaid's people sent it up with an EYES ONLY/ASAP because the damage limitation measures are extraordinary. Nobody seems to know whether Fox was *our* double, or Canada's. If he turns out to be Canada's, this whole mess is going to land on *your* desk—your people aren't supposed to let this sort of thing happen, not on American soil, anyway."

That put Gallen on the defensive. He'd heard the bitch was almost as good as a man with a gun. And he'd heard other things—about her sexual acrobatics with General Teddy Westin from the Army's SAVE program; with Noah Neely, old enough to be her grandfather; and with Quaid from Counterintelligence, everybody's wild card and one contributor to Blaustein's sleepless nights. A couple of Harrison Quaids could make the sort of difference no individual was supposed to be able to make any more, in the modern age of the Great Game, when electro-optical capability— Communications and Signals Intelligence in all its subcompartments—was vaunted as the make-all and break-all of intelligence gathering.

Of course, when you were a Special Services II officer of Blaustein's rank, and running an agent of influence like Jim Crossfield, you knew better. No Event Alarm Tables, no Automatic Interrupt with however-many bells and whistles, could make the difference that a Human Intelligence team like Blaustein and Crossfield could. But even Blaustein had a controller—that was the way of KGB.

And he had to be able to convince that controller, Genya Posner, that the threat Gallen had made, savoring lemon sorbet served in swan-shaped bowls between courses, was real.

It had seemed *so* real at the time that when his poached salmon came, it had tasted like cardboard. Now, an hour later, sitting alone in La Maison, the car dismissed to deliver Gallen back to Langley, sipping an after dinner brandy and waiting for Genya to saunter over from a neighboring table— Genya, here because Blaustein had pushed the panic button under his desk in his Langley office and the meet had been electronically arranged by the mechanism of his secretary's calls for reservation and limousine—he tried to compose himself.

KGB was Blaustein's life; he firmly believed that he *still* believed in the shining concept of World Socialism which had led him into the labyrinth as an undergraduate. But men grow old and sore and calluses appear on youthful fervors: Blaustein had seen too much, worried too much, and accomplished too much by nefarious means to entertain the delusion that he—or anyone else—was irreplaceable. So when he spoke with Genya, he'd have to be very forceful, very careful and, most of all, very confident.

If Directorate V's boys were to be kept at a distance, if Special Services II was to continue as his support system and his benefactor, Genya must never realize that Blaustein's forearm was cramping under his jacket, that there was sweat rolling down the back of his neck under his hairline. No, Genya Posner must never even guess that Blaustein was, at this moment, the most frightened he'd been since Crossfield's election—the night he'd realized that he was actually going to be running the President of the United States.

He tried to review his accomplishments—the socialization of America well under way, the creation of a Western Socialist Republic, not by the wasteful method of war or even the primitive revolutionary techniques of terrorism applicable still in the Third World, but by Active Measures, the molding of public opinion, the manipulation of the mass consciousness of a nation whose very citizens were natural Communists: in the melting pot where nothing had melted, in a polarized America consumed by greed and factionalism and unwilling to share its wealth, Scientific Socialism had found its greatest challenge. And Blaustein, his greatest goal.

But that little Jew-bitch Gallen and the reports of a dead someone named Fox (*if* Gallen could be believed and Fox *was* dead; the woman had been somehow unconvincing) were about to undo decades of work and millions of rubles and the most carefully conceived covert action program ever launched by the USSR—the Thirty Year Plan for the Neutralization of the American Menace.

"Kurt? Mind if I join you?" Posner's English was better than Blaustein's—he was a graduate of the US & Canada Institute, a five-year resident of Washington and a fellow at Georgetown, one of America's top Soviet-watchers, a man whose defection had been so "embarrassing" to Moscow that no one in US intelligence had even suggested doing less than embracing Posner and the expertise he represented with open arms and without reservation. A big, handsome, sandy-haired Slav with a full beard and polished nails, Posner was happily running to fat in the decadent West.

But Kurt Blaustein knew that this was the same Posner who had overseen the execution of the last of the Afghan rebel leaders personally—who had, shortly before his "defection," interrogated certain prisoners in Kabul in the time-honored Iranian fashion (hot pokers up the rectum, it was whispered, for the men; rats in the women) and successfully extracted from them names and locations where all previous interrogators had failed.

"Please, Genya, sit down. Let me buy you a drink." Blaustein's greeting was hearty. The perfectly-manicured fingers which were Posner's trademark, with their clear nail polish giving a shine to each ridged nail, still gave Kurt the creeps. It was whispered in the Services back channels that Genya had a fetish about keeping his hands clean—small wonder, but it was disconcerting, nonetheless, to Blaustein.

"Vodka, why not?" Posner's lips quirked in their nest of beard. He didn't say "Wodka"—his "V" was perfectly enunciated, a matter of pride.

They spoke of the approaching Summit until the waiter had come and gone, and then Posner leaned forward, hamlike forearms on the table, big shoulders curving forward as if to protect his chest.

"So, I'm here. You dine with that Jew-snake, and this is my business?"

"Ever hear of somebody named Fox? A supposedly dead and assuredly dead-end GS-11 until recently stationed somewhere in Turkey? Or a certain dead former Politburo member named Kunayev? Or a Canadian corpse toe-tagged Stevenson?" Blaustein spat the accusations out as if he were slapping Posner open-handed: backhand, forehand, backhand, forehand.

And the big Slav responded as if he'd been struck by someone as much smaller and weaker as was Blaustein: his shoulders hunched higher, his neck seemed to draw in on itself, he raised his chin and slitted his eyes: "You did not need to know."

"Wonderful. It's all true, then?"

With one hand, Posner tossed off his vodka in a gulp, then sat back and shrugged eloquently. A bad-boy smile played at the corners of his beard-shadowed mouth.

Blaustein reminded himself that Soviets—all Soviets, and most especially KGB—loved nothing so much as a good deception.

Since Posner wasn't going to answer with more than a look of pitying amusement, Blaustein hissed theatrically: "Then perhaps you don't need to know what *I* know. Sorry to have disturbed you." He raised his hand, not quite signalling for the waiter, but threatening to do so.

Posner shook his head infinitessimally.

Blaustein found that, without conscious volition, his own chubby, hairless hand lowered until it was palm-down on the restaurant's pink linen tablecloth.

"Tell me what you have to tell me, and how I can help you, Kurt," Posner suggested, now the kindly advisor.

Kurt Blaustein tried not to be affected by this change in demeanor, but relief shuddered through him. He knew he was being played, but the response-pattern had been set up years ago and had worked so long, so successfully. . . . He said bluntly: "We've got to take out Gallen, Quaid, this bas . . . Fox . . . before it's too late."

"We?" said Posner disbelievingly. "Fox? Too late?"

"We. Fox isn't dead—not if Gallen's personally trying to convince me he is and that he's sent out some mysterious after-action report to an un-specifiable civilian somewhere. Fox is a psycho, a killer. My bet is he's holed up someplace where they haven't been able to get to him yet. We've got to find out where and finish what Directorate V started. And I mean 'finish': that's Gallen and Quaid in the bargain. And we've got to hurry. There's no time to—"

"Kurt," said Posner, "you know we do not work that way. Such undertakings must be tasked . . . tasked from Moscow. Orders come down to us; they do not go up *from* us. Now you are worried, tired. You have been under much strain. This Fox and Stevenson . . . they are one and the same. There is no Fox. There is no problem. Gallen and Quaid may be trying to test the waters, cause us to misstep. We *must* not—you must not."

Blaustein rushed to explain, hoping he didn't sound like a burned-out paranoid. "Fox relayed a message from Kunayev—all about Crossfield, me, the whole penetration. Gallen's smart. She's float-ing the legend that Fox is dead, but I don't believe her: they've got him—at least he's alive and they know where; they're going to pull something at the next NSC meeting. She as much as told me I'd better be on the next plane to Moscow." Blaustein bit his lip: until those words had been spoken, he hadn't realized that he wanted exactly that: out, *now*. The way they'd always promised him, if something went wrong, or when it was over—however it ended. He wanted that Black Sea dacha he'd been promised, and wanted to spend the White Nights in Leningrad. And most of all, he wanted Gallen, Quaid, and everybody else who even suspected him, dead.

"You know that's impossible now, Kurt—the Summit is too important. The Cooperation Pact which will come from it will change the course of history . . . the face of the world. Thanks to you." Avuncular, as he must be, Blaustein's controller ran a finger around the rim of his empty glass and said, "Since you really don't want an Aeroflot, then what do you want?"

"I want Gallen and her people neutralized—in a hurry," Blaustein repeated flatly.

"If that is what you want," Posner responded as coldly as if they were wheeling and dealing over a grain sale rather than human lives, "you'll have to take care of it yourself. You have the resources. We tried to prevent this—Stevenson, you know. We handled Kunayev. That is all we can do, all Moscow has tasked. If there is a botch here, it's yours: someone named Platt, wasn't it? A very messy matter in your Istanbul station."

"So you know about that?" But how? Blaustein hadn't reported it. The hair rose on the back of his neck.

"We keep tabs on you. This is our assignment. For your protection, of course, whenever possible. But for ours, always." Fish-eyed, Posner pushed back his chair. "Thanks for the drink, Kurt. Good luck."

"But what about? . . ."

The waiter was approaching as Posner unfolded to his full height and said, "The answer, my friend, is 'no.' But we have faith in you to do what needs to be done, using the resources of the American government at your command."

And he left Blaustein—speechless, dumbfounded, and shaking so badly he could hardly sign the check when it came—all alone.

When Gallen drove herself home from Langley after dinner with Blaustein, there were too many cars in her driveway and too many lights on inside her small, secluded home up in the Virginia hills.

Doubly puzzling was the fact that the security system wasn't breached; her dashboard monitor would have indicated a breach or forced entry.

She parked in the peach orchard a hundred yards from her doorstep and walked quietly up the side of the driveway, carefully avoiding the motion-sensors which looked like fist-sized rocks scattered on her overgrown yard.

But when, pistol in hand, she got close enough to see the license plates on the mid-sized American cars, she also saw three Suzuki motorcycles in her open garage: Quaid was giving his usual hundred-and-twenty per cent.

She reminded herself that she must appear to know the babysitters who would undoubtedly greet her at the door and got out her keys.

The steel-lined oak door opened before she'd touched key to lock. "You're late, Ma'am. We were beginning to worry," said a flint-eyed woman who was pretty in a large-boned way. "Let me take your coat."

The "maid" had her eyes on Gallen's Detonics. Shai didn't explain, just snapped it back into her SMZ holster as a brown-eyed, brown-haired man in his early thirties who might have been the unfamiliar woman's twin came into the hallway and said, "Hiya. We've got plenty for a late dinner, if you want one. Your houseguest and his doctor ought to be done in five or ten minutes; I bet they'd like some food." He held out an envelope with no writing on it.

She took it, opened it, and read their code names, work names, division ID, and cover names from the slip of paper inside. When she had memorized the information, she handed the slip back to him.

She wasn't hungry, but she told "Mike and Mary" that a late supper was fine with her, trying to stifle her annoyance.

She needed about three hours alone in her study, taking notes on exactly what Blaustein had said and done, making predictions from those notes which she could log into her directorate's dual-coded data base. She might not be around to explain things if Blaustein overreacted.

Instead, she'd been invaded and couldn't even complain: she'd been in situations before where counterintelligence types housesat her so she knew that every step she took was going to be audited and controlled from now on, thanks to Quaid.

The only consolation was that Quaid was on her side . . . she was pretty certain of that, anyway. After a two hour dinner with Blaustein, she wasn't certain of much.

"I'm going upstairs to change," she told Mike.

"Fine. We've got everything torqued down. You won't need that—" he said boldly, eyeing the bulge of her holstered firearm "—while we're here. It might make your guest nervous, his doctor said."

"When I want advice, I'll ask," she snapped and, without apologizing, took the stairs two at a time.

To get to her bedroom, she had to pass the guest

room. She stopped long enough to put her ear against the door. All she heard were two male voices murmuring in low conversation.

By the time she'd changed into jeans and a sweatshirt, washed the makeup from her face, and padded barefoot toward the stairs again, the guest room door was open. Inside was a clutter of pill bottles, luggage, strewn clothing, and M-1, her twenty-five pound cat—but no Fox.

She found Fox in her eat-in kitchen with his doctor, a man she didn't know.

Mary was putting out hot and cold meats and salad; Mike was lounging crossarmed against the refrigerator.

No one had bothered to tell her how much the doctor knew or from what division he'd been seconded to her. Gallen paused.

Fox, who'd been sitting facing away from her with his elbows propping him up on the table, shoulderblades painfully apparent beneath a heavy oiled sweater, turned in his seat.

His gaunt face lit up, his eyes steadied on her: "Shai? Hey, Shai! Christ, am I glad to see you—"

Her heart wrenched: Fox was so weak that he had to use the table and chair for support as he stood up, but he was determined to get to her.

She saved him the trouble in two quick strides, pushing him back down into his chair. Then, not caring who was watching, she put her hands in his hair and pressed his head against her, then bent down and kissed him on the forehead: "It's all right, Larry. It's going to be okay now. We're going to take good care of you."

She let him go and Fox craned his neck, trying to focus his eyes on her face. " 'S okay. Shai, sir, I'm sorry I couldn't make them—"

"Ssh, Fox. You did just fine, or you wouldn't be

here." Her voice wasn't as steady as it should have been. When she looked up and away from Fox, the doctor watching them blinked and visibly shrank from her glare: "Did *you* do this?"

"I—some of it," said the doctor, his jaw squaring. "He's in better shape than he looks. When the drug residuals flush—by later tonight and at the latest early in the morning, he'll be in good shape. If he'll eat. Won't you, Mister Fox?"

"Yessir, I'll try, sir," said Fox, his voice a monotone now. It was the voice of any prisoner who knows his only choice is to obey.

Shai Gallen had seen too many interrogations in too many wars to be able to take the state of Larry Fox calmly—this was peacetime, putatively. At least, it wasn't Beirut or Basra, not the Bekaa or the Galilee. "Get out of my sight," she said to the doctor. "If there's anything you need to tell me, leave a note."

The doctor put down his fork with a clatter. "Director, I was following instuctions. I hope—"

"Yeah, yeah, I know. I even accept it. This isn't a formal rebuke, I just don't want to look at you while I'm eating. You'll probably get a commendation if you're out of here by the time I count to ten."

Still standing beside Fox's chair, she put both hands on his shoulders again and closed her eyes, counting through moving lips but silently.

She heard the doctor's chair scrape, then the rustle of his clothing as he moved wide of her and a short sotto voce exchange between him and Mike. Finally the back door slammed.

When she opened her eyes again, Fox's babysitters were watching her as if she were pointing a gun at them. "Don't stand there," she said. "Finish up and go watch TV or something."

Mary hustled, setting out a pot of coffee, and then taking off her apron in prelude to leaving. Mike didn't move until the female babysitter tugged on his arm and whispered, "Come *on*. Don't you know when you're not wanted?"

"Orders," said Mike.

"Your orders will send you to Central America tomorrow sharp if they don't come from me from here on in," Gallen said pleasantly, with a final pat on Fox's shoulder, as she slid into the chair catty-corner from the field collector.

She barely noticed when the others left. She was watching Fox try to follow what was going on around him with what must have been a gargantuan effort.

And he *was* making sense out of what was happening to him, for as soon as the two strangers left, he put his elbows on the table again and buried his face in his hands.

She watched, trying to decide if he were crying or just shivering with cold. She was planning to put this man back in the field as bait. In fact, she'd already done it, though the field was, for the present, her own home and in it, barring an airstrike, he was safe from his enemies, if not his friends.

For a moment, it didn't seem worth it and her stomach rolled as it had once or twice in the Beirut war. But then she remembered Blaustein and Quaid and how much was at stake, and said, "Larry, come on, you've got to eat and then we can go to bed."

He slid his hands down so that only his bloodshot eyes were visible. "Eat, yeah, I don't know . . . my stomach isn't . . . there, you know? I'd rather . . . Christ." The hands came down all the way and she could see him battle to keep his expression mild while his eyes were screaming questions at her: *Why did you do this to me? Is it over? Is this a trick? Can I trust you? Are you just playing me?* Out loud, he said only: "Yeah, I better eat. But you got to tell me one thing first, okay?"

"Okay, Fox. I'll tell you one thing, you'll eat, and we'll go to bed. In the morning it'll all look different." Shit, this kid—he was thirty-two now, not nineteen, and it didn't change a goddamned thing—this kid was getting to her like nobody had gotten to her for years and she was letting it happen.

As hard as Fox tried, he couldn't keep his stare steady, his eyes kept defocusing: "Do they . . . do *you* believe me now? Or am I crazy?"

Shai Gallen lowered her head and put a spread hand in her hair so that her palm propped up her forehead and all she could see was her dinner plate. She stayed that way until the film of unshedable tears blurring her vision receded; to make that happen, she had to forcibly remind herself that Fox had killed his station chief and at least four other people scant days before. Then she looked him straight in the eye and said, "Larry, there wasn't a moment that I doubted you. I believed you from the start."

"Then . . ." He cocked his head, trying to process the information she'd given him and reach a conclusion he could understand, ". . . tell me why did you do this to me?"

"SOP," she said in an emotionless voice. "Now eat, and I'll do other things to you that'll begin to even the score."

"I . . . I don't know if I can. But sure, I'll try, honest."

She didn't know whether he meant that he couldn't eat or couldn't do other things.

He did eat, and she chewed cold roast beef in a dry mouth to keep him company.

Upstairs, an hour later, in her bedroom instead of his, she took him into the shower with her and kissed the white, hairless spot below his left nipple, which wouldn't tan: "The Shai Gallen memorial scar, isn't it?" she teased, and then slipped her hands around his hips: he'd had fuzzy buttocks in Beirut; he still did, she found out as she began to soap them.

Not long after, under a down quilt, she turned sideways and snuggled his head between her breasts, telling him that he was safe now, that he was going to be all right, that he just needed sleep.

Larry Fox needed more than sleep: he desperately needed something to cling to, something to get him through what lay ahead.

Gallen had to make sure that she was it.

Harrison Quaid met Noah Neely in front of the Old Executive Office building, an imposing structure that made Quaid think, every time he saw it, that it, rather than the White House, should have been the seat of US government—its columns were stout enough and its historicity apparent enough to make dignitaries accustomed to Buckingham and Versailles properly respectful. But it wasn't the President's digs; the Old Exec was the warren in which the rodents ruled—the scrabbling, scheming rabble of both Houses who would foul their own nests for a line of good press or an edge in the next election.

Watching Neely, Coordinator of Crossfield's Intelligence Advisory Board, scuttle down the steps toward him, his laden briefcase held away from his body for ballast, his suited form as perpetually wrinkled as his high forehead and his Burberry forgetfully flapping against the February chill, Quaid wondered again how America could have stood so long and so strong under the stewardship of amateurs and academics. With luck and a little ruthlessness, that was about to change. . . .

Quaid pushed away from the fender of the borrowed limo against which he was leaning and held out a hand mottled with cold. "Doctor Neely, so good of you to make time for me—"

"Nonsense, Mister Quaid," Neely's birdlike head shook in jerky negation; his voice was high and squeaky with just a hint of rasp, probably from the pipe he now struggled to light against the Washington winter wind. "No one I'd rather see— what with nearly everyone still out on recess, it's been damned quiet: what good's an intelligence advisor when no one wants advice?" This last was mumbled through clenched teeth around the slimy stem of an ancient briar as Quaid himself opened the limo's door and motioned Neely inside, then followed.

The driver, Quaid's own, had been well briefed. The limo purred away from the curb in Teutonic satisfaction at itself: the elected officials might be forced to Buy American—cars whose engines and transmissions were worn out in thirty-five thousand miles—but the Agency bought what worked, and worked well: the Mercedes 600 was not only best-of-breed, but armored from gas tank to reinforced bumpers, and shielded from microwave eavesdropping besides.

And if the Mercedes, like Sonny Quaid, was not quite what it seemed and somewhat overpowered for cruising slushy streets with Administration favorites inside, then no one remarked on it: those who knew Quaid's counterintelligence affiliation

expected both efficient paranoia and overprepared-
ness; those who didn't saw only one assignation of
many facilitated by another Mercedes with a
silver-and-black European license number in place
under a bolted-on red-white-and-blue DPL plate.
And whatever was assumed by any who'd seen the
meet go down—even those who watched everything via overflying reconnaissance photo-return
satellites to satisfy President Crossfield's unslakable
thirst for security in an increasingly insecure
America—wasn't a problem to Sonny Quaid. He
was possibly the one man in Washington who was
absolutely certain that his true function wasn't
known by another living soul. He'd made sure of
that.

The limo drove past the White House with its
concrete, waist-high barricades and electro-optical
defense system that would target and trigger
mounted and barely-camouflaged machine guns
on any intruder with a gross weight of more than
thirty-five pounds.

Neely clucked with exaggerated distress: "You'd
think they'd have managed to find a way to secure
the Lawn which wasn't so. . . ."

"Daunting?" Quaid supplied the missing word.

"Flagrant," Neely corrected. "We may be a nation under seige from within, but we oughtn't to
look like it, Mister Quaid. Tell your people that.
Those damn machine guns your sort rammed up
the Secret Service's butt give the perception that
we're even more shaky a nation than we really are.
And with a new Summit scheduled—"

"That's why we need 'em, sir," Quaid said
laconically. "If the Secret Service could manage to
be either secret or servicable, we wouldn't; but an
attack on Our Peerless Leader between now and
the Summit—or *during* it—could get my record

censured. So it's personal, you see. The rest of you can do as you damn well please but—if I can be blunt, sir—I don't fuck up, and I won't be ordered to, not for God, Country, or what's left of the American Way."

"It's that certain then, you think—an attempt on Crossfield's life, I mean?"

"Nothing's certain, sir," Quaid replied, settling back against the punched leather of the Mercedes back seat and stretching out his hand to push a button which caused an automated bar to slide out of the console between driver and passenger compartments. "Drink, Doctor Neely?" The satisfaction Quaid felt at that moment had more to do with Neely's willingness to take the bait, to be led where Quaid wanted to lead him, than the serendipity which forced the Mercedes to a halt as a pack of bundled-up demonstrators filed into the street, oblivious to traffic lights and crosswalks. Quaid saw women from The 52% with sharpened broomhandles desultorily disguised by placards demanding everything from "Equal Representation For Equal Votes" to "Unilateral Disarmament NOW" to "Woman Power in the White House—Use Us or Lose Us."

Quaid read one of the slogans aloud: "Men Start Wars, Only Women Can Stop Them—Impeach Crossfield and All Male Oppressors." Then he turned the full power of his stare on Neely and added,"You think these skirts are kidding? Our infiltrators say that it's 'heads, you lose; tails, you lose,' for this Administration—just a matter of whether its the Bund or The 52% who storm the White House first."

"We're *giving* them what they want," Neely said dourly, reaching toward the bar where Quaid had made sure a bottle of Neely's favorite brandy, laced with a psychotropic drug which made a subject suggestible, was waiting. "All we can do, within reason. How peaceful do we have to show ourselves to be? Isn't it enough that we're dismantling the space-based lasers, the railguns—our entire space-borne Strategic Defense? Shutting down the manned orbital station? God knows the Europeans who bought into that project think it's *more* than enough."

Though the questions were rhetorical, Neely, pouring his drink with hands shaking despite the Mercedes's competent heater, was getting away from the subject Quaid wanted to broach.

So he said, "Not nearly enough, and you know it. Not when the ladies' rallying cry is 'Don't Let Your Babies Grow Up To Be Soldiers,' it isn't. It's the Women's Movement—or at least one woman—I want to talk to you about."

Neely's eyes, yellowed and bloodshot like a boiled lamb's at a Saudi dinner, fixed on him. "Woman trouble, Quaid? That's hardly in my line."

"This woman's most exactly in your line—it's Shai."

"Shai?" Neely repeated, sipping his brandy, which sloshed against pleated bluish lips as the last of the demonstrators passed with an angry punch on the Mercedes hood and the limo rolled smoothly into gear.

Neely knew, Quaid realized, that Shai Gallen and Sonny Quaid were lovers; he also knew Quaid's wife of twenty-years, Lucille. Harrison Quaid still lived with his spouse—there was a son, security, and the dual leash of habit and responsibility around his neck. The couple had drifted apart through the years but Quaid never admitted failure. And Lucy wasn't a failure—she was so complacent, so circumspect, that no agent of his sort could have asked for a finer foil: she asked no questions that he couldn't answer and, so far as he knew, engaged in no dangerous speculation. And he'd been able to keep her clear of the drift toward militant feminism. She was a good Washington wife, so grateful when he fucked her lately that he tried not to recall that it was because, somewhere deep down, she knew he had some side action she wasn't capable of competing with, and unwilling to confront him with that or any other facet of an Agency employee's existence that might be classified.

But Neely knew because Neely was Shaitan's sole confidant, though neither had ever admitted it. So Sonny had to lay this feed out very carefully, keeping in mind that Neely would believe it, despite the letter his brother Owen had received from Fox, because Neely would assume that if Quaid, who was bedding her, had doubts about Shai Gallen, they must be serious doubts indeed.

"Shai," Quaid confirmed with a heartfelt, frustrated sigh. "She's got this cockamamie idea that Crossfield's a . . . Jesus, it sounds so crazy I can't even find a way to say it that isn't prejudicial . . . a Soviet agent of influence."

"What!"

Neely's exclamation was a bit too vehement, a trifle forced—so that meant Shai had been talking to him about it, or at least hinting about the degree to which she was taking Fox seriously. Or that Owen Neely had shown his brother Fox's letter. Fuck-all!

"That's right, sir—you know how torqued down she can get. She's got some data, and she's reading it all wrong, and she wants to run with it. As a matter of fact, your brother Owen's got some of the same data—"

"Pardon?" Neely interrupted. "Owen has *what?*"

"There was this letter," Quaid said, spreading his big hands with just the right mixture of chagrin and exasperation on his face, "that a street man—an operations officer of ours, going nowhere fast in a Turkish backwater—sent to your brother, sir. Full of crazy accusations, delusions about high-level meets with ex-Politburo members and wild claims that Crossfield's a Soviet mole. That was right before this line officer killed his wife, four or five—we're not sure how many—Turkish nationals, and blew the hell out of his station ... with his station chief inside. Maybe you heard about it. Anyhow, your brother got a letter from him, which we'd like destroyed, of course."

"Of course," Neely murmured, a barely-concealed expression of pain on his face that looked as if it were accustomed to being there: being the elder, smarter half-brother of the flamboyant Owen Neely hadn't been easy for Noah.

"But it's Shai—her reaction, her. ... Sir, she's bought this crazy story, for all the wrong reasons. Seems she and the line officer in question were ... more than friends. A long time ago, yeah, but you know, she's a still a woman. And she's my superior officer, so I can't say squat when she's not thinking straight. And Doctor Neely, you know that if I'm coming to you with this, I'm concerned. Shit, I'm more than concerned—I'm scared to death for her. There's not much in the way of operational capability she hasn't got, or can't get if she thinks she needs it. And she thinks she needs it."

Neely put down his drink on the burled caddy and pursed his lips. "And you don't think she's reading the data right?"

"What I think, sir, is that she needs a rest. She's a chronic overachiever and she's looking for a simple way to solve America's whole problem. ..."

Quaid waved a spread hand at the Washington administrative buildings the Mercedes was passing. "And there *ain't* no simple way. She's got a problem she can't solve, and it's eating her up inside. So she's found a way to look at things which fits some data, but more importantly, fits her need to *act*. Remember where she came from—she doesn't know how to stand around and wait while a country goes to hell in its own handbasket. Not a country she loves. And Shai dearly loves the good ol' US of A, make no mistake about that. . . ." Letting his voice catch, Quaid trailed off and looked away from Neely, out the window beyond which sleet was beginning to pour from a leaden sky.

"And you," said Neely in a gentle and intimate tone, "love her, Sonny. . . . No, it's all right. We all do, at least those of us who know her well."

Quaid screwed up his face in a grimace of pretended pain: "Doctor Neely, don't make any assumptions. I'm a married man. She's my respected superior and my good friend, that's all. But—"

Neely smiled avuncularly. "I wasn't implying anything else, Mister Quaid. But in the matter of President Crossfield's . . . shall we say . . . affiliation, then—you don't think she's right? She maintains that he's exacerbated matters with his Equal Americans program to the point where—"

Noah Neely was neatly avoiding any mention of what *Owen* Neely's reaction might have been. Blood, even half a share of blood, was still thicker than water. And Noah Neely didn't want Owen's name brought into this any further. *Okay, then, old fella, we'll play it your way. With the unspoken agreement that you'll fall into line about Shaitan, of course, we'll leave your brother to you.*

"She's *right*," Quaid replied sardonically, "altogether too much of the time for me to discount her analysis out of hand. But *this* time she's wrong, Doctor Neely—dead wrong. And that's where this obsession of hers is going to get her—dead—if you can't help me talk some sense into her. She's backtracking from an unjustified, if convenient, preconception—breaking one of the cardinal rules of intelligence. And this time, what she's coming up with is a one-eighty from what I'm reading on the same data base."

"So you're giving me a dissenting intelligence opinion? Formally?"

"Formally? Hell, no, sir. I'm looking for help saving Shai, not setting up a power play. I read the same data and my analysis is that the USSR has plenty of reason to want Crossfield dead. More specifically, to want him assassinated—as long as it's not a Soviet national who pulls the trigger or the pin. Assassination can really screw up a country. It sure as hell would screw up the Agency if someone of ours was implicated in such a plan— whether it failed or succeeded." Quaid let the care with which he was choosing his words become obvious. "You know, or you'll soon know, that this line officer, name of Fox, claims to have met with Abdulhamid Kunayev—the Politburo honcho—shortly before his death. The take from that meet was minimal, and just the sort of data with which to set up someone like Shai. Do you understand what I'm saying?"

Neely's whole head, to its crown, was wrinkled like wadded newsprint as he flicked a glance at the driver and murmured, "Not exactly—or *too* exactly." Lighting his pipe, he met Quaid's stare with one that could have cut diamond. "I'm assuming, though, that this is an official and highly confidential meeting between the head of the Counterintelligence Staff and the Coordinator of the Intelligence Advisory Board. Which wasn't what I was assuming ten minutes ago."

"Yes sir, Doctor, you're right. What I'm saying is that I think Shai's being set up by the Soviets as an unwitting agent of KGB's Directorate V— that they're running her through data feed, that Kunayev, via Fox, was the final provocation, bait to dangle in front of our Ops division in hopes that we'd bite. And Shai bit—hook, line, and Operation LEMON PLEDGE."

"*Quaid!*"

"You know the op in question, then? It's about to go on line and all of us, in my estimation—and that includes me because I won't let her take this kind of fall by herself—are going to end up the most famous traitors in history . . . and the biggest dupes. We've let Soviet intelligence maneuver us into a position from which the only 'next' move on our part is to take the President of the United States out of play."

"Assassination?" Neely's whisper was hoarse. "She's talked to me about Jim Crossfield obliquely, of course, but *this*—"

Still no mention of brother Owen. Quaid wasn't sure if he dared allude to the possibility of Owen Neely being drawn into an assassination plot. "Sir, I just want you to know what's up next. Somebody has to talk to her, and if it's you . . . well, you've got to make it look like you've figured this out on your own. Find a way to keep your brother's name out of it. Somehow. Or else . . ."

"Or *else*?"

You didn't "or else" a man like Neely, Quaid realized almost too late—the guy was just too damned sharp. "Or else, sir, I'm going to help her do her job, as she sees it, and with your tacit assent and support. Because if you can't stop her, nobody can, and that makes you a co-conspirator, doesn't it?"

The driver of the Mercedes pumped the brakes in time to avoid hitting a small group of Bund demonstrators wearing swastikas, chased out into the street by police with clear Lexan shields, helmets, and tear gas and riot guns.

But neither man noticed. Neely was examining his knuckles and Quaid was waiting, deadpan, for the IAB honcho to fold and come into line.

Damn, it felt good to win one against an opponent as good as Noah Neely—even with a little help from psychochemicals.

"So, maybe we could talk about how we ought to handle the upcoming NSC meeting, Doctor Neely. Some way we can disenfranchise Shai's spy-hunting expedition before it does the ultimate harm it could." *Before your redneck brother puts Fox's letter on the fucking agenda, buddy.*

Noah Neely nodded at his gnarled knuckles like a beaten prisoner ready to sign any confession handed him.

Use the resources of the US government at your command, Genya Posner had said—it wasn't an exact quote which kept running through Kurt Blaustein's head and that bothered him a little: Mustn't panic, old son. But then, when you panicked, you couldn't think at all. And Blaustein was thinking, in situ.

Sitting in his office on the fifth floor at midnight, waiting for Snyder from FBI to return his call, he chewed his nails. There *was* a civilian listed as Fox's next-of-kin—a civilian who wasn't kin. A lawyer named Alden, the obvious choice for a button-down letter of the sort Gallen had alluded to.

So all right. He wasn't going to call Genya and

ask for help—tasking would have to come from
Moscow, he could accept that. He didn't dare seem
to be losing his grip. But tasking could also come
from his office, via FBI's Domestic Antiterrorist
Group. The Special Agent In Charge, Snyder, had
been involved with terrorism for twenty years, having worked on the Letelier murder when a search
of the U.S. Code had finally determined that the
F.B.I. had jurisdiction. He wouldn't ask too many
questions. He'd be thrilled to have a chance to
loose his dogs. Pick up Alden, was all he was asking.
The guy might or might not be dangerous, so go
prepared, he'd say. Friend of a known terrorist,
he'd say, who'd blown a CIA station abroad. And
Fox was certainly that.

Snyder of the plaid sports jackets and the Cats-
kills weekends would be thrilled to be included.
Blaustein normally didn't play golf with Jews, let
alone fuck around. But these days, nothing was
normal.

And Blaustein would try anything in the way of
alternatives before having to inform Jim Crossfield,
direct, that there'd been a little snag which would
probably end in Crossfield's impeachment and sub-
sequent execution.

What would it be? Firing squad? Electric chair?
Something special, no doubt, for a Presidential
traitor. And for Blaustein, too.

When the phone bleated its soft, electronic alert,
Blaustein jumped in his seat.

Then he snatched the receiver while keying a
white-noise generator with his other hand. "Yes?"
he snapped.

"Kurt? Snyder, here. What the hell's so hot it
couldn't wait eight hours?"

Blaustein's pulse was pounding, but he sat back
and smiled at his cork-paneled walls, a faraway

look in his eyes. "Snyder, I hope you're on your secure line. Because you're going to love this."

Neutralizing Glenn Alden was going to be a pleasure. Quaid was on a roll. Since his interview with Noah Neely the day before, his toes and fingers had been tingling; he was stimulated to a degree neither drugs nor sex could match. Even now, in an Agency Wagoneer on the way to Alden's office, he was filled with a nearly euphoric self-assurance.

It was almost enough to mask the low-burning fury in his belly that had ignited this morning when he saw the way Shai continually looked at the skinny fuck-up, Fox.

He'd stopped by her house—which ought not to be used as a safe house, but which was the only place Lawrence Fox was safe from Harrison Quaid—and found Gallen and Fox out back shooting paper targets in the snow.

Shai was obviously convincing Fox, who ought to be in some nice permanent box being debriefed while his brain was gelatinized, that her protection extended not only to his life, but also to his career.

Anybody who'd give that fuse a gun and stand within range was torqued down too tight to be trusted, or outright in love. They'd handed Quaid a nine millimeter and walked up twenty yards to check their scores, and he'd stood there thinking how easy it would be to put a couple rounds through each of them: first Shaitan, then this damned kid who'd come out of nowhere and muddied everybody's water. Quaid could have finessed the details so it looked like Fox shot her and Quaid had shot Fox after the fact.

But he didn't. He didn't like her fucking around

with some damned kid and she was going to find out just how much he didn't like it.

So he'd been polite and even agreed to help her cover "the Fox base," as she called it: do whatever was necessary to make sure that Albert Stevenson took the rap for the carnage in Turkey—including Platt's death—once the confusion about who was who and who was dead and alive cleared away.

And he'd have to appear to be doing that—or delegate the work to subordinates. Otherwise, she'd sense something was really wrong, that he wasn't as adult as he pretended about her, their relationship, or anything else. But even if she did pick up on the jealousy heating up his groin, she'd never look beyond it: he was going to pull off the most complex intelligence maneuver of his career, one which would change the course of history.

Of course, no one would ever know, if things went well—no one in America and, after a while, no one abroad. Sonny Quaid wasn't a counterintelligence officer for nothing—he had the widest nets and the most efficient operatives on three continents at his command.

But right now there was Alden, something he had to do personally.

Alden did business out of 2430 E Street, probably oblivious to the fact that the address had once been that of the Office of the Coordinator of Information—the birthplace of the OSS.

The townhouse which now occupied the spot was one of half a dozen desultory reproductions built after the whole block was truck-bombed in '92 by Armenian terrorists but the street itself was no wider: Quaid's backup team of twelve—six CI boys and six levied from the Support Activity's preemptive-strike roster via an FBI back channel—looked innocuous on the slushy narrow street. Even with their Bug Doctor Exterminators truck parked in the driveway of the townhouse adjoining Alden's and styrofoam coffee cups in their hands, the three agents with the commo truck looked exactly like what they pretended to any but Quaid's critical eye.

The three on the roof opposite the target building—one sharpshooter and the two legs of his triad—were nearly invisible and the man and woman chatting, grocery bags in their arms, on a stoop two doors down from Alden's, were all Quaid could have hoped for, as was the fellow fixing a flat tire on one corner while his partner, cassette player on his belt and headphones over his ears, spread rock salt around the base of the E Street signpost, head bobbing to "music" coming in on a shielded sideband from the Bug Doctor truck.

The balance of the team—Quaid's driver and the other passenger in the Wagoneer's back seat behind the driver—would probably be the only ones to see any action, and they were war-game precise, taciturn in the presence of their chief as the four-wheeler glided to a stop before Alden's ground floor office.

The driver shifted enough to check his crossdraw holster and murmured a terse "go code" into what looked like a CB mike on his dashboard. His partner sat on Quaid's left because the backup always sits behind the driver when a dignitary is in the car, both to ensure the driver's loyalty in any ensuing crisis and to facilitate a clear line of sight in the event that shooting is required. Both men were just back from Central America, short-haired and tanned six-footers with faded eyes behind sunglasses polarized to cut Washington's snowy glare. They functioned like two parts of the same well-oiled gun with hardly a word necessary between them.

With any luck, Quaid wasn't going to need anywhere near the amount of firepower he'd requisitioned for what seemed on the surface a simple pickup. But Glenn Alden had once been Foreign Service and Larry Fox seemed to make everything he touched explode into violence. Therefore, by the time-honored rule of guilt-by-association, Alden was as likely to escalate matters as not—as far as Quaid could determine, the two were the best of friends.

Any friend of Fox's being an enemy of his, Quaid had given orders that, should Alden come out of that verdigris-painted door before Quaid, or come out alone, or should neither come out within the twenty minutes allotted by Quaid to the meet, Alden was to be summarily dispatched, even if that meant blowing the entire premises to hell.

When you went hunting in America's urban jungle these days, you needed all the edge you could get. It reminded Quaid of his teens in Nam, sometimes—the bottom line being that you needed to be sure that, if you bought the farm, somebody was going to even the score posthaste.

And right now, Quaid thought grimly, getting out of the Wagoneer without a word to the two wolves backstopping him, the score was Fox, five; Quaid, zero.

But that was about to change.

Inside the lawyerly office whose outer door boasted a gilt-carved sign and inner door bore a modest brass plate bearing the legend, "Glenn K. Alden, Attorney at Law," a pale and harried junior clerk with his tie stuffed into an argyle vest was being harrassed by a svelte black secretary wearing fashionable mirrored contact lenses and electric purple lipstick.

"... can't *go* home, sweetcakes, until every line of that chickenscratch of yours is loaded onto disk—or did you think *I* was waitin' on your ass so's I could cart your work on home and do it for you? Those days are *long* gone, man, long—Oh, sweet Jesus, who's this, now?''

Quaid was no happier to see the two subordinates in Alden's reception area—he'd waited until nearly four o'clock, despite the groans of his shooters outside about low-light conditions further hindered by reflected streetlights and snow, so that he could find Alden alone.

But there was nothing for it. "Jack Sneed. Counselor Alden's expecting me."

And that was true enough, as the woman found out while Quaid's mind reformulated everything: unless he wanted to blow up the building with these two inside, he'd have to be more careful. He hadn't bothered attempting to disguise himself—he hadn't thought he'd need to, there hadn't been time for the sort of beard, hair and eye alteration which worked, as opposed to the cosmetic stuff which tended to make a person look just enough out of the ordinary to ensure a clear memory in any otherwise casual observer.

By the time the black woman's generous lips parted in a professionally cold smile and she levered her ample bottom out of her chair to escort him into Alden's sanctum, Quaid had decided that the lapse was coverable—*if* no shit hit the fan here. If it did, a couple more casualties weren't going to make or break the security of an operation which by then would be ultra-overt.

So on his way in he managed to bump up against a row of lateral files long enough to set his briefcase filled with thirty pounds of C-6 and a radio detonator against the nearest cabinet—if he wanted to blow the building, it was now merely a matter of depressing a stud on the tunable wrist-radio he wore which was so much more than the civilian-issue unit it resembled.

"Mister Sneed?" Alden half-rose from his executive desk chair, hand outstretched. "Gracie, you and Doug can go on home now; I'll probably be here all night—"

Quaid stepped across the carpet to take Alden's plump hand as if oblivious to the secretary's protestations that she couldn't leave until "Dougie finishes—somebody's got to teach that boy some responsibility."

Alden squeezed Quaid's hand and rolled his eyes heavenward, then sighed. "Gracie, don't argue with me in front of a client. Take Doug to dinner and finish up—on my tab."

The secretary, obviously mollified and pretending not to be, withdrew, grumbling good-naturedly in her velvet Georgian accent.

Alden, as the door closed and the two were alone, grinned ruefully, running spread fingers through unruly black hair that was retreating from his forehead. The lawyer was paunchy, winter-pale and of that particularly inbred appearance so common to WASP intellectuals born on the Atlantic seaboard: his small featured face with its soft chin, close-set droopy eyes, and sensitive mouth was the sort Quaid had seen in more US Embassies abroad than he cared to remember: this one had a pedigree, if a minor one, that guaranteed a ring with his family crest somewhere and lots of college "pals" with whom he still kept in touch.

"Smoke?" said Alden, and tapped an ironwood box on his desk with his left hand so that Quaid saw the ring he'd anticipated, though not closely enough to read the Latin legend under its family device.

The dossier Quaid had seen had been cursory,

unspectacular, boring in its mid-level details. Alden specialized in corporations involved with technology transfer, a particularly dicey area of corporate law what with the tightened restrictions by the Commerce Department. "No thanks, Counselor," Quaid replied. "I'd like to get right to business, if you don't mind."

Alden consulted his wristwatch, took a cigarette from the box, and hesitated. "If you don't mind my smoking, I don't mind you keeping me late. I have to admit," he added over the flame of his lighter, "that I'm curious—I don't usually get 'emergencies'—not my bailiwick. Your office said it was urgent, but I did take the liberty of checking, and I can't find 'SigSec Industries' listed anywhere in my—"

Quaid reached into his breastpocket and tossed a leather card-sized bi-fold onto Alden's desk: "We've got a mutual problem. Can we check to see that your people have left?"

Frowning at the leather case, Alden slipped a finger between the flaps, raising one side far enough to see the credentials, not of CIA, but of CSS, an agency with a much lower profile. Then he said, "I was afraid it was something irregular—your people are masters of innuendo. Hold on a minute."

With unexpected grace for a man whose body showed signs of too many hours at too many desks, Alden rose, checked the outer office, punched up a security block on his key-pad lock, and returned, murmuring, "That lock's not anything fancy. May I assume that you know what you're doing, and have made the necessary provisions?"

Even though the tone was questioning, Quaid didn't answer—he was here to *ask* questions: "How good a friend is Larry Fox?"

Alden's face was expressionless but he sank into

his chair and leaned forward. "*Is*? Not 'was'? That's
something, anyway. Some misguided souls have
been trying to convince Larry's parents that he's
dead. He's a friend, Mister . . . Sneed. In every
sense. So if Larry's the subject of this meeting,
you're going to have to do the balance of the talking.
I can't violate the confidences of a client, you—"

"Crap, Alden. Fox is no client of yours, we know
that. And we know about the letter. And we know
that you two are friends. The question is, just how
good a friend are you ready to be to him?"

"That's what you came here to find out?" Alden
sat back with a wary look.

"Your friend needs help—maybe on-site legal
counsel, maybe just some concerted moral support.
What's your calendar like for the next week or
so?"

"Damn, Larry. . . ." Alden put his fingers to the
bridge of his nose. "What's he got to do with the
Central Sec—never mind, sorry I asked. I suppose it
wouldn't do any good to point out that if Fox is
alive and being held somewhere, as you're implying,
in the continental US, without having been formally charged with—"

Quaid shook his head pityingly and moved to
pick up the leather bi-fold.

Alden's hand closed on his wrist: "Okay, okay,
Mister Sneed. Just tell me what you want—the
letter doesn't exist . . . I destroyed it. Larry can get
. . . nervous. Right now, I'm in the middle of arrangements to get his wife's body flown home,
dealing with distraught parents, trying to fend off
various accusations—unfounded, no doubt—from
foreign powers as to what he's done and where. As
a favor to his parents. Because we *are* friends. So,
if you'll just tell me what kind of help he needs,
and where I can find him—"

"Come on, Alden, you know better than that."
Quaid bared his teeth. "Write a note saying you're
off to Switzerland on routine but unexpected business and come along. Now. You won't have a second chance. This is the equivalent of Fox's one
phone call, and if you say no, he doesn't get another.
You're the one person he's anxious to see. So we're
asking. Once. You want to help your friend, or let
nature take its course? It's up to you."

"I've got a wife and—" Something in Quaid's
face made Alden hesitate. "Jesus Christ, Sneed—*if*
that's your name—you know this isn't the way
things are done. But then, you don't care, do you?"
Alden was squinting, though the light in the room
hadn't changed. "You don't *want* me to come with
you, do you?"

"Smart boy. That's right, I don't. I can't see that
your buddy Fox deserves any kind of help—he's a
traitor and a multiple murderer." Harsh words, a
hole card played early, but Quaid wanted to get
Alden out, now, without a fuss. So he needed to
push hard and make Alden angry enough to push
back.

"You know that a man's innocent until proven
otherwise, don't you?" For one reason or another,
Alden was scribbling something on his desk pad.

Quaid didn't want to look too anxious or interested. "Maybe that's true for civilians, but you
know Fox wasn't that. . . ."

"You bastards," Alden gritted angrily, signed
his name to the note before him with a flourish,
and stood up. "Give me enough time to stop off at
my house and pack an overnight bag, and I'm
yours for the dura—"

"No dice. Call your wife and tell her you've got
to fly to Switzerland to personally oversee the
release of a mistakenly quarantined shipment bound

for Abu Dhabi—we've backstopped it. There is such a shipment, it's sitting on the dock surrounded by Customs agents, and you were involved in the paperwork. Want me to name names?''

"Bastards." Alden shook his head. "No, don't bother." He stabbed at his speed-dialer as he snatched his phone's receiver from its cradle. "Honey, I've got to go out of town. Now." He paused, grimaced, then continued: "I know it's Timmy's big game. But it's business. I'll bring you a Swiss watch, one of those ones made out of a gold coin." He paused again and smiled proudly at something said on the other end. "That's my girl. Hold the fort. I'll call every night, honest."

Then he cradled the receiver and his smile bled away. "All right, hot shot, let's go see Larry. And remember—I've got to call home every night." There was a glare of defiance in the droopy eyes of Glenn Alden and a set to that soft mouth that made Quaid reassess the man.

But he'd attained the objective without premature violence—Alden hadn't bolted into the street or drawn a weapon in an echo of Fox's paranoia.

Section 101 of the National Security Act of 1947 created the National Security Council and directed that: "The function of the Council shall be to advise the President with respect to the integration of domestic, foreign and military policies relating to the national security so as to enable the military services and the other departments and agencies of the Government to cooperate more effectively in matters involving the national security."

Section 102 of the Act established the Central Intelligence Agency, the appointment of its Director (DCI), and subsection (c) gave the Director of Central Intelligence discretionary authority to fire employees "when necessary or advisable in the interests of the United States"—preemptorily and without regard to governmental procedure.

Section 102(c) was very much in Gallen's mind as she sat in the White House's Blue Situation room across from Luftsen, her DCI, and waited for Crossfield to appear: somebody's head was going to roll today.

She could see it in Dick Luftsen's bony Norwegian face across which the skin was drawn so tight it seemed that as soon as he spoke, or even smiled, the parchment-white skin would split and fall away, leaving exposed the muscle that animated the skull beneath—Luftsen's mournful tautness always preceded a termination order. It remained to be seen only if the unlucky about-to-be-*ex* officer was Galen herself, Blaustein, on Gallen's left, stroking his moustache so fondly it might have been a cat, or one of the Defense or FBI or State honchos who made up the even dozen who awaited Crossfield's entrance this morning, pouring tepid coffee into cups bearing the Presidential Seal and ruffling the red-bordered documents in front of each place at the oval rosewood table. If it were someone from another department or agency, Luftsen still would have been the first to know.

Of all those present—from the inspection-ready, crew-cut Army Assistant Chief of Staff for Intelligence for Human Systems, General Theodore Westin, who was also head of Army's SAVE Program (Sensitive Activities and Vulnerability Estimates), to his antithesis, perpetually rumpled Noah Neely, Coordinator of the Intelligence Advisory Board, sitting beside his brother Owen, Crossfield's National Security Advisor near the head of the table—only Gallen felt, and *was*, out of place. So maybe it *was* Shai—her career, the demise of which Luftsen was so obviously mourning.

Staring absently at the American flag drooping from its standard in the far corner of the room, Shai Gallen considered the possibility that, as soon as Crossfield came in, she was going to be summarily terminated, told to hand over her cards and keys in exchange for an envelope containing her severance pay. One part of her mind argued that it would be a relief—she'd be off the hook, LEMON PLEDGE would never go on line, and she could get the fuck out of the country on one of the various blue, black and red passports she'd squirreled away for just such an hour of need. Take a commercial flight to Andorra and to hell with the world. But her operational self rebutted that then the world *would* go to hell—and so would Larry Fox, unless she could dummy up enough ID to get a Caucasian male of his celebrity out with her.

Through what seemed hours but was actually forty-six minutes of interminable waiting, Gallen never once thought that it wouldn't matter to the world if she wasn't around to tweak its security agenda or run LEMON PLEDGE to its abhorrent conclusion: Shai Gallen was still too much of an intelligence professional to entertain the thought that her efforts wouldn't make a difference—perhaps *the* crucial difference—in the day-to-day making and unmaking of history that, as Deputy Director of Operations, was her responsibility. But she was the only officer present who wasn't usually and routinely present at such meetings, and the only one who knew for certain that Jim Crossfield was something more than an idealistic bumbler making his way into American history books.

So it seemed to her in some sense diabolical that Crossfield was late, though she hadn't sat in on enough NSC meetings to know whether it was unusual. As it seemed to her that Luftsen kept staring at her covertly out of the corner of his watery midnight-sun eyes, and that Owen Neely kept flicking glances her way as he chatted with his brother as if the younger Neely had never gotten Fox's letter and the elder had never been privy to Shai's qualms about Jim Crossfield, the Equal Americans programs, or—via Sonny Quaid—the death's-bed message of Abdulhamid Kunayev, ex-Politburo member.

Damn you, Crossfield, you pinko Commie whale-loving traitor, show the fuck up! Gallen prayed silently, thinking that if something didn't happen, and soon, she was going to *make* something happen: stand up, ask for the table's attention, punch the electronic stenographer's "record" button, and confess—or accuse, or quit, or some damn thing; *any*thing that would get the matter of Crossfield on today's agenda so that if she *was* terminated here, the information she had on Crossfield wouldn't be tainted and neutralized, deemed sour grapes or the parting shot of a disgruntled ex-employee. But she didn't. She just lit a cigarette and poured more translucent coffee into her cup. You'd think the White House staff could make a cup of coffee strong enough that you couldn't see through it all the way to the bottom of your cup!

For nearly fifty years, the President had presided over meetings of the NSC personally, supported by his Vice President, Secretary of State and Secretary of Defense. One of the NSC's primary purposes was to provide a direct link to the President for the military and nonmilitary directors of the various departments and agencies concerned with national security.

For nearly half that long, it had been common

practice to start before the President's arrival, to get the mundane business out of the way with the National Security Advisor presiding. And this meeting of the NSC's Special Coordinating Committee/ Working Intelligence Group should have been no different. Owen Neely should have opened the proceedings with some distasteful joke about ants fucking elephants, as he'd done at the last meeting Shai had attended, when she'd been responsible for presenting a National Intelligence Estimate dissenting opinion.

But Owen just sat there chatting with Noah sotto voce while the FBI Deputy picked at pills on his plaid sport coat and DIA's three-star representative examined his agency's seal—thirteen stars over a globe speared by a torch surrounded by angled circles, the whole mess resting on what Shai knew were supposed to be sheaves of grain but which she could only think of as a rocker of scrambled eggs—on the wooden place-marker in front of him.

There were few moments in her life when Gallen had even noticed, let alone regretted, that she was the only woman somewhere or other. But sitting at that table, with tension filling up the silence so that it roared in her ears, she felt suddenly isolated by her gender: with Blaustein on one side of her and the robot-stenographer on the other, she had no one to whom she could whisper chattily, even if she'd been able to think of anything to say which wouldn't blow the lid off the meeting about to commence.

She caught Luftsen staring at her dourly and met his gaze, holding it well past the point of discomfort, so that she was startled when the door behind and to her right opened and Crossfield and Jennings, his black VP, entered—looking for all the world like an Eighteenth-century gentleman and his footman in their stylishly Edwardian clothes.

The men at the table rose and Shai rose with them: no use pointing up the gender gap. Murmured greetings went round. Jim Crossfield's crinkly smile seemed forced and there were bags under his clear, steady eyes as he sat and told his staff, "Be seated, gentleman—and lady," and Shai cringed inwardly.

Blaustein, hopping his chair forward, prodded her, "Engage the stenographer, dear," as if Shai were his secretary.

She stabbed the button with more force than was necessary and the stenographic computer bleated in protest, a machine's equivalent of "You don't have to tell me twice." But its lights went on and chased each other across its face as, voice-actuated now that it was powered up, it took verbatim minutes, including hems and haws.

"Old business, guys?" Crossfield said with his customary proletarian bonhomie.

"Mister President," said Dick Luftsen, rising to his full height, a jumble of angles and joints that stooped because the world was not made for men who stood six foot four, "before we proceed—"

The room fell silent; even the robot-stenographer paused, its cursor blinking in startled anticipation.

Shai's throat tightened; her skin seemed hot all over. Steeling herself, she dared to throw an interrogatory stare Noah Neely's way. The frail shoulders shrugged quizzically, but Noah's perspicacious eyes cautioned her: *Wait and see.*

"Yeah, Dick? What's up?" Crossfield said, not impatiently, but with encouragement in his voice.

"Sir, at this time I find it...." Luftsen's voice caught as if his prominent Adam's apple had fouled in his white collar. He looked down, took a single sheet of paper from his crocodile briefcase and handed it to the FBI Deputy next to him, who obediently passed it along toward the head of the table without looking at what he held.

"I—I'm submitting my resignation, Sir. Effective immediately, if you'd be so kind. So if you'll excuse. . . ." Whatever else Luftsen was saying in a voice audibly thickening with emotion was lost in his own movements as he prepared to flee the room and the shocked responses coming from the men at the table.

"You're *what?*" Crossfield's voice cut across the subdued mutters. Silence followed as the President scanned the letter before him and then snapped a commander's stare across Luftsen's face so accusatively that the DCI flinched as if struck.

But Luftsen raised his head and held his ground, frozen in mid-backstep: "Sir, I can't be more specific than what's in my letter. I beg you, accept my resignation before. . . ." Luftsen shook his head, raised both hands and lowered them so that the croc briefcase he held banged against his knee, and seemed to be about to faint.

"Right, then," Crossfield said soothingly, though Shai noticed that his color was rising: the famous temper, held barely in check. "Do you want to tell me if it's the Summit, or the Kalahari Reception Station junket, or some other damn thing that makes you think you're 'no longer qualified to serve in your present—or any other—capacity?' "

"No Sir, Mister President, I don't." There was some echo in Luftsen's voice now of the archly commanding tone that had occasionally awakened Gallen at odd hours with flat demands for explanations. "It's my health. That's all I'm willing to say. And now, sir, *if* you don't mind—"

"Jesus fucking *Christ*," Blaustein whispered so

low that Gallen was certain no one farther away could have heard. The deputy director was staring, not at Luftsen, but at the empty chair across from them which would, in all likelihood, now be his.

Shai chanced a glance and saw a pensive, delighted smirk come and go, only half hidden by Blaustein's moustache. *No shit*, she thought and found that her fists were clenched, her nails biting into calluses on palms accustomed to being unconsciously savaged. She spread her fingers forcibly and put both hands flat on the table, half expecting to hear Crossfield say in his Commander-in-Chief voice, "But I do mind, I mind very much, Dick. Sit down and tell me what the trouble is."

But Crossfield said no such thing. Rather, he told Luftsen, "I'm sorry, Dick. For all of us. Of course, your resignation is accepted. We'll cut you a bonus check if we can find a way to do it . . . you've another three months, though, until you're eligible for pension. What say we keep you on as a consultant until—"

Luftsen was retreating, reaching out for the doorknob, when he raised his hand before his face as if to shield some emotion from the crowd and said, "No, I tell you. No. Just leave me alone, you bastards. That's all I want."

Crossfield blinked in shock, the door opened, Luftsen bolted through it.

Shai had a glimpse of a disconcerted Marine—his rosy, smooth-shaven cheeks and his wide, startled eyes—before the door closed.

Then she looked past Blaustein, who was breathing evenly and preening his moustache as if he'd just lapped up a bowl of cream, toward the President.

Jim Crossfield said evenly, "Well, damn. I guess

that's that. Anyone know what's wrong with him? He's not been looking well? . . ."

Vice President Jennings suggested cancer, but no one seconded the guess. Shai saw Owen Neely pass Crossfield a note and Crossfield turn to Neely, saying, "Surely, Owen. As soon as we're done here, we can steal a few minutes." He checked his Baume & Mercier. "The chopper's picking me up out back at noon, though, so we'd best get started."

Then Jim Crossfield addressed the room generally, "Well, gentle—staff," he amended, with an impish nod to Gallen, "let's table the old business. We'll have to pre-empt Senate hearings on a new DCI and appoint Kurt as our pro tem. Probably give you a shot at the seat permanently, if you'd like it, Kurt?"

Blaustein's modest, self-effacing comment that he'd "served my country long enough to be willing to go on serving in whatever capacity the President sees fit to want me," didn't hide his palpably feline pleasure.

Shai thought, when Blaustein turned to her and prompted her to hand him CIA's agenda and the National Intelligence Estimate from which he would begin his report, that she saw naked triumph glittering in his eyes.

They weren't more than fifteen minutes into the meeting when the same pink-cheeked Marine that Shai had glimpsed outside the door opened it abruptly and a Presidential aide came bustling in, white as a sheet.

The meeting quieted instantly.

No one protested that it was highly irregular to have an aide interrupt an NSC meeting.

When the aide had finished whispering in Crossfield's ear, Crossfield dismissed him.

Pincering the bridge of his nose between two

fingers, Jim Crossfield took three deep breaths, lowered his hand, and looked squarely at those gathered around the table. "People, Jack Luftsen just blew his brains out in the damn parking lot. And I want—no, I *demand* to know why."

Everyone started talking at once; the FBI deputy was on his feet, officiously informing anyone who would listen that domestic matters were his purview and he'd begin a full investigation as soon as the President gave him leave to start.

Crossfield, standing also, said, "Right, right. Let's do that. This meeting is dismissed. We'll get back to this other business later."

It wasn't until she was following Blaustein, at his order, out the door, that Shai realized she hadn't read her dissenting opinion on the Soviet threat into the record—that only Blaustein's Assessment analysis had been entered.

But there was nothing that could be done about it. She had a glimpse of Jim Crossfield and Owen Neely headed toward the Oval office, heads together, as she got her coat and followed Blaustein obediently toward the waiting staff cars.

For some reason or other, when the cold hit her and she stepped out under the portico, she started thinking about Larry Fox again. Fox, who needed her even more now that Blaustein was Director of Central Intelligence, with nobody to answer to for the immediate future—not until Congress came back from recess, if then.

Then she admitted that she damned well *knew* why she was thinking about Fox now that, as far as she could determine, Jim Crossfield, a Soviet penetration agent, had just made Kurt Blaustein, the man running that agent, into the second most powerful man in the conduct of American policy at home and abroad.

*   *   *

Quaid was whistling as he escorted Alden out the door and down the steps toward the waiting Wagoneer, its lights on in the lowering dusk. A gray, unlighted Oldsmobile pulled away from the curb and hissed through the slush past the Counterintelligence team chatting across their 'grocery bags.'

"Mr. Alden," Quaid was saying, "we already have clothing in your—" when the street shattered in the racket of submachinegun bolts, bullets hammering sheet metal, and the moan of ricochets balked of a kill and furious. The Oldsmobile was being riddled point blank by Quaid's people with suppressed Uzis still shrouded in the paper bags which had concealed them.

The CI chief gripped Alden's shoulder with his left hand and kicked the lawyer's legs out from under him so that Quaid was on top when the two men hit the slushy sidewalk, his right hand of its own accord drawing the .45 holstered high on his hip. There were more cars moving, too many, and the street popped with what sounded like machine-gun fire but was in reality a single shot: the sharp-shooter on the roof opposite had put a round into the passenger compartment of the Olds. Though a suppressor absorbed the muzzle blast of the power-ful bolt-action rifle, the shock wave of the super-sonic bullet itself echoed sharply among the façades.

There was a yellow flash on the roof as the mixture of super-heated powder gases and oxygen in the rifle's yard-long suppressor burned off like a trip flare a fraction of a second after the shot. The woman with the Heckler and Koch submachinegun she had snatched from the baby carriage hosed the sharpshooter's position while her partner's burst snapped over Quaid and Alden to cut down the CI team firing from the stoop.

The gunman in the Wagoneer had already leaned across his seat to throw open the back door and Quaid's wrist radio was competing with startled bleats from the squirming lawyer—but first things first, and in the hot silence as nothing moved but him, the CI chief put two shots into the man with the baby carriage and two more into the woman as she turned, her face distorted in the red flash from the gun muzzle.

The Wagoneer's driver had opened his door for a shield while the long-barreled revolver in his hand slammed shots into the pair of black cars which had pulled into E Street even as the Oldsmobile started down the block in the other direction. The windows of two-inch Lexgard could not be rolled down, and nobody on Earth could do useful shooting through the punch ports in the armored sides. The muzzle blasts of the two handguns, his and Quaid's, were momentarily the bass notes in a chaos of bolts and receivers clanging on suppressed submachineguns and the shriek of the Oldsmobile— it was anybody's guess what the CI team had seen within to cause them to open up—rending itself to a stop on a building front. Then a machinegun cut loose from the ground floor of the corner building across the street.

When his immediate targets had gone down, the woman crushing the baby carriage as she sprawled backwards, Quaid had risen to a low crouch— holding Alden by the coat collar and ready to thrust the lawyer into the Wagoneer like a sack of rice. The machinegun raked the passenger compartment from the windshield back in a shower of sparks. Lexgard crumbled and the bullets sailed on through plates of titanium body armor which should, on a good day, have stopped a cal fifty. Concrete on the sidewalk and the stone foundations of Alden's townhouse powdered with a dry, burning odor and a sound like bones breaking.

Quaid's jacket was afire and the armored Wagoneer rocked on its springs with the impact of bullets it could not stop. The CI chief put a knee between Alden's shoulders and slammed him back down as he himself rose to sight over the car's front fender. The driver was on his knees, gripping the upper edge of the riddled door to keep his torso upright; his partner, flopped on the back seat, seemed to have shrivelled like a spider in a candleflame when bullets took off the top of his head. As they would Quaid's, when he—

The man fixing his flat tire on the corner was FBI, and it was with a twelve-gauge shotgun that he cleared the room from which the machinegun was firing, even as the muzzle tracked back toward the CI chief.

"Wait!" someone screamed: the FBI liaison man from the commo van, running toward Quaid with his hands raised, "they're—" and was shot by one of the men spilling from the black cars which had collided, hood to trunk, when bullets starred the windshield of the leading one.

The spotter and the commo man of the countersniper triad had been equipped with automatic rifles. At least one of the men on the roof had survived the initial burst of submachinegun fire, because he now emptied his thirty-round magazine on the wedged cars and the men in business suits jumping from them with guns in their hands. The sustained fire probably burned out the barrel; but there were more where that gun came from, and the sleet of light bullets ricocheting through metal and flesh was the perfect way to disrupt what was left of the organization of the attacking team.

There had been four men in each of the cars. The one who did not go down—dead, wounded, or rightfully terrified by the high-angle fire—dropped as Quaid put two rounds into him and changed magazines without needing to have counted shots consciously.

Instinct was a fine way to operate—because when you tried to think, you found there was no way out of a rat-fuck like this.

Except instinct's answer: to get out and worry about the side-effects later.

Glenn Alden lay with his chest and palms flat on the concrete and his arms splayed out like a lizard's forelegs. His face was turned upward, pale as dough in the half light save where it was touched by blooddrops or glittering fragments of metal sprayed by the machinegun fire. His staring eyes held an expression Quaid had seen only once before, and that in a virgin's.

Quaid tapped a preset of his wrist radio twice with his trigger finger—confirmation codes were required on every position of this particular unit—and called, "Scramble! Scramble!" Then he ducked so that the car body was again between him and the gunfire that sputtered like sparks in the waste of a recently burned forest. "Keep low and pray," the CI chief snarled to Alden; but his words were ahead of his intent, for with an iron grip on the bunched shoulders of Alden's coat he dragged the lawyer after him onto the front seat of the Wagoneer.

The transmission was in Park, the motor purring quietly. The headlights flooded the street and the two bullet-riddled cars of the interdiction team. The glass-thermoplastic Lexgard sandwich set behind the windshield had disintegrated, but the windshield itself was still there—albeit holed and starred to opacity. Quaid cleared a swatch large enough to drive by, using the butt of his pistol and ignoring the scrape of the glass on his wrist as he swept it away. The safety glass fractured into ragged file-edges, not razor blades; and anyway, he had more immediate problems than the possibility he was going to bleed out through a slashed wrist.

The Wagoneer's driver, his chest shot to doll-rags, lay beneath the open street-side door. There was no reason to pick him up, just another dead man at a scene littered with them; but Sonny Quaid had left too many bodies behind in the past not to retrieve this one when it was just a matter of leaning down, his right elbow hooked as an anchor around the glassless windshield post, and jerking the flaccid corpse over his own lap and onto the floor of the passenger side. It did not occur to him until afterward that the dead body was now tangled with Alden, huddled in the same corner.

The commo van pulled from its driveway with the wavering squeal of its power-steering belt rubbing as the driver locked his vehicle into a tighter turn than the designers had intended. Nobody shot at it, for a wonder, despite the fact that it skidded close to the pair of black cars and the gunmen sheltering beside them. The windshield was already marred with a milky oval where a ricochet had spun through it, but it could still have been a civilian vehicle.

The van fishtailed and swept the Wagoneer with its lights as it came abreast. The instrument and courtesy lights of Quaid's vehicle had been disconnected when it was rebuilt to its current purposes, so as not to silhouette its occupants for hostile eyes. For that reason, it was only in the flash as the van passed him that the CI chief saw the scrap of metal on his dashboard.

Quaid swore through clenched teeth as he slid the gear selector into Drive with a hand which still gripped his .45. Cramping the wheel hard left, he floored the gas pedal and let the turbocharged engine roar against the mass of the Wagoneer's plating. The tires had cores of nitrogen-charged Kapton foam, blowout proof and almost as bullet resistant as the Lexan armor. The big car twisted away from the curb in a deceptively sharp acceleration curve, stable enough for control as both axles found purchase despite the wet street already chilling to ice as the sun set.

A burst of automatic fire rang on the right quarter panel and side as the Wagoneer turned its back to the black cars. It was just a submachinegun, though, no threat to the titanium or the plates of undamaged Lexgard on that side of the car.

A disk of mild steel, its edges milled by the rifling of the machinegun firing it from the corner building, lay on the Wagoneer's dash. It was the push-plate from a tubular penetrator, meant to drop away at the muzzle when it had accomplished its task of driving the depleted uranium tube of the projectile itself down the bore of the gun. The armor-piercing ability of such rounds was thirty percent higher than that of saboted sub-caliber projectiles, but proper airflow demanded exotic machining on the interior of the thin-walled tubes. It was limited-issue ammunition; and issued by no one at all except on orders from someone very high in the government.

The United States Government.

Alden was squirming beside him. "Stay *down*,"

Quaid snarled, his hand tight on his gun butt, as the car roared through the dusk toward the home of Shai Gallen: the only person who both knew where Quaid was going and who could have approved use of tubular penetrators for the interdiction. . . .

Jim Crossfield, President of the United States, felt an attack of colitis coming on as he shepherded Owen Neely through newly-carpeted private halls to the Oval Office. Crossfield's wife had been given a special award by the White House domestic staff, a good-humored citation handlettered on parchment for the "most extensive and continual redecoration in our Nation's history."

The errant memory fled, leaving Crossfield chagrined but bolstered: like his faithful wife, Crossfield loved living in America's most historic home, loved leaving his stamp on it, loved everything about his life as First Executive but the portions having to do with Kurt Blaustein. An error on the side of humanitarianism—no, morality—in Crossfield's youth still cast a pall over everything the President did, everything he was. He couldn't quite remember when he became sure that his new "allies" weren't CIA after all . . . though in a way it didn't matter—the help had been necessary and it would have come with strings, no matter who provided it.

"I'm sorry, Owen, what was that?" Crossfield interjected into a pause yawning between him and his outspoken National Security Advisor, who'd suddenly fallen silent as Crossfield reached around the shorter man to tap the lockplate which needed his handprint to admit them to the Oval Office from the rear corridor.

"I said, Mr. President, that the way things are

going, we're about to snatch defeat from the jaws of victory, that's what."

"Don't let this Luftsen thing shake you, Owen. Dick must have had a damned good reason. We'll find out what, you have my word on it." Crossfield tried to summon his trusty smile, but it felt spiky on his face, as if well-trained muscles were threatening to cramp. Maybe it wasn't *all* Blaustein's fault, though Jim Crossfield now knew enough about intelligence-community parlance to know that the US President was being referred to, in KGB circles, as an "induced double," if not worse. Maybe he'd asked for it, flirting with Marxism at Harvard, cozening favors out of then-Professor Blaustein which led to letters of recommendation which in turn led to his first State Department post as a commie-watcher. . . .

"Commies, dollars to doughnuts—whole place is crawlin' with Commies, fer Chrissake," Owen Neely said. "I don't *blame* Dick, myself—"

"What?" Crossfield snapped because it seemed just then as if Owen Neely, of the gaudy silver prize-buckles with horses' names on them and the lizard roach-stompers, was reading his mind. Shutting the door behind them, so the two were alone in the newly refurbished Oval Office, Crossfield eased behind FDR's desk and slapped toggles set into a panel of black leather whose LCD display winked encouragingly: security unbreached; videotape engaged and rolling; urgent messages, none.

"I said. . . . No, I didn't, Jimbo." Neely didn't wait for permission to be seated. Crossing his legs in a chair given Crossfield by the People's Republic of China, he toyed with the silver tip of one cowboy boot, looking up at his President almost ferally from under a jutting brow: "I got this letter, this frigging crazy letter, from some CIA boy name of Fox." Neely paused, staring at Crossfield like an interrogator waiting for visual confirmation that he'd hit a nerve.

"Fox? Yes, go on, Owen." Quizzical and a trifle impatient, annoyed because he had no time for one of Owen's rambling stories—not when he'd just slipped Blaustein neatly into the DCI's chair without the slightest notion of whether Blaustein had arranged for it to become vacant: "What's this got to do with? . . ."

"Just hold your horses, Jimbo. You know, my dad used to say that there's more horses' asses in the world than there are horses."

Crossfield hated being called "Jimbo," but usually he could deal with Owen's down-home egalitarianism. Today there was something else there. "Holy mother of God, Owen, *will* you get to the point? We've got a dead man in the parking lot who used to be the head of Central Intelligence and you're telling me what your daddy used to say?"

Owen Neely sat back, both booted feet on the Kashmir rug, and shrugged. "Dick Luftsen had good reason, perhaps. Cancer of confidence, could be. Seeing that he got wind of what was in this letter *I* got from one of your Turkish mission staffers. . . ."

"Which *said?*" Crossfield's exasperation, barely in check, put an edge on his tone that could have cut silk.

"That you're a Red, Jimbo. A cocksuckin' Russkie. A spy for the Bear—"

Crossfield couldn't think of anything to do but laugh, loudly and campaign-heartily enough to justify the flat-handed slap at his desk-top display which turned off the recording equipment and, with the tap of a finger, began erasing the last five minutes' worth of tape.

Owen Neely laughed along with him, but neither as determinedly nor as long.

When Crossfield wiped his eyes, the National Security Advisor said, "That's what I thought, at first. But then I got to thinkin'—where there's smoke, there's smoke, I always say. We know you're no Sov-lover. But sometimes where there's smoke there's fire. We ever do any real checking on Kurt Blaustein, Jimbo?"

We? "Oh, come now, Owen," Crossfield said clearly.

Neely was leaning forward, elbows on his knees as if watching one of his teams at a championship horse-pulling contest. "I'm coming, Mr. President, to the point—as you requested.

Whenever the good-ol'-boy gloss fell away, Owen Neely made Crossfield distinctly uncomfortable; when Owen's watery little eyes glittered like his big brother Noah's, Crossfield had learned to take care. So he only gestured magnanimously, decreeing that Owen continue, hoping that the beads of sweat on his palm didn't catch the light.

"Point being," Owen Neely said from the depths of his capacious belly, "that if Dick Luftsen, once I asked him, came up with any suspicions of his own—I'm not saying 'proof,' mind you—that your prof, Blaustein, is some kind of Russian spy, then I'd understand how come he decided to check out early and avoid the rush. Hard as hell to convince anybody of something like that, wouldn't you say?"

"I'd say, Owen, that if you and Dick Luftsen were colluding to keep something of this magnitude from me, I'd be very disappointed."

"Colluding, my ass. Dick told me this morning that he couldn't prove squat to anybody's satisfaction. The implication being that he'd proved it to his own."

"Is there some paperwork I can see—a report?" Crossfield leaned forward.

"Not a damned thing," Neely sighed regretfully. "Too sensitive, he said."

"That's what I thought," Crossfield said cynically and rubbed his neck as if in disgust. "So, then, if there's a Soviet plot here, it's probably to sow the seeds of distrust within my Administration—we can't have something like this floating around. . . . Owen, let's drop the subject until the FBI's done with an *impartial* investigation. Ten-four?"

"Consider it dropped . . . until then, Jimbo. Now, if you want my advice on how to minimize the repercussions from Dick's . . . death . . . then let's talk about appointing a new DCI who's confirmation hearings might not bring anybody's suspicions—groundless or not—to light. We can't afford the embarrassment. *You* can't." And Owen Neely bared his teeth in something which only an idiot would have classified as a smile.

Crossfield almost lost his own temper, then. No matter the means, no matter the caveats, James Crossfield's administration was going to bring peace to a troubled world. Unilateral disarmament by the US was going to set a new moral standard. And if the Soviets were anxious to help him claim that high ground, then what of it? Jim Crossfield wasn't in an eviable position, but he was damned well going to make the best of it. He could feel his intestines spasming, but he ignored it. Damn Blaustein: this was no time to screw up. And damn Kurt again for having no more vision than the rest of the KGB and CIA—no more than Dick Luftsen, who'd succumbed to suicide, the coward's way out: who, for the price of a fifty-cent round, had bought himself an endless sleep from which no one could wake him in the middle of the night with horrific reports and insane projections of just how close to Nuclear Zero-hour the world was coming; who was going to his nice, peaceful grave with the appropriate blazon draped over his coffin and medals for valorous service in little velvet boxes left behind with a wife who'd never be allowed to understand how, when or why he won them. Not that Luftsen was sweating any of that. Not anymore. . . .

The male receptionist in Blaustein's liaison office in the White House was so near a double for the muscular homosexual in the same job at Langley that the two could have been brothers. In fact, there was no biological relationship—but Blaustein wondered whether the men's sexual relations with one another did not sometimes seem to be a complex form of masturbation.

"Your calls are arranged on the screen, sir," this one said primly, his hands linked in a neat V on the mahogany desktop.

"All right," Blaustein replied with a brusque nod, thoroughly disinterested in why the receptionist seemed peeved. Now that he had time to think about it, Luftsen's death had possible implications more important than Blaustein's own appointment as Acting Director.

Even as he reached for the door of his inner office, however, the receptionist said, "*One* of them even wanted to call you out of your *meeting*, sir. I told him he was a fool if he thought that *anything* the FBI had to say to you was more important than the President, whatever they claimed the priority was."

Blaustein paused and looked back at his receptionist, who met his gaze for only a few seconds before looking down and pursing the smug line of his lips into an expression of nervous concern. "Was the call from Special Agent Snyder?" Blaustein asked with the voice of an executioner.

"Yes, sir," said the receptionist, looking up, hopeful that Blaustein's fury was reserved for Snyder, a hope which his superior's expression immediately dashed.

"Have your personnel jacket downloaded to my terminal," Kurt Blaustein said. "Then you can leave." He closed the door behind him abruptly, but the man in the outer office was too shocked to have made an immediate protest at his abrupt termination anyway.

The liaison office had a window for prestige, but it was invariably blocked with internal lead shutters as a security requirement. As a result of the lack of sunlight and infrequent use, the room had the musty odor of something recently dead. The KGB agent's hand was trembling as he reached out to touch Snyder's number in the upper left-hand corner of his video display.

The FBI man would not have tried to break in on an NSC meeting if the interdiction had gone as planned.

Blaustein tried to relax in the old-fashioned swivel chair as his computer put the call through automatically. The act of tenting his fingers and composing himself physically as he faced the video display—though of course there was no video pickup at either end of the line—helped considerably to calm his mind, but Blaustein's palms were chill with sweat.

"Eight-two-four-four," said the speaker harshly.

"Good evening, Special Agent Snyder," the professor replied. "Kurt Blaustein here. You needed to speak to me?"

"Wait a minute," Snyder said; and even as Blaustein wondered whether or not the statement were rhetorical, he heard the bang of the FBI agent's door through the telephone speaker. "Blaustein," Snyder's voice resumed, "do you know what the *hell* you got me into? There was a firefight on E Street this evening, a fucking *war*, and it was my people on both sides."

"The arrest of—" Blaustein began, loosened marginally by the fact that Snyder's *words*—whatever they meant—were not the words that he had expected. Casualties were not even regrettable, not when they were taken by the button-down brigades of the Justice Department.

Snyder, whose attitude was sharply different on that point, snarled through the interruption, "I've got four dead and six in critical, Blaustein, *critical*—I'm not talking about folks with ribs taped where their chicken vest kept a slug from blowing a hole in them!"

"Agent Snyder," said Blaustein as his hands wrung each other but his voice held stern, "did you or did you *not* arrest Alden as you were directed to do? I'm asking you as Deputy Director of Central Intelligence and your superior for this mission." In panic, he failed to use his new title.

"*No*, we don't have your goddamned terrorist suspect," the FBI agent said; "we've got over a dozen casualties and your *own* people have Alden, that's who. Because things in your shop are so fucked up, you tasked it *twice*—and my own people shot each other up." There was a pause which Blaustein could not fill because his tongue was sticking to the roof of his mouth. "Did I mention we got a couple of yours, too?" Snyder continued.

"The one who could still talk hasn't yet, but my people—the survivors—that Sonny Quaid requisitioned say they were all working together, us and the CI boys."

"Well, you can count on me to cover you if it's humanly possible, Snyder," said the KGB agent as he got up from his chair and began to pace, trusting the balance program in the telephone receiver to keep his voice steady. "I suppose you prepared a suitable cover story before you authorized the missions." He rubbed his palms on his shirt front, darkening it with patches of sweat but not drying his hands for more than a moment.

"What do you mean *you'll* cover me, you son of a bitch?"

"As the only man who approved both these unfortunate missions," Blaustein said as coolly as if fear had not drawn up his surface muscles so that the skin prickled with goose bumps, "I shouldn't think you'd need *me* to draw a diagram, Agent Snyder."

There was a strangled sound at the other end of the phone line before the FBI agent managed to articulate, "Now *wait* a minute, it was *your* people who tasked these. My boys just provided support and—"

"And killed quite a number of the wrong parties, from what you tell me," acidly interjected the man speaking from the White House office. "Listen, Snyder, I'm perfectly capable of cleaning my own house—but the fact remains that you either signed papers on both interdictions, *or* you authorized them without proper paperwork. I'm going to cover you, I say, but only if you'll tell me *exactly* what happened and what cover story you've prepared."

For a moment, there was no sound from the wall speaker but the whisper of distant static. Blaustein pressed his palms tightly against his face, then took the ends of his crushed moustache between two fingers and the thumb of either hand and drew the waxed hair out again.

"Right, it was rival motorcycle gangs fighting over drug territory," said the FBI agent in weary defeat. "Fuck. Motherfuck. We'll string the press for another two, three days, then let it die. . . ."

"You'll handle the Capitol Police?" the Acting Director said sharply. He had stopped pacing and now faced the pickup with an imperious expression as invisible to his listener as had been the earlier signs of panic.

"Yeah, goddamnit, we've handled the locals, but *you've* got to goddam take care of the flak in the administration from what *does* leak out," Snyder snapped in reply. "Word's going to leak, and we're not going to roll over and play dead if you smart-asses don't yell 'national security' and put a lid on it."

"You'd better run through the incident," said Blaustein, pacing again as his feeling of triumph over the lesser danger melted before a wave of unease at larger questions. "I'll expect a written report within twenty-four hours, with updates as they come in."

"Goddammit," Snyder repeated, but he was too thoroughly beaten to argue. "All right, yeah. Your man Quaid requisitioned a team through ISA about three hours before you called me directly. No way in *hell* anybody over here could have known it was the same pickup—Quaid briefed the boys personally. He was going to bring a fellow out of the building, maybe no problem, but the fellow was going to leave either in custody or dead. No other options."

Kurt Blaustein, who had not seen a corpse since

his father died in 1972, nodded in cool appreciation of something as far from his real understanding as the core of the sun was. "Go on," he said aloud as he paced.

"So they were in position before the second team set up to arrest this Alden for you," Snyder continued. "When he came out, our guys moved and one of Quaid's own people cut loose and called an alarm. Everybody—*everybody*—was all primed for a gang of terrorists, and Christ, you couldn't recognize your mother as dark as it was ... so the shit really hit the fan."

"And Alden," said the KGB agent as he stood stock still and closed his eyes, "the terrorist—was *he* killed?"

"Hell, I *told* you," Snyder replied with more spirit than moments before, "Quaid got him and drove off. Maybe he stopped one, god knows there was enough flying around—but don't ask *me*, Blaustein, ask your own boy."

"Thank you, Special Agent Snyder," said Blaustein distantly, squeezing his hands together like a pair of soft, pink sponges. His head was bowed, his eyes still closed. "You cover your end and I'll protect you from here."

"You'd damned well better, buddy," the FBI agent said. There was the click of a disconnection through the telephone speaker; then the brightness of the other numbers and messages on Blaustein's video display came up to equal that of Snyder's.

"Well, that's going to be all right," said the KGB agent in a normal voice, with his eyes squeezed shut and his fingers twisting hard enough on the tips of his moustache to stretch his upper lip. Had Gallen picked up Alden because he could support Fox's story—or because there was *no* story, beyond unprovable suspicions that damned blond bitch had come up with and the whirl of violent activity she had aroused to screen that lack of proof.

Was this firefight itself part of her plan, a way to embarrass the DDCI within the intelligence community—of *course* the story would leak!—and to goad him into further mistakes?

A phone rang, and it took Blaustein two rings in his state of terrified uncertainty to realize that nothing *should* be ringing here in his office, only a muted chime and an entry flashing on the display. He opened his eyes and it was, of course, the intercom in the center of the desk. Only one person could be at the other end of that line. Blaustein swallowed cautiously before he pressed the key and said, "Yes, Jimmie. What can I do for you?"

"You can get in here right now," responded James Crossfield in an unexpectedly taut voice. "Kurt, you're supposed to be protecting me, and I swear if the wheels come off now I'll. . . ."

"I'll be right there, Jimmie," said the President's case officer in a smooth, unctuous voice.

He broke the connection and paused for a moment to settle his suitcoat so that it covered the patches of sweat and body oils he had wiped onto his shirtfront. Then, with a brisk stride and his habitually cool expression, he started for the Oval Office.

James Crossfield was behind the desk and very coldly presidential when his case officer entered the big room. No one else was present and the door shut with the dense resilience of an air lock at the pull of the uniformed guard outside. Blaustein did not speak until he had cocked one fluffy white eyebrow in the direction of a corner vase—translucent blue from the outside but clear to the video camera within it.

"They're off, of course," said Crossfield, "do you think I'm an idiot?" But he glanced at the controller inset into the desk top. Presumably there were no red gleams from the light-emitting diodes indicating live cameras—the room was fitted with at least three of them—but the KGB agent would have been happier if he could have checked the display himself.

It would have been better yet if Crossfield's vanity or suicidal perversity had not caused him to install the system, activated by sound or motion unless the President deliberately switched it off. Something as potentially dangerous to the operation should not have existed, much less been under the sole discretion of an agent like Crossfield.

Did one ever *really* control the president of the most powerful country on Earth?

"Owen just left," Crossfield continued grimly.

"He was his usual charming self at the NSC meeting, wasn't he?" Blaustein said in seeming nonchalance, seating himself on the corner of the broad desk in order to preserve a height advantage over the agent he was running and to eviscerate Crossfield's attempt to dominate the discussion from what was literally the seat of power.

"He told me you were a Russian spy," the President said. His eyes glanced across the gleaming, immaculate desktop, looking in vain for something that his fingers could fumble. When he found nothing there, he took the double-barreled derringer from a side pocket and ran his palm over the case-hardened frame. "And he told me Dick Luftsen had 'cancer of the conscience'—trust Owen to coin a phrase like that." Crossfield turned his derringer's barrel toward his face and stared into it cross-eyed. "Owen thinks Luftsen took the 'clean and honorable—even noble—way out.' Do you?"

Kurt Blaustein held his breath until Crossfield continued, "A fellow named Fox, a CIA agent, of all things, told him *I* was a Commie, Kurt; but good old Owen knew that couldn't be true. He figures where there's smoke, though. . . ."

Crossfield stood up and glared at his case officer. "What did we put you in as DDCI for, Kurt?" He slammed his right hand down on the desk, the hand with the gun so that the butt banged on the wood and dented it. "What the *fuck* is going *on!*"

"Yes," Blaustein lied easily as his right hand smoothed the tip of his moustache, a toying motion and not a strangling grip, "the Fox business has been dealt with by now, but there were of course side effects which have to be damped down in their—"

"Kurt, you didn't *tell* me about Fox!" interrupted the President, speaking now with a voice that was under control but still held an edge. "What else is there that you aren't telling me about?"

"I didn't tell you it was raining yesterday in Atlanta, Jimmie," said the case officer with an effort to avoid glancing at the pistol—an aberration, like the cameras, which was beyond the power of Crossfield's "controllers" to affect. "For god's sake, you're the *President*, you can't be told everything. All of this goes back to Kunayev's defection, a one in a million occurrence on which you were fully briefed—in *both* capacities."

Blaustein caught and held Crossfield's eyes as his fingers stopped playing with the moustache. "And if the ripples from that are still spreading, then they're also becoming weaker in any real terms."

Crossfield sat down abruptly, grimaced at the derringer, and dropped it back in his pocket. The dent in the ebony desktop was an accusation. "Kurt,

I don't like this," the President said toward his hands before looking up again.

"None of us do," agreed his case officer soothingly, "but we've solving this problem just as we've solved all the earlier ones." He took a deep breath when his subject looked away again; then, certain that Crossfield was relaxed, Blaustein got up from the desk and walked to one of the matching chairs beside it, black leather and black wood.

"Judging from the NSC meeting today and some other rumors I've been hearing," the DDCI continued as he seated himself normally, "I'll be making some changes in the Agency's top management." He smiled across the desk, his hair and moustache a fringe of hoarfrost suiting the expression. "I have a particularly amusing choice for a 'lateral shift' into the Public Relations Office. I'm sure the job as public spokesman for the Agency will be a delight to her."

"You'll want to get rid of Owen," Crossfield said.

"Nothing of the sort. He's perfect where he is."

"But he *knows*—"

"He *knows* nothing," Blaustein interrupted tartly. "He's been *told* something that no self-respecting journalist or political leader would listen to ... unless, just possibly, you gave weight to the story yourself by firing your long-time friend and political advisor."

"Yes ...," the President said, drawing out the sibilant and touching his tongue to his upper lip at the end of the word. He looked at a floral arrangement across the room. "I can see that you would be hesitant to order the, ah, permanent removal of a man who has been a close associate of mine for so long ...?" His eyes flicked sidelong toward his case officer.

"Good God," said Professor Kurt Blaustein, "I

wouldn't think of it. It—" He paused and organized the words before he spoke them. "That would be even firmer support for Neely's wild ideas than replacing him as National Security Advisor. Who knows who he's repeated his notions to already? His brother, business associates, newsmen—anybody!"

"Kurt," said the President in a tone as hard as the dented wood his finger was tracing, "I'm not going to have people in public positions talking about communist moles in my administration."

"I *said* we were going to solve the problem," Blaustein responded more sharply than he had intended. Crossfield's ruthlessness had shocked him and made tremble the illusion of order with which the KGB agent had surrounded his life for so many years. His left hand rose as if to touch his face, but he brought it back onto his lap. "The way to keep Owen Neely from talking is to tell him not to talk in a fashion he can understand, not by—by any sort of violence." He stood up. "I'll see to it that that's taken care of immediately. Among other things."

Crossfield snorted. "You'd better be prepared for—other eventualities, Kurt. You don't know Owen like I do."

Blaustein strode to the outer door, but he halted there with his hand on the marble knob and looked back at the agent he controlled. "On the contrary, Jimmie," he said, "I know him much better than you do. That's why I'm sure we'll have no difficulty in silencing him."

Crossfield's face was as stark as a stone from a stream bed as he watched the door close behind his case officer.

*　　*　　*

When Shai Gallen finally got home after overseeing the FBI's search of Luftsen's office (which had turned up nothing in the way of suicide notes but plenty in the way of files no FBI types would ever get clearance to so much as open), it was sleeting again.

The weather suited her mood. She was more confused than she could remember having been since she'd left Israeli Intelligence.

And so were Mike and Mary, who were out of their depth preparing the menu she'd left for dinner—a menu for an intimate little dinner party she'd decided upon this morning when she'd been in a more optimistic mood—before Luftsen had either blown his brains out or been murdered by somebody capable of making it look like a classic case of suicide.

The circumstances of Luftsen's demise didn't really matter, but the result—Blaustein's promotion—wasn't going to be good for Shai Gallen.

This morning, she'd been thinking how nice it would be to have a civilized dinner, bring Alden on board carefully and properly, show Fox that she meant what she said—that she could and *would* do her best for him—and Sonny that this whole Fox affair was strictly business.

Which it wasn't. God, how she wished it was. What did she need with Fox beyond a lure to flush Blaustein? Why did she care about a GS-11 whose record showed him so ambivalent about his work, so unstable, so damned unnecessarily dangerous? He was still the skinny kid with the murderous grin who was fool enough to stop a bullet meant for her on the Green Line. You didn't promote guys like that, you retired them: CIA wasn't the Green Berets; Agency personnel needed brains, not machismo. You kept your profile low and your fucking head down. Survivability was everything.

Shrugging out of her down jacket and oiled sweater, listening to Mary carp about "popovers with strawberry butter, for shit's sake. What does she think this is, the Waldorf Astoria?" and Mike retort, "Just be cool, all right? With Quaid at this party, everything had better be ultra-perfect, or I'm the one who'll get ultra-fucked," Gallen tried to tell herself that the qualms she was having about using Fox for bait had more to do with his condition when he'd come in than with any real emotion on her part.

She couldn't afford to get emotional about an asset like Fox. Couldn't afford the kind of emotion she was feeling, anyway. You could love them for a distance, your field collectors—talk them through the rough spots and promise perks you knew you could deliver, even promise undying loyalty because they were knowingly putting themselves on the line for you—but you should never, ever let yourself care the way she was beginning ... no, damn it, the way she'd already *begun* ... to care about Fox.

She wanted to run away with this skinny, vicious little psycho—somewhere, any-damn-where—and grow old listening to his voice. That was just great. If it didn't get her killed, that was because she wasn't in the field anymore. It was going to lose her whatever else she loved—her job, her equilibrium, her ability to affect the perceptions of policymakers and to keep better than a hundred other agents alive. And she was *letting* it happen.

Fucking dinner party. Next she'd be buying him pajamas. It just had to stop. But she didn't know how to stop it. She'd loved Ariel Sharon and it had made her crazy—before that she'd loved an Israeli pilot who'd gotten himself shot down over the Shuf. After Sharon's removal as Defense Minister, she'd decided that, from then on, her love was reserved for countries, operations ongoing, and specially competent agents. She'd married a man whom she didn't love in the way that women obsessively loved men, on purpose and because doing so left her mind and passions clear to be posited where she willed.

She hated the feeling of being out of control—of caring, selfishly, for a single person to the exclusion of relevant factors and even logic. There was no future in it and she was going to put an end to it if she had to stand over Fox's grave to do it.

Sonny, who was impartial, said that putting Fox out was going to be a sacrifice play—that they'd probably lose him. On her way to check the linens and stemware on her dining room table, she consoled herself: Fox would in all likelihood be dead before he ruined her career. And she'd probably cry, though she hadn't cried for better than ten years. Then she could get on to new business. So if she was doting on the kid, maybe it was okay. She had to keep thinking about him as a kid, because the man in the room upstairs had eyes that wouldn't be lied to and a trustful smile reserved only for her.

When she'd told him she'd take care of him, he'd believed her enough to be troubled by the disparities in their positions—as if it mattered that she outranked him, as if they had time to worry about little problems that civilians had. He'd said, last night, "But I don't have anything to offer you," and she'd thought, *Just your life; let's hope it's enough*, and hated herself both for caring and not caring.

Even her cat liked Fox, and M-1, her twenty-five

pound Persian, didn't like anybody but Gallen herself. The cat hated Sonny; when the Deputy spent the night with her, they had to be careful to hang up his clothes, or M-1 would defecate on them.

As she climbed the stairs to change, she missed M-1's kamikaze act: the cat invariably rubbed around her ankles as she mounted the staircase so that both of them were in constant danger of a crash to the slate landing at its foot.

M-1 must be in Fox's room—the door was open. She had an impulse to sneak by and tried it.

"Yo? Hey, babe?" Fox, cat draped over his arms, stepped out to block her path.

She couldn't believe that it didn't bother her when he talked to her like that, as if she were some skirt he'd picked up in a bar or one of a line of twats so long he'd gone to the generic rather than risk calling one by the wrong name. Or that she was disappointed because she'd wanted his first sight of her this evening to be in her slinky black dinner dress. Hell's bells, she was losing her fucking *mind!*

She smiled tightly, "I've got to change—dress for dinner. So do you, cowboy. Now, don't *do—*"

His fingers closed on her left nipple, his hand brushing against the holstered Detonics snuggled against her ribs. She wouldn't have put up with that sort of behavior from Sonny—or from anyone else. Astounded at herself, more confused than ever, she raised a hand to brush his away, found she couldn't—didn't want to—and leaned back against the wall, eyes on his fingers as he rolled her nipple between thumb and forefinger.

"Want me to stop?" he murmured, laughter in his eyes that wasn't offensive but should have been.

"No," she heard herself say, then took control

with an effort of will. "Fuck you, *yes*. Alden and Quaid are due here in—" The act of lifting her watch to read it pressed her arm, her pistol, her breast and his hand together."—forty minutes. We want you looking like a willing guest, not an internee."

"Alden? Glenn's coming?" Fox demanded. His fingers did not slip away, but his attention was no longer on them.

"We thought you needed a friend," Gallen said, looking down at the hand motionless on her breast as an excuse not to meet Fox's eyes. Only the unimportant part of her statement was true: Fox did need a friend, and he had none in this house, not now . . . "Sonny's going to ask him. Of course—" she added as she looked up at the man's trusting face, her hand patting his against her "—you're movements won't be. . . . You'll both be under wraps, pretty much."

"All right," Fox said with enthusiasm, giving her a light kiss and lifting his hand away. "*All* right," again as he disappeared into his bedroom, still hugging the huge black cat to his chest.

After she'd showered, brushed out damp hair, slipped into a black Galanos over only pantyhose, and buckled high-heeled sandals at her ankles, she found him leaning against the doorframe.

"Suit fits," she approved neutrally, retreating toward the bathroom where her makeup was.

"You mean, I'm really this thin? Black's not my color—except at funerals." He followed, his jaw squared, the tension there making it seem more pronounced. "What's with the black tie bullshit, Shai? Glenn and I are old—"

"We need to make him comfortable, send some signals as to what kind of situation you're in here and how strongly we feel about you. I—"

He came up behind her, sliding his hands under her arms, cupping her breasts. "When did you say Mister Quaid would be bringing Glenn? He's—"

"Ma'am! You'd better get down here. Now!" came the voice of Mike, the male babysitter, from the foot of the stairs.

Gallen felt as if somebody had thrown her in an ice-cold shower, and not simply because she heard the door open, running feet, and the sound of a motor.

Fox's glance met hers, suddenly suspicious and distant in the mirror, and he took his hands away.

He was loping toward the front door, with a gait that said he was still favoring one leg, before she could think to forbid him.

She was slow in her heels; he made the ground-floor landing before she did.

She heard him breathe, "Fuckin' A," and then, "Christ," and then she was following him out the door into the murky, sleeting night.

The Wagoneer skewed before her doorstep looked like it had been shipped straight in from Central America: no front windshield, lots of chewed-up quarter panels, one headlight out of the entire complement unshattered and throwing unsteady light.

But her porch lights were good, and in them she had one detailed look at Sonny Quaid, blood smeared over his face and hands from too many cuts, trying to untangle what seemed to be one living and one dead man from the Wagoneer's passenger side, where the open door hung crazily, so full of bullet holes that the flashlight Mary was holding sent rays through it as if it were a mirrored ball in a disco.

Gallen moved more quickly than she knew through the slushy gravel, oblivious to the cold, taking stock: rents in the sheet metal; punctures also in the titanium plates beneath and that should *not* have been; no glass to speak of; Sonny's big back occluding her view of everything but the stains where blood had clotted on his overcoat.

And the living guy was Alden: she recognized the WASPy face from Alden's dossier photo as she reached Quaid's side and whispered, "Sonny, what the *hell* happened? Are you all right?"

By then, Fox had made his way around the car, knifing between the two babysitters and talking excitedly, his voice high-pitched, to his friend, begging him to "let me get you out of there, buddy." And to the babysitters: "Get the *fuck* away from him, you bastards. Just get your goddamned hands off him," over and over.

"*I'm* all right, Shai." Quaid straightened up and looked down at her, face set in a rictus Shai was used to seeing only behind shelled revetments. "Get your friendly fuse, there, out of the way, and we'll bring Counselor Alden in and patch him up—he took one in the butt. It's not that serious, but he's shocky. A little bit too real for him."

So she ran around the car and tugged at Fox's sleeve. He pushed her away as if she were a minor, nameless annoyance. Out of the corner of her eye she saw Mike draw a snub-nosed revolver from behind his hip. She raised one hand to forestall the babysitter and tried again: "Fox," she said quietly, laying a hand on his suited arm and rubbing it back and forth gently. "This isn't your fault. It's not going to be a problem unless you make it one. Come on, now, cowboy. Step back and—"

"*Not* a problem? Tell me about it! You walk Glenn into a—" Biting off his words in mid-sentence, Fox knelt down and began crooning to the stricken lawyer, still entangled with a corpse on the Wagoneer's deck.

She squatted down beside him, then knelt abruptly, finding no purchase for spike heels in the treacherous mixture of snow, mud and gravel. "Larry, look at me."

Hands under Alden's armpits, the line officer hesitated and then squinted at her sidelong. "Yeah, Shai, I'm listening."

"Good. That's fine. Now, your friend needs gentler care than you're giving him. Let go. Let Mike and Mary take care of him. You and I will go in with Sonny and call a doctor. Okay?"

Fox stared into her eyes as if by pure intensity he could undo the reality before him. Then he blew out a breath and in a low, distant monotone bristling with desperate control, said, "Yeah, okay Shai." Then, harshly, to the babysitter: "All right, man, take him."

At that moment, the lawyer groaned and opened his eyes, while the babysitters were moving in and Mike grasped Fox by the shoulder.

"Larry? Larry, man, is that you?" Alden's eyes roved, struggling to focus. "They said you—Shit, my ass hurts. You there, Larry?"

Fox shook off the babysitter's grip and Shai thought she was going to have to start all over again. Sonny was right—Fox was a fuse, a crazy.

The fuse said, "Right here, Glenn. Right here. We're going to get you in the house, get you a doctor, get—" His voice broke; he shook his head fiercely though Alden surely couldn't have seen the gesture.

Sonny Quaid, leaning on the steaming hood of the Wagoneer, shook his head too, but in disgust. "Shai, get your goddamned 'asset' out of there so we can get the fucking casualty into the house!"

Quaid's tone snapped Fox to his feet and she heard Fox mutter something unintelligible as the asset from Turkey staggered back, bumped her, and then fixed Quaid with a stare: "Soviets, sir? Like Alvin Stevenson—meant for me? Is that it?"

Quaid snorted and hawked into the snow: "Fuck no, kid. You're looking at the best efforts of our own FBI."

Shai was pulling on Fox's hand, trying to get his attention, defer all speculation until later, when they were indoors and warm and Sonny didn't look like some soldier on the nightly news.

So she almost had Fox to the door before Quaid's words penetrated. Then she demanded: "FBI?"

Quaid was on Fox's other side, not touching the field collector who'd killed his station chief in Turkey, but obviously ready to intervene if Fox made a move toward Shai. The big Deputy's face looked ruddy, almost as if he had a bad sunburn that was peeling, due to the dried blood and sleet and, in places, specks of metal and concrete on his cheeks and among his five-o'clock shadow.

"That's why they call 'em the Fuckin' Bunch of Idiots, ain't it, boss?" Quaid's fury was barely in check.

Gallen understood that: she and Harrison Quaid were both bad losers; it was one of the things that made them so good at their jobs.

They crossed the threshold as Fox echoed, "FBI?" from behind them, but neither operations officer paid any attention.

Fox pressed the knuckles of his hands together as he stood in the driveway, but he followed the babysitters and their charge into the house after what he was sure was no more than a few seconds.

Glenn was already face down on the carpeted

floor of the living room, his trousers and under-shorts cut out of Mary's way with a knife which must have been very sharp indeed. There was a medical kit open beside the injured man, and Mike, holding down the small of Glenn's back with one hand, had just slapped the uninjured buttock with a morphine injector. Larry Fox swore under his breath as his friend twitched, but he couldn't quarrel with the fast, professional treatment.

There were two holes in the right cheek of Alden's butt, an entrance and exit only a finger's length apart and joined by a track of purple bruising. There was a smear of dried blood across most of the bared skin, patterned by the weave of his clothing, and there was a fresh, thick, seepage from both ends of the bullet's path—but nothing life-threatening, nothing guaranteeing permanent disability.

Fox knelt by Alden's head while Mary squeezed colorless antibiotic cream on both of the puckered bullet holes and Mike stripped the covering from a prepacked gauze wad.

Glenn clutched at the carpet; though the ointment was only a cool touch, shock and fear had scrambled the brain's expectation from physical stimuli. Fox took the nearer hand between both of his and said, "I think it's going to be okay, man. Gonna hurt, but I think it's okay."

Glenn opened his eyes. "Larry?" he said, gripping the hands that caressed his. "Goddamn, he said you needed help but I didn't have a *clue*. Goddamn." He let his head lie back on the floor, and though he didn't close his eyes again, morphine and trauma were already leaching away the consciousness behind them.

"Shouldn't 'a come, man," Fox said, squeezing shut his own eyelids. "*Jesus*, I'm sorry about this."

The lawyer raised his torso abruptly, bringing angry exclamations from the babysitters taping the gauze pack in place. "Jack Sneed, Larry," Alden said, "I got to thank him."

"Sneed?" Fox repeated in surprise.

"The guy you sent for me, the big guy," Alden explained.

"Sir, will you *please* lie down," Mary said in a sharp voice.

"I thought he was a real bastard," Alden whispered, obeying either the babysitter or the chemicals surging through his system, and letting himself droop flat again, eyes closing. "But when it started, he saved my life, lay right on top of me and drove us away while I hid. He's the sort of friend you need now, Larry. . . ."

"What I need," said Larry Fox too softly for even Mike and Mary to hear him, "is you in one piece again. That's all *I* need."

"—get that doctor we had for Fox out here," Gallen insisted as she and Quaid stepped into the hallway.

"—sure I don't need any doctor. Sic that quack on Alden, if you want. You and I have got to figure out why this happened, and what we want to say about it. There's more American bodies on E Street than I'm willing to account for as DCOPS; 'terrorist shoot-out' might barely cover our asses—*if* Snyder'll play along. If he doesn't, you can tell him for me that I'm planning to personally shoot his balls off with 'limited-issue armor piercings,' tubular penetrators and all. Or let 'em bite the damn bag on this one—say we don't know shit about what happened—for all I care."

"—could care less about covering any FBI mess," Gallen was talking at the same time, "if *they* don't care to tell me just who ordered an interdict and fucking *why*. Otherwise, Sonny, as far as I'm concerned, you're bunking in here or at Zero-profile Site One for the duration; we scramble everybody we can trust, including Noah Neely; and we're into operational phase on this go—we'll run LEMON PLEDGE until either we're dead or they're dead."

"I second *that* fucking motion," Quaid grinned bleakly and he grabbed Shai's elbow to spin her back against the wall, his .45 in one smooth motion drawn and pressed against the soft skin under her chin, forcing her head up.

"Now, Shai," Quaid gritted, "you want to tell me why you tried to kill me? And don't worry about Mike and Mary—I picked 'em. Cards go down, they're on my side of anybody's table."

"I didn't, Sonny. I don't know any more about this than you do." It wasn't easy to retort with the cold muzzle of Quaid's threaded .45 pressing against the tendons behind her jawbone, but it was eye-contact, not words, that were going to convince Sonny Quaid that Shai hadn't set him up.

And Quaid spent long moments looking at her, while she tried to judge which way his internal battle was going. Quaid, like Gallen, wanted an immediate target now that he'd been hurt; he wanted to win this one, find a culprit and vent righteous wrath. And he'd have to decide for himself that Shai wasn't the person he was looking for—no amount of conversation or protestation could do any good: both of them were professional liars, manipulators, nearly peerless deception agents.

So she didn't try to do more than relax her body as much as possible and let him think things through.

As suddenly as he had grabbed her, Quaid flung

himself away from the woman. "God *damn!*" he shouted to the opposite wall, then punched it with the heel of his left hand.

When he looked at Gallen again, the counterintelligence chief said, "Shaitan, you're going to push too far one day. You're really going too far."

She turned away, not because of the words, but because she was afraid she saw the beginnings of tears in Sonny Quaid's eyes.

OPERATION LEMON PLEDGE

Quaid spent half that night on the Fox/Alden/E Street debrief—which turned into a private brainstorming session with Gallen because Dick Luftsen had blown his brains out while Quaid was involved in an unwitting FBI reduction-of-force on E Street and, as a result, Kurt Blaustein was Crossfield's new Acting Director of Central Intelligence.

The Agency doctor who'd tended Fox took Quaid aside after he'd swaddled Alden's bottom—ostensibly to pick splinters of metal and concrete out of Quaid's face—and said, as he dialed a setting on a hand-held electromagnet and ran the humming device over Quaid's jaw, "Sir, I'd appreciate it if you'd call someone else next time. I can't write this up, Gallen says, and the situation's getting very . . . polarized, you understand."

Quaid, ignoring the needle-sharp pricks along his jaw as metal fragments, some too small to see, tore their way out of his subcutaneous layer to

221

join the magnet attracting them, grunted, "No, I
don't understand. Who's polarizing it?"

Gallen's kitchen, an affair of Delft blue and yellow tiles with ditsy little ships and tulips and
lighthouses on them, was lit by fluorescents. In
their harsh light, the doctor's complexion was waxy
yellow; every hair on his long nose stood out black
and every vein on his alcoholic-red cheeks shone
purple as he leaned close with needle-nose tweezers to remove by hand the shards of concrete which
the magnet couldn't lift from Quaid's abraded face.

"Who's polarizing it? Come now, sir. This house-
call is so Top Secret, I've been told, that I'm forbidden to log it. What am I supposed to do if someone
beeps me?" He tapped the beeper on his belt with
his left hand while probing deep in Quaid's cheek
with the tweezers in his right. "Say I'm busy patch-
ing up a butt-shot civilian with enough legal recourse to make public knowledge of whatever you're
doing here, the entire . . . situation? A situation
that various supergrades aren't going to be rippingly
pleased about, unless your face and Counselor
Alden's bottom aren't the result of what I think
they are: today's E Street—"

Quaid said, "You're not paid to think. You're
paid to doctor. The assumption—Blaustein's or anyone else's—is that you're doing your job. CI doesn't
answer to anybody, not even Blaustein himself, on
specifics, unless it's through me." A grunt came
out of Quaid unbidden; it felt as though the medic
had removed the Statue of Liberty from beneath
his right eye.

"Hurt, did it?" said the doctor with more satisfaction than solicitousness. "Sure you wouldn't like
a local anaesthetic?"

"No thanks. My nerves are plenty frayed as it is.
Go on, get the rest of 'em out. Then go home and

tell your wife you had a couple late ones with the boys."

A long-suffering look came and went on the Agency doctor's face. "I've never been involved in anything like this before, you know. It's one thing to monitor psychochemical interrogations or patch up foreign—"

"Don't tell me your troubles. You could have had a nice civilian practice—doctoring old ladies with arthritis and politicians with gouty feet. It's too late for second thoughts, unless Blaustein's ready to stick a needle in your arm?" Quaid laid the question carefully, at the end of a long line of emotional triggers, then waited.

"No, it's not that—this one's going to pinch a little; don't flinch."

"Right," Quaid said dryly while the doctor probed with what felt like a twelve-inch hot needle and pain lanced up into his brain from the sensitive skin around his upper lip.

"It's not that, *yet.* . . ." the medic continued, and Quaid realized that the man wanted assurances that he'd be protected from whoever was doling out the sort of punishment he'd been brought here to treat. "Blaustein personally put a team together to handle the Luftsen autopsy and I should have been on it—they *expected* me to be there. I had to do some pretty fancy footwork to get out of it. Can you promise me that what's going on here—that what I'm doing—is fully cleared?" Straightening up, a hand to his back, the doctor held out the bloody hemostat for Quaid's inspection. Between its pincers was a jagged piece of concrete with little gobs of flesh stuck to it.

"You bet," Quaid said, wiping his sweating upper lip reflexively with the back of his hand, which came away blood-streaked as the doctor looked up.

"Don't *do* that, please. I've only got three more to go; if you introduce a septic—"

"When will Alden be fit to travel?"

The doctor grimaced. "He's fit for a smooth automobile ride to the nearest facility, as long as he doesn't put too much pressure on the wound. He could use another pint or two and a few days rest. What kind of—"

"And Fox? Status report?" Quaid wasn't here to answer questions, not about Blaustein's bumbling progress toward defeating OPERATION LEMON PLEDGE through standard KGB countermeasures, not about the legitimacy of Gallen's CI moves, not about Fox or anything else. Though he'd have given his eyeteeth and half of his trigger finger to know whether Blaustein knew so much as the name LEMON PLEDGE, or was just moving from point to point, like an avalanche that fortuitously buries everything in its path—in this case, Kunayev, Platt, Sabanci, various Turkish and Tadzhik nationals, a Canadian staffer named Stevenson, half of FBI's "elite" antiterrorist squad, and maybe (though there was no damned way to prove it), Dick Luftsen.

It would have lightened Sonny Quaid's mood if the doctor torturing him for God and Country, Glenn Alden and Larry Fox could be added to that list. But you lose more than you win in the Game—a rule of thumb which seemed to be holding annoyingly true.

The status report on Fox was guarded—the doctor thought his patient had flushed most of the psychochemicals and that stress-related imbalances in his blood chemistries were beginning to normalize—in other words, that Fox could be expected to behave in his "normal range." But the doctor, true to form, was unwilling to hazard a guess as to what Fox's normal range of behavior might be.

Another item of business running true-to-form was Shai Gallen. When the doctor opened the slatted kitchen doors with a flourish and announced that he was done, Gallen was all over Quaid: kissy-face to the max, cooing and petting and letting him know how much she cared, while M-1 rubbed around his legs with uncharacteristic affection.

"Sonny, let's go upstairs. We'll move them in the morning—Alden's half-drugged and Fox needs some time to calm down. And," a smile danced at the corners of her mouth, "so do I."

He didn't argue. The bitch about Gallen was that, when all was said and done, he'd rather lay her flat than any ten other women he could think of, his wife included. She was good in bed, not simply by nature, but by acquired expertise, and not even that bothered him.

The muscles she'd developed weren't only in her thighs, but it was a more than physical stimulation which kept him coming back to her despite the sure knowledge that someday their affair was going to reach Number One on Quaid's list of problems to be solved.

It was that, when he spread her legs, he was entering a sort of forbidden zone: Gallen was his equal in some ways, or as close to an equal as Quaid could acknowledge—equally smart, perhaps; equally dangerous, for certain.

So when he said to her, "Jesus, Shai, we're going to kill each other one of these days," in a hoarse voice as he entered her, he knew he wasn't being misunderstood.

She said, "Sonny, shut up and fuck me," and it was just one more double entendre in a relationship he hadn't the strength to break off—or the courage.

As long as they were lovers, she wasn't going to roll over and decide he was the enemy—at least, he didn't think she would. As long as he was one of her close confidants, he had a chance of staying on top of things. As long as LEMON PLEDGE was an operational feasibility—and especially now, when it was going on line—he had to stay on top of things.

He kept trying to figure out some way to save her, though—to spare her the inevitable end of an operation she wouldn't let slide. He didn't want to think about her fine body lying lifeless, whether it was through a calm, State-sponsored execution, methodical and supposedly humanitarian, or by virtue of some street-corner shoot-out like the one he'd been in today.

When she pulled his head down to her breast, salty with perspiration, and he could hear her quick heartbeat and a low growl of climax begin deep in her chest, he really wished he hadn't come up here tonight. It had been easier to think about end-game strategies when Fox was monopolizing her time and affection.

But then, he admitted as he bore down on his own sphincter muscles and delved as deeply as he could into her, she'd know that.

When they lay side by side, her head in the crook of his arm, she began to talk about the move in the morning, and about Fox's future, and he felt something shrink and then harden inside him.

"Shaitan, I'm going home for a while—get my things, lay some deep context with my wife, in case anybody noses around asking questions." He rolled away, off the bed, and began searching for his clothes.

"Shit," he muttered. In passion, they'd forgotten—*he'd* forgotten—to hang up his pants and M-1 had found them.

"What?" she said, and: "Oh, *no*, Sonny. I'm sorry. I'll rinse them—"

And she was out of bed, turning on lights as she went, his soiled pants in hand, toward the bathroom.

M-1 was curled up under a Greek Revival chair in one corner, an eye cocked at him balefully, tail lashing.

"You're dead, motherfucker—history," Quaid promised M-1 under his breath and wondered how the hell that overweight hairball could manage to look like it was smiling at him.

An hour later, in dried but still redolent pants, he wheeled the shot-up Wagoneer out into the predawn gloom: he couldn't leave it at Gallen's, and he didn't want to call for an Agency tow-truck and another car.

Fox had been awake when he left, puttering around Gallen's kitchen in his skivvies as if he were still in Turkey.

"Hiya, Quaid, Shai. Couldn't sleep." Fox's boyish grin had made Quaid want to strangle the GS-11 on the spot.

The kid didn't seem jealous, hostile, tense, or even crazy right then, but he was too damned proprietary about Gallen's kitchen to suit Sonny Quaid, who'd been lying in with Gallen for years and still wouldn't think of raiding her refrigerator uninvited at four in the morning, or scanning for news on her World-band, or of feeding that damned cat cold rack of lamb from the plate Fox had made for himself and set on the table.

There was small talk Quaid found unreasonably annoying, coffee prepared by Fox he couldn't drink, and an awkward farewell—Shai wouldn't give him more than an upper-class hug with Fox looking on.

Quaid's last image of Gallen's house was one of that damned kid leaning against the staircase, half naked, with a ten-inch carving knife gleaming in his hand and Shaitan walking toward him, her high rump swaying under a red satin kimono.

Hell, Quaid thought to himself, bundled up but shivering at the wind roaring through the blown-out windshield, a wind even the Wagoneer's sub-arctic heating package couldn't warm, *maybe they'll make it to Zero Site One. And maybe that damned psycho will slice up the whole lot—Gallen, the babysitters, and Alden—before they get there. And maybe I don't give a shit.*

But he did, and ambivalence gnawed at him all the way home like a rat caught between a hot pan and somebody's belly during an African interrogation session.

When he got home, dawn was breaking. Still, Lucille was grateful to see him, smudge-eyed with worry, and bereft of questions, though she covered her mouth with her hand when first she got a good look at his face. Somebody had called, and she had a number for him.

He knew whose it was, and it meant he had to go right out—it was the kind of return call he made only from payphones. Lucille hugged him at the door and she was trembling.

He thought it might have been because of the implications of the wounds on his face, or because she'd glimpsed the ravaged Wagoneer parked outside on the circular drive, or heard the news reports of the E Street fiasco. He was pretty sure she couldn't have seen the bodies of the Wagoneer's former driver and his backup, shrouded in Army blankets as he'd directed because neither of the babysitters he'd given Gallen had the clout or the clearance to avoid questions and explanations while delivering shot-up corpses to Langley—not a pair whose ID said they had been seconded to the Agency through ISA, not after what had happened to their teammates on E Street.

But it wasn't his face, the car, the bodies or the evening news that was bothering his wife.

He knew because she managed to say what was on her mind: "You still love me, don't you, Sonny?"

And he was so relieved he managed to put some fervor in his response: "More than ever, Lucy."

And he did love her, although maybe not the way she meant. She was his wife and he'd take care of her, no matter what happened. He said that, too, and didn't understand why, when he looked back through the spidery shards of the remaining fly-window on the Wagoneer, she was standing on the threshold, clutching her flannel bathrobe, with tears rolling down her tired, forty-ish face.

When Quaid had left Gallen's a little after four in the morning, he'd looked like the devil incarnate and the farewell stare he'd given Larry Fox was full of death.

When Gallen left, two hours later, for her Georgetown office, she looked like an avenging angel and the kiss she gave him was full of life.

Alone in her house with the two babysitters who wouldn't talk to him, M-1 who couldn't talk to him, and Glenn Alden, who by doctor's orders wasn't supposed to be disturbed, Fox paced the carpeted halls until the sun came up and Mary started fixing breakfast, muttering about the mess he'd made in the kitchen.

He retreated upstairs then, thinking that he

wished he had a gun. He'd never carried one in Turkey, though there were those who did. More trouble than it was worth, he'd said. The truth of it was, he hadn't wanted to think he lived in a world of lethal violence, because he knew very well from the Lebanon what he was like when he got into that mindset.

Ed Platt and a variety of Turks and Russians had learned what Fox was like in that mode. It might be that President James Crossfield had that lesson yet to come.

He considered watching the news on the TV in his room to see if it reflected in any way the briefing he'd been privy to last night, when neither Gallen nor Quaid were too concerned about who overheard what. Then he heard Mary coming up the stairs, stepped into the hall and saw she had a tray in hand, and barred her path: "For Glenn? I'll take it."

The woman seemed about to spit at him, but she handed over the tray with only, "You're so anxious to do my job for me, 'sir,' why don't you do the dishes when you get done delivering this?" and stomped back down the stairs.

Whistling, Fox took the tray into Alden's room, balancing it on one hand while he opened the door.

Mike, sitting just inside the door, looked up and frowned.

"Changing of the guard," Fox said lightly and very quietly: on the double bed Mike and Mary had been sharing, Alden lay stretched out on his side, chest rising and falling evenly as if in deep sleep. "Go get yourself something to eat."

"Where's Mary?" Mike said uncertainly, but stood up.

"Downstairs. Go on. He's my friend, after all."

Mike flicked his head toward the wounded lawyer. "I'm glad I'm not—look where it got him."

Fox didn't respond, just stared at Alden's baby-sitter until the tall dark man left, closing the door behind him.

Alone with Alden, Fox fought a moment of vertigo as all the self-recrimination and doubt he'd been holding in abeyance threatened to overwhelm him. His throat tightened and memories flashed before him, out of sequence and as wrenching as if his mind were trying to vomit them up: Kathie being blown to shreds in their apartment; Sabanci, bled out over a latrine, swinging slowly back and forth; a hand coming at him, horny with callus; Barker's face as his hands were bound behind him; Platt, terror-stricken in the mission's vault; Shai, toying with her glasses in a musty Glebe Road motel room. And Shai again, her face swimming because Fox was too drugged to be able to focus his eyes, telling him "It's all right," after a three-day interrogation that hadn't been all right at all.

And now Glenn, shot up and brought into something that wasn't his fault, and wouldn't have been any of his business except for Larry Fox.

He wasn't sure if he was sorriest about involving Alden—when he dreamed about Kathie, he still woke up in a cold sweat, even after three days of virtually complete R&R, broken only by Gallen's visits. But he felt pretty bad about what had happened to his friend and he hadn't had any time alone with Glenn to say so, or explain anything.

So he took the tray to the bedside table and turned on the massive Chinese porcelain lamp with happy little coolies dancing around it. "Hey, Glenn? Rise and shine." What did you say at a time like this?

Glenn opened one bleary eye, then closed it:

"Larry. I had the damnedest dream. . . . Ow!" Rolling to his back to stretch, Alden had put weight on his bandaged right cheek.

"Oh, man, I'm sorry about . . ." Fox trailed off. About what? What *could* he say? About the hole in your ass, old buddy? About siccing my friends and enemies on you? About you, half-drugged, sitting in on last night's very classified brief/debrief? About the way Quaid was looking at you like a piece of incriminating evidence that ought to be disposed of? He continued lamely: "Brought you some breakfast."

The whole place was assuredly bugged by at least Gallen's people, who weren't exactly handling things with kid gloves. As for other listeners. . . . He hesitated to finish the thought, because suddenly his mind went into gear—a familiar gear that said, *Run like hell. Take Glenn and get the fuck out of here—go to ground. Gallen can't help you. She's fighting for at least her professional life. And it's your fault. Quaid's right. . . .*

Then Glenn levered himself up and, groaning exaggeratedly, rubbed his face with both hands. From behind them came a muffled, "Larry, old son, I used to think you had all the fun. Now I know better—" Alden shifted squarely onto his left hip, cocked an elbow, and patted the sheet beside him. "Slide that tray over here, friend, and let's have some Channel 13 with breakfast."

There wasn't any broadcast on 13, just snow and white noise. It took Fox a second to realize that Alden would know that, then he grinned, "Good idea, Glenn," placed the tray carefully and went to turn on the TV set.

With the volume control up full, they might well be shielded against bugging devices. If not, there was nothing for it—they had to have this conversation, anyway.

When he came back to Alden's bedside, Glenn said, "There's a notebook and pen in my suit coat . . ." and pointed to the partly open closet.

Fox, sheepish because he should have been thinking of these things (*he* was the Agency collector; Glenn just liked to read spy novels), went to get the notebook.

When he handed it to Alden, Glenn wrote, *Get us out of here?* while saying, "You don't think that Gallen woman was serious last night—about dumping those corpses in the Wagoneer on Blaustein's desk?"

Fox shook his head and took the pen, writing, *Where to? Where's safe?* as he said, "She might, don't kid yourself. I don't really know her that well, though."

"Could have fooled me," Alden teased wryly, a gleam of laughter flickering in his eyes as he scribbled, *Anywhere that isn't a war zone.* "If I don't call my wife tonight, they'll be dragging the Potomac for me. Sneed—*Quaid* knows it, too. Didn't it strike you odd how Gallen kept insisting that it was Blaustein who was behind what happened to me—to Quaid and his guys—on E Street and Quaid kept chalking it up to crossed wires?"

"Chalk it up to *my* bad luck," Fox said ruefully and meant it. "And yours for knowing me, I guess. Sorry 'bout that." Both of them were afraid of emotion; and Fox could care less about eyebrows rising at his offhand callousness if the conversation were reviewed on tape. Besides, he was concentrating on his answering scribble: *You're right—it's a war, but I don't know even who's declared it, who to trust except Shai. Wait till she gets back.* He handed the pad back to Alden, who crumpled the single piece of paper in his fist, then said in an exaggerated imitation of Peter Lorre: "You must eat this, now, before my very eyes!" and offered him the sheet on which they'd both written.

Fox held out one palm for the ball of paper, then tore the next three blank sheets off the pad and took all of them to the bathroom, where he methodically tore and flushed the lot.

Coming back, he said over the roar of the toilet, "Glenn, I say again: I'm sorry, man. But I didn't know where else to turn. . . ."

"I've always wanted a scar like this—'wounded in the line of duty.' I'll get lots of mileage out of it. Forget it. We're friends, aren't we?"

"Oh yeah. Hey, Glenn, did the doctor give you any shots?" Fox rubbed his arm, where three warm bumps just below his shoulder joint were still tender.

"Shots? You mean as in tetanus, or as in rabies?" When Fox didn't answer, Glenn added, "No, I don't think so, anyway. Why?"

"I don't know, no . . . yeah, I *do*—that is, maybe I'm going somewhere soon . . . like Africa or somewhere . . . and I sort of wondered whether you were, too. You're in this pretty deep now, Glenn, and—Aw, fuck it." It had been hard to ask the question, and now Fox regretted it. He'd heard the Kalahari mentioned, but not to him directly. And nobody would tell him just what his part of LEMON PLEDGE was going to be, or when or where he was supposed to do whatever he was supposed to do. His mind shied away from speculation. He shouldn't be assuming anything, not now, not at all. And he shouldn't succumb to the impulse to use Glenn like some kind of secular confessor—Glenn was in enough trouble because of him.

"Check," said the lawyer. "Let's talk about what

that little session I overheard last night—between you and the Agency brass you hang out with—means and what a citizen in your position can command in the way of Constitutional rights. And you can turn the TV off while we do it."

Fox noticed, for the first time, the anger seething in his friend, an anger that had been there, but which Fox's own guilt had deemed meant for him. He should have known better: Glenn was his friend and somehow it made him feel better to know that a little thing like a slug up the ass couldn't change that.

Glenn Alden angrily tapped CLEAR on the living-room telephone's automatic dialing pad. "I can't raise repair service, much less my house," he snapped. "I don't know about you, Larry, but I'm beginning to get cabin fever."

Fox looked at his friend, considering the dangers of a world in which people shot at other people . . . and, more prosaically, the air temperature and the probable state of the road surfaces. The shooting was an aberration, despite reminders by the aches of his own body and the leprous patches of styptic cream on Alden's face where Mike had plucked out bits of glass and metal with tweezers. Fox had ridden motorcycles regularly for so long that the ways they could kill and maim the unwary were matters of perpetual concern.

"Me, too," he said aloud. "How's your fanny?"

Alden grimaced. "I wish it belonged to somebody else right now, but it doesn't hurt *more* if I sit than if I stand. Can't walk any distance, though."

"Then let's go for a bike ride," Fox said. "Ought to be a pay phone around that's working. Trouble with all the fancy hardware—" Lord knew how many different ways the communications at Gallen's house were shielded—"is that it doesn't work a lot of the time."

Mary, who had disappeared with Mike a few minutes before strode back into the room. "I don't think you'd better do that just now, sir," she said with no more obsequiousness than the bare 'sir.' She began keying a number into the telephone Alden had just given up on.

"That doesn't work," said the lawyer. "That's why we wanted to get out. Part of the reason."

"Look," said Larry Fox, angry at the way the "maid" ignored his friend, "the bikes are here to be used. You want to tag along in the van, that's fine, but—"

"Mike, this line doesn't work either," the woman called toward the hallway. The handset slipped when she tried to replace it in the cradle, and slipped a second time before her fingers managed to align it properly.

"Gail," called Mike's voice from the study at the far end of the hall, "are the curtains drawn in there? We've got movement in the back again and this time it's not going away."

"Who's Gail?" asked Alden before Fox touched his friend on the shoulder to silence him and to reassure them both by the contact. The livingroom drapes were closed, but all three of them checked with nervous eyes to be sure of what they already knew.

The maid swore very softly and took a small pistol from a pocket concealed in the folds of her dark skirt.

Glenn Alden sucked in his lips for a moment, then said, "I suppose there's some sort of emergency communications system in this house?" his voice rising on a note of hope as well as question.

"Not any more," Gail/Mary responded grimly,

even as Mike stepped into the livingroom carrying
an automatic rifle in one hand as he tried to stuff
an additional loaded magazine into the pocket of a
quilted jacket which was not intended for the
purpose.

"We've got to get out of here," said the male
babysitter.

"You'd better get us guns, too," Larry Fox said,
then turned from Mike to Alden and added, "Glenn,
can you shoot?"

"Mike, if they're waiting out there we don't have
a prayer of getting clear," the woman snapped,
looking up at her partner as her free hand opened
the cabinet beneath the telephone.

"I don't know," said the lawyer, answering a
question more basic than the one Fox had thought
he was asking. Alden splayed his fingers and
squeezed together their tips, watching the exercise
with determination.

"M-Mary, they're not just out there to make us
nervous. If we don't make a break now—"

"The house is safer than the van!" the woman
said, taking a worn Beretta Brigadier from the
cabinet and handing it to Fox. If the heavy pistol
weren't the one Shai had worn in Israeli service, it
was one just like it, thought the young CIA officer
as he took the weapon.

"Wait a minute," he said, waving a hand between the two babysitters to interrupt the argu-
ments poised on the open mouths of both. "There're
three bikes—do either of you ride?"

The babysitters glanced at one another, the
woman blankly and the man with a grimace of
self-disgust which cleared as he said aloud, "But
that might be it, the diversion . . .?"

"We can't let him do it," the woman said, glancing from her partner to the curtained windows,

then toward Fox himself striding into the kitchen where the motorcycle helmets sat atop the refrigerator. She followed her charge, continuing over her shoulder to Mike, "She'd have our *scalps*. We're supposed to be guarding him, not sending him out to get his—"

Gail/Mary probably had enough control over her tongue not to have completed the sentence in any case, but Glenn Alden chose to forestall her by limping past and saying, "Got room for a passenger then?"

Fox paused with the black dome of a full-coverage helmet in his hand and looked back toward his friend. Gallen's cat, M-1, curled on the counter, raised up and butted his head solidly against the man's wrist to get attention. Fox absently kneaded the thick ruff of fur at the cat's throat, setting the Beretta down to do so.

"Look, he's got a damned good chance," said Mike, following the others with more positive enthusiasm than anybody else in the house showed at the moment. "He goes out the *side* door, the bike ought to clear, and off through the orchard. We give them about two seconds to think about that one and we go *bam*, straight up the drive before they're set again."

"Glenn, this time I don't think the extra weight's a great idea," said Larry Fox with a false smile and a horrifying mental vision of the bullets hitting him, plucking him and the huddled passenger off the bike as it, riderless, careened through the night. The van probably had more than just the usual sheet metal for protection . . . but at least it had the sheet metal.

Gail/Mary swore again. "Then we'd better do it while the garage is still clear," she said angrily. She stepped to the outside door.

"Hold a minute," Fox said, nervous at what he was about to say and nervous that he had to say it, but they weren't bikers and they couldn't have been expected to understand the *fragility* of a motorcycle. If he tried to run through woods in the dark, he'd be lucky to get twenty yards before being slammed to the ground by an obstacle which a car could have bulled through with only cosmetic damage. "The side door, sure. But I turn up the drive then. You pull out and cut for the back. It's as likely to confuse them, and it's a lot more—I think it'll work better for me."

"We'll rendevous at—" Gail/Mary began.

"The office of the Best Western on Glebe Road," Larry Fox interrupted, the only location he could think of instantly which was not a government building. He was not going to try to memorize the out-of-the-way address of another safe house; and for that matter, he wasn't going to trust himself to another Agency location just at the moment.

Not that he was likely to reach the end of Shai Gallen's driveway alive.

"Garage is clear," Mike echoed after glancing at the telltale he wore as a lavalier, previously hidden beneath his shirt.

"Larry," said Glenn Alden and tossed one of the down jackets he had retrieved from the livingroom. "Don't freeze to death, hey?"

"The pistol," Mike reminded, gesturing toward the Beretta still on the counter. M-1 reached out in an attempt to grab both attention and the pointing finger.

"Come *on*," said Gail/Mary, opening the door down into the garage. The van's iridescently-polarized panels hid the motorcycles on the other side of it.

"Goddamnit!" Fox snapped, "I don't have a free

hand for it, do I? Doesn't matter." Even if there were a holster for the big service pistol, he had neither time to strap it on—nor need, as he had said too bluntly. He was going to die, and of course everybody did—and he just wished that everybody'd stop fucking *around.*

Fox bolted into the garage, catching his heel on the last step because the helmet cut off a cone of his normal downward vision. He caught himself with a palm against the side of the van. Someone touched his shoulder and he turned, peripheral vision limited also by the helmet that would not stop bullets however much Fox wanted to believe that it would. . . .

"From Mike," said Glenn, offering a snub-nosed revolver, an alloy-framed Smith and Wesson like the one Fox had carried through the Lebanon. "Keep your pocket warm, too. I'll lug the big one."

Larry Fox fumbled as he thrust the snubbie beneath his jacket, into the pocket of his shirt where it rubbed the scar left by the earlier weapon. "Keep your head down," he said as he turned back to the motorcycles. Neither man attempted to shake hands or meet the other's eyes.

While the van doors opened and closed behind him with a satisfying, bank-vault, inertia, Fox gave his attention to his own vehicle. Only one of the three bikes was suitable for the present task. The first was a dual purpose machine with low gearing and a long-travel suspension for use in the woods. The second was a touring bike with plush seats and enormous, vibration-free power—the machine he would have chosen to carry Glenn and himself to a pay phone and cups of convenience-store coffee.

The third motorcycle was one Fox had read about but had never dreamed of stepping astride as he now did. He choked the single carburetor and the engine fired with only a quick dab at the electric starter.

The bike was dimensionally as small as the Jawa he rode in Turkey, and it weighed far less because the frame was hand-built from boron composite and most of the engine, a half-liter square four, was ceramic. Between the cylinder banks nestled the crankshaft-driven supercharger which was the heart of the bike, literally as well as figuratively. When the AMA opened Superbike racing to blown engines, Suzuki had homologated this model. It had promptly blown the doors off normally-aspirated machines of twice the displacement as well as the competition's attempts to meet the new rules with exhaust-driven turbochargers. The supercharger's instant response across the whole powerband made it the hottest thing on wheels. Quaid must have pulled some strings to get one of the few copies not in the hands of factory racing teams.

It did not make its rider bullet-proof, however.

Fox closed the choke lever and straddle-walked the bike to face the pedestrian door at the side of the garage. With just the van and the motorcycles inside the three-car structure, maneuvering was easy enough—but there was still the problem of how to open the inward-swinging panel against which his headlight now cut a rectangle of brightness. Even as he poised, Mike stepped into the side-scatter of the light and reached for the latch with the hand which was not on the pistol grip of his M16. Fox blipped his throttle and nodded. The engine between his legs responded with an intake whine like the squall of a hungry tigress.

Mike snatched the door open.

Fox's launch was complicated by the fact that he needed to turn in the slush and dead leaves just outside the door. Concentrating on that made it possible to ignore the threat of shots which he could not have heard over the engine anyway. Everything but the instruments and the wedge thrown by his headlight was impenetrably black by contrast; it would have been easy to pretend that there was nothing waiting but the night itself. . . .

The Suzuki's clutch was lightning sudden and the engine so peaky and willing that Fox overshot his intended turning point by several yards. When he braked on the slick surface the back end broke away, forcing him to pivot on his right foot like a dirt-track racer. The bike spun in a rooster tail of mud and wet leaves. A spark flicked across the field of view of the rider hunched on the solo seat—a round fired by a marksman fooled into believing the motorcycle was headed off into the orchard as it had been initially pointed.

Fox gave the engine a full handful of throttle. It responded like the wing of a bumblebee hovering, converting enormous power into vibration with scarcely the least component of forward motion. The rear wheel spun and howled, skidding from side to side in soil like a snake throwing itself across a sheet of glass. Spray from the wheel mounted thirty feet in the air and dribbled back into the glare of the headlight.

Then the tire caught the edge of the concrete driveway and shot the vehicle ahead with a suddenness that would have stripped Fox away were it not for the step molded into the seat to hold his butt against even that level of acceleration. Front wheel a hand's breadth off the ground for all the rider's attempts to shift his weight to anchor it, rear tire shrieking and burning in a cloud as opaque as the spray of moments before, the motorcycle tore a path down the driveway.

Past the gunmen who stitched the air and the

garage door behind him from the heavy cars waiting in the street; past the attaché case left midway along the drive, just beside the concrete.

The vibration of an engine revving to twelve grand blurred the distinction between Larry Fox's bare palms and the rubber grips, making of bike and rider an extraordinary unity. The sport fairing and low bars doubled him over the gas tank in a fetal position which seemed more natural than anything else could have at the moment. The car parked to the left of the drive was a lump of darkness with the smoky red glare of muzzle flashes at its heart, submachineguns firing through ports beneath the armored windows—unable to track a target moving as fast as the motorcycle, even in a low-deflection shot.

He was going faster than he dreamed at the end of the drive, too fast to make the square turn into the street. He chopped the throttle and clamped down on the brakes anyway, laying the bike over to the left in what he was sure would end up a low-side get-off rather than a turn. For a moment, the bike and rider poised as inertia balanced the grip of the tire's contact patches against the pavement. The back end shimmied in snow packed in the curb cut, but the wide tires had tread most of the way up their sidewalls: they were intended, like the motorcycle itself, for purposes which would have been abuse for most similar items. They bit and held as Fox, a perfect target for that instant of stasis, dropped the hammer again.

He had not felt so much alive, so powerful, since before the first punch doubled him up in Mehmet Sabanci's shop. He short-shifted, unable to believe that the crank spun as high as it seemed to want to or that the engine was not in the heart of the powerband when it was accelerating him like a catapult. The quiet street was a tunnel the width of his headlight; and Larry Fox, oblivious of the possibility of other traffic and the killers behind him scrambling in vain for a shot, punched his course down that tunnel in triumph.

He was alive. Dear God, for the first time he was *alive*.

As soon as the sidewash of the motorcycle headlight flecked the translucent doors of the garage, Gail/Mary shifted the van into Drive with the engine already turning 4,000 RPM. Stray bullets punched across the garage, one of them humming like a cable stretched to parting when it ricocheted from a beam. Then the van's blunt nose smashed its own way through the fiberglass paneling. The door's bolting mechanism held for an instant before it spun sideways toward the front of the house, a set of giant shears which sectioned a gunman who had jumped from cover to blaze away at the motorcycle.

The van's back door was swinging. Alden reached to grab it across the sprawl of Mike and his M16, jumping back into the vehicle even as it accelerated. The driver braked hard and spun the wheel left, toward the side of the garage and the hope of at least piercing the immediate cordon. Breaking inertia slammed the door and flung the lawyer toward the front of the van. Bullets were hitting in sudden packets like the first touch of a rainstorm, but the armor held though side panels rang and the glass starred above them.

Shards of fiberglass fluttered in the air while the van rocked on its beefed-up suspension under the level of turning force Gail/Mary was demanding of it.

Then the doughnut of plastic explosive in the

briefcase further up the driveway went off in a blinding flash. The shockwave shattered windows for a half mile in every direction and forged the twenty-pound steel plate with it in the case into a white-hot projectile ripping through the poised van the long way.

The aluminum block of the transverse engine disintegrated as it took the first shock of the steel bolt. Molten gobbets of it sprayed the passenger compartment along with a fine emulsion of the fuel and lubricant. The projectile itself made no more of the van's Lexan-toughened rear window than it did the chest of Glenn Alden through which it had flickered a microsecond earlier.

The impact lifted the front wheels, but the vehicle still spun ten degrees further into the turn it had begun before the explosive mixture in the passenger compartment bulged the sides against its red-orange pressure. A man from one of the waiting cars ran forward and emptied his submachinegun into the van from ten feet away. The sharp muzzle blasts were completely overwhelmed by the roar of fuel and plastics and bodies burning.

Cars began to pull away from the curb, still picking up additional passengers. The gunmen of Directorate V had been temporarily deafened by their own mine, even those who were protected by the armoring of the vehicles; but they did not need to hear the sirens to know that emergency vehicles were on the way.

Alone in the house, Shai Gallen's cat began to yowl.

Gallen had been invited to "tea in the executive dining room, 1600 sharp."

She spent the day fishing for confirmation that it was, as Quaid was certain, an interdepartmental screw-up that had caused the E-Street mess, reading the headlines in the paper which decried this latest incidence of domestic terrorism, and trying to get Special Agent Snyder on the phone—an impossibility, for some reason—to help her batten down the details of the impromptu terrorist deception Quaid had started and then left to her. Sonny's secretary said that he was home sleeping. Shai didn't blame him.

It was a weird day in Gallen's Georgetown office: all her incoming calls had to do with the Kalahari Power Station junket Crossfield was making just before the Summit; none of them had to do with E Street. Somebody should have brought E Street to her attention, for clearance to act if nothing else, but nobody did. It was as if Shai Gallen existed in a counter-universe in which E Street had never happened. If not for the print and electronic media, like a dog with a bone on the subject, she could have convinced herself that she'd dreamed the whole thing.

Maybe, she told herself, it was Sonny's people, shielding her. After all, domestic matters were the province of the CI staff, only her problem if they couldn't handle it. So she shuffled papers and talked to various Regional Commands abroad, handling standard stuff and waiting for Noah Neely to return her call because Noah could take her mind off the meeting with Blaustein set for 1600 hours at Langley.

When she got back from lunch, Noah's office had called and left a message: Doctor Neely wouldn't be in his office all day. Would Mrs. Gallen consider dropping by his house for cocktails after work? When Shai questioned Noah's assistant, she learned that Crossfield's Chief Intelligence Advisor had taken on the responsibility of arranging Dick Luftsen's funeral, since Luftsen's wife was a pill-popping neurotic, and that, the assistant was certain, was why he wasn't available.

She had to accept the excuse, as she had to ignore the ominous implications of her summons to Langley, and the fact that no one from Langley had called her office all day, not even Sonny's CI people.

When she got to Langley, the sun was setting and the squat office building looked altogether too much like the new KGB headquarters outside of Moscow.

Getting out of her car, rebellious enough to leave it right in front of the building under the OFFICIAL USE ONLY sign, she swore to herself that, when this was over, she was going to tote up her unused sickleave and spend a month in Bora Bora or Andorra—someplace out of the Continental US where nothing ever happened and where nobody could find her to convince her otherwise.

She'd never imagined that Blaustein would have cleared the supergrades' dining room: there was nobody in that yellow-papered expanse but Blaustein, presiding over a buffet that included Bismarcks and petits fours, cucumber sandwiches and fruit paté, but had nothing so simple as a piece of dry toast, which was all Gallen's stomach could tolerate.

She took a croissant instead and filled her tea cup, conscious as she made her way among the empty tables set for fifty that Blaustein looked like nothing so much as Humpty Dumpty before the fall, down where the windows met and she had a great view of the parking lot lights coming on, chasing back the early dusk and illuminating the trees beyond.

The nice thing about Langley was that you could

bring your gun to tea—everybody was equally paranoid above the third floor, and there wasn't a metal detector in the room. Angleton used to handcraft fishing flies and gun leathers, refuse to write up reports on his ongoings, and, some said, open America's mail. That was how they'd gotten rid of the best DDO in CIA's history, anyway . . . by claiming he'd initiated a program of domestic surveillance in disregard of chartered restrictions. Gallen fully expected to find herself slapped with some similar trumped-up charge and summarily separated, on the spot, somewhere between the time Blaustein waved her to the seat opposite him and the time he finished his Bismarck and tea.

Otherwise, there'd have been no need to clear the room of diners and yet have so many big waiter-types lounging around the buffet and in the doorway to the kitchen.

So when Blaustein said, "My dear girl, you're looking very tired this evening," she didn't answer, just nodded.

"Rough night?" Blaustein postulated.

It was so obvious a taunt that Shai pulled her croissant apart, holding it almost at eye level as it unwound and the soft middle came away in her hands: "Nothing I can't handle, sir. Condolences are in order, I suppose, despite the fact that you've benefitted most directly from Dick's . . . death." She wasn't about to say "suicide." If Blaustein wanted to see her come into line, he'd better show her a damned good reason.

"Thank you, my dear," the Acting Director said pedantically, folding his hands in the face of death so that he looked like nothing so much as a medieval gargoyle. "And now, to business. We're embarking upon the inevitable reorganization that attends every change in Directors," Blaustein purred. "And, my dear, I've got just the slot for you—one which will make use of your many god-given talents, which we've been wasting in clandestine services. We want you out there where you can shine, where you'll be able to represent the entire Agency, be the spokes . . . *person* we want and need right—"

"Kurt, I want you to know that I have no intention of transferring out of Directorate. If you want a new DDO, that's fine, I can understand. I even approve. But I'm not willing or able to—"

"Let me be the judge of that."

Gallen dropped the croissant she'd been holding and it made a dull *ping* as it hit her plate. She put her head in her open palms and blinked back unwanted, girlish tears. She'd never been fired from any job; she wasn't prepared for the way it felt to look at someone and know they were going to discharge you for poor performance—even when that someone was Blaustein and his definition of performance differed so radically from hers. She kept from biting her lip or throwing her food at him with an equal effort of will—the last she managed before chemical panic, generated by her stalemated impulses to fight or flee, took over and she sat, numb and helpless, unable to summon a cogent thought, as Blaustein intoned her fate.

"We want you in the public's eye, my dear. We want and need a new image and President Crossfield agrees with my assessment that you're the perfect asset to project that image. You'll be lobbying Congress, dealing with the Senate Intelligence Oversight Committee, disseminating information to the press corps. Public Relations, my dear, is the power base of the future—"

"Publicity?" she managed to whisper, aghast: you couldn't do worse to a covert operations specialist. She had an impulse to quit, to tell Blaustein what she knew about him and that the press was going to get an earful of *all* she knew—about Fox's Turkish adventure, Crossfield's double nature, Blaustein's attempt to interdict the Alden pick-up, the whole shooting match. And that frightened her enough to force adrenalin into her system and free her mind from the cold numbness of panic.

Carefully, she said, "Unless you want an ex-Politburo member named Abdulhamid Kunayev to become an American hero, Kurt, you'd better rethink this transfer."

She'd never even considered threatening Blaustein this directly. Once she'd said it, her stomach dropped out, gone she had no time to wonder where, and she was left listening to her own breath quicken in an agonizing silence as Blaustein split his Bismarck with one quick and deadly slice of his knife.

"What's that?" he said after he'd forked, chewed, swallowed a bite, and patted his lips daintily with his napkin. "I didn't quite hear you?"

"I said, sir, that I'd rather remain where I am. I've got a number of sensitive black ops ongoing which won't run well under anybody else."

"I see. Well, we'll have to wait until you roll up those nets, then, won't we? How long do you need to clear your decks? A day? Two? A week?"

"A month," she sighed, wondering if she were a coward or a fool or both, wishing she could get angry enough to just end things then and there—manage to get herself thrown bodily out of Langley, kicking and screaming. She had a fantasy of drawing her carry-gun and shooting a neat hole in Blaustein's shiny forehead. But she didn't. She couldn't. There were too many others at stake—Fox, Alden, and Sonny Quaid to name just three.

"A month," Blaustein repeated avuncularly. "My dear, we could destabilize Switzerland in a month. Make it two weeks. We can't have this sort of thing . . . shoot-outs on Washington streets. . . . Counter-intelligence failures, my dear, are ultimately *your* failures. Let me make this as painless as possible for you. I'm going to send your replacement over to begin some on-site training as soon as we've decided on the man. Tomorrow, probably. Make him comfortable, will you? Don't sulk. Remember, we're all together in this. For the good of the Agency, it's imperative that he know all your most sensitive cases like the back of his hand . . . including this Fox matter."

Dropped in at the end of everything else, while she was still reeling, the mention of Fox thrilled her nerves like electroshock. Shai found herself admiring Blaustein's skill for a moment. But she couldn't react. She had to act. She said, "I won't be in the office at all this week, Kurt. I've got a great deal of homework and plenty of unused sickleave. Send your boy around the first of next week and we'll break him in . . . assuming things are still going the way you think they should." She smiled at him. "And now, if you'll excuse me, I've got a shop to run."

Her chair caught in the pile of the rug as she pushed it back and nearly toppled.

Kurt Blaustein's flat hand thumped the table so that flatware jumped and stemware teetered. "You haven't been dismissed, Gallen—not yet. Don't push it. *Sit down!*"

But as she was standing there, feeling blood rush blazing to her cheeks, considering offering an immediate resignation, one of the big boys who'd been lurking in the kitchen came hustling over.

"Sir? Sorry to disturb you, but?. . ." The col-

legiate-looking Security-type must have been a half-
back once, Shai decided. To see that much muscle
so timorously hesitant struck her as ludicrous. What
the beefy youngster really wanted was to whisper
in Blaustein's ear. For all she knew, maybe he did,
after business hours. . . .

"Just spit it out, Ralph, whatever it is. Can't you
see I'm in conference?" Blaustein was as much
astounded as annoyed by the interruption.

"Yessir." Ralph glanced quickly at Gallen, then
at his boss. "There's been some sort of explosion at
Mrs. Gallen's house. The report's garbled, but—"

"There's been *what?*" Blaustein's fury was blis-
tering as he interrupted.

But Shai wasn't in any mood to appreciate
Blaustein's theatrics. She was already running
toward the elevator full-tilt, smoking wreckage and
severed limbs and twisted bodies dancing before
her eyes, memories of Beirut superimposed on the
pastoral landscape of her hill-crest home.

"Ah," said Lucille Quaid as her husband poured
himself another drink, "the Porters are selling their
house in McLean, you know, with Trav taking early
retirement. . . ."

"Lucy, I don't want—" Quaid began. He would
have continued, '—to think about that just now. . . .'
Or ever, if the truth were told, think about moving
to one of the enclaves of upper-level Agency house-
holds in which a wife *could* talk to the neighbors
about what her husband did . . . to the extent she
knew. Lucille Quaid knew damned little, but she
probably knew why her husband would never agree
to move from where they now lived, an awkward
drive to either Langley or the District proper, but
within a mile of Shai Gallen's similar dwelling.

Quaid didn't have to complete the angry sentence,

because a telltale in the study began to chirp. No matter what the circumstances, all activity in the house was going to stop until the CI chief learned what had caused the alarm. He set his whiskey down, the liquid sloshing to the rim but not quite over, and ran to the study whose simple code lock was not meant to exclude serious intruders—only his family.

Lucy remained where she stood, pressing her teeth against the knuckles of her left fist. Sonny hadn't said anything, he never did; but she had seen the Wagoneer, and she could see now that he had not stripped off his holstered .45 the way he usually did when he got home.

The study was lighted by a pulsing bead in the handle of what looked like a cheap plastic attaché case by the wall. Quaid did not bother to turn on the overhead, though he latched the door with instinctive care before he squatted to open the case. The inner face of the lid was a map drawn in liquid crystal and scrolling downward automatically. Overlaying it were data lines and a cursor, projected much as the head-up display of a combat aircraft would be. The alarms, light and sound both, cut off as soon as Quaid thumbed the latch.

The case was a tracking terminal as sophisticated as the navigation system of a cruise missile—which it in fact resembled. At the moment, the terminal was being powered by line current through an induction pad, but the case itself was a plastic battery which could keep the unit running for over twenty hours of continuous operation.

A coded microwave transmitter had been planted in the headlight nacelle of each of the three motorcycles Quaid had provided for the amusement of Larry Fox—during the hours he was not in Shai's bedroom. The transmitters remained quiescent until the bike to which each was attached was fired up. At that point a continuously-updated signal was beamed to the Navstar satellite net which responded with positional data precise within a meter—anywhere on Earth.

In the case of a cruise missile, the navigational fix would have been used to update the inertial guidance system in the weapon itself. For use with the tracking device, the satellite signal came instead to this portable terminal where it was received not merely as digital information but in the form of an orange dot on the face of a map moving continuously beneath it. That analog capacity depended on the necessary background being in the terminal's database, of course—this unit would have to be reprogrammed before it could work to its full capability in Tokyo, for instance. But for the moment, the terminal was accurate within the limits of the US Geological Survey for all points inside a hundred-mile radius of Shai Gallen's house.

There might be a glitch in the system at that, though, because the analog display was unreeling beneath the orange pipper at a rate which seemed absurdly high for curving secondary roads. He'd chance it anyway. Sonny Quaid had not planned this, not really, but if the opportunity were offered he would not pass it by.

He thought of Gallen's face as she'd winced away from sight of Fox, that murderous, incompetent *kid*, being debriefed under chemicals. It wasn't going to be a chore; that he was sure of.

Quaid slammed the door behind him as he strode from the study with the attaché case closed in his left hand. Lucille was waiting in the entrance hall but he did not bother to kiss her, only paused to snatch a sport coat at random from the closet. "Back when I can," he muttered as he pushed open the storm door.

The night was cold and the breeze curling around the porch had teeth. Quaid did not stop to don the jacket, however. Time enough to do that when he was in the car and able to set the tracking terminal down on the seat beside him.

For the moment, he just clamped the flapping garment against him with his right elbow, so that it hid the pistol from any neighbor who chanced to be looking out at this hour.

The COMINT (Communications Intelligence) van that Shai had "borrowed" from Central Security peeled up her driveway toward her, skewing dangerously to avoid the last tow truck pulling its burden of wreckage—twisted axles and crumpled quarter panels—without the benefit of warning lights.

Gallen was sitting on her front steps with M-1 cradled against her, the big Persian's chest pressed to hers, his forelegs locked against her neck like a frightened child's. "You're a coward, M-1, you know that?" she murmured into the cat's ruff as he burrowed against her neck, his cold nose wet because he was purring and, when he was purring, M-1 drooled.

The cat was in better shape than she was—at least he felt safe in her arms. She'd felt anything *but* safe as she sat there and watched the meat wagon drive away with what was left of Alden and the two babysitters; she'd felt downright violated as she'd watched the Agency's crack Security squad comb the premises with as few telltales as they'd have employed in a hostile nation—no searchlights, no double bubbles, no fuss, no mess.

Everyone had been at pains to keep the profile

exceedingly low, to keep the press and the local cops out of it, to keep things deniable so that, in extremis, it might be claimed that nothing ever happened here. It was all achingly covert—as covert as you could manage after such a goddamn big *bang*.

Except for Blaustein, of course—Blaustein was about as covert as a shoulder-launched neutron missile, what with his entourage and his damned limousine, she thought dreamily, her mind drifting into a technical consideration of missiles, shoulder-launched and otherwise, of the sort Tech Services thought might have blown that reinforced van to Kingdom Come in her driveway.

She'd been grateful, on arrival, to find out that the report she'd received at Langley was wrong— that it wasn't her house, just the van and her people.

Now she felt a little guilty for caring less about human lives than her furniture. But it wasn't the furniture, her books, or even the cat in her arms whose safety had been paramount in her mind as she'd raced homeward: all she'd been able to think about was Larry Fox.

Fox was gone somewhere on one of the motorcycles, as now everyone else was gone—everyone but M-1 and the occupants of the COMINT truck pulling up before the front steps.

She'd used her wrist-communicator, on her way here, to requisition the truck through a parallel channel. She probably should have done it prior to her talk with Blaustein, because there was something not quite right about Sonny lately, but she hadn't. And Blaustein hadn't removed her from Operations officially, not yet. Though she had no doubt that, left to his own devices, he would. So she'd gotten the truck by calling in a marker owed her by a one-star general she'd occasionally had congress with—somebody beyond Blaustein's power to hurt should the matter of her authority to utilize the vehicle come into question.

She winced as she got up and M-1 growled, digging his claws into her neck. The cat didn't want to be put down yet. But it was the memory of tea with Blaustein and her imminent transferral to Public Relations which had made her shudder. Everybody's cards were on the table, now. Blaustein had made it a him-or-me situation and Shai Gallen hadn't missed the point.

Someone else might assume that her removal from Directorate was just a natural outgrowth of Luftsen's death, Blaustein's promotion, and Quaid's fuck-up on E Street, but Shai never assumed the obvious. And Sonny Quaid never fucked up. So there was a piece missing somewhere.

That missing piece was what had prompted her to commandeer the COMINT truck now idling before her and to make its surveillance target Sonny Quaid, not Blaustein or Crossfield or the Soviet mission on Embassy Row. She had to know if Sonny was unknowingly being maneuvered by Blaustein or if there was another factor at work here, something more diabolical than the Blaustein/ Crossfield link.

She was certain about Blaustein, now, as she'd not expected to be for days or weeks. But she was also uncertain about Sonny now, as she'd never expected to be.

Maybe Harrison Quaid was simply jealous, maybe he was burning out, maybe he was an innocent victim of some slick attempt by Blaustein to draw attention away from himself, to turn Shai's suspicions on her own organization and abort LEMON PLEDGE from within—for security reasons, the only valid shut-down grounds for an operation like PLEDGE.

She carefully extricated M-1's claws from first her left shoulder, then her right, and put the cat down on the flagstones: "Go on, M-1, go savage some rabbit or something."

With a baleful glare at the COMINT van, M-1 flounced away, tail high but lashing.

The missing piece she was looking for might be in the COMINT boys' report. There was bound to be something that didn't compute. She'd given the Com Specs access to everything she had: her scramble codes, her in-house bugs, her whole personal nine yards. If there was a missing link, they'd find it. And something inside her kept warning that there *had* to be one. Sonny wouldn't have put himself in the middle of a firefight just to cover his ass: when bullets fly, they don't always go where you want them to, and Sonny was a combat veteran of too much experience not to know that. And yet, things shouldn't have blown this badly; it was as if the whole CI component was concentrating on getting Shai Gallen canned, no matter what the cost.

She wasn't willing to accept human error and yet she wasn't willing to accept collusion between Blaustein and Quaid, because E Street was too unlikely a result of that.

So she'd sicced the COMINT boys on her lover, trusting her instinct.

She found, as she walked over to the truck and its side doors opened to reveal the men and electronics within, that one part of her wasn't anxious to hear an answer she might not like.

And she couldn't think of one she *would* like: Fox was gone somewhere on one of the bikes and Sonny wasn't home—she'd tried him. Blaustein had made the "mistake" Shai had hoped he'd make, on E Street, but too big a mistake and the wrong sort to do Gallen, who still thirsted for hard evidence, any good.

And Alden was dead by the mechanism of a brutally effective device, delivered systematically in the most obvious Directorate V fashion.

She shouldn't be spying on her own people, she thought wildly for a moment, despising herself and all she stood for, as she climbed into the van and one of three COMINT officers—the senior analyst by his rumpled civilian clothes and casual wave—motioned her to his console.

The van was state-of-the-art. The main terminal the analyst sat behind was alive, its screen divided into two Status areas set between Command sidebars above an Options table activated by a light pen to minimize mistakes.

Its Event Alarm Tables had already been replaced by Emergency Override; Shai had missed only the ringing bells and flashing highlights of the Automatic Interrupt sequence.

Now, by ID code and location, Sonny Quaid was being tracked.

"What the fuck? . . ." she breathed, leaning forward, her hand on the analyst's shoulder.

The analyst turned his short-haired head toward her and screwed up his face into a grimace: "Ours is not to wonder why, Ma'am. If you'll sit down at that other console there," he pointed to a chair on a roller-track beside his console and stabbed buttons before him without looking at them, "we'll run some highlights—what triggered the Override sequence once we got the scramble decode and fed in certain key words—and you can decide for yourself whether this guy is trouble. System thinks it's got a bad guy. And, whatever he is, he's on his way to the Glebe Road area, which is where, according to your in-house bugs and the tracers on his bike, your houseguest is going. I've got a couple phone calls for you to listen to, now that we've got them unscrambled, as well as . . ."

"Shit," she whispered, and squeezed her eyes shut. When she opened them, the secondary terminal was flashing data at her as fast as she could handle it, and she was being handed a headset. "Glebe Road, Mister," she called out to the driver without looking away from Sonny Quaid's recent itinerary, phone log, and requisitions list. "Fast as you can manage."

One of the other two Com Specs closed the van's side doors, but not before the driver put the heavy truck in gear and it lurched forward, throwing Gallen into the back of the chair because she was off balance, unzipping her down jacket to check the batteries on her Detonics' laser sight and thread the can which suppressed noise and flash onto its squat muzzle.

Quaid, alone in the mid-sized Ford—a government motor pool car with no frills and an engine which stumbled every time he gassed it—was doing what a minimum staff of two was required to accomplish safely. The terminal lay on the seat with its lid open toward him. He drove fast for the darkness and the road conditions; making quick glances to the data lines overlaid on the display, Hooes at Silver Brook rippling into Hooes at Pohick, since the LCD map and legend were unreadable under the circumstances.

Quaid sat with a slight forward hunch as if he were trying to pull the steering column out of the firewall, the posture a legacy of years of driving while wearing a heavy pistol in a hip holster, as it rode now. Looking at the terminal meant looking back; he looked anyway, and the car twitched each time he did so, barreling along the narrow highway.

Pausing to check his bearings would put the CI chief even farther from a quarry who already seemed to have the legs of a helicopter. He'd been a fool to put a machine that hot in Fox's hands! But he hadn't known, hadn't *dreamed*, that he'd want the kid that bad . . . and want him alone.

The Beltway was a broad ribbon visible across the face of the liquid-crystal display. When it scrolled down to meet the orange cursor, Quaid was afraid that he had lost Fox for good. In a wallowing cow like his present vehicle, he hadn't a prayer of overhauling a reckless motorcyclist with the breadth of a divided highway to dive through. The bastard couldn't outrun the transmitter, of course; but he could be out of the terminal's database in well under an hour. Why in *hell* hadn't he thought to put self-destruct mechanisms in the bikes for a situation like this?

The driver of a pick-up truck headed in the other direction laid on his horn as his right wheels splashed mud and gravel from the shoulder of the road. Quaid ignored the protest, though his reflexes snatched the car back onto the proper side of the road. He was shouting in triumph, because the Beltway was slipping on toward the bottom of the terminal screen. Fox was headed on into the District proper, almost certainly planning to hole up there.

That meant he would be waiting for Sonny Quaid, whatever he *thought* his plans were.

Alexandria had always seemed to the CI chief to be one of those places where they rolled up the sidewalks at 10PM, but there was enough traffic now to keep him from noticing at once when the LCD stopped moving beneath the pip that was

Fox's motorcycle. What Quaid *did* notice when he stopped for a traffic light—angry but unwilling to run it, not now when the risks outweighed the gain of a few seconds—was that there was a blue dot near the bottom of the display as well as the orange one in the middle. He had finally brought the terminal into the same reference frame as his quarry.

Quaid accelerated across the intersection while the light was still amber toward the cross street. His big body was pumping with more adrenalin than he could burn off, so that his fingers clenched and unclenched from the ring of the steering wheel and his buttocks squirmed against the fabric of the seat. In Quaid's mind flickered stroboscopic images of Fox: ID shots from his file; the man himself, face bruised and dark, bruised-looking circles around both eyes; the same face, pared even closer to the bone by drugs and fasting . . . and the hands that had killed with the icy willingness of guillotine blades kneading the shoulders of Shai Gallen as she clung to him, the bitch, the—

Blue dot and orange merged on the terminal display. Parked beneath the neon OFFICE sign of the motel across the street was a red and white motorcycle, tiny looking—new to Quaid because its provision had been a delegated responsibility, one of the things he had ordered done because Shai had wanted it. . . .

He pulled the Ford up hard in front of the bike and got out, closing the terminal as he did so.

The office front was brick to waist height with glass panelling above. For a moment, Quaid could see only one person within the lighted interior, a clerk of Middle-Eastern appearance behind the counter which was itself set off from the anteroom by a panel of wire-cored double glass. It would keep a thief from smashing his way into the cash register, thought the CI chief as he walked toward the door, but it was not bulletproof. The cold wind snapped at him and lifted the tails of his sport coat.

Even as he reached for the door with his left hand, Quaid saw Fox slouched in one of the low, cushioned chairs along the front wall of the office. The young field collector looked even worse than Quaid remembered him. His head was slumped forward and his hands were knitted together as if each were the other's only hope of safety in a maelstrom. He glanced up and stumbled to his feet as he saw the glass door start to open and the CI chief illuminated through it by the overhead fixtures.

"S-Sir," he called to Quaid as the night clerk waited in stiff expectancy, "is Glenn all right?"

The headlights of a van jouncing into the parking lot scattered themselves among the glazed surfaces of the office in a myriad of images. Quaid swore, but it wasn't going to stop him: he'd planned on two, but he was hot enough now to scratch the whole city if that's what it took. The kid was watching him in puppyish longing, and it wasn't even Gallen he was spending his last breath worrying about. Wouldn't that piss her off if she—

"*Sonny!*" shouted the familiar voice from the parking lot, "Sonny. . . ." again, muted, because the door had closed behind Quaid.

He glanced over his shoulder, but there was nothing to be seen except his own reflection in the glass, his face a ghost of itself with all the color washed from it by the fluorescents.

It didn't matter. Quaid turned again from Shai Gallen to Fox. The CI chief swept his hand toward his right hip, shifting his body left as he did so to help clear his coattail from the holster it covered.

The door shattered behind him and the white star of a bullet hole splashed across the panel above the counter. Fox was diving for the floor, his hands groping for something beneath his quilted jacket.

The bullet couldn't have hit the inner glass, thought Sonny Quaid, because his own body was in the way—and the second round struck within a hand's breadth of the first as the clerk disappeared behind the counter screaming and the whole of Quaid's chest began to burn like a block of dry ice.

Goddam nine-millimeter, he thought, penetration up the ass but no stopping power ... but though his thumb unlocked the safety of his own .45, his hand no longer had the grip strength to hold the heavy automatic which slipped toward the floor in a slow-motion arc.

Quaid turned. As his knees buckled beneath him, he saw through the hole blasted in the door panel the face of Shai Gallen over her hands linked on the grip of the pistol with which she had just killed him.

Shai watched Sonny crumple with as much dissociation as she could manage, but it wasn't enough.

The first time she'd killed a man, it had been in wartime, a head shot because she'd been trained that way and, though she wasn't the greatest paper-puncher, all she'd learned snapped into alignment when she'd turned a corner in Sidon and found herself face to face with a teenager pointing a rifle at her. She'd been sighting—front sight, rear sight, forehead of target directly above bridge of nose, all in perfect alignment—and squeezing the trigger on a half-held breath before her mind had time to tell her heart that the kid before her had eye-brows that met over the bridge of his nose and acne pocking his face, that he was too young to grow a beard, or tell her anything else that might have allowed her to hesitate a fraction of a second too long.

And then the recoil from her Brigadier shocked up her arm and the kid's forehead disappeared to be replaced by blood and bone and bits of brain, all neatly framed in her sights for an instant and her mind's eyes forever.

When you shoot somebody close at hand, you never forget it. And the first one haunts you at every opportunity.

Certain things, she always noticed, and this time was no exception: the truly amazing amount of blood a human body can hold, the visible shrink-ing of the person as if a soul were an actual thing and its departure made some difference to the bulk discerned by a human eye. This time, because Sonny was face down on Spanish tile, the blood just seemed to keep seeping, so much of it that her stomach lurched as she reached for the door with one hand and stepped over Sonny Quaid with a conscious effort of will that separated the corpse in its widening pool of blood from the person, so much larger in life, she'd known.

With the Detonics still in her strong hand and trained on Fox, who had frozen with his hand inside his quilted jacket, she slipped indoors, glanc-ing away from the wide-field sight picture the Detonics offered—of Fox's emotionless, strained face—toward the counter, behind which nothing seemed to move.

"Larry, let's go," she said harshly. "Now. Move!" She had no idea what the young collector had made of what he'd just seen, but she had to get him out of there, fast, before the foreign type be-hind the counter came popping up with a shotgun or a Saturday-night special.

And she needed to keep moving, keep acting. If she let the significance of what had just happened overtake her, she might stop moving altogether. And there was no time for that.

Fox blinked in the fluorescents, first at Gallen, then at Sonny, then turned his head toward the counter.

"Jesus, Shai, I, you fucking killed him—"

His hand, inside his jacket, moved.

"Larry, I said *now!* Hands where I can see them. Come on, cowboy, *move.*"

"It's your choice if you want to do it." Fox's voice was deep and his chin outthrust. His hand didn't come out from under his jacket. He didn't move.

"Fox, Christ, if I wanted you dead, you'd be dead. Now do what I tell you while there's still time!"

Please, God, don't let him stop to see if Sonny's really dead. Don't let him play hero when he doesn't understand and I can't explain. Don't let me shoot him.

Fox, eyes steady on her and a muscle ticking in his jaw, brought his right hand out empty and, both hands spread well away from his sides but not exactly upraised, came toward her, stepping around Quaid's body but not avoiding the pooling blood.

Gallen, hyperacute in crisis, noticed droplets splashing and a skid as Fox's heel slipped on the blood-slicked tiles.

Then Fox was closing on her and she backed out of the door, Detonics still trained on the man com-ing after her.

A voice behind her said, "Need any help, Ma'am?"

She didn't glance around; she recognized the voice of the senior analyst from the COMINT truck. "Let's get our friend, here, and his bike, in the van."

"Affirmative," said the voice. "Let's go, sonny."

The analyst's unfortunate choice of words brought tears to Shai's eyes she hadn't thought herself capable of shedding. But that was all right: the analyst had come up beyond her and was briskly patting down Fox, then moving him toward the van, Fox's weapon—a snubby that could have been his own before it stopped a bullet in Beirut—in his hand, and talking as if to himself.

"Shai? What's going on?" Fox's voice, trailing behind him on a puff of visible breath as he was frog-marched toward the van by the analyst, was full of everything she didn't want to hear: mistrust, accusation, confusion.

She didn't answer. She just kept her gun trained on the counter beyond the starred glass in case the clerk popped into view. She could see a reflection of the analyst's progress, with Fox in tow toward the van.

Then she began to make sense of the analyst's mutters: he must have a body-mike on him, because the other two Com Specs were already sprinting—one from Sonny's car, with a portable COMINT case under his arm—to load the bike into the van.

It wasn't until then that she realized that she was sighting down the laser guide at nothing more than the glass beyond which Sonny Quaid lay dead, that the clerk wasn't interested in being a hero, that the van's motor was racing and the senior analyst was calling her name. Carefully, almost in slow motion, she safed her weapon, unscrewed the suppressor, and snapped both can and gun into her holster.

Then she ran like hell, flat out, and leaped up into the van, away from it all.

And skidded to a halt inside.

The COMINT truck wasn't made to accommodate a bike or a prisoner, which was what the Com Spec with Fox's gun thought he had. Shai Gallen wasn't made to accommodate the look that Larry Fox gave her. All the work she'd done, all the confidence-building measures she'd employed, had gone down the tubes in that instant when a man Fox trusted had reached for his .45 and Shai had made a split-second decision with no time to prepare her agent, and no explanation handy if she'd been able or willing to give one.

Oh Christ, Sonny, why'd you have to make me do that?

At least the collector wasn't giving the Com Specs any trouble. He was sitting where he'd been told to: by the bike's front wheel, legs crossed, hands laced above his head.

The junior analyst, with a neutral, " 'Scuse me, Ma'am," squeezed by her to close the doors.

By then, the truck was already speeding down Glebe Road and Fox had resumed staring at her accusingly.

She said, "Fox, he was going to shoot you. Think about that."

"So you say. This guy going to shoot me instead?" Fox craned his neck to look defiantly at the analyst who had one knee on the seat of his task chair and his gun hand leaning on its back, pointed close-range at Fox's head.

"He's going to put his gun away as soon as we're sure you're all right, Larry," she heard herself say.

"I need you. You can have your gun back, as soon as we've talked this out."

"What's to talk out? People keep getting killed and it's all for a good reason, right?" Fox's eyes were flat and empty, the eyes of the fuse Sonny'd proclaimed that he was.

The analyst in charge said quietly, "Ma'am, we could use some orders. The General said do whatever you wanted, for as long as you wanted, and unless I miss my guess, none of us are going to be home for dinner."

She flicked a glance at the Com Spec in charge. It was the first time she'd really paid attention to him, and what she saw was someone quite ready to take PLEDGE anywhere she asked him to. She'd seen his type before, and mentally thanked her friend of a few raucous evenings for knowing what kind of help she might need better than she did.

"Let's try the Langley parking lot, gentlemen—or as close as you need to get to log onto the CI database without anyone knowing. . . . We *can* do that with this," she waved a hand at the equipment around them, "can't we?"

"Mister Fox here could do that with this equipment, Ma'am," said the analyst with a touch of pride.

The analyst's assistant came up behind him and murmured, "I'll take that, sir, if you like." The two together were nearly a pair: medium height, trim and clean shaven, fair-haired and clear-eyed. And ready, if not anxious, for all the action they could find. The assistant had sergeant's hash-marks behind his eyes and a nondescript sweater over a plaid shirt and jeans.

"Want to tie this guy up, Ma'am? Is he friendly, or what?"

"No, he'll be fine. Won't you, Fox?" she was

going to have to tell him about Alden at some point. But not yet. Not until they had a bed—or just a few minutes in private.

"Don't you trust me, Shai?" Larry Fox wanted to know.

None of the alarms had gone off, but something brought Owen Neely bolt upright in the bed of his room above the garage to call, "Marie?"

The overhead light went on with a shock and a dazzle which did not affect the man in reflective sunglasses in the doorway. Neely reached for the bedside table, but the drawer was already open and a man stood in sunglasses there as well, a black whose hands dwarfed the single-action Colt he had already removed.

"Big man's gun," said the black as he rotated the cylinder between thumb and forefinger, letting the heavy cartridges drop out into his palm with oily clicking sounds. Neely could not tell whether the tone was one of approval or mockery. "Ought to remember there's a law against these things, though."

The intruders wore dark suits which would have gone unremarked at a working-class funeral. There were striations of scar tissue noticeable on the knuckles of the black as he spilled the ammunition and the emptied revolver back into the drawer. The man who had turned on the lights now walked, carrying a briefcase, to the other side of the brass-framed bed which Neely had special-ordered to fit a king-size mattress.

"What in the hell—" the National Security Advisor blurted, starting to rise just as the intruders sat down on the bed. Their weight on opposite sides of the tiger-striped satin sheets bound him unless he were willing to squirm out the top like an undignified butterfly emerging from its cocoon.

"Nice pajamas, Owen baby," said the man who had turned on the lights. He flopped his briefcase onto the bed and cocked one leg up onto the mattress so that he could face Neely squarely. The only weapon either man had displayed was the advisor's own Colt, but the pair projected an aura of power and physical danger which Neely knew better than to challenge.

"There's a safe behind the award," said Neely carefully, nodding toward a wall plaque of black laminate reading Contractor of the Year in scrollwork lettering. He looked from one of the reflective, smiling visages to the other, twisting his body to be able to do so. "There's three grand in it, small bills, no alarm. The jewelry's in my wife's room in the main house. That's got a time lock, and even *I* can't get into it now."

He did not think the men were burglars: he *prayed* they were.

"Relax, Owen," said the black, "we don't want your money." He gave a playful pat to Neely's bare scalp.

"Just want to show you some pictures, old buddy," his partner said, and he spun a thick 5×7 from the briefcase onto the chest of the man in black silk pajamas.

Neely had heard a whisper of sound as the man tossed the photograph. Now, as he lifted it himself, the temperature of his trembling fingers activated a mechanism within the mounting, and the picture said in a voice even thinner than that of the child who had made the recording, "Hi, I'm Alice. I'm thirteen now, but when I was nine Mr. Owen Neely took me up to his room over the garage. He had me drink something, and I think it was wine, and then—"

Neely threw the photograph down as if the smiling face, still girlish and as innocent as he remembered it, had grown fangs and bitten him.

"Plenty more where that came from," said the man with the briefcase. He fanned a sheaf of at least a dozen similar photographs and dropped them beside his victim. The grinning visages had the aspect of skulls, not seductiveness, now as Neely stared at them in fascination.

"I won't touch them," said the balding man in pajamas. He squeezed his hands together so that the wedding band and the Masonic ring he wore on opposite ring fingers glinted alternately as one palm washed the other.

"Won't you?" gibed the black. "That's not what *they* say."

The man with the briefcase took out a further photograph. Instead of offering it to Neely, he held it himself so that the face framed by blond ringlets was toward the National Security Advisor.

"My name is Susan Merricks," the tiny voice sing-songed, "and I am ten years old on March 27. Yesterday I was up in Mr. Owen Neely's bed with him and I won't tell you what he did to me. But there was a, a—a recording device in the brocade on my dress and it heard everything I said and he said." There was a short pause. The mechanism began again, "My name is—" but shut off when the man dropped it on top of the other prepubescent smiles.

Owen Neely rubbed his face with his hands, but he was too wide awake now to take the childish step of trying to escape reality by covering his eyes. "All right," he said in a voice which was mechanically harsh and without emotion, "how much are we talking about?"

"If we didn't know better," said the man with the briefcase, "we'd believe you didn't think about anything but money." He brushed through the array of photographs with a thick forefinger, setting their voices chittering as a background to his rumbling laughter.

"We just want you to keep your mouth shut, brother Owen," said the black man as his fingertips wriggled the advisor's scalp playfully again from behind. "Just forget you ever heard the name Lawrence Fox and none of this has to go to the papers."

"What do you know about Fox?" Neely demanded, twisting his head around sharply to face the black.

"What we *know*," said the man with the briefcase from the other side, "is that we're here to give you a message—that's all."

Even as their victim spun toward that speaker in turn, the black intruder picked up with, "Keep in mind, dear buddy, that we're not *just* talking about losing your family and your job."

"We aren't even talking about jail," added the man with the briefcase.

"It's what's going to *happen* to you in jail," continued the black, "the way some folks without much to lose feel about child molesters."

"One of these kids was up in your room in New Orleans," said the Caucasian. "I can just guarantee you an interesting time if you're committed to Angola Prison." He grinned so broadly that Neely could see he was missing three side teeth in his upper jaw. "Some of the folks I was in with are still there, and they'd just *love* to meet you."

The men got up simultaneously, and the release

of their weight made the mattress pitch like a gaffed swordfish. "Take care, Owen baby," called one of the intruders as the pair stepped toward the door.

"Let's hope for your sake you never see us again," added the other.

The men walked out of the room, the man with the briefcase pausing briefly so that his partner could precede him through a doorway which looked small for men of that size even one at a time.

They did not bother to turn out the light behind them. Owen Neely sat, facing the brightly-colored photographs. His eyes were not focused on them, and his mind was so disoriented that it was five minutes before he got up to pour whiskey into a large glass.

It was three o'clock in the morning when Ralph tiptoed into Blaustein's office to awaken the Acting Director.

"Your overseas call's waiting, sir," said the big youngster with gentle diffidence.

The lights in Blaustein's office were blazingly bright and the pudgy supergrade had been lying with an arm crooked over his eyes, stretched out on his wine-colored leather sofa, for better than an hour—not sleeping, thinking.

Now, taking his elbow away, Blaustein blinked like a cat accustoming his eyes to the brightness. Then he smirked. The sight of Ralph usually pleased him, and tonight, despite the gravity of matters pressing, was no exception. Rank Has Its Privileges, and Ralph was one of them.

"Thanks, son; go see if you can rustle us up some breakfast, will you." The casual order had no hint of question about it, but the tone and syntax were those Blaustein reserved for his favorites, of which Ralph was currently one. A smart boy, as well as being attractive, and one whom Blaustein felt a duty to protect. Ralph had put through the call efficiently and without even a raised eyebrow.

Damn Posner for picking *now*—the worst possible time—to brush up on his falconry in Abu Dhabi with a bunch of rag-heads who had nothing better to do than hunt the Houbara bird to extinction. It was so inconvenient that Blaustein wasn't about to put Posner's absence down to coincidence.

Levering himself off the leather sofa, he knocked three of its loose cushions to the floor and cursed them. The sofa bed, all twenty thousand dollars of it, was a perk he'd fought for. Right now, he'd gladly have set fire to it, as long as certain files were feeding the blaze.

On his gleaming, black composite desk, a red "Hold" button was blinking patiently. Blaustein sat down and stared at it awhile before he stabbed three buttons in turn—Privacy; Scramble; and Erase, which defeated the phone's automatic log function—and picked up the receiver.

"Genya?"

In the pause before he got an answer, Blaustein could hear the bounce of satellite transmission and a background of crosstalk in a dozen languages.

Then a voice, pained at having been identified directly, without the use of its owner's code-name, said, *"Te Tchto ohuel?"* Not "Da," or "Allo," but a Russian expression, difficult of translation, which meant something like, "Have you lost your cock?" Colloquial Russian was one of the—if not *the*—most scatalogical tongues in the world. Blaustein, who refrained from profanity in most situations because he was proud of his vocabulary in three languages, nevertheless replied: "You son-of-a-bitch. Don't you think you owe me a goddamned explanation?"

Again a pause in which Blaustein fancied he could hear the magnetic waves of space beating upon a distant shore, and during which he twisted his Harvard class ring on his finger, which was beginning to sweat. Posner better not be playing him, out of the country because somebody in Special Services II had decided Blaustein was expendable . . . .

Genya Posner's voice replied, "An explanation? Of what, my friend?"

"Of *what?* Of a Directorate V hit on Shai Gallen's net—on her goddamned *premises*, that's what! When I asked you to take those bastards out, you told me you couldn't get tasked for it. Then you go ahead and—"

"Kurt! Get hold of yourself."

Blaustein, receiver cradled between shoulder and ear, was gripping one hand with the other so hard that his ring was digging into his fat, short fingers painfully. He fairly yelled into the phone: "Get *hold* of myself! If I go down, *friend*, you and as many of the ten thousand *agents provocateur* you've got in my country are going with me. And that means your precious Jim Crossfield, in the bargain. I want to know why I wasn't consulted about you people blowing a truck full of American citizens to hell in my frigging backyard. At just the wrong time, in just the wrong place. How am I supposed to—"

"Kurt," Posner's airy voice undulated across thousands of miles, "we're not prepared to shield a conversation of this magnitude, not here. Please believe me, no one intended—or *intends*—to jeopardize you, not your position, not your cover, not your usefulness. What was done was not my doing.

You are most valuable of all persons, especially now, with the Kalahari station opening and the Summit being so—"

"Genya, I want an Aeroflot jet standing by, twenty-four hours a day, from now on until I tell you different, at National. Just for me. In case I want to take a little trip. And if I find out it isn't there, I'm going to take measures. As you said before, I do have the resources of the American government at my command."

It wasn't exactly what Posner had said, but it was a threat with teeth.

Genya was rattled enough to spurt a number of conciliatory phrases in Russian before his professional poise returned. "I am coming home very soon now. Immediately when I can arrange this. You will wait, and we will solve our great problems, as always we do. There are . . . other interests . . . in Special Services as well as in your CIA, you know this. We have other agents, other nets. It was not through me that this occurred. Tell me the extent of your damages."

Blaustein's cheeks puffed out and he repositioned the receiver with one hand while the other played absently with his moustache. That was better; Posner wasn't bullshitting him: America's favorite Soviet-watcher was truly rattled.

"All right, Genya. I'll give it to you straight: I was about rid of Gallen when this hit went down. Now I don't know what I'll be able to do. The papers are going to make lots of hay with this, there's no stopping it. We're going to be in the spotlight—the whole Agency. We may even hear questions about my effectiveness, and then there's the Soviet Menace theme. . . . On top of Luftsen's suicide and E Street, Directorate V's making it look more like Latin America than DC here lately.

"And you would like me to do what?" Posner's voice was icy, distant. And Blaustein recognized the emotion behind it: if an agent gets in too much trouble, the first thing the case officer does is disengage emotionally, in preparation for disengaging unilaterally and completely.

"I'd like you to find out who's tasking these other operations on my turf and tell them, for me, that if it isn't stopped, CIA's going to have to go after the perpetrators—and *find* them. Do you understand me? I'll want some fucking Turks or Bulgarians or some such—about a dozen sacrificial lambs. And if I don't get them, there's going to be an abrupt and definite cooling in American/Soviet relations, because if KGB's not going to play by my rules, I'm not going to play by theirs."

"Now, Kurt, my good—"

Blaustein hung up on Posner and found that his hands were shaking, their palms slick with perspiration. There *were* things he could do. None of them were particularly survivable for him personally—his career as a Soviet hunter would probably be short and end spectacularly. He could have a number of Soviet diplomats declared Personae Non Gratae, send some counter-counterjamming trucks out to Long Island and screw up the transmission/receiving gear installed in the mansion belonging to the Soviet mission to the U.N. He could, and would, do that much tonight, to show that he was serious, that they weren't playing with field collectors and moribund ex-Politburo members now.

He stabbed the "Call" button on his desk-top display and waited for Ralph to answer. He would let the FBI rough up a few of the dips, he thought as he made a list of targets, the way KGB had scared the piss out of an American Deputy Chief of

Mission and his wife a few years ago. Blaustein needed to show himself to be a hard-liner, tough as nails on any sort of Soviet espionage because, if worse came to worst, he was going to claim that he'd been running a double double game: letting the Soviets think they were running him, and through him, Jim Crossfield, while in reality manipulating the Soviet intelligence apparatus to the benefit of America.

The only really difficult part of setting up a fallback like that was building Crossfield's confidence enough to allow the President to pull off his end of it, to realize that he'd be a hero, not a villain, if he played his presidential cards right. And they could blame all the failures—the Bund, the food riots, The 52%'s wanton partisanship—on Soviet active measures, which was the absolute truth. And the truth usually played pretty well . . . .

Where *was* that boy? Ralph was usually prompt, he loved to please, to be petted, to be . . . .

Ralph shouldered his way in with a tray in his hands and a piece of teletype printout between his teeth so that it was hard to judge his expression. Blaustein concentrated on the muscles stressing the tight sleeves of the youngster's Fila polo shirt. Blaustein was beginning to feel better and, feeling better, to conjecture how he might release some of the tension that had been building in him all evening, and which his call to Posner had not sufficiently dispelled.

"Put it down here," Blaustein purred, patting his desktop. "Pull up a chair. . . ."

As soon as the laden tray was on the table, while Blaustein was reaching forward to peek under the plate's cover and see what egg-based delicacy Ralph, an accomplished cook, had prepared for him, the big youth took the flimsy out of his mouth and said, "Sir, you'd better look at this right away," in a tone which told Blaustein that, whatever the news was, it was going to spoil both his late supper and his plans for after-supper recreation.

The flimsy bore a facsimile of the *Washington Post*'s morning headlines: "CIA Superspy Gunned Down In Motel"; "Bomb Guts Government Van, Killing 3"; and an abstract of the Op/Ed page, which reminded the readers of Luftsen's recent suicide and tried to make connections between it, the incident in Gallen's driveway, and the death of the agent in the Glebe Road motel, wondering if the Agency itself were not under siege and questioning the safety of the Soviet General Secretary and his entourage during next week's Summit.

"Ah, crap." Blaustein rested his chin on his palm, then looked up at Ralph, whose face was full of commiseration. "No chance of getting them to pull these, not with the *Post*."

"No, sir," agreed Ralph unnecessarily.

"Well, get me Snyder on the phone. It's time to remind the American people that terrorist attacks on American soil are the purview of the FBI. We'll see how he likes a hair-suit when it's tailor-made for him. Tell him I'll expect to meet with him directly after Luftsen's funeral."

"Yes, sir," said Ralph, scribbling notes.

"And, Ralph," Blaustein said silkily as the big boy got up to expedite Blaustein's orders.

"Yes, sir?" There was disappointment, almost resignation, in the handsome youth's face.

Blaustein didn't quite understand it until he asked his next question: "We don't happen, by any off chance, to know who this 'superspy' we lost was, do we? Or do I have to ask Snyder, or the Capitol Police?"

"No, sir, I—that is, we do," Ralph stammered,

then blushed, continuing: "It was Harrison Quaid, sir. We've got Security down there right now, but the unofficial report is that there was only one witness, and all he saw was a blur beyond the window: Quaid was shot through the door to the place. There was another witness, but he ran off. And the clerk's worried about his Green Card status, so he isn't lying. He hit the deck and covered his ears and said lots of prayers, thinking he was dead. By the time he got up, all he saw was taillights."

Those words drained Blaustein of everything he'd gained in the last half-hour: his buoyed confidence due to aggressively planned fallback measures, his pleasure at seeing that handsome face blush—*every*-thing.

With Sonny Quaid dead, he couldn't implement Gallen's lateral transfer. Right now, he needed somebody who knew exactly what the CI staffer had been doing, and that wasn't Sonny's direct superior, a paper pusher. It was Shai Gallen.

By the time Blaustein's eyes refocused, Ralph had slipped out of the office and closed the door softly behind him, leaving the Acting Director to puzzle out a statement he could give the press that wouldn't be patently as thin as piss on a rock.

About sunup on the day of Dick Luftsen's funeral, Noah Neely succeeded in calming his brother, Owen, enough to prevail on the stricken fool to show Noah the "evidence."

When he'd fingered the third photo of a young girl and heard a squealing voice tell tremulously what Owen had done to her, Noah sat awhile, bent forward as if studying the photos laid out on his petrified-wood coffee table, sickened and distraught.

"I'm going to blow my head off, Noah, I really am," said Owen in a thick voice.

Noah turned his head and socked Owen with a glare which would have sobered an hysterical matron. Noah's albatross, his younger, incorrigible brother, looked away and bit his lip, shaking his head.

Noah said without a trace of sympathy, "You know, when you used to say at cocktail parties that, 'You've got to get 'em before they've got fuzz on 'em,' I always thought you were doing it to make me uncomfortable. You stupid bastard. You poor, stupid bastard." Noah Neely wanted to retch, but his stomach was empty.

Failing that, he wanted to strip the cowboy accouterments—from silver collar-tips to crocodile, custom-made boots—from his brother and beat the hell out of him, the way he'd wanted to beat in Owen's face for forty years

Instead, he asked drolly: "Well, what shall we do about this? Pay off the parents? Send each of these young lovelies to private schools with on-ground therapy in Europe at our expense? Audit the parents' tax returns? There's always some short hair to grab. . . ."

"Could we?" Hope flickered and died in Owen's eyes. He wrung his hands, then groaned like a dog just hit by a truck. Then, amazingly, his face turned white and Owen Neely started to cry.

It wasn't until that moment, as Owen deflated like a balloon, sobbing, and tried to lay his head in his older brother's lap, that Noah realized he loved his sibling, despite years of embarrassment and different mothers. Maybe it was the sort of love one reserved for anyone who had the grace to know when bluster was useless, when all was lost, when tears were the only human refuge; but even if that were all, Noah Neely was deeply moved. And, these days, with his country in crisis under Jim Crossfield's stewardship and the geopolitical situation near its boiling point, Noah was grateful to feel more than the dull despair to which he woke every morning, exhausted from too little sleep, to face a globe's worth of problems no nation as divided as the US, let alone a single man like Noah Neely, could hope to solve.

He found himself saying, "There, there, Ownie, we'll fix it. We'll find a way," and stroking Owen's pomaded fringe of hair.

The crushed man, racked with sobs and reeking of nervous perspiration no deodorant could conquer, whined brokenly, "I don't know how. Where to start. *How* to start. . . ."

When Noah's aide-de-camp came tapping on his door apologetically, the elder Neely was relieved at the distraction. He had to think and *couldn't* think with the trembling body of a fifty–year–old man cuddled up against him like a child's.

Once Owen had straightened and stumbled off toward the "john" adjoining Noah's cherry-paneled study, Noah hit the remote which disengaged his privacy lock and called, "Come."

The door opened a crack, the ADC's freckled face peeked in, saying, "Sorry to disturb you, sir. You've got visitors—Mrs. Gallen and a friend. They say it's urgent."

"Why not?" Neely sighed, glancing toward the closed door behind which his brother, by the sound of it, was washing his swollen face in cold water. "Stay here with him. I'll see to Gallen. And send over to Owen's for a clean suit. I don't want him out of my sight for a while." As he spoke, Noah Neely gathered up the incriminating videographs and headed with them toward his wall safe where, behind a Turner, he locked them away. "He'll be going with us to Luftsen's funeral, then staying on here for a few days."

The ADC nodded and Noah knew he could leave his brother in capable hands. There were still, thank God, some men who didn't need a diagram to be effective. Neely had had other ADC's, but none as competent as this one.

He headed down the hall, dredging up his best smile for Shai, remembering what Sonny Quaid had told him about her intentions toward Crossfield and wishing everybody's buck didn't always seem to stop with him.

He was about to go back into the study and ask where, in the rambling old house, his ADC had told Gallen to wait, when he heard voices from the kitchen.

When he got there, he saw a van through his kitchen window. Out of it, two men were offloading a fancy motorcycle.

Closer to hand, Shai Gallen was leaning against the sink, looking dishevelled and pale, her hair stringy and wetter than it should have been, considering that only a few snowflakes were drifting in the dawn. There were bright spots like frostbite on her cheeks and at her temples. And, although nothing Shai did had surprised him in living memory, Noah was startled to realize that she was field-stripping a pistol with some difficulty, laying piece after piece on his kitchen counter.

Beside her was a young man Noah Neely didn't know, one of those ragged, emaciated-looking types Neely expected to see on TV in demonstration footage, not in his home. The fellow, in a quilted blue jacket, was watching him steadily, head slightly upraised and jaw outthrust, arms crossed over his chest and hips jutting forward, as if Neely were his mortal enemy

"Good morning, Shai. I don't believe I know your—"

"Noah, I don't have much time," said Gallen, dropping the handgun's heavy barrel onto his kitchen counter.

Noah Neely shut his mouth and walked to his automatic coffee maker, pouring himself a cup and watching the men outside stow the motorcycle in Neely's garage.

Shai turned to face him, hands gripping the sink. "Noah, this is Larry Fox, one of my line officers, and he's got some information for you. Tell your story, Fox, from the beginning—from the Galata Tower."

The man looked at her sidelong with an expression that sent chills up Noah's spine. This was definitely not one of Shai's lovers. This was someone she was running, and running hard; right up to the edge of the man's ability to cope.

"Yeah. . . ." The thin man's jaw worked and he looked at his muddy boots. Then he raised his head to Neely and began to speak in at first halting, then rapid-fire, bursts.

Noah Neely never remembered sitting down at his kitchen table, but he remembered every word of Fox's outrageous story about Kunayev and his flight from Turkey and—though Shai shaded her eyes and then covered her mouth when the man she'd brought here deviated from the speech she'd told him to make—the fellow's own opinion.

"So you see, sir," Fox said coldly, as if talking about a stranger and not himself, "by the time they—CI, I guess it was—got through with my chemical debrief," he spat the words as if they tasted foul to him, "I was hurting pretty bad. I didn't know if I believed my story, myself. But now I do. I have to. Sonny Quaid—you'd know him sir, I bet—he's dead, you see. A friend of mine, Glen Alden—" he could have been discussing somebody who chanced to work in the same office; except that Neely watched the man's eyes as the lips spoke the cool words "—he's dead, too. And both the babysitters."

Noah didn't interrupt; though he had to smother an exclamation of surprise when Fox started dropping names of recent casualties, the professional part of him knew better than to stop the flow from a man like Fox. Once silenced, it might not be possible to get him talking again. And the pain and confusion there, the loss and resignation, were all too real. Fox might have been manipulated, but he wasn't consciously lying.

"So you see, sir, Shai'd like it if you believed me, and helped us do . . . what we're going to do. Because we've got to do it, or none of the rest of it makes any sense . . . all those lives, wasted."

Fox paused, Gallen took her hand away from her mouth and touched the tall, thin man's shoulder in a gesture meant to be confidence-building, but Fox said one more thing that Gallen wasn't expecting: "And, sir, since she's killed Sonny, and all, to keep LEMON PLEDGE on line, I don't think you'd want to cross her on this one. But then, I guess you'd know that, too, wouldn't you?"

"Shit, Fox. . . . Go wait in the van." Gallen's dismissal was abrupt and she accompanied it with a hand signal given through the window to one of the three men in the van who were watching her, the doorway and the driveway, with calm alertness.

Neither Neely nor Gallen said anything until the door slammed behind Fox and one of the men in jeans took him by the arm companionably.

Then Gallen said, "I thought you ought to know. So you could cover your ass, if you won't help us." As she spoke, she put all the pieces of the pistol except the barrel in her coat pocket.

"You've left a piece, Shai," Noah said, pointing to the grimy barrel on the counter.

"That's the gun barrel that killed Sonny. Easiest thing to do with it is get rid of it . . . I can get another."

She's a hardballer, Neely reminded himself. The gun barrel, evidence, was going to be left in his hands. "And that—" Noah Neely pointed to Fox, beyond the window, sitting inside the van staring back at them, "is the gun-barrel that's going to kill Jim Crossfield?"

Gallen shuddered. "If I hadn't put your security system in myself, if I didn't *know*, better than I know that I'm going to die someday, that you couldn't record the National Anthem in here, I'd be terrified."

"But you're not? You expect me to believe that this . . . let's be polite . . . this field collector of yours knows what he's talking about?"

"More than that, Noah. I want to leave him here, have your ADC clean him up, slip him into a slot I'll arrange to be empty in Crossfield's Secret Service. I want him with Crossfield wherever the President goes—on the Kalahari junket, and then at the Summit. I'll arrange all the documentation. Fox is your nephew and you've been trying to slot him; we'll make him . . . ex-Team 6 ought to do it, don't you think?"

"Shai, I can't . . ."

"You've got to," she said, taking one step closer and locking onto Neely's eyes with her own, blue and hard as sapphires. "I'm so hot I'll be lucky if I don't spontaneously combust within the week.

Blaustein thinks he's going to put me in Public Relations—laterally fuck me over—and the only recourse I've got is not to let him get close enough to tell me until this is over. So it's me and my boys, there, and whatever we can do with the van. And you'd be surprised, Noah, just how much we *can* do with it. I got some evidence on tape from sitting in the parking lot at Langley while Blaustein made a phone call that'll ease your mind. Destroy after one listen, understand?" She produced a cassette and put it next to the steel barrel on his kitchen counter.

Noah Neely was reeling from too many revelations, too close together. *Destroy after one listen*, she'd said, and her words reminded him of Owen, in another part of the house, and of Owen's plight. "Shai, you didn't really shoot Sonny?"

"You bet I did." Her voice was emotionless. "I'll live with it. All I can tell you is that I wasn't wrong. I need this Fox inserted. That's what I came here for. Are you going to help me or do I go somewhere else?" As she spoke, she was fingering the gun barrel on the counter top. "You can just throw this in your trash now, if you don't mind. I need an answer."

Neely replied, "I don't mind telling you that I didn't need this, not right now. But yes, I'll help, on one condition."

"I'm not in *condition* to work my standard miracles, Noah," she said with a weak grin that fled as quickly as it came, "but I've told you my troubles, so I suppose I'm obligated to listen to yours."

"It's about my brother Owen," Neely began hesitantly. "Someone . . . visited him last night. Made threats. It seems he'd gotten a letter from someone, a letter that said substantially what that

young man said here a few minutes. . . . Oh, my!
Shai, what did you say that man's name was?"

"Larry Fox. Mind if I have some coffee?"

"I've been remiss. Please, help yourself." He
wasn't even looking at Gallen, but down at his
own gnarled hands as he began to tell Shai as
delicately as possible what sort of threats had been
made against Owen Neely and how seriously Owen
had taken the men who'd broken into his home.
"So you see," he finished uncomfortably, because
Shai was sitting across from him, poker-faced, just
listening as if he were telling her about some every-
day affair and not the ruination of his brother's
life, "there's little chance that it's not the same
man—your Larry Fox, and the Lawrence Fox someone is so anxious for Owen to forget."

Shai only nodded, turning her coffee cup in its
saucer.

"Sonny thought you were overreacting, you know,
Shai. He was against this . . . early retirement
matter. Is that, if I may ask, why you, ah? . . ."
Was there a delicate euphemism for murder? Neely
didn't think so.

"Greased," Shai supplied a pornographic verb.
"I greased him. Shot my lover, my best friend, the
only person I've ever trusted in this damned
country—with the exception of you. I shot him
because I had evidence that he was going to kill
Fox and I couldn't afford that. Not when Fox is *my*
best shot—and maybe yours." She leaned forward
and Neely could see the veins standing out on her
forehead and blue, pulsing tracery sharp against
her temples. "But 'why's' aren't important—not
even if you believe me, which you probably don't.
But I think you'll help me anyway, because I'll do
my best to source this problem your brother's
having. And because, given what you've heard and

seen tonight and what you're *going* to hear when you give that one-time tape a listen, you can't be sure that I'm *not* right—that Owen's problems, as well as mine, aren't coming from the very top levels of this administration—from Langley's top floor and the fucking Oval Office itself."

"Shai, you can't *do* this ... it'll be the end of you. And worse—relations between Israel and the US. . . ." Neely chose his words carefully. With the Bund in the ascendancy, Jews were very sensitive, Israel was nervous, and Shai was as protective as a lioness when it came to the star-crossed little nation which had bred her mother.

"Don't you think I've thought of that? Don't you think I know I'm not going to survive this, that *we*," she included herself and a nation half a world away in a single breath, "may not? But where's the choice?" she said bitterly. "America won't survive a revelation that its President is ... what Crossfield is. And you and I would never live long enough to prosecute it in the courts. Assassination is the only way."

"I've never been party to anything like this before. . . ." Noah Neely spread his hands in dismay.

Shai hooted. "You haven't? In the flesh, you mean. Operationally. When you knew the targets personally. Well, your brother's never had his honky red-neck ass on the line before, has he? God knows you've signed off on enough recommendations to promote counterinsurgency abroad. What do you think that means to the people who control those governments you don't like? Pink slips?"

Neely heard steps, then Owen's voice called out: "Noah? Hey, Noah, who's the company? If we're going to the funeral, we'd better get crackin'."

Shai was on her feet and at the door: "Fox? Can I leave him? Will you backstop me?"

Noah had no alternative but to say, "Yes. For now."

Luftsen, a one-time admiral, was being buried with full honors at Arlington.

The limousines just kept on coming, long lines of them like warrior ants with glowing eyes in a serpentine processional among the gravestones and the snow.

It had been easy to get the COMINT truck past the intense security: that's what COMINT was about. The SAVE credentials the driver showed to the Marine guards, there to keep the press at a respectful distance, weren't questioned.

In fact, they were welcomed: "Glad to have you aboard, sirs," said the Lance Corporal who waved them through, a horse-faced boy-soldier with nervous, darting eyes obviously expecting the Bund or The 52% to make his life miserable by trying to disrupt the burial of an Establishment honcho as they tried to disrupt every solemn or official moment which was bound to have press coverage.

Shai Gallen just ducked her head and hunched over one of the rear consoles while the driver jockeyed for position on a hilly slope above the proceedings and the senior analyst gave her a running commentary on what she didn't dare look up to see.

The three newest members of Gallen's reshet hadn't introduced themselves, and Shai hadn't asked their names. There was a feeling in the van, a familiar feeling she'd felt behind revetments and in trenches, an unspoken superstition that whispered: *don't get too familiar, don't make close friends, somebody's going to die and most likely whomever you care the most about.* Anonymity might keep Death at bay.

So the senior analyst, whom she now realized was about her own age and who had a thin, white scar cutting his upper lip and running up along his nose to end just below his eye, was called "Sir," by everyone; Gallen was "Ma'am"; the junior, who had a longer jaw and a white line around the third finger of his left hand where a wedding band or some other identifying ring had been recently removed, was referred to as "Buddy"; and the driver, who was darker, with a Mediterranean strain in him that made Shai feel unreasonably confident of his performance, was "Mac"—not a name, an *un*name, a protective generic because, in all likelihood, what survivors there were of this operation were going to have to forget it as completely as they could.

The three had been briefed, to the extent that briefing was possible and advisable, by General Westin, the man who'd seconded them to her—who hadn't told her he was giving her soldier-spooks from the Joint Chiefs Support Activity and who hadn't told them that they'd be working directly with CIA's beleaguered and soon-to-be-ex DDO.

There had been a flicker in the senior analyst's eyes of dawning comprehension when Fox called her "Shai" in the van, the ghost of a smile in them thereafter. She resolved, as the senior asked her to "pop up to verify these ID's, Ma'am," to thank the General extensively in whatever fashion seemed appropriate if—*when*—she came out the other end of this one. If she'd had time to think things through and better anticipation of the way things were likely to go, she'd have tried to get just their sort of actors from JCS's exclusive little shop, men who had no loyalty more general than the Joint Chiefs and who, as far back as Nam, had raised internecine warfare among the services to new Machiavellian heights.

The senior analyst, when Shai sat up straight, had a light pen behind his ear and a look of parental pride in his eyes as he walked her through her options:

"Console One," he said, taking the pen from his ear and pointing to the quadranted, twenty-one inch screen in front of him where simulations of the scene below the rise on which the truck was parked were displayed in shades of red. "HF, VHF, UHF coverage; ten to nine-seventy-five MHz; AM/FM, NBFM, S.C., demodulation modes with auto-warning of other jammers, so we're anti-detect; 40dB available attenuation of incomings, so you have whispers and farts along with screams of anguish if you want 'em; sensitivity and stability select enough so that we can counteract any limousine-internal countermeasures and give you everything said inside, right off the glass; lock-on, once you tell us who, so we can't lose 'em in a crowd; optional video, audio, and data storage connects to consoles Two and Three."

The junior analyst turned in his task chair, parallel to the driver's seat where Console Two was showing real-time video split-screens: a closeup of the grave site, a mid-range of the mourners exiting their limos, a parallel shot of the honor guard and the phalanx of chairs where the dignitaries would sit during the funeral, and a wide-angle panorama of the entire area downslope from the COMINT van. The junior said proudly, "We can give you look-down shoot-down, if you've got the TacAir to supply the overflight. And there's a KH-15 due to eyeball this area in—" he glanced at his onboard chronometer "—six minutes, real-time, so if you want to see what NSA's getting . . . what the hawk sees . . . we can give you that, too, Ma'am."

"That's enough, Buddy," said the senior a bit ruefully. "She knows what she wants, and probably more about the spook-balls up there than we do." He glanced reflexively at the ceiling, as if he could see through it and beyond, to the arcing domestic and foreign surveillance satellites, photo-return and computer-image, Crossfield's administration had put into orbit.

Shai's gaze followed: one of the things making her stomach queasy was that she *did* know just how extensive and capable the overflight satellites crisscrossing DC were: even the low-orbitals, the KH-15's, could give photo-reconnaissance of Blaustein porking one of his bevy of quail at midnight in total darkness—as long as he wasn't doing it at Langley or Meade. That was why she'd gone to Langley with the van when she'd had to pick a safe location, but she couldn't spend the rest of PLEDGE's run camped in a parking lot. There were better than a hundred COMINT vans in service; she was counting on that, and the fact that no satellite could pick up the van's license plate number—you'd need a side-looking, aircraft-borne system for that. So if she wasn't buzzed on the road, and if the van was really zero-signature, as the senior analyst had assured her, nobody could tell even how many warm bodies were inside it, let alone the use to which nearly a million dollars of Federal SECRET/NOFORN electronics was being put.

And Shai did know exactly what she wanted to do with all the equipment around her this morning. She started to tell the senior, and he leaned forward: Gallen had a habit of lowering her voice when what she was saying was crucial and the senior analyst was straining to hear.

"Give me lock-ons, audio-visual, of Crossfield, Blaustein, Snyder, both Neelys, and—Shit."

As she'd been listing her targets, the analyst had been circling the various figures. Some, like Crossfield, were still in their limousines; some, like Noah Neely, were already clustering around Luftsen's heavily-veiled widow.

Now, as the analyst paused, Shai tapped the screen with her fingernail: "That's Lucille Quaid, isn't it?"

The senior analyst said only, "I don't know. But if you want her, we can give her to you," as he tapped follow-on codes and enabled audio-visual recording linkage so that, behind Shai, a reel of magnetic one-inch tape began to rotate on its transport.

"I want her." Shai paused for a second and made up her mind: "I also want to send your buddy out to Blaustein with this." She pulled a miniature audio-cassette which they'd made earlier from her pocket and began scribbling a note: *When you listen to this, you're going to back off and wait for instructions.* "It may be risky, but I'm going with him as far as that copse there. He collars that Quaid woman, tells her Shai wants to talk to her, and brings her to the copse, leaves her with me and comes back here. Any trouble you can't handle, and you're on your own. Drop all the data in your commanding officer's lap and tell him it's my parting gift. Copy?"

"Affirmative. Bud, you just volunteered."

"No sweat, sir. You're having all the fun, anyway." The junior analyst started to shrug into his coat and paused, both arms in his sleeves but the jacket at his elbows: "Side arms, Ma'am? Need 'em?"

"With the honor guard, there, ready and able? This isn't the OK Corral, Buddy. Try your invisibility cloak, if you've got one."

The joke wasn't meant to be funny, but the senior analyst chuckled as he punched "Play," and three conversations occurring simultaneously below filled the van.

Getting her own coat, she tried listening, knowing that the senior analyst was effortlessly separating each group, that trained ears could follow what sounded to her like babble. But she couldn't, not with the closer distractions of the junior analyst moving to open the door and the sanguine driver coming aft to relieve the junior at his station while both men engaged in the inevitable banter of their breed.

"Bring me a sandwich and some coffee, Buddy? There's always great food at funerals."

"I'll bring you sòme 10W-40 if I see any, Mac, but civilians don't tend to serve it, not at high-class do's like this one."

Behind their voices, she could hear Crossfield, saying, "Kurt, I'm getting awfully tired of funerals. I want you to promise me it won't happen—"

And Blaustein interrupt, "Have you seen Snyder? He's the one to talk to. You do remember that the last antiterrorist EO gave his unit priority over—"

And, from another quarter, Snyder's voice, "I *know* she's here, but I've been told in no uncertain terms that we're not to be the ones to tell her. She doesn't know. As a matter of fact, *we* don't know—not yet. Like it said in the *Post*, the name's being withheld until relatives can be notified by the proper authorities, whoever Blaustein decides *they* are. . . ."

Then Shai was letting the junior analyst give her a hand as she stepped down into the slush from the van's side door and the two of them sauntered, gearbags in hand and glassine credentials the junior had produced hanging from cords around their necks so that they looked like part of the beefed-up security contingent, toward one copse of many meant to screen the cemetery's sections from each other so that it wasn't immediately apparent just how many dead heroes America had found need to honor.

From his gearbag, the junior handed her a one-ear headset with attached throatpad mike and a control box the size of a pack of playing cards. "If you want to talk to me, press the white button. If you want to talk to the van, press the red button—Mac can get that four-wheeler down here to pick you up so fast you'd think the truck was Stealthed. If you want to monitor any of the transmissions we're taking, press the numbered switches. If you want everything at once, depress that stud and hold it down. Want to repeat those instructions back, Ma'am—just to be sure you've got 'em?"

She had them, but she did as the junior asked. "Do I pass, Buddy?"

"With flying colors. I'll do the drop, hook the lady and be back in a flash," the junior promised, leaving her by an ancient oak.

She watched him trot down toward the dignitaries, hands in his jeans' pockets against the cold, conspicuously unconcerned, with just the right amount of command in his body language to defer questions before they were asked.

Still, she listened to his circuit almost exclusively as he approached Blaustein, threading his way among gentlemen in rubber boots and storm coats complaining about the inconvenient timing of Luftsen's death and would-be gentlemen in trenchcoats bitching to each other about the cold and the nature of their bosses, and women chattering nervously about Luftsen's age and apparent health and wishing their own husbands would stop drinking and jogging and working so hard, because even though it was a documented fact that married men lived longer, Dick Luftsen was a victim of stress and none of these men seemed to realize that their wives were the best anti-stress medicine a man could have.

The junior's breathing began to deepen and slow as he proceeded. Watching, her hand on the tree bole, Gallen could judge his progress. When she heard, " 'Scuse me, Mister Vice President," she could see the junior ducking his head as he passed the Black who would soon be America's Commander-in-Chief, if PLEDGE ran to fruition.

She held her breath as a man barred the junior's path and asked, "Can I help you, Mister?" and the junior replied, "ComSec. Need to find Blaustein. Know where he is?" and the Secret Service agent replied, "Right this way, then."

Gallen leaned against the tree, weak with relief: this would only work if the junior gave Blaustein the cassette without undue fuss. Then she pushed away from it and stood squarely, depressing the All-Com switch which gave her all the input the van was taking. It was a long shot, a desperate measure, anyhow. If she had any brains, she wouldn't be out here, playing against these odds for purely personal reasons of guilt and desperation. She'd be back in the damned van letting an expendable junior officer try to avoid becoming a statistic.

But she wasn't. She couldn't. It had something

to do with Blaustein and the very real countermoves she was trying to field, countermoves which
might well be her only hope of salvation. But it
had more to do with Sonny Quaid.

And she'd better face that, and admit that she'd
had no intention of doing more than sitting with
the senior in the nice, safe, armored COMINT van
until she'd seen Lucille mincing through the crowd,
handbag clutched in both hands, looking drab and
drawn and fighting a private, silent battle with
terror as she looked fruitlessly among the crowd of
Agency honchos for her husband.

*Shit, you're crazy, Gallen. That little mouse is going
to get you blown. Why didn't she just stay home and
fret?* But Lucille wasn't at home, and Shai might
be able to avoid the funeral because of Blaustein
(avoid Blaustein, at least until he'd listened to the
tape), but she couldn't avoid Lucille Quaid, not
when Sonny's widow hadn't been told and it was
Shai's place to tell her.

Even if Shai hadn't killed the crazy bastard,
she'd have owed his wife at least that. For all the
nights Sonny hadn't come home to Lucille because
he was with Shai, for the son Lucy had whelped
that shackled Quaid to her more surely than iron—
for the man Shai still respected, she'd discharge
her duty as best she could.

The junior's voice cut through the general babble and Shai tapped her hand-held selector onto
his channel, screening out all voices but his and
Blaustein's: "Director Blaustein, sir, this is for you
personally," said the junior.

"Who? . . . Oh, ComSec. Fine, son. Thanks. A
tape, is it?" Then Blaustein's voice changed and
Shai couldn't tell whether he'd read the note or
pocketed the cassette. "What's your name, there?
Hey, son? . . ."

Shai held her breath and heard the junior analyst cursing sotto voce, while occasionally he murmured an apology to someone he jostled.

She realized she'd been on the wrong channel for what she wanted to hear and flicked through the numbered switches until Blaustein's huffy voice selected itself out: ". . . nice looking boy like that ought to have better manners, Jim."

And the President replied, "You know, Kurt, I'm not at all interested in your fag ego problems at the moment. He's just a messenger. Forget him. I want to know why, with thirty thousand men at your command, you can't find your own Deputy in a town as small as D.C. It doesn't look right, her not being here. And who the hell's going to deal with Lucy—"

"Gallen'll turn up. She's on the rag, I'll bet. You know how they are when their hormones start acting up. I haven't seen hide nor hair of her since Luftsen's suicide interrupted her opportunity to read her precious 'dissenting opinion' into the NSC record."

"Well, maybe she's right. If I'd have known they'd start this damn thing an hour late, I'd have stayed away myself. Where do you think the Reverend Whomsoever *is*, anyhow?" complained the President.

The junior was separating himself from the crowd, Shai noticed as she looked up from the channel-selector she was holding. And he had Lucille Quaid with him.

Shai instantly regretted her impulse, but it was too late. She could abort, but what would the junior say to the woman who wanted to know, Shai found as she pressed the right button, "if this is about my husband? Did Sonny send you?"

She listened, for what seemed hours, to the

junior's channel as he helped Lucy Quaid up the slope, a steadying hand on her elbow.

Whatever she missed, whatever was relevant, would be neatly arranged and presented to her by the senior analyst on demand.

Shai could afford a few minutes to prepare for an encounter she might well find, later, had been one she couldn't afford at all.

When she stepped out from between two trees, Lucille Quaid's blue-white hand flew to her throat. "Mrs. Gallen. I thought—Sonny. Is there? . . ."

"Go on up, Buddy. I'll be there in a minute," Shai told the junior, who did as he was told without argument.

When he was out of earshot, Shai said, "Lucille, I've got bad news. Do you want to hear it standing up?" There was no place to sit but in the mud or the snow. Shai should have thought of that.

Lucille Quaid took one step backwards and Shai wondered how firm her footing could be in muddy pumps meant for city streets. Her eyes were wide and her fingers at her throat seemed to be squeezing it tightly. So tightly, in fact, that her mouth worked without a sound.

Shai realized that it was possible the woman might faint. She took a step forward, arms out, ready to grab Lucille if she fell, and said, "Sonny's dead. He was killed in the line of duty. You may have seen something about it in the papers. We couldn't release the name and I wanted to tell you myself. He died in action, valorous service, and we're all very proud of him."

Lucy Quaid glared at Gallen as if about to leap on Sonny's mistress and tear her throat out.

Gallen stayed very still, arms still spread wide. "Come on, Lucy, this is a tough one, and Sonny was always telling me how tough you are. Make him proud of you one more time. He'll get a medal but you're the only one who'll know it. We—" Gallen's voice broke and, as she cursed herself, Lucille Quaid half fell, half stumbled, into her arms.

Shai held the larger woman as Lucille Quaid's body convulsed with animal grief, strangled little yelps of loss and pain that were so eloquent that Gallen, too, started to cry, in her own way: silent, covert tears that rolled down her face unheeded.

Nobody should have to do this, Shai thought to herself. Nobody. But somebody did and, after a few minutes, when Lucille's weeping subsided and she could stand on her own, Gallen mouthed some meaningless phrases and sent her back down toward the funeral, now in progress.

Climbing back up the slippery slope toward the van, Gallen swiped angrily at bushes and melting ice, sweeping up slush she pressed against her lips and eyes to try to erase signs of purely human weakness she couldn't afford to admit, even to herself, that she had.

The first chance Blaustein had to listen to the cassette the gung-ho ComSec kid had given him was after the funeral, on the way to the wake being held in Blaustein's prestigious Embassy Row home.

Most of the mansions on Embassy Row were either missions belonging to foreign governments or chanceries, but Blaustein had argued that CIA needed a place to entertain foreign dignitaries and that the former stucco-and-wrought-iron Libyan mission was just that sort of place. After all, we weren't in a cloak-and-dagger era, Blaustein had argued. And he could point to numerous successes achieved during his time behind the Deputy Director's desk. The adage ran that "there's no such thing as a friendly intelligence service, just intelligence services of friendly governments," and Blaustein's government was very friendly indeed and wanted to be perceived as such.

But the note wrapped around the tape in his hands was far from friendly, and when, having broken the elastic band securing it to the cassette, he read it, he had the presence of mind to pull up the Lexgard window between him and his driver and play the tape on a hand-held, shielded dictation unit he kept in the limo's bar.

When he was done listening, his hands were shaking. The note was unsigned, and that was more terrifying even than the voices on the tape. *Why* had he spoken so thoughtlessly, so forthrightly, with Genya? His mind raced. Was the tape Soviet made, an attempt to coerce him back into line? Or was it something worse? Was it from another government's service, a government who could use this tape to get anything it wanted, within Blaustein's ability to provide, for as long as he lived and as long as Crossfield was in office?

Blaustein's stomach rolled. It was still rolling, making it impossible for him to think, three Maaloxes later, when his Lincoln pulled into his Embassy Row driveway and he saw Snyder waiting for him.

The FBI man was looking cross. Blaustein had been short, even nasty, with him before the funeral. How long? An hour, two hours, ago? Blaustein's sense of duration was shot to hell and he prided himself on never having to wear a watch.

He got out of the car without a word to the chauffeur and shambled up the walkway toward Snyder on the steps.

Beyond the FBI man, he could see caterers bustling

within and a few early arrivals—mourners not close enough to Lufsten to have gone to the funeral but who wanted to pay their respects: a Saudi woman in a leopard-fur coat, a Charge d'Affaires from the Federal Republic, the standard types.

He saw but did not note the van parked down the street in front of some mission or other. It was a world away and his own world was crumbling.

Was it Snyder? Was Snyder out to make himself the Hoover of the '90s? Was Snyder that smart, that capable? Searching the hawkish face of the FBI's finest, Blaustein could only think, *Jews. Damned Jews. We've got to do something about them. Jews are ruining my life.* Yet, somewhere he'd heard that Snyder was German.

"Hello, Snyder. Why not come inside?" Blaustein, shoulders squared, put forth his best front. No use in cowering, none at all. One had to be perceived as effective to be effective.

"Because if you're going to chew my tail off about this Quaid thing, it might as well be where everybody in the community doesn't have to hear it," Snyder said.

Blaustein was so relieved he had an impulse to deposit a loud, wet kiss squarely on Snyder's lips.

"Oh, yes," he said instead, "I did want to talk to you about the Quaid matter. Let's keep it quiet. Find Gallen and tell her it's her job to break the news to Quaid's wife. Put some of your best on this, but don't expect too much in the way of results. It's clear to me that some foreign service is trying to disrupt the US/Soviet Summit—and you know that it could be any of a dozen Third World contenders. So it's nobody's fault. Let's just try to keep our profile low, if you understand me."

Snyder said, with a mixture of relief and incomprehension, "Thanks—for being so frank, I mean. We'll do our part, Director. We'll need a new liaison, of course, but that's Gallen's responsibility, I suppose?"

Blaustein didn't treat the statement as a question, though Snyder's words had had an interrogative inflection. He dodged: "Let's go in and eat. Funerals always make me hungry."

And he did eat, because he was dizzy and the relief he'd experienced at finding out that Snyder wasn't his enemy-of-the-cassette-tape had him giddy to boot.

So he wasn't prepared when, forty minutes later after the house had filled with the truly important among the community and the self-important who always tried to be where their betters were, first Noah Neely and then Shai Gallen herself confronted him.

Each interaction was brief, and each confounding.

Noah said: "Kurt, I need a favor." Behind him was his brother Owen, obviously drunk, weaving on his feet, and staring at Blaustein with huge, baleful eyes.

"Anything, Noah, anything within my power."

"Which is considerable, at the moment," Noah Neely observed and Blaustein's blood ran cold. It was Neely; it had to be. Blaustein never should have sent those thugs after the brother of a man like Noah, an old CIG vet, a stone pro. If it weren't for Crossfield, he wouldn't have. He was about to begin wheedling—anything was negotiable, and Jesus God, Blaustein had enough sexual skeletons in his own closet—when Neely went on:

"My nephew's in town, looking for work. He's ex-Team 6. I was hoping that if a slot came vacant in any suitable position—the Agency, FBI, or Secret Service—you'd give his dossier first consideration."

"Certainly, Noah, I'd be glad to. Your family's been the source of so much talent, how could I refuse?" With bated breath, Blaustein waited for Neely to drop the other shoe. But he didn't. Noah just thanked him and turned, took his child-molesting nerd of a brother by the arm, and melted into the crowd.

Then there was Gallen. Gallen, who came late, dressed somewhat informally for the occasion, and must have come in through the kitchen because that was where the houseboy took him to find her.

"Kurt," she said without preamble. "I took care of Lucille. You can release the name."

"Gallen. Where have you been? We've got unfinished business to discuss. I'm afraid I was harsh—"

"Kurt, I'm in the middle of something. I can't stay. I want you to turn on your TV tonight at 2350 hours. We'll take it from there." And she started toward the kitchen door.

There were too many eyes and ears on them: black women in caterer's uniform, dishwashers and the inevitable few diplomats' wives who always congregate in kitchens, no matter whose. Blaustein couldn't make a fuss. He couldn't demand a clarification or make her stay. He couldn't yell at the woman in field pants and down jacket and stall-mucking boots, demanding, *Is it you, you bitch? Is this your damn cassette? Are you the one who's got me by the balls?*

Gallen certainly didn't look like a dragon lady, a Mata Hari, or anything much more than an outdoorsy girl with color spots in her cheeks and knots in her long blond hair.

He was overreacting, Blaustein told himself, and helped himself to the Tattinger being poured into glasses on silver trays. But then his hand brushed the pocket of his suit coat and he felt the plastic of the cassette in his pocket.

It had to be *some*one. Whoever it was, they'd contact him soon. Someone with more balls than Noah Neely and more smarts than that little twat from Operations. When she did call in next time, Blaustein was going to whip her ass into line. Right into line. Make it clear to her that she was on probation so that, as soon as all this was over and he didn't need an old hand of her sort, he could pick up where he left off, fire her and clean house in the Agency.

The only question was whether he'd still have control of his own destiny by then.

"The *White House?* We're going to closed-circuit this right into the *White House?*" breathed the junior analyst, aghast but impressed.

It was 2340 hours, no time for second thoughts. No time for a balky subordinate. Gallen glanced at the senior analyst, his countenance, like all of theirs, stripped of years by the amber and red work lights of the van's electronics.

"Just get ready to break into the cable circuit when we Zero," advised the senior, beyond whose head Shai could see the master control read-out pulsing as he fine-tuned every piece of equipment.

Even the dark-haired driver, Mac, was on station in what Shai had come to think of as *her* task chair: she leaned between two vertical transports against the van's side doors while, in front of Mac, Console Two was sweeping incoming NSA message traffic—separating, displaying and logging by priority groupings all satellited communica-

tions worldwide which contained the key-words
Shai had gleaned from Blaustein's private file in
Langley's database the night before: *MUZYKANT*
(Musician), somebody's Russian cryptonym; *GLAVA*
(Chief), someone else's, Kalahari; *KAFIR*, which
could mean any of the Bantu-speaking South African tribes or the Nuristani Afghans, but also meant
"infidel" in Arabic and might have something to
do with the Kalahari notations, because the south
African plateau referred to by that name extended
from western Botswana throughout eastern Namibia, as well as a number of phone numbers, including all of Crossfield's private lines.

In spite of herself, Shai was impressed by the
team's skill and the capabilities of the COMINT
van parked, this evening, in Meade's NSA lot among
a dozen others. The van was giving her everything
Cheltenham and Meade were monitoring which
might interest her, whether the point of transmission was Sri Lanka, Dubai or Manchuria; the analysts were giving her full cooperation and, with
the exception of Mac's single comment on the hu-
bris of turning the White House's cable system
into a transceiver under their control, not blinking
a collective eye.

Shai didn't blame Buddy for balking when the
program to take control of the White House's TV
cable started to run: all of them could and would
be summarily shot if they were caught.

But they wouldn't be caught—not alive. And the
upcoming scare she was going to give those privy
to the van's private-stock transmission—Crossfield,
Blaustein, and her friend, the General—served them
right: it was one matter when unknowing civilians
subscribed to cable services that could be used,
even when their sets weren't turned on, to monitor
goings-on wherever such connections existed; it

was another thing for professionals, who *knew* that any such system could effortlessly be subverted to provide high-quality surveillance, to allow their homes . . . their bedrooms, in some cases . . . to be coupled into such systems.

"Just be cool, Buddy," the senior advised his subordinate. "It's not something you'll want to tell your grandchildren about, but I've got to admit that it's one hell of a show we've put together for 'em. We'd get Pulitzers, if any of the press ever caught wind of this."

"Honest to Pete, they won't, Sir," said Buddy to his boss—Buddy's task was to make sure that there was no leakage, that the closed-circuit was really closed, scrambled and impervious to any attempt at unauthorized monitoring. He shifted in his task chair. "Ma'am, you about ready with that final edit? We ought to load the tape. . . ." He tapped his wrist, indicating that time was getting short.

Gallen had been ready for better than five minutes; the splicing block and editing tape she'd been using were above her head on top of the transport rack. She took the reel of one-inch from under her arm and passed it to Buddy, who kissed it and threw her an ingenuous grin before he got up to load it.

"Here we go, then; let's calibrate."

As test tones and pictures filled the COMINT van, Gallen watched with only cursory attention. Something about the cryptonyms she'd found in Blaustein's Ops file bothered her: it was one thing for a DCI to be keeping tabs on something like the Kalahari power station; it was another for him to have exhaustive specs. And then there was KAFIR. She'd have heard about KAFIR if it was Agency sanctioned; and if it were an operation, it was lacking the two-letter area-designator, or prefix, which all running operations must have to be logged and followed. The two Soviet cryptonyms, MUZY-KANT and GLAVA, were obviously asset-designators, from their usage in messages the exact meanings of which were still unclear, and also lacking CIA's in-house filing data. Whatever KAFIR was, it was going to culminate soon, and MUZYKANT and GLAVA were responsible for it.

The two most likely time-frames for KAFIR were the Kalahari junket and the Summit. And whichever was meant, Gallen had to figure out how someone else's ongoing operation might impinge on her own, and soon. Anything Blaustein was involved in was bound to be something Gallen wasn't going to like.

"Ma'am?" the senior analyst said for the second time. "It's 2345 and counting. Want a ringside seat for this?"

"Yeah, sure thing," Gallen said, forsaking the wall against which she'd been leaning. Now that the shit was about to hit the fan, she was wondering if she oughtn't to wait until she had more data.

But the only intelligence failure that was irremediable was that of acting too late. And Gallen had already paid too much in bringing PLEDGE this far. She wasn't about to quit now.

"Okay, Sir," she grinned with more insouciance than she felt. "Let the good times roll."

Around her, heads bent in unison as the team prepared to send the program and take the responses from every viewer as they were uttered.

Jim Crossfield was alone in the study adjoining his White House bedroom, watching the NPT *Panorama's* special broadcast on today's hottest newsflash—the Soviet incursion over the Manchurian border into Red China—and not feeling very good about it.

Rachel Joplin's fat purple lips seemed to be articulating his doom as the camera panned in on her black, shaven-headed face while she explained, "British intelligence sources report that this incursion, supposedly in response to Red China's 'brutal' takeover of Hong Kong, began some eighteen hours ago by land, while, at sea, a task force of nuclear submarines and Soviet warships headed for Hong Kong left its exercise area in the Sea of Japan, and has been confirmed by eyewitnesses in the Pacific theater as well as by satellite photos. Meanwhile, US intelligence and our State Department refuse to comment. The Soviet Union insists that no such incursion is taking place, and an official TASS report suggests that the entire story is a 'reprehensible British provocation, baseless and of only propaganda value,' but at the same time admits that the 'oppressed people of Hong Kong cry out for help as the boots of British oppressors are lifted from their necks only to be replaced by the sandals of the Chinese perverters of socialism.' "

The black woman faced the camera grimly, without blinking while, behind her, the set's backdrop dissolved into a map with large arrows tracking Soviet land and sea forces on Chinese soil and in Chinese waters.

Crossfield pulled his bathrobe around him and, suddenly cold, stabbed a button which opened a locked drawer beside him. In it was a bottle of Glenfiddich he saved for special occasions and the .357 derringer he liked to stroke when he needed to remind himself that there was a way out of anything.

He took out both, and uptipped the four-figure

bottle of whiskey whose top was a sculpted silver stag's head, as if it were Ripple, slugging two inches of the Scotch before he came up for air.

By then, the black harpy who was currently the woman he most detested in all of America, the bane of his life, was telling him and millions of viewers that she was about to "give America its first look at BBC's footage, then—" a self-satisfied chigger smile "—our own Don Welles will moderate a satellited discussion of these events—"

The screen went blank just as Crossfield pointed his derringer at it and said, "Bang."

Blank. Just like that. Crossfield, liquor fuming in his belly, looked for a moment in puzzlement at the gun in his hand, then realized that the screen wasn't pulverized, just snowy, and began to laugh out loud.

First luck of the day—a miserable day, what with Luftsen's funeral and then meeting Noah and Owen Neely at Blaustein's afterward, now this.

Damned Soviets. Couldn't they wait? What was he supposed to make of this? If they wanted him to look good, and they should, this wasn't helping. Like Blaustein wasn't helping. Blaustein had been looking pretty frayed, lately. Almost as if he were losing his grip. For not the first time, Crossfield had a vision of Blaustein laid out in a coffin, his cherubic, fat-cat smile painted on his face, while around his corpse Crossfield danced, victorious.

Maybe, after the Kalahari, during the Summit, he could find out to whom in the Soviet government one complained when one was an agent of influence and didn't like one's handler. The KGB Chairman ought to be safe enough.

Liquor-musings prevented Crossfield from immediately noticing what had replaced NPT *Panorama* when transmission resumed. Then he sat bolt upright as Reuters-type computer script filled the screen and began to scroll downward.

Jacknifing out of his chair, gun in hand, he stalked forward, close to the offending set which was displaying a "letter" addressed to Blaustein and which said: "WE KNOW ALL ABOUT MUZYKANT/GLAVA/KAFIR/POSNER/CROSSFIELD. YOUR ONLY OPTION IS TO FOLLOW THE APPENDED INSTRUCTIONS TO THE LETTER. CODE KEYS WILL FOLLOW.

And the rest was a cryptographer's nightmare. But Crossfield didn't even wait to realize that. He shot his TV at such close range that glass and sparks showered him.

Oblivious, he ran howling into the bedroom, demanding, "Get up, you lazy cunt. You're sleeping and my life's at stake. What's Snyder's number, damn it? And Noah Neely? Get *up!*"

By the time Crossfield's wife had knuckled her eyes, every light in the White House was on, every panic button pushed, and Vice President Jennings was being rousted out of bed by the Secret Service, while the President himself screamed at his Attorney General on the phone: "I don't give a flying *fuck* about the First Amendment! I want *Panorama* off the air. I want that black bitch jailed—I don't care why, sedition, treason, whatever. I want whoever was involved in broadcasting that slander buried so deep that God himself'll never find 'em!"

Blaustein, too, had been alone at 2350 hours, as he'd been instructed by Gallen.

Now, in the bathroom, he repeatedly flushed the toilet before which he knelt, although the bile and heavy food he'd vomited had long ago been swept away. He couldn't remember Gallen's exact words to him this afternoon. *Watch TV. We'll be in touch.* Something like that. But he couldn't remember just what.

He huddled on the tile floor, terror-stricken, his mind frozen in panic. He'd thought, when the news about the Soviet invasion came on, that was what she meant. And that had been bad enough. Genya hadn't even bothered to warn him it was going to happen. The damned Soviets had been playing him, too, using him. Crossfield should have been informed—Blaustein should have been informed. They should have been given a briefing on how to react, given time to prepare.

He tried to get up, but his knees seemed to be made of jello. He could still salvage something—his own ass.

He could run for the Aeroflot jet he'd demanded be waiting for him at National. He could run like hell.

But he couldn't, he realized—not until he figured out who was doing this to him. It could be the Soviets themselves. Maybe Blaustein had outlived his usefulness. Maybe Crossfield was muscling him out. Maybe. Maybe.

And then he did get to his feet. Stumbling into his bedroom, he tried to dress himself but found that his fingers couldn't perform simple tasks like buttoning buttons or zipping his fly.

He slapped on his intercom and winced at the tremulous breathlessness of his own voice: "Ralph, come up here and help me. Order the car, too. Immediately."

He didn't know where he was going, he just had to move, to do something.

He'd go to Langley. Destroy all his files. Wipe the whole damned Ops computer. He could do it. He *would* do it.

And then, as Ralph came running up the stairs, the doorbell rang. And rang again.

Blaustein, holding his pants around his waist with one hand, bolted out the door to stand at the head of his staircase, looking down at Ralph, caught halfway up them, wearing only BVD's and a worried Cocker Spaniel expression.

"Sir, should I get the door?"

"No. Yes. Yes, get the door, Ralph."

When Ralph opened it and one of the men standing there said, "Secret Service," Kurt Blaustein voided in his drawers.

Fox couldn't keep Glenn Alden's death out of his mind. Sitting in Noah Neely's livingroom, in clothes Crossfield's Chief Intelligence Advisor had paid for and Neely's ADC selected for Fox as if Fox were really Neely's nephew, wasn't helping.

Glenn was dead and it was his fault and he was alone in an empty living room, thinking about it. Yeah, he'd do what he said; yeah, he'd play Secret Service agent; yeah, he'd be Shai's kill factor. But Glenn shouldn't have had to die to make it happen. Quaid had known what he was doing; Stevenson was in the business; Platt and Sabanci—even Kathie, though he didn't want to think of the most probable way she had become involved—were combatants of a sort. But Glenn was just an innocent bystander until Fox sent him that letter. And now Glenn was dead, too.

It was a damn waste and it was his fault. He got up, jerking the fancy belt around his new slacks a notch tighter, and parted the curtains on the livingroom's bay window, looking wistfully toward the garage.

From the other room, he could hear voices: Neely and that narrow-assed Yalie of an ADC. Earlier, at

dinner, they hadn't talked to him; they'd talked at
him, then left him alone. He was assumed to be
tame but not civilized.

There was nothing for him to do right now, so
Shai had just shelved him, stashed him someplace
safe.

But *was* it safe? Some damn thing was going on
in there—the phone had rung three times in quick
succession; the lights on its mate by the window
were blinking like a Christmas tree's. He'd have
picked up the receiver, but some of these units let
the conversationalists know when another instrument entered the circuit. He didn't want to cause
any trouble.

He kept thinking about Glenn and the babysitters
and the firefight in Shai's driveway. Then he started
thinking about Shai's house. And M-1. The poor
cat.

He looked at his watch which read 0-dark-20
hours. It wasn't that late. He'd take a run over to
Shai's and if she wasn't home, at least M-1 would
be fed. There'd been nobody there to answer the
phone when he'd received permission to call her
an hour ago.

Yeah, that's what he'd do. Then he could talk to
Shai when she got home. He didn't know what
he'd say, even what he *ought* to say to somebody
who'd done what she'd done and said it had been
to keep him alive.

He let the curtain fall, glad that the night was
clear, and headed for the coat closet where his
quilted jacket was. There'd been a leather jacket
he'd liked at the Neiman-Marcus where the ADC
had outfitted him, but evidently budding Secret
Service agents didn't wear bomber jackets because
the ADC had winced when Fox tried it on.

No sweat, he thought, slipping into his blue

quilted jacket and tiptoeing through the kitchen, the breezeway, and into the garage.

The garage-door opener worked silently, and he wheeled the hot bike out and down the driveway with his neck prickling. He didn't know why he felt he had to sneak away. After all, nobody'd told him he had to stay here twenty-four hours a day. But he knew Neely wasn't going to like it that he'd left.

He'd call from Shai's, if it felt safe. He wasn't exactly a law-abiding citizen. Neither was Gallen, not after Glebe Road. And Neely was involved. He'd never imagined the air could feel so thin up here among the supergrades, never wanted to find out what it would be like to play with the big guys—and girls.

At the end of the driveway, he slipped the helmet over his head, a leg over the bike and fired it up. The feline snarl was comforting. Give him freedom, a reasonably dry road and the snubby he had in his pocket, and he was ready for anything. Only he wished somebody would tell him what the "anything" was, what they were saving him for.

The bumps on his arm had gone down, the warmth of vaccinations faded. What had he been vaccinated against? Rabies? Typhus? The Tasmanian trots? He drove as sedately as the peaky engine permitted down the residential street with its artsy streetlights and its manicured houses, almost all dark, except for porch lights, this late at night. D.C. still rolled up and snored like a small town after ten.

So it wasn't unusual perspicacity that made him look twice at the two mid-sized Fords, which passed him, headed for Neely's, which rode steady as tanks on pursuit shocks, the way State Police cruisers did.

He didn't turn his head, just watched in his rearview mirrors as the two cars pulled up to Neely's and men jumped hastily from both vehicles' back doors.

There was a stop sign and like any good citizen he paused at it, watching to see if the men knocked on the front door or stormed the place.

They knocked, all of them on the front stoop—no one went round the back. Okay, he thought, then it's not big trouble for Neely.

But he was glad as hell he wasn't there to find out what the guys in sport coats wanted, this time of night, with Crossfield's intelligence advisor.

He pulled slowly out into the intersection and headed for the Beltway, thinking that, even if Shai's place wasn't any safer than Neely's, he'd been right to leave when he had.

Instinct. Sometimes it's all you can trust.

Instinct was telling him, when he reached Gallen's, to walk the bike up the drive, so he did.

There were lights on, but there'd been lights on when he left. There was a van—full-sized, not the mini-van the babysitters had had before—parked in front of the house. And Shai's Wagoneer was there.

He stowed the bike in the peach orchard where he could get to it quickly and walked up to the garage, one hand on the snubbie, and hesitated.

He could sidle up to the door without being seen, peek in the windows, and run like hell if it were trouble. But if it were trouble, then where would he run? He hadn't had anyplace to run when he'd contacted Gallen. Things were worse now, not better.

In the end, after too much indecision, he slid the

snubbie back in his pocket, walked up to the front door and knocked.

The COMINT van's driver opened it and said: "It's our little lost sheep. Come on in, Foxy. The party's just beginning."

Shai came darting from the other room: "Fox! God, you gave us a scare. Come on, come in. We've got little enough time to brief you if you want in on this."

"This? What? I—" He stepped inside and M-1 was immediately present and accounted for, stretching up to his full height, paws on Fox's knees and claws digging

"That thing's not a cat, it's a dog," Buddy grinned, greeting Fox with a desultory salute as he joined them. "Some timing. We were just about to make room for you in the Secret Service. Want in?"

Buddy had on some kind of swat-team outfit and was carrying a capture gun of the sort used to shoot tranquilizing darts into animals in the wild. He tossed it to Fox: "Know how to use this? Bet we can suit you up. You're just about my size, 'cept skinnier."

Mac closed the door, saying: "How'd you get here? Fly?"

Fox ignored him, picking up M-1, who began immediately to purr, as an excuse to look around for Gallen. She was leaning against the far wall next to the senior analyst from the COMINT truck and the two had their heads together, whispering.

She saw him looking at her and broke off, coming toward him: "Fox, do you want in or not? You don't have to . . . we're going to pull one of Crossfield's SS boys out of play and stash him—no killing. Just holding—at Zero Site One." Her brow was knitted.

"Conceivably, I can avoid murdering a total stranger," Fox replied. "Is that what you mean, Shai?" When he tensed, M-1 stopped purring.

"I mean that you're already in deeper than you may have expected to be." There was something haggard about her, harried and shut down, that made him know she was fighting for her own life at this point. He didn't know whether that ought to make any difference to him when he'd seen her calmly blow two large-caliber holes in a man she'd been making love to the night before, but it did.

"I'll do whatever you need me to do, Shai. You know that." M-1 began flailing and Fox let the cat hop out of his arms.

"Yeah," she said in an odd way, on a choked breath. "I know, cowboy. I know." Then, more loudly: "Okay, gentlemen, let's go bag ourselves a Secret Servant."

Mac took Fox by the elbow: "Right this way, and we'll turn you into a bona fide night stalker."

Just then, as Gallen was shouldering a gearbag and saying, "We'll wait for you in the van, Fox, Mac," the phone rang.

Everybody froze and the men looked at Gallen, who closed her eyes, opened them, and said, "Don't answer it. It's bound to be Crossfield's office or Blaustein, telling me they want to take a meeting, ASAP. And that's not my idea of a real good time."

When he got outside, dressed in somebody's extra Kevlar-filled coveralls, both car and van were idling and Shai was in the Wagoneer beckoning him.

"Change of plan," she said when he opened the Wagoneer's passenger door. "You're riding shotgun with me."

He slid the capture gun between the leather buckets and got in. "Not funny."

Gallen swiped at her forehead, muttered, "Sorry," and put the car in gear, wheeling into line behind the van as it glided down the drive. "I thought we ought to talk. We may not get another chance."

He didn't say anything. He knew missions like this weren't survivable—not when the targets were national leaders. Booth, Oswald, Sirhan . . . *Fox?* Dead crazies, right? Only Israel's Mossad, in recent history, had been able to get in, scratch, get out and get away with it. And Fox didn't want to kill anybody, right now. Too much killing. There were too many holes inside him where friends and loved ones had been torn away. So he just looked at Shai's patrician profile while the road lights played on it and hoped against hope that she wasn't going to tell him what he already knew.

She didn't. She said, "Fox, where are we?"

"On the Beltway, almost. . . ." The barrel of the capture gun was unreasonably cold but he kept one hand on it, and one eye on the side-mirror, riding shotgun like she'd told him to do.

She didn't even smile. "I want you to know that . . . damn, this is hard to say. . . ." Eyes on the road before her, she began again: "Look, Larry, I'm sorry I got you into this. I can't afford to lose you, I can't let you out, and I've got no right to feel the way I do about you when—" Then she did look at him, out of the corner of her eye, for an instant, pleading for help.

"Yeah, I feel it, too. But it doesn't help. It doesn't change anything." Neither of them could even voice the words: whether it was "love" or "death" they wanted to talk about, or some unholy mixture, the realities behind the words cancelled one another out so what was the use?

"Given the situation," she sighed, "I need to brief you. Stuff you shouldn't need to know. But if something happens and you end up on your own, I want things to make sense to you. You can always get the Com Specs' boss to back you. . . ."

"Nothing's going to happen like that." They tailed the van along the on-ramp and the Beltway stretched before them, lightly trafficked this late at night.

"Whatever. We've arranged to put you in the Secret Service, you know that. You're to hit Crossfield when he takes the reviewing stand at the Kalahari station inauguration. We're going to try to have a Frisbee standing by. If you can make it that far, we'll do the rest."

"Fine," he said dully. Right. Shoot the President of the United States at close range and then sashay calmly through a crowd of American, Soviet, African and Arabian security personnel, steal some vehicle or other, and try to make it to some desert airstrip in broad daylight with no cover, probably not even a knee-high bush, for miles.

"There's something more," she continued. "In fact, there's a lot more. The senior analyst and I," she motioned with her hand, unnecessarily, to the truck they were following behind a narrow space cushion, "looted Blaustein's database. If we've got the cryptonyms right, Blaustein's being run by Georgetown's Genya Posner. Together, they've pulled something funny on this Kalahari station deal; the related data is every damned thing you'd want to know if you were building something like a massive energy weapon which could double as a solar power station. And they've given the Soviets all the go codes to change frequencies. I'm not talking about 60 Gigahertz atmospheric-absorbable weaponry, here. I'm talking about a bona fide doomsday weapon."

"Oh, great. Shai, don't load this on me. I don't need to know why . . . don't feed me like a civilian. It's not going to make any difference." *Not when I'm dead*, he thought but didn't say. "I've got all the reason I need right now." On impluse, he reached out to touch her shoulder.

He was startled when she lowered her head, kissed his fingers, then brushed her cheek against his hand, all without looking away from the road. When she raised her head, she said, "Larry, I'm not betting on being around to explain this to you later. And, no matter what you think, you've got a good chance of making it through this—as good as any of the rest of us have. And if you *do* get through this, I want you to use those keywords I gave you to convince the Joint Chiefs to use the railgun to shoot that damn power station to hell."

The railgun wasn't supposed to exist anymore. Fox craned his neck toward the starry night sky. Crossfield was supposed to have scuttled all the space-based defenses. The electromagnetic railgun launcher, powered by a homopolar generator coupled to an onboard nuclear reactor/turbine system, had onboard phased-array radar and long wavelength infra-red to guide the projectiles it could fire, at velocities above 10 km./sec., at satellites in orbit or nuclear-armed ballistic missiles.

"So you're telling me we've still got one?"

"I'm telling you what you need to know. If I'm out of play, those boys up there will take your orders. Until it's over. Your wrist transceiver's going to be updated and you're going to want to make sure nothing happens to it." She took her eyes away from the road and stared at him for too long, considering the speed at which she was driving.

"Fox, I don't intend this to blow—we're going to bring LEMON PLEDGE home and give this country its first black President, because we don't have any choice."

"Said I was aboard, Shai," he remarked. He guessed he'd said that one time or another. He'd been aboard ever since he closed the vault on Ed Platt. "You don't have to convince me."

He thought she might have said, "Well, I've got to convince myself, then," but he wasn't sure. She reached over to lay her hand on his thigh and, unreasonably, he felt better.

At least he told himself he did.

He felt really odd, thirty minutes later, sitting in the Wagoneer with the capture gun trained on a doorway while Shai stood on the doorstep and waited for the target to answer his nightbell.

She was counting on him not to miss, she'd said. The COMINT truck was parked a little down the street, the two junior officers deployed in the shrubbery around the Secret Service agent's house ready to snatch the target and stow him in the van.

He didn't understand at first why Shai couldn't have shot the dart into the Secret Service agent from close range. And then he did: when the porch light went on, so did a metal-detecting arch built into the trellis: he could hear it from the street, reacting in muted tones to Shai's car-keys. Even a side arm would have triggered a much louder warning, which must have been why Shai had left hers on the Wagoneer's dashboard.

The sights on the gun weren't bothered by the sudden change in illumination: what had been a greenish, night-sight image adjusted itself so that the red laser dot still appeared in the middle of the scope's crosshairs—but not on the target. The 8-power scope allowed him to see the target's mouth attempt to smile despite his obvious irritation at being awakened.

Then Fox squeezed the trigger and the stock kicked his shoulder with more force than he'd expected, although the report was more of a thump than a bang and unlikely to arouse interest even at this time of night.

Fox found that he was weak with relief. He could have hit her. They said it was just a knock-out drug but you couldn't trust what they said. Not what she said, either. And he hadn't wanted to hit her. Watching her matter-of-factly put her person at risk, walk unarmed up to the agent's door, risk her anonymity—for all he knew, her life, since these honchos were playing for such damned high stakes and no one, not even Shai, could be sure how much information the opposition had or how much resistance to expect at any point—to insert him in Crossfield's Secret Service, he'd realized that he'd have done anything in his power to protect her from whatever was behind that door.

But she'd never let him do that. And she was right, they had no business feeling any way at all about one another. He especially had no right to feel protective about his Ops Director—he was just a line officer, a field collector.

He watched the two Com Specs dart out from the shrubbery, scoop up the man who fell so slowly and walk him like a drunk to the COMINT van while Shai closed the target's front door with gloved hands and walked at a measured pace to the Wagoneer.

"Nice shot," she said casually as he leaned across the seat to open the door for her and she got in, putting the Wagoneer in Drive with one hand as she closed the door with the other.

He didn't say anything as he stowed his weapon.

He was nauseated and his palms were sweating. It was one thing, he realized, to have his own butt on the line; it was quite another to watch a woman he ... cared about ... take chances a woman ought not to be taking.

But there was nothing he was going to be able to do about that, except maybe put himself in the way of another bullet meant for her like he had in the Lebanon. *If* he happened to be around when the opposition realized that, as long as Gallen lived, none of them were safe.

When Gallen arrived at the NSC's Emergency Session, she didn't seem to understand what was going on.

Crossfield watched the woman especially carefully because Kurt was sure she was part of the problem. Or so Kurt had told him. But Blaustein, sweating visibly and mopping his forehead intermittently, was entirely too nervous. Crossfield had known Blaustein too long not to realize that the Acting Director of Central Intelligence wasn't levelling with him.

Gallen, in a skirt for once, sat down with a nod and punched up the log of the meeting's proceedings on the LCD screen set into the table in front of her place while, simultaneously, Snyder was giving his opinion on Crossfield's proposition that the entire broadcast incident was the work of Communists.

For all Crossfield knew, the standard ploy might be the truth. Kurt was too nervous. And, beside him, Vice President Jennings was squirming uncomfortably: there were lots of Black communists, and the proposal to arrest and try as a subversive the black woman from NPT hadn't sat well with Jennings, a former ACLU staffer with a law degree.

No one at the table seemed to want to confront the issue of how and why security had been breached so flagrantly in the White House.

Snyder was saying, "—people have determined that only the White House, Blaustein's Embassy Row residence and your place, General, received the transmission. We—"

Crossfield exploded: "Does that make it all right, then? What's the matter with your people, Snyder? Security's your province." He let his mouth rant on auto-pilot, watching first Gallen then the general across from her, askance.

The two were having a bit more eye contact than usual, but that didn't mean anything.

When Noah Neely came back from wherever he'd gone, a dripping umbrella in hand because, outside, it was finally raining—not sleeting or snowing, but raining, a sure sign of spring—he tripped on the rung of his chair and stumbled, saving himself with a stab of his umbrella as if it were a cane.

His whole Cabinet was falling apart, Crossfield thought as Blaustein yelped, "Ouch! Damn it, Neely, that was my foot! Watch where you're brandishing that thing."

Neely, looking old and frail and visibly shaking, widened his sheep's eyes and murmured a broken apology.

Bunch of geriatrics. Crossfield couldn't take any more. "Gallen," he interrupted Snyder's attempt to defend himself from Crossfield's implication of incompetence. "Have you got anything to add to these proceedings? Does Operations have any idea what this message means?" And he read it with as much innocence and cache as he'd have used in a campaign speech: "WE KNOW ALL ABOUT MUZYKANT/GLAVA/KAFIR/POSNER/CROSSFIELD.

YOUR ONLY OPTION IS TO FOLLOW THE AP-
PENDED INSTRUCTIONS TO THE LETTER. CODE
KEYS WILL FOLLOW." He glared at Gallen, the
famous fighting glare that had won him the highest
office in the land. "Well, did they? Have the code
keys been transmitted? Surely, we could intercept
such a transmission?"

"Surely, if it were sent. But it hasn't been, not
by technical means. So we don't know any more
than you do—those of you who received the transmission." Her delivery was deadpan.

"And your whole cryptology department can't
crack this code?"

"It's a sophisticated matrix code, sir. We'll crack
it eventually. Has anyone looked into a linkage
among the three of you?"

She looked from Crossfield, to Blaustein, to
Westin, the one-star general who represented the
Joint Chiefs, and who'd have been a four-star long
since but for his refusal to accept further promotion.

The skin around Westin's eyes crinkled and
Crossfield remembered the rumors that Gallen and
Westin played house every once in a while.

"We're all going to the Kalahari start-up, Shai,"
Westin offered. "That's all I can think of."

Gallen nodded and stabbed at the keypad in
front of her before turning to Blaustein: "Sir? Any
ideas?"

"None, Deputy." Blaustein's dislike for the woman
he'd been about to fire before people started dropping like flies in his Agency was ill-concealed.

"And you," the woman said to Crossfield, "Mister
President? Do you have a guess, a suspicion, anything we could use as a starting point?"

"Not a damned thing," Crossfield said shortly,
"beyond the scenario Kurt proposed: Third World

crazies trying to ruin my image, distract the people from the monumental value of the Summit."

"Mister President," Neely said slowly, "I have no theory, but a recommendation."

"Go ahead, Noah," Crossfield said, suddenly uneasy. Neely's body was aged and fragile but his mind was still a deadly weapon. "Perhaps you should cancel your trip to Africa . . . until all this subsides and—"

"*Absolutely not!*" Neely's suggestion was so unexpected that Crossfield's temper, already on a short leash, broke free. "I'm going to inaugurate that station and bring the benefits of civilization to those dark—" He flicked a glance at Jennings, but the black Vice President hadn't caught (or refused to notice) the slip of Crossfield's tongue. "—to the Less Developed Countries of South-West Africa: it's America's gift, the only thing that can halt the spread of Pan-Islam. And I don't need to tell you what those strategic minerals down there are worth."

Crossfield sat back, waiting for Blaustein to speak up in his favor, to assure all present that CIA was up to the job of protecting Crossfield's entourage anywhere in the world. But Kurt was rubbing the back of his neck and staring off into space, so that it was General Westin who assured Crossfield that "DIA's going to have AWACs and air support, special forces on site, the whole nine yards. If we're now talking about the Kalahari," Westin stood up, "I've got a briefing prepared, with your permission, sir?"

Crossfield waved a hand in assent and leaned back in his chair, watching Neely. What a damned weird thing for Neely to say—what an obvious slap in Blaustein's face. It was probably because Blaustein had pushed Owen Neely too hard, blackmailing him with underage sexual partners, and Owen had run to his big brother for help in getting Blaustein off his back.

Crossfield let his mind wander back to MUZY-KANT/GLAVA/KAFIR, wondering if one of those code-names were his. He'd have asked Kurt if he thought he could get a straight answer. But Blaustein wasn't giving any straight answers lately.

Resolving to find some way to rid himself of Blaustein, Crossfield turned his attention to the Kalahari briefing. He needed to make sure that the trip went off without a hitch.

When the NSC meeting was finally over and the participants were leaving, Westin asked Gallen to lunch.

Her gut cramped, but she agreed. She had to talk to Westy, anyhow. It was just that she couldn't remember when she'd last slept and she'd wanted to talk to Noah.

Neely came up behind her as the cars were being brought around and gave her a fatherly hug, whispering, "We're on target, my dear. Your insertion's complete, my ADC just called. And don't worry. It's a fait accompli."

She wanted to ask, *What? What's a fait accompli?* but there wasn't time.

And when Westy settled in his staff car beside her and hit the privacy button, he was even more mysterious.

"Bet you're not hungry. Let's go to my place." The horse-faced general grinned lasciviously.

This was no time to pay back favors, Shai thought wildly. Something must have shown on her face, for the general said: "Just so I can brief you, dear. You wanted a Frisbee, and some other support. We need to go over the details."

"Frisbee'd was a nickname for AWAC; Shai relaxed. Noah must have meant that he'd arranged the logistics with the general.

By three o'clock that afternoon, Shai Gallen was putting on her clothes after a shower with the man who'd given her the COMINT truck and the Com Specs and perhaps a new lease on life.

"That's some operation you're running," said Westin who'd been content for years with one star, his eyes sparkling. "If you were a man, I'd adopt you—the son I never had."

"You like me better the way I am, don't bullshit me," she said and wished she hadn't been sharp. Buckling her belt over the dress she'd worn so that she'd look calm, collected and prepared at the Emergency Session for which she'd been none of those, her throat tightened up.

In General Westin's bedroom was a window and she leaned her head on the glass, staring down at the muddy grounds where snow was melting under a pelting rain: "I really want my singleton to make it, get out of this alive."

"We'll do our best. You ought to be thinking about yourself." Liver-spotted hands slipped around her waist from behind.

"My*self*?" She laughed harshly and suddenly all the fears she'd been suppressing surfaced. "There's only one thing I want, and that's out. I want to go home, take my cat, and run like hell. But there's nowhere to run."

"That's right," said the old warhorse. "There's not. Not for any of us, if this doesn't work. You've just got pre-op jitters. Happens to the best of us. Come on, lady, and I'll buy you a cup of coffee."

It didn't seem like a cup of coffee was going to help, but somehow, in the general's company, it did.

*   *   *

When Aeroflot landed Genya Posner at National, a car was waiting for him.

And that was bad, because he hadn't been expecting—hadn't wanted—a car. He liked to take anonymous taxis, liked to keep his profile low.

But the car was there and Ralph, one of Kurt's chickens, was insistent that he get into it.

Perhaps they had pushed too hard, too soon. Perhaps this was the end, Posner thought gloomily, alone in the back seat of the limousine as it sped toward America's capital. Perhaps Blaustein had realized what KGB could do—planned to do—with KAFIR.

The Soviet agent leaned forward to look out the window. Such a beautiful country. Such a rich and wasteful, spoiled and arrogantly beautiful country. What a wonder it would be when both superpowers shared the same ideology. What a relief to his economically stressed motherland.

Blaustein's usefulness was nearly over, the work nearly done. Whatever threats or schemes Blaustein fielded could be countered. KGB had seen to that. In Abu Dhabi, Posner had been briefed, told many things that, until now, he had not needed to know. And what he had been told was enough. He was proud of what he'd done, content with it—even should Blaustein balk and, balking, stop all apparent progress, it was too late to undo what had been started. The great enemy, America, was all but on its knees.

The sun was just breaking through the clouds and Posner was reminding himself to tell the Aeroflot dispatcher that there was no longer any need to have an entire jet sitting idle, ready to wing whither at Blaustein's whim, when the limo in which he was riding disintegrated, turning into an orange fireball so quickly that neither Ralph, the driver, nor Posner, the passenger, had time to suffer more than an instant of agonizing flash as the explosion sent shrapnel and their pureed bodies at speeds of up to five thousand feet per second in every direction, causing a dozen cars around them to crash into one another and twice that many secondary fender-benders as the fast-moving traffic tried to avoid the crater in the left lane.

Blaustein was on his way to National himself, driving a nondescript fleet car and sweating like a roasting pig.

He'd spent the afternoon in his office, trying to wipe files. But he couldn't decide which ones. He might need to call up data at some future date, data he could put to good use in Moscow.

After all, he was still Acting Director of Central Intelligence, as far as anyone knew. And he'd played this last operation by the book. He'd left a message saying he was taking a few days accumulated sickleave, which he had coming. He'd not been *ordered* to go to the Kalahari. Nobody would miss him.

He'd sent Ralph for Genya, and Ralph had a cassette to give MUZYKANT, a cassette on which the appropriate threats—countermeasures, actually—were detailed, as well as a list of demands.

So, it was over—all but the payoff.

Blaustein wiped his lips. He didn't understand why he was sweating so much, why he was so dizzy. His chest and throat were tight and his left arm had pins and needles running up and down it. He couldn't take any more stress, that was all. He'd be fine once he got on the plane. He pulled out to pass another car and his mind began to wander:

could the Aeroflot pilot be persuaded to change their destination? Take him to the Aegean? Blaustein deserved a little rest before he had to confront the KGB Chairman on Dzerzhinsky Square.

There were flashing lights up ahead—some sort of accident on the other side of the median strip had caused a huge jam and traffic was being diverted.

He had to slow his Ford to a crawl and follow red cones set up to route the outbound traffic into two lanes so that the inbound traffic could jounce over the median and use the other two lanes.

Traveling at five miles an hour, it was going to take forever to get to National. Blaustein wiped his forehead again. He had a pain behind his eyes, as if the air pressure were too great. Maybe he was coming down with something, he thought, as his car and the traffic crawling before it came abreast of a clot of tow-trucks with flashing lights that were trying to separate tons of twisted metal, some of which looked like it had come from a war zone, not a traffic accident.

He'd just gotten by it when his left arm went numb. Damned arm, falling asleep. It was good he was getting out now, while he still had his health.

Blaustein had made the decision to cut and run while sitting in the NSC's Emergency Session, watching Gallen. It wasn't that he thought the twat could ever beat him; it was that it didn't matter to him to prove it, not enough to stay. Crossfield was going to find out who GLAVA and MUZYKANT were, it was just a matter of time. And then he was going to find out about KAFIR—a technical collection file of whose purpose Blaustein and even Posner himself had been given only the briefest hints by their masters. About KAFIR—

Blaustein slumped forward in sudden agony, his

forehead on the steering wheel, his body convuls-
ing as a massive coronary ripped through him.

During its progress, he depressed his accelerator
pedal to the floor and his car rear-ended the one in
front of it.

By then, Kurt Blaustein was beyond help. The
poison injected through the tip of Noah Neely's
umbrella was very classified and undetectable by
autopsy. It had a number, but no name, in Technical Services, where the unbrella had originated.

Rank did have its privileges, and Noah Neely,
who'd been in the community since CIG's formation,
hadn't even had to fill out a requisition form to
save his brother's reputation.

Somewhere in the world, twenty-four hours a
day, a National Airborne Command Post E-4A,
a modified 747 with airborne launch equipment
for the United States' nuclear arsenal, is always
flying.

This one, designated Air Force One, had half her
full complement of ninety passengers aboard. One
of them was Larry Fox, alias Lincoln Neely Ford.

Fox kept trying to read the briefing book on the
Kalahari trip, but the problems of the non-Tswana
peoples, the migrating Bantu and the civil wars
spilling over from South Africa and Rhodesia,
couldn't hold his interest. If the authors of the
Secret Service briefing seriously expected Fox/Ford
and his dozen compatriots to successfully spirit
Crossfield, by land and under fire, across the
Kalahari's desert and dry grassland to Serowe, a
tribal village of thirty thousand natives, and from
there to the Botzam road which led from the
Zambian border to Gaberone, Botswana's capital,
those authors were kidding themselves.

If there was going to be trouble—from the

South Africans, the Cuban-supported revolutionaries in Zimbabwe, the Namibians, or any of a score of white mercenary armies-for-hire that circulated in the South, a dozen Secret Service agents with Mini Uzis in attache cases weren't capable of stopping it, not with ninety-six rounds of 9×19 per man.

Of course, Fox/Ford also had his desert-issue SIG and two extra clips on his belt. If he could have taken the insertion/extraction/logistical/tactical problems of the venue seriously, he might have been as jumpy as the old Service hands around him.

But he couldn't. He only needed one 220 grain KTW bullet to do what he had to do. What came after wasn't going to matter to him a whole lot.

Still, there was a nearly imperceptible red dot on his map of the staging area, a dot that appeared on his copy alone (he'd checked the agent's next to him when the fellow went to the head) and marked the location of the Frisbee he'd been told would be waiting for him at the airstrip.

So he tried to ignore the other agents around him, the banter of the dignitaries and functionaries forward, where Crossfield was holding forth, and commit the best route to the construction airstrip to memory. But his mind kept balking. It wasn't the distance or the terrain—he'd probably be able to see the Frisbee from the steel reviewing stand, opposite the technical control center, where he'd be stationed. But by the same token, every one of the other agents around him would have a great view of the assassin as he broke for safety. Damned desert. There just wasn't a way around it; Larry Fox was going to get himself shot to pieces sometime around 1300 hours tomorrow, local time.

"Hey there," said the agent who had the seat next to him as he came aft with two steaming plastic cups and handed one to Fox, "take this. The tour's got champagne, but—" the agent, sitting down in the seat next to Fox's, reached into his back pocket and produced a hip flask "—we're not entitled. This isn't exactly by the book, but? . . ." He held the flask poised over Fox's cup, ready to pour whatever booze neither of them should be drinking into Fox's coffee.

It was the first overture of friendship any of the old Service hands had made, so Fox nodded and said, "Just a taste won't hurt, I guess. Nothing's going to happen up here that I'd need quick reflexes for—except grabbing my flotation cushion." He smiled at the Secret Service agent, who was wearing his sunglasses even though it was night outside the plane's window.

"Nothing's going to happen that you'll need quick reflexes for, period," the other said forcefully, pouring a generous dollop of brandy into Fox's cup and then his own. He sipped and sighed. "You know, Ford, it's not that we're standoffish. It's just that this is a hell of a time to get a new man, and some guys don't like the way your uncle, up front, muscled you into a slot most of us worked years for."

At least somebody was being honest. Fox said, "Thanks for saying so," while relief beat the brandy and caffeine into his system and taut muscles relaxed: the way they'd been treating him, he hadn't been sure whether some of them might suspect something. But it was just the old pecking-order blues, one more time.

Feeling better, he slipped his .45 out of his holster and, balancing his attaché kit on his knees, began the process of strip-and-clean, saying, "This thing's digging into my hip something fierce."

The other agent brushed his sport coat back to reveal a canted belt-holster. "Get you one of these, if you like, when we get home. Beats the hell out of anything else when you're sitting, armed, most of the time."

Fox looked at the agent's high-tech holster and thought, *Yeah, until you've got to get it out to use it.* What was going to happen to Larry Fox wasn't going to happen while he was sitting on his duff.

He took another swig of the coffee and asked, "How many other security forces do you think there'll be—besides the Soviets and the Cubans, I mean?"

Beyond, he could see the dignitaries and functionaries and staffers milling around a buffet with plastic champagne glasses and helping themselves to chateaubriand and pate. Back here, it was roast beef sandwiches and light beer. Most of the agents were sleeping or writing notes on pads of onionskin with USG watermarks and raised gold-leaf in the left-hand corner which said in boldface: ABOARD AIR FORCE ONE beside a relief of the Presidential seal.

Up front, only two of the agents were on duty, staring back toward the tail of the plane from their posts against the forward bulkhead, faces impassive. Fox was trying to practice that look, peculiar to the breed, when "Uncle" Noah came back to use the facilities—or to reassure him—and said, "How're we doing, Linc?"

"Oh, fine, Uncle Noah. Just fine," Fox said; his discomfort at being singled out was as appropriate to a beneficiary of overt nepotism as to what he really was—an inserted assassin awaiting his moment. Neely was going to have some problems after this one blew—but Larry Fox was the wrong man to worry about that.

He dozed off wondering whether the sense of detachment he was experiencing, the feeling that he was living a bad dream and whatever happened in it wasn't going to matter in the real world, came with the territory. He'd find somebody else who'd been tapped for a walk-up if he got through this, he promised himself, and ask the bastard.

If he got through this.

Shai Gallen, who'd flown to Sri Lanka with Westin in a "prototype," a black wasp of an aircraft with red NASA designators on its tail that wouldn't fool anybody who knew his transatmospheric spyplanes, began unzipping her pressure suit as soon as the onboard ladder started descending and the canopy rolled back.

The suit was squeezing her guts together and her neck ached agonizingly from all the G's they'd been pulling. Her mouth was dry and her pulse rate well over one hundred. It hadn't been the plane's speed which frightened her; it was the physical stress, coupled with the knowledge Westy was just too old to have reaction-time quick enough to make a difference if the X-TAV prototype hit any clear turbulence.

All she'd been able to think about—at least until they pierced the atmospheric envelope and she saw the way the stars looked from inner space—was that these old warlords had a habit of killing themselves in classified aircraft.

But then Westy had started talking to her in raspy, short breaths about the conclusions his study group had come to relevant to the "capability and intentions of KAFIR and its controllers, dear. If there's one place we can talk with absolute security, it's up here in Peregrine."

It took her a moment to realize that "Peregrine" was the aircraft arcing over the curving Earth at better than Mach 12, another to understand that she was in this plane, with this man, because whatever he wanted to say demanded such irregular and inordinate security procedures.

She and Westy should have gone in the E-4A with the others; she'd wanted to be there, for Fox. Be with him, even if they couldn't acknowledge one another. But Westy had ended all chance of it. And, on the ridiculously short flight to Sri Lanka, where they were to meet the Frisbee and the Com Specs seconded to Gallen's reshet, the General had deigned to tell her why.

"Shai," he'd said, his words sounding like grunts because of the G-force as he wrestled with the big black bird swooping downward, "we're reasonably sure that Rockwell Number One is going on line as a weapon, not a power station, in the very near future."

"You mean that the Soviets will enable it during the test? Use it against Crossfield's party? But why? They'll have their own dignitaries on site. The casualties ... the trauma. What would be the point of—" Then she'd stopped talking and started thinking. Somebody had blown away a limo with Genya Posner in it: Blaustein had suffered an all-too-timely heart attack. Maybe the Soviets were nervous about Crossfield, now stripped of controllers and contacts. Maybe Westy was right. But it didn't make operational sense—you don't use a weapon for display, not one as awesomely capable as the Kalahari power station's specs whispered it could be.

"Probably not during the test, no." Westy's gritty voice had a touch of laughter in it. "Not unless we help them along a little."

"*What?*" she gasped, and not because the Peregrine was diving toward denser atmosphere.

"My dear, I'd like your professional opinion. . . .
If we were to enable and demonstrate the weaponry in the Kalahari satellite, could it be floated
as an aggressive hostile act by the Soviet Union?
Could we blame Crossfield's assassination on them
and handle the questions as to why they'd sacrifice some of their own?"

"I . . . suppose. With the specs we've got. It's
their project, their—Jesus, Westy, how do you know
they're *not* planning the same sort of thing?" She
paused but Westin didn't reply. Then she added,
"Yeah. Sure, we could surface them, no matter
how the station demonstrated its aggressive potential."

"And our diplomatic posture at that point?"

"After something like that? Break off diplomatic
relations while letting them argue that it was an
American failure, an accident caused by our slov-
enly security practices and an attendant scheme to
divert attention from our own failure. Cancel the
Summit for sure. But why are we gaming this?
. . ." She asked, not because she hadn't guessed,
but because she wanted to hear Westy say it.

"Because," came the voice from the pilot's seat
in front of her, "we're going to make sure that this
demonstration of the power station's capabilities
is complete. Then we're going to use the railgun to
shoot the sucker right out of the sky. As we must,
of course. Since they can't be allowed to unilaterally assume control of space, *or* divert control of
American technology. That's why I wanted you up
here. You've got to make sure you're in the control
bunker, under all that concrete, with me. And I
want you to realize what's at stake here, before—"

Before you try to warn your agent off, she finished
his sentence silently, unable to speak because her
mouth and throat felt as if they were lined with

shards of glass. *Oh, Larry, what have I gotten you into?*

That had been better than an hour ago and Westy and she hadn't spoken since. The old general knew what Shai was going through, what sacrificing lives of subordinates for no good reason could do to a commanding officer. And yet, there wasn't a choice, not really. They'd gone through hell to insert Fox in the Secret Service and get him slotted on the podium behind Crossfield.

If Shai tried to pull him out, somebody would smell a rat.

She said, on the runway as she finished unzipping her suit and took a deep breath of Sri Lanka's perfumed sea air, "What about Noah? Does he know? Can we save him, at least?"

"Noah would stand there beside Crossfield willingly, Shai. So would I. So would you." It was night in Sri Lanka and the stars shed light that glistened on Westy's eroded face. "So would your man Fox, if he knew the extenuating circumstances. Give him a chance to do what he's volunteered to do, Shai. He's paid for it."

She was thinking, *A chance to die? To fucking fry? For no good reason? For no damned reason at all?* when the AWAC which would be the real control center for operations at the Kalahari test site fired up its engines and an oval of light appeared in its side as the door was opened for them while a jeep came speeding to hustle them aboard.

There were all sorts of types milling around the steel reviewing stand in the middle of the Kalahari. It looked more like a political rally or a football game than a technological breakthrough waiting to happen, Fox thought. Except for the sand, and the fact that there wasn't a football gridiron, just a huge collection base station of transformers and domes under a sand-screen that seemed to be the size of Texas, on the far side of which was a concrete ground-control station and what seemed like miles of stun fence, it might have been the Army/Navy game, there was so much excitement in the air.

The excitement reserved for the Secret Service was the meeting and greeting of the Soviet, Cuban, Angolan, Zambian Namibian, Saudi Arabian and Libyan Secret Services.

They had their own trailers—a little park of them like miniature hostile nations. There were metal-detecting arches everywhere, and, despite the Administration's determination to make this a show of good faith and good fellowship, every single guest had to be run through the gauntlet of every security service.

The agents had been on-site since dawn, checking everything out with mine-sweepers and electro-optical vans and trucks and hand-held detectors of a dozen sorts. It reminded Fox of the COMINT van and he felt just as uneasy as he had when he'd been in it. High tech of this sort was all classified, and Fox had never had that kind of clearance, or the schooling to apply for it. It was all just bells and whistles to him.

The realization that half the Saudi security force was Western—Brits, Aussies, Frogs—came as a bit of a shock. The Saudis were here to see if they wanted to buy one of these installations—they were probably the only non-superpower on Earth who could afford one. One of the Brits thought he recognized Fox and Fox had had a heart-stopping moment when the guy yelled, "Hey, Mate!"

He'd been in Turkey long enough to have met his share of Brit Special Air Services personnel, which was what the fellow looked like he was. But the buddy-buddy gleam in the Saudi security chief's eyes faded on closer inspection and Fox didn't even have to deny that he was Fox. The guy just apologized and wandered away.

There were too many Blacks to suit the Secret Service's agent-in-charge, and he was going through his roster looking for someone who could tell a Ndebele from a Shona. That wasn't Fox, either.

Finally, Fox snuck away and hid in the trailer, staring out at the desert through his polarized glasses and hoping, irrationally, that one of the vaccinations he'd been given had been against malaria.

He cleaned the SIG again, checked his attaché case with its Mini Uzi, satellite-link secure phone/modem, and handie-talkie. He reseated the button mike in his ear. He spent some time in the head, but nothing happened.

He'd never been this nervous before. But he'd never done anything like this before. The closest he'd come had been with Platt, and that hadn't been coldly premeditated. That had been something about honor and revenge.

This was just a walk-up.

If he did, by some miracle, make it to the Frisbee he could see, fifteen miles away as the buzzard flew, gleaming on the flat plain in the unrelenting sunlight, he could probably make a living doing this sort of thing. If he could just stomach it.

The trailer door opened and shut. "Ford? Ford, damn your ass, didn't your uncle tell you we work for a living?"

"Yeah, yeah. Can't a man take a shit in peace?" He flushed the chemical toilet and fussed around with paper and soap and water he didn't need.

Finally, he splashed cold water on his face and opened the door.

The man waiting was the agent who'd given him the brandy aboard Air Force One. "You all right, Ford?" The other agent took off his sunglasses and peered at Fox. "Heat getting to you? My shirt's soaked under this damned coat."

Fox said, "Something like that. Sorry," and slipped past the agent out into the blazing sun.

About ten minutes later, one of the Brits clapped him on the back, joined him by the ten-foot stun fence and said, "Bloody hell. You'd think somebody'd have had sense enough to tell your Crossfield that you don't schedule for noon in a sodding desert, what?" The Brit had a huge nose and piggish eyes, a receding chin that seemed part of his wrestler's neck.

Fox shrugged, "Bunch of idiots," and grinned.

Suddenly there was a scuffle, then shouts behind them. Fox and the Brit turned and ran full-tilt toward a cloud of dust rising from the sand.

When they got there, Fox had his SIG out and the Brit had snapped a Sterling submachinegun out of a web holster on his hip and was shouting like a bobby or a drill sergeant, "What's all this now? Come on, blokes! Clear off!"

The "blokes" turned out to be two Blacks settling a family quarrel on the spot, Fox and the Brit found out when they'd collared the men in dashikis and dragged them round through the security enclaves until they found someone who spoke the requisite language in the Botswana security tent.

Fox tried to melt into the background—he'd just done what, under no circumstances, he should have: drawn attention to himself. He was congratulated, his name was asked, and the Brit thought he'd found a buddy and asked him, "over to our place for a spot of iced tea, hey?"

He didn't know whether he dared refuse, whether he'd gotten lucky or unlucky when his own people came looking for him and he was dressed-down for "grandstanding."

He hadn't been. But he'd been thinking about hiding in one of the Brits' lorries. He could have managed it—hidden out and gone AWOL. If the Brits wouldn't have him, the Frogs would. He could have tried it.

The lost opportunity to become a living deserter before he became a dead assassin obsessed him as it faded.

Back at his own trailer, as Crossfield's Vertical Takeoff and Landing aircraft cut the Muzak beginning to blare from loudspeakers on poles and Land Rovers and armored Chevy Suburbans came crawling through the gates in greater and greater numbers, the Secret Service agent in command gave everybody the de rigueur pep talk: "It's never routine. Don't assume anything. Watch the Libyans especially. Okay, boys, let's get to it."

And they got to it, which meant that Fox had to take his position near a gate only Crossfield's car would use, then trot alongside the Suburban as it nosed at three miles per hour through the crowd up to the reviewing stand.

There were mikes on the stand, red-white-and-blue bunting, and above it the flags of half a dozen South African nations hung limply beside those of Saudi Arabia, the Soviet Union and the Pan-Islamic Republic of Libya.

Fox, waiting to open Crossfield's door, considered nonperformance one more time and then gave in. He'd shoot Crossfield, just like Shai had told him to, at close-range with the SIG on his hip. He really didn't have to worry about what he was going to do after that. The podium was fourteen feet deep and there would be, when the Soviet Vice Marshal of NII 13 and his entourage joined the others, more than thirty-five security people up there with him.

So it was just a matter of going through the motions.

Crossfield's door opened and the jut-jawed face broke into a crowd-pleasing smile. The President's blue eyes were proud, glittery, untroubled.

He looked up at Fox for a moment, nodded, and got out of the car. Fox and three of his fellow agents closed around the broad back in its tropical worsted, TV-blue suit as smoothly as an airlock and, each agent looking toward a different compass point, they buffered Crossfield as he made his way to the steps in back of the reviewing stand.

The one thing a Secret Service agent needed to know, Fox thought, was how to walk backwards, to know where you're going when you're looking where you've been or have no intention of going.

Noah Neely, he noticed, was getting out of the next car, ready to follow. A page hurried up to Neely, handed him a message and pointed to the control bunker. Neely nodded and followed the man with the red-white-and-blue armband in the opposite direction.

A change of plan, Fox realized. But it didn't matter.

As Crossfield mounted the steps to the tune of "The Star-Spangled Banner," and Fox followed, the ersatz agent's palms began to sweat.

In the control bunker, Neely had been handed a further message: *Stay put. S.*

At least it was cool in the electronics-filled operations center—a necessity for the equipment, not the operators. Neely sat down where the page, a dark-haired, Sicilian type with military posture and manners, indicated.

He asked no questions. His heart was aching and he was filled with despair. You just couldn't do it—you couldn't force peace, nor amity, nor reason, nor even armed neutrality among nations. Neely had spent his whole life doing things he detested for goals he revered. Now, about to watch an American intelligence service—CIA, for years referred to as "the President's intelligence service"—assassinate its own leader, the goal finally seemed unattainable, the means insupportable. Noah Neely would have changed places with James Crossfield gladly, if he could.

When the page, who'd introduced himself as "Mac," slid one of those new-fangled electronic briefcases in front of Neely and said, "Sir, if you'll just pick up the handset, you've got a call," Neely did as he was told.

A facsimile of Shai Gallen's face appeared on an LCD video screen no bigger than Neely's wallet. The voice coming from the receiver against his ear said, "Noah, where are you? Where's your nephew?"

He told her, puzzled but too distraught to think about why he should be.

"I'll be right over," she said, and the screen went blank.

Gallen and Westy were still arguing about it when the senior analyst from the COMINT van—Gallen still thought of him as "Sir," in lieu of an offered name—said, "We're go," leaned back from his console, hands behind his head, and grinned fondly at the bank of controls before him in the

AWAC. "You want your boy, Ma'am, you've got . . . seventeen minutes, thirteen seconds to get him."

Westy shut his mouth, threw up his hands and said, "Dear, I'll wait two minutes in my car for you. Then I'm gone." And the General stomped out of the AWAC.

"Buddy," Shai said, "what's the closest safe distance?"

"Shit." Buddy, at the secondary console, punched up a simulation and waved at it. "System thinks it knows but it doesn't." His stabbing finger showed her concentric circles around the designated blast area. "That much power, through atmosphere. . . nobody's ever tested anything like this that we know of, that right, Sir?"

"Sir" said, "That's right. You've got thermals to consider, fragmentation if everything doesn't just melt. There are a certain number of explosive elements, ammunition that's going to cook off if it isn't vaporized, that sort of thing. I'd say it's still either make it to the control bunker or hit the dirt and pray, Ma'am."

"Okay," she said. She handed Buddy a cassette: "Send this to Noah Neely when Westy and I stop at the gate for our security check."

"Roger, Ma'am," said Buddy laconically, but he gave her the high sign as she grabbed her gearbag, slung it over her shoulder and ran for Westy's staff car.

No matter what she thought, or what she regretted, it was too late to change plans or stop the operation in progress in the AWAC. The Kalahari power station was going to show its true colors by blowing away everybody on the desert reviewing stand and probably half of the senior press corps, and then the electromagnetic railgun under the

AWAC's control was going to blow the power satellite out of the sky.

But she was going to do her damnedest to make sure that Larry Fox didn't get blown away with all the rest. It wasn't an emotional decision; it was operational: Shai Gallen didn't want to try living with herself if she didn't try to save Fox.

Fox saw Westy's staff car approaching: generals will be generals, and Westy had his flags on his front fenders. Anyway, he was looking for it. The old bugger was late and Fox's boss was bitching. Fox couldn't afford anything to be out of the ordinary.

In his pocket, his strong hand was feeling very large and unwieldy as if it were self-conscious. But it was just that all his attention was posited on the action to come: draw the gun which already had one up the spout, shoot Crossfield in the back of his seamed neck, and jump off the reviewing stand. If the fall didn't break his legs, somebody was sure to shoot him, but it was the best plan he'd been able to come up with.

He'd thought of throwing himself on Crossfield, trying to bluff his way through it by shooting at one of the other security types ranged around their charges. But it was just a fallback plan. It wouldn't work any better and he didn't trust himself to be able to pull it off. It might work if the actor was inhumanly cool and a better-than-average liar. Fox was neither.

Besides, he didn't want to blow away some innocent bystander. Not just to stay alive.

When Westin's car got through the gate, it didn't come around to the back of the stand. It stopped halfway between the stand and the concrete ground-control station. Westy got out of one door and somebody else got out of the other.

It took Fox a moment to realize he was looking at Shai Gallen, in chinos and riding boots and a safari jacket. Then he squeezed his eyes shut. *Dear God*. He was glad she hadn't told him she was going to come watch him die.

He was trying to figure out if he could get angry enough at her for doing this to him to quit—stand there and let Crossfield give his speech—when Shai started trotting toward the reviewing stand just slowly enough not to arouse untoward suspicion and Westy ducked into the bunker.

Just then, Crossfield stepped up to the microphone and the music died.

The President began, "Ladies and gentleman, this is a historic moment in world history and I'd like to begin by pointing out to you that no one nation is responsible for the good we're going to do here today—and tomorrow, and for hundreds of brighter tomorrows in an energy rich future—"

Fox stopped listening. It was within his assignment to check out anything unusual, and so he did: craning his neck, he saw Shai, credentials prominently displayed, waiting while one of the American agents tried to convince his Soviet counterpart that the writing in the glassine wrapper which the Russian couldn't read allowed the bearer to do anything she damned well pleased, including climb the reviewing stand.

Gallen looked up and Fox thought to look away. Crossfield's speech was ringing in his ears and he had to get back into position. If she wanted to wish him Bon Voyage or whatever, it was just too damned late.

But she waved imperiously, then pushed at the shoulder of the American agent twice her size.

The agent scratched his head, looked up toward Fox, and suddenly there was static in the button mike in Fox's ear: "Ford, get your ass down here. I'm coming up to cover for you. You've got an urgent message, so I'm told."

What the fuck?

But he did what he was told, heading down the stairs as the other agent came up. The man who was replacing him said coldly, "I don't know what this is about, but you're going to have the shortest career of any Secret Service agent in history."

Meanwhile, below, Gallen was looking at her watch, then up at him, squinting, a hand shading her eyes.

When he reached her at the bottom of the stairs, he noticed her lips were dry and sticking together as she spoke: "Come on, your uncle's had a stroke or something and he's asking for you."

Her voice was so loud it must have carried, but she wasn't saying anything that made relevant sense. It was some sort of abort, he guessed. But then why was she tugging on his arm, urging him to hurry?

He held back, wondering if he dared ask her anything the way he was wired for sound.

Her head snapped around so that her blond hair whipped his chest: "Ford, this is an emergency. Now, *move!*"

He knew that tone. He matched her pace and watched her chest rising and falling. She kept glancing at her watch.

Just as they were in the stairwell leading down to the ground-control station's heavy door, Gallen muttered, "Shit. Hit the deck," and tripped him so that they both fell down the stairs and he landed on top of her in a tangle, his nose in her hair.

Then something blocked his ears and a shockwave buffeted him and a sound like a giant match striking followed, just before something sucked the air from his lungs.

In the ground-control station, everything froze. Neely was at the polarized glass window and it seemed to him he was back at White Sands. Only at White Sands there weren't people melting along with the girders and the concrete. He'd closed his eyes reflexively against the flash, but what he'd seen had been enough.

Around him, equipment was exploding, circuits frying in sympathy, men yelling and cursing and the hiss of fire extinguishers was everywhere.

Tears were running down Neely's face. He'd seen Shai and Fox come toward the bunker but they'd never made it in the door. He forced his eyes open, forced himself to look at the destruction he'd been party to creating—at the reeling, burned figures in the foreground, those who'd been lucky enough not to be on or under the reviewing stand when it melted, portions vaporized, portions exploding, portions falling.

Now there was a red-white sea of glass where the stand had been and all around the edges the scene might have been from some lost Breughel.

He couldn't see too clearly, thank god, because he was weeping uncontrollably.

So he didn't realize until somebody elbowed him in the back that Westy was screaming to be heard over the din of the technicians trying to salvage what they could of the ground station.

He turned around and there was Westy, his face blistered as if he'd fallen asleep in the sun. And beside him was Gallen, hair singed but smiling, with the Fox boy leaning on her, looking shocked and white-faced.

Neely didn't realize that the boy was in pain until Westy yelled into his face, "Let's get out of here, fool," and tugged him away from the window so that he saw Fox's back, as Shai turned carefully, supporting her asset, where his shirt had been burned away to reveal second and third degree burns beneath.

Still, the boy was moving—alive. And somehow it made Neely feel better—as General Westin pantomimed in the din that Noah follow him and they hurried through the confusion of the power bay to a rear door beyond which Westy's car was waiting— that Gallen and Fox weren't dead, even though so many others were.

But it's always the ones you know—the faces behind which lies something worth saving—that you fear for. Gallen was one such. Fox, Neely was sure after only a short acquaintance, was another— the boy had plenty of sand in his craw.

James Crossfield, on the other hand, was not such a man. As a matter of fact, Neely thought, watching Gallen and the page named Mac ease the badly burned operator into Westy's staff car, Crossfield hadn't been worth all the lives and equipment destroyed to make an end to him. In fact, he probably wasn't worth the fifty-cent round Larry Fox had been dispatched to pump into him today.

But then, if there was one thing an old pro learned about intelligence operations, it was that you do what you have to do. Whatever works, works.

And in the car, where Gallen was unashamedly cooing over Fox with tears streaming down her face and Mac applying some respectable first aide from Westy's kit in the back seat while, up front,

Westy stared ahead with steady eyes, Noah Neely was feeling a lot better about America and the life he'd dedicated to keeping her free as the staff car sped unobstructed toward the Frisbee gleaming on the airstrip fifteen miles away.

EPILOGUE

Even Israeli television carried President Jenning's cancellation of the Soviet Summit and, two weeks later, his announcement of a new Strategic Defense Initiative which would reassert America's control of space, "Our most crucial asset, so long as the Soviet Union persists in active measures aimed at destabilizing free governments everywhere as a prelude to world domination." The velvet face of America's first black president was grave, his delivery stirring as he assured a worldwide audience of "America's vigilance. Our new Space Command, headed by General Theodore Westin, will have as its top priority the defense of the communications and power satellites of all free nations."

The face of the President on Fox's hospital-room TV screen flickered, then disappeared to be replaced by an Israeli commentator's, and Fox thought, as he finished packing: *Well, it wasn't for nothing, then:* the skin grafts and the time spent in an Israeli burn tank, the goo and the pain, the delirious nights when he was sure Gallen was sitting with him.

But she couldn't have been, because his memory was of a woman with tears in her eyes and Gallen didn't cry—not over somebody like Larry Fox.

The white door to his hospital room opened, admitting the sound of men and women talking in the corridor. Then one of his doctors, a Sephardic Jew half his size and twice his width, stuck his long nose in: "Ready, I see. This is good. A nurse with a wheelchair will be right along. But before you go, one visitor, yes?"

Fox, for the first time, looked beyond the doorway.

Noah Neely was standing there, all eyes and wrinkles and teeth because his paternal smile was so wide.

"Noah? Sure, yeah. What are *you* doing in Tel Aviv?" They'd brought Fox to the nearest burn treatment facility with which the US had good relations—and where security could be assured, he'd assumed though he hadn't been told.

Neely had on one of those tropical cotton suits that wrinkled the moment you looked at it and the old man was carrying a canvas-and-leather folio. Noah Neely was the first representative of the American government that Fox could remember seeing since he'd been here, although his Israeli physicians had assured him that the good ol' US of A was picking up his tab.

Now he looked at Neely, who didn't say a word in greeting, just came in and closed the door, nearly on the doctor's long Sephardic nose, and thought, *Here it comes. Whatever it's going to be.* But he couldn't think what they were going to do to him: he was no longer an employee of CIA, he was willing to bet. But that wasn't anything; he didn't care about that. He didn't want his citizenship lifted, his visas limited, or a long stay in Leavenworth, however. His gut tightened and the skin grafts on his back began to burn.

Neely, still unspeaking, joined Fox by the bed and began unzipping his portfolio.

Fox said nervously, "They say I'll have to come back for a bunch of check-ups, and maybe more grafts, later." He didn't know where they were going to get the skin for them—his thighs and his calves had given all they had to give. It didn't look as bad as it felt. It still felt like hell, where it wasn't numb. They said the feeling would come back, but he wasn't sure he believed them.

Neely pulled a piece of White House stationery out of the folder and handed it to Fox, his huge brown eyes very bright.

Fox didn't read it; he tossed it on the bed contemptuously. "Noah—sir. Why don't you just tell me what this is about?"

The old man smiled again, so widely that it seemed his face might crack. "Read your commendation, 'nephew.' It's from President Jennings himself." Neely reached into his pocket and pulled out a blue velvet presentation box about two inches long. "Or maybe you'd rather see your medal first?"

Christ on a crutch! Fox sat down on the bed, one buttock wrinkling the commendation letter from Jennings, and opened the box Neely handed him. In it, on a black ribbon, was an Intelligence Star. "Damn," said Larry Fox. "Damn."

"You're pleased, then. They want you to be." Neely sat down on the bed beside him and it sank unreasonably under the frail old fellow's weight. "*I* want you to be. I need a favor, Larry."

Fox let the medal, which bore no inscription or

identifying device that marked it as CIA's most coveted decoration, fall into his lap. "I gave in the Kalahari, Doctor Neely." What they probably wanted was silence. He figured they could have that from him, now that Glenn was gone and even Kathie . . . but he wasn't going to tell them so.

Stiff, formal, and laced with hostility Fox couldn't control, his words hung in the air a long time before Neely said, "Don't think harshly of us, Fox. We did what we had to do. So did you. And the favor I need is above and beyond. It's not your government asking— it's me. And, though you don't owe me anything, I did do what I could to help. . . ."

"Say it. Just say it," Fox said.

"It's Gallen. I want you to talk to her for me. She's submitted her resignation and I think she's being hasty. . . ."

"Maybe," Fox said, closing his eyes briefly, "she's finally realized that it doesn't help, not any of it." He didn't mean that. But he'd said it. "And anyway, I'm not going back to the States for a while. I've got to stay here where my doctors are." He was assuming things: that the commendation letter and the star meant he *could* go back to the States—or anywhere—whenever he wanted; that there were no travel restrictions on him; that they were going to do him the consummate favor of leaving him the fuck alone. But they wouldn't do Gallen the same favor, never in a million years.

"You don't know then?" Neely responded incredulously: "She's been here the entire time you've been in hospital. She was, I've heard, in this hospital, nonstop, twenty-four hours a day until you were out of danger. Don't you remember? Surely you must."

He remembered some stuff, yeah. But he'd thought

it was the Dilauded they'd been pumping into him. "I was . . . pretty under the weather." He looked at his fingers, which of their own accord were turning the velvet presentation box round and round, stroking the plush. "So, she's here. Maybe that's her business. It's sure not mine. And if she wants out, maybe that's a good idea, too." He looked up at Neely defiantly. "Nobody should have to do this shit. Nobody."

"Somebody does. Always." Neely's voice was thick. "It's not to her benefit to leave, not now, not when Jennings will give her anything she wants—the DCI's desk, carte blanche . . . anything. After all, LEMON PLEDGE did make him President."

"You mean it's not to the Agency's benefit if she leaves now."

"Gallen has more enemies than she's prepared to admit—not just KGB but many other agencies, over the years, have built up reasons to put her in their target files. How long do you think she'll live if she separates, the way she wants to, with no coverage, no support? It doesn't have to be obvious—a car accident, a 'natural' death. You've seen enough action, Fox, to know that I'm telling the truth. She can't walk away mad. Somebody's got to convince her of that."

"Well, Doctor Neely, you'd better get started on it, then, hadn't you? As for me, I'm out of here. Out of *it*. I figured you people would pink-slip me, but if you want, I'll write you a resignation letter myself."

"Larry, take a six month leave, full pay, and then we'll talk again," Neely said as he stood up and one of his joints cracked like a stone hitting a windshield. "I'm sorry you won't come with me to Shai's. I know she'd love to see you."

"I . . . can't," Fox said.

But in the end, he did. Not because Neely kept making sheep's eyes at him or because of the six months' leave at full pay, but because Neely might just be right—Shai ought to think about her own security. You've got to be alive to feel any way at all about things. And, anyhow, he had unfinished business of his own with Gallen, who, if Neely could be believed, had made herself his personal babysitter until he was well enough not to need one.

Goddamn woman. If she was going to sit by his bed and cry, she could have at least done it when he could see her, not just when he was so doped up he'd thought he was dreaming.

Gallen was digging in the court behind her seaside pension, looking for Roman coins or shards of pottery, or whatever she could find. She wiped her brow with a forearm and leaned on her shovel when she heard the car drive up, then looked around at the holes she'd made. *Admit it, girl. You're just trying to dig a hole deep enough to crawl in, one you can pull in after you.* The old hotelkeeper wasn't going to be real pleased about the mess she'd made of the walled garden behind her bungalow. Oh well, she could always fill in the holes when she decided to leave.

She heard the knock on the door and, though it stiffened her spine, ignored it, wiping her hands on her jeans and going to the two-by-six on which she'd set out her strainer, brushes and other amateur archeologist's paraphernalia beside the 1st-century Roman coin she'd found along with a few potsherds.

The maid that came with the place would run interference for her. The maid was a treasure and would have been surprisingly so if Shai hadn't expected Mossad to be covering her while she was in Israel.

But it wasn't an Israeli whom the maid led out through the patio doors.

Shai looked away toward the Mediterranean, dark as her eyes today. Fox and Neely, together. She thought about trying to vault the plastered mud-brick wall and run but you couldn't keep running. If she had to make a stand, this was as good a place as any; this was where it had all started, anyway.

"What's up, guys?" she said, not turning.

Only one pair of feet approached. When Neely said from close by, "Shai, don't you think you ought to reconsider? At least talk to us about it. I do. Larry does."

She was angry, unreasonably disappointed that it was Neely, and not Fox, who was standing within arm's reach. She turned on her heel and said coldly, "I don't want to talk about it. There's nothing to talk about. I'm out. Done. Finished. Used up. And if you, or Fox, think different, it's your misconception."

"We need you, Shai, America needs—"

Shai's harsh laugh cut him off. "Don't say that to me. You've got your new President; he's dismantling the Equal Americans program, I hear. So there's a chance for democracy, not some parody of it based on greed, not socialism in disguise." She had to blink repeatedly and then found she couldn't say anything at all. She moved away from Neely, to the ancient wall, and leaned against it on one stiffened arm, head down. "Go away," she said, trying to get the words out clearly, trying not to choke up and make an ass of herself. "Leave me alone. I'll be home when I've cooled down. I've got to pick up M-1."

There was the sound of feet shuffling and Neely's voice said, from farther away, "Whatever you say, Shai. I hope you'll come and see me when you get back to Washington."

She could only shake her head and try not to move. She was praying that Fox wouldn't come over and try to change her mind, too.

Watching Fox was what had made it all just too damned much. Fox, in an Israeli Intensive Care Unit: Fox, doped out of his mind. Fox, who kept talking to dead people in his delirium—his wife, Alden, Sonny. And who kept trying to save Shai from something happening in his nightmares. Over and over.

She felt a hand at the small of her back and she didn't move. It wasn't Neely's hand, not from the way her body reacted.

"Damn, Fox," she said, "not you, too."

"Hey, babe. Look at me."

She panicked for an instant, then she turned and leaned back against the wall where they wouldn't be touching one another, arms crossed.

His face was drawn and stubbly, but he was grinning. "Good for you," he said in a low voice.

It was that voice of his that made her so crazy. She put a hand to her forehead. "Larry. . . How do you feel? All right?"

"Good enough, Shai. Better than I thought I would, hearing you tell Neely what you did. . . ." He moved a step closer. "They wanted me to help convince you to stay. I don't know if I could have, but I *do* know that I've got six months' paid leave to think about what *I'm* going to do. They gave me a star, Shai, a damned medal."

She tried to smile and found that, despite everything, she had to touch him. She ran her fingers along his jaw. "I know. You deserved it—you deserved more, but that's another issue. Where will you go, on your leave?"

He turned his face into her hand and kissed her palm, then his fingers closed on her wrist. "I was thinking that we've got a lot of thinking to do—and talking, maybe."

"We?" She didn't let herself consider it; he was a fuse, a line officer, and she was . . . an *ex*-supergrade, a damned civilian with short odds. "You go put your life together, Fox. You could get some consulting or security work. . . ."

He smiled impishly. "I bet we could, at that. If we talk things out and it seems like the thing to do. If you want."

She tried to pull her wrist away but she didn't seem to have the strength. Was this part of the game? Put him on her for coverage? To bring her **back in?** She looked into his eyes for a sign and saw more gentleness, more hope there than she'd ever seen.

"I have to go back to the States, soon," she muttered, flustered. "Got to get M-1. He doesn't like to be babysat any more than I do."

"Yeah, you know," Fox said casually, pulling her by the wrist until he could slip one arm around her waist, "I was thinking about that, too. Bet that touring bike is still in your garage. America's a beautiful country. I've got the feeling that if we went home, there'd be nobody looking over our shoulders. No matter what we wanted to do."

"M-1 likes you, too," she said unsteadily, and leaned into his embrace, pressing her head against his shoulder. "And M-1 doesn't like just anybody. . . . Maybe we could . . . talk about it."

He raised her head to see her eyes, his finger

pressing gently under her chin. "We will," he promised, and kissed her while, overhead, a trio of jets broke the sound barrier, headed out over the Mediterranean on patrol.

Coming in May 1985 from Baen Books—Poul Anderson's
first Terran Empire/Polesotechnic League novel in years!

THE GAME OF EMPIRE

Dominic Flandry has fought the good fight—but now
he is of an age more suited to deciding the fate of
empires from behind the throne. Others must take up
the challenge of courting danger on strange planets
filled with creatures stranger still . . . and such a one is
Diana Flandry, heir to all her father's adventures! Here
is an excerpt from THE GAME OF EMPIRE:

She sat on the tower of St. Barbara, kicking her heels
from the parapet, and looked across immensity. Overhead,
heaven was clear, deep blue save where the sun Patricius
stood small and fierce at midmorning. Two moons were
wanly aloft. A breeze blew cool. It would have been
deadly cold before Diana's people came to Imhotep; the
peak of Mt. Horn lifts a full twelve kilometers above sea
level.

"Who holds St. Barbara's holds the planet." That saying
was centuries obsolete, but the memory kept alive a
certain respect. Though ice bull herds no longer threatened to stampede through the original exploration base;
though the Troubles which left hostile bands marooned
and desperate, turning marauder, had ended when the
hand of the Terran Empire reached this far; though the
early defensive works would be useless in such upheav-
als as threatened the present age, and had long since
been demolished: still, one relic of them remained in
Olga's Landing, at the middle of what had become a
market square. Its guns had been taken away for scrap,
its chambers echoed hollow, sunseeker vine clambered
over the crumbling yellow stone of it, but St. Barbara's
stood yet; and it was a little audacious for a hoyden to
perch herself on top.

Diana often did. The neighborhood had stopped
minding—after all, she was everybody's friend—and to

strangers it meant nothing, except that human males were apt to shout and wave at the pretty girl. She grinned and waved back when she felt in the mood, but had learned to decline the invitations. Her aim was not always simply to enjoy the ever-shifting scenes. Sometimes she spied a chance to earn a credit or two, as when a newcomer seemed in want of a guide to the sights and amusements. At present she had no home of her own, unless you counted a ruinous temple where she kept hidden her meager possessions and, when nothing better was available, spread her sleeping bag.

Life spilled from narrow streets and surged between the walls enclosing the plaza. Pioneer buildings had run to brick, and never gone higher than three or four stories, under Imhotepan gravity. Booths huddled everywhere else against them. The wares were as multifarious as the sellers, anything from hinterland fruits and grains to ironware out of the smithies that made the air clangorous, from velvyl fabric and miniature computers of the inner Empire to jewels and skins and carvings off a hundred different worlds. A gundealer offered primitive home-produced chemical rifles, stunners of military type, and—illegally—several blasters, doubtless found in wrecked spacecraft after the Merseian onslaught was beaten back.

Folk were mainly human, but it was unlikely that many had seen Mother Terra. The planets where they were born and bred had marked them. Residents of Imhotep were necessarily muscular and never fat. Those whose families had lived here for generations, since Olga's Landing was a scientific base, and had thus melded into a type, tended to be dark-skinned and aquiline-featured.

A Navy man and a marine passed close by the tower. They were too intent on their talk to notice Diana, which was extraordinary. The harshness reached her: "—yeh, sure, they've grown it back for me." The spaceman waved his right arm. A short-sleeved undress shirt revealed it pallid and thin; regenerated tissue needs exercise to attain normal fitness. "But they said the budget doesn't allow repairing DNA throughout my body, after the radiation I took. I'll be dependent on biosupport the rest of my life, and I'll never dare father any kids."

"Merseian bastards," growled the marine. "I could damn near wish they had broken through and landed.

My unit had a warm welcome ready for 'em, I can tell you."

"Be glad they didn't," said his companion. "Did you really want nukes tearing up our planets? Wounds and all, I'll thank Admiral Magnusson every day I've got left to me, for turning them back the way he did, with that skeleton force the pinchfists on Terra allowed us." Bitterly: "*He* wouldn't begrudge the cost of fixing up entire a man that fought under him."

They disappeared into the throng. Diana shivered a bit and looked around for something cheerier than such a reminder of last year's events.

Nonhumans were on hand in fair number. Most were Tigeries, come from the lowlands on various business, their orange-black-white pelts vivid around skimpy garments. Generally they wore air helmets, with pressure pumps strapped to their backs, but on some, oxygills rose out of the shoulders, behind the heads, like elegant ruffs. Diana cried greetings to those she recognized. Otherwise she spied a centauroid Donarrian; the shiny integuments of three Irumclagians; a couple of tailed, green-skinned Shalmuans; and—and—

"What the flippin' fury!" She got to her feet—they were bare, and the stone felt warm beneath them—and stood precariously balanced, peering.

Around the corner of a Winged Smoke house had come a giant.

The Newest Adventure of the Galaxy's Only Two-Fisted Diplomat!

THE RETURN OF RETIEF

KEITH LAUMER

When the belligerent Ree decided they needed human space for their ever-increasing population, only Retief could cope.

$2.95

BAEN BOOKS

See next page for order information.

A BRAND-NEW
NOVEL BY THE
BESTSELLING
AUTHOR OF
DRAGON'S EGG

Robert L. Forward

THE FLIGHT OF THE DRAGONFLY

"His SF-scientific imagination is unsurpassed...this is a must!"
— *PUBLISHERS WEEKLY*

"Outshines *Dragon's Egg*...rates a solid ten on my mind-boggle
scale. If there were a Hugo for the most enjoyable alien creation,
the flouwen would be frontrunners." — *LOCUS*

"I much enjoyed *The Flight of the Dragonfly.* Part of my
enjoyment came from knowing that the man damned well
knows what he's talking about...." — *LARRY NIVEN*

384 pp. • $3.50

The future is NOW!

Distributed by Simon & Schuster Mass Merchandise Sales Company
1230 Avenue of the Americas • New York, N.Y. 10020